SO THIS IS WAR

USA TODAY BESTSELLING AUTHOR

MEGHAN QUINN

Published by Hot-Lanta Publishing, LLC

Copyright 2024

Cover Design By: RBA Designs

Cover Illustrations By: Gerard Soratorio

Prologue

LEVI

"I want him off my fucking team. Now!"

My testicles shrivel into dust as Coach Wood screams at Andie Lintour, the general manager for the Vancouver Agitators.

Spittle flies off his lip.

Eyebrows are slanted like knives, ready to strike.

And the veins in his neck protrude, making me question if it will be his hands that choke me or the scary, pulsing veins.

"Will, we can't—"

"He was fucking my daughter! We can do whatever the hell I say."

Did you wince? Because I did.

I know what you're thinking. *Posey, you're about to lose your life at the hands of your fuming, spitting, hulking-out coach.* And your assessment of the situation is a fair and accurate one.

Because yes, I've never felt closer to death than at this moment right now.

To bring you up to speed, yes, I was fucking his daughter.

1

Yes, it was in the locker room.

Yes, it was out in the open where anyone could walk in.

Was it stupid? Absolutely.

Have I lost my mind? One hundred percent.

Do I have any defense? Not one.

Nope, this was pure stupidity. This was a move by a desperate man brought to his knees.

A weak man.

A man with no morals.

A man infatuated with a woman he can't control himself around.

"I understand the circumstances," Andie says in her calming voice, "but we can't get rid of a player because he was having relations with your daughter. Posey is one of the best defensemen in the entire league." If I wasn't so terrified, I'd puff my chest. "He's under a no-trade clause. Even if we wanted to get rid of him, we couldn't."

I'm not sure if I should be grateful for that clause because, at the moment, it wouldn't hurt to at least escape the darkness of death clouding Coach Wood's expression.

"Then he's benched," Wood says as he looks me in the eyes, nostrils flaring. "Did you hear that, you bologna-loving mother-fucker? You're benched."

I swallow deeply as I dig my fingertips into the armrests of my chair. Not sure why he had to drag the bologna into this, but I don't bother asking as the vein in his bald head looks like it's maxed out on stress. "I, uh, yes, I heard you the first time," I say, causing him to grow angrier.

"Once again, Will, I don't believe we can do that. We pay him a lot of money—"

"We do." Will paces his office, and every time he goes near me, my ass clenches in anticipation of a ninja knife hand right to my trachea. "We pay him plenty of money, so why don't we just put him on the injured list, say he has a sore toe, and then he can figure out with his agent what he's doing for next year because he sure as fuck won't be playing on my ice."

Now, is Coach Wood being a touch extreme? Some might say yes without any context because who really wants to bench their starting defenseman? It's not the smartest move as a coach, but the man has a good reason.

And sure, I shouldn't be taking his side. I should be defending myself and the ability to have sexual relations with anyone I damn well please, but here's the thing . . . the situation runs a little deeper than what you see on the surface.

It's more complicated.

I didn't just fuck some random girl on an arbitrary day in our locker room.

The coach's daughter was riding me, completely naked, in the middle of the locker room after he struck a deal with me to hire his daughter as my assistant to teach her a lesson.

And before you even ask, no, the lesson was not on the science of how the penis meets the vagina.

It was a tough lesson about life.

So yeah, this really is on me.

Raises hand Yup, I take the blame.

Guilty.

The only question is, how the hell am I going to get around this? From the way he spoke so cruelly of my precious bologna, I don't think offering him a daily sandwich—made by yours truly —is going to mend the severed ties we've created.

Nope, this will take a monumental, epic proposal of apologies, especially if I want to stay on this team. Which I do. My boys are here. My life is here.

She's here . . .

Which means I need a plan.

But I swore I wouldn't get them involved.

I said over and over again that I wouldn't use their idiotic advice or poorly constructed ideas, but I think desperate times call for desperate measures.

It's time to call on the Frozen Fellas.

Chapter One

WYLIE

A year ago . . .

"I'm so excited you're here," Sandie, my best friend, says as she pulls me into a hug. "And I can't believe your dad let you catch a ride on the team plane."

"It took a lot of begging," I say as I adjust my gold top in the hotel mirror, making sure my breasts are exactly where I want them. "But he caved when I said I wanted to visit with you. He's always loved you."

"Because I wasn't the one getting us into trouble in high school."

I shrug as I sift through my pouch of lipsticks, trying to decide what nude color I want to wear tonight. "I helped us live life. Can't complain about that."

"Your dad did."

I chuckle. "Because he's a cranky old man who got divorced nearly twenty years ago and has refused to find love again. That would make anyone cranky."

"He's found love," Sandie says. "In hockey."

I roll my eyes because ugh, hockey. Growing up with a single father infatuated with the sport, I could have gone two ways. I could have grown to love it as much as my dad or utterly despise it because it took my dad away from me for nearly half of my life.

Can you guess which one it is?

"I hope his love affair has been worth it." I go for my honey-suckle lip color, knowing it always makes my lips look the best.

"Seems like it has. I mean, you flew here on a team plane. Which, hey, you didn't tell me about the flight. Did you meet any of the players?"

"No," I say glumly. "Dad forced me to board way before any of the players. He made me sit in the back with the staff, then made me wait to deplane until after all the players got off, so zero interaction."

"Was he afraid you might try to intermingle with them?"

"You know him, he's always worried about me."

"Probably because he caught Sebastian in the house several times in high school when he shouldn't have been there."

I chuckle. "Remember the time Sebastian climbed out the window in his underwear and sprinted down the street just to avoid my father's wrath?"

"Yes, I still recall seeing him sprint past my house, his long hair flapping in the breeze. He joined track right after that."

"And became All-American his senior year. He should be thanking me for opening his eyes to his speed."

Sandie laughs. "Poor Sebastian. I wonder what he's doing now."

"He's in Portland, Oregon," I answer when I finish my lipstick and sit on my bed across from Sandie's. "I think he's working as an assistant coach of a track team, so yeah, he owes his career to me too."

"You've done him favors left and right." Sandie chuckles.

"Just here to help." I smirk and take in her dress. "You know, you could borrow one of my outfits. Show off a little bit more breast . . ."

"First of all, my breasts would drown in your dress. And second of all, I don't want to show breasts like you do." She points at the strings that crisscross over my exposed cleavage, holding the front of the shirt together. "That's just asking for trouble. Aren't you afraid something will slip out?"

"No." I shake my head. "You know me, I couldn't care less about being naked. I wear clothes because it's the law, not because I want to."

"Hence the top." She brings her hands together. "Now, what did we talk about?"

I roll my eyes. "That this night is about you and me, and I'm not to go off and try to flirt with anyone. Come on, Sandie, do you really think I would do that?"

"Uh, yes." She nods.

"I'll have you know, I've matured since the last time you saw me."

"Says the girl who is not wearing a bra tonight."

I never wear a bra. "And this top was for you. I wanted to show you how strong fabric can really be."

"Ah, yes, can't wait for you to sneeze because that will be the real show."

I laugh. "Seriously. Just you and me tonight, okay?"

"Okay."

We both stand, Sandie in her cute red dress that hits her mid-thigh and me in my gold top and wide-leg black pants with three-inch heels.

Sandie looks up at me. "I remember when we used to be the same height."

"Add some heels to those flats, and we will be." I link my arm through hers and guide us out of the hotel room. Purses in hand, we make our way to the elevator.

"So where are we going?" Sandie asks.

"I thought we could hit up the bar downstairs for food and then go to a drag show I heard about."

"Ooo, sounds like fun." The elevator dings, and we both get on. I press the button for the ground floor as Sandie turns toward me. "What if we run into your dad at the hotel? Do you think he's going to make you change like he did when we were in high school?"

I laugh and shake my head. "I'm a twenty-one-year-old woman in her first semester of grad school. He doesn't have that kind of control over me anymore."

"Says the girl who had to sit in the back with the staff on the team plane."

"That's different," I say. "That was his territory, and I was doing anything to get a ride here to see you. Now that I'm here, it's free game."

"I like this side of you," Sandie says. "Not so scared of your dad and living your best life."

"Well, possibly my best life." I lean against the elevator wall as it stops and an elderly couple gets on. "I don't know if I'm into what I'm studying."

"What do you mean?" Sandie asks. "You're getting your master's in business. I feel like at this stage, you should be really into it."

"The only reason I applied for grad school was because of my dad. But what am I really going to do with a master's in business? It's so . . . broad. And then where do I go from there? Sit behind a desk all day?"

"Doesn't he want you to do something in the Agitators front office?"

"Yes, like business-to-business sales or something like that. Not something I'm entirely into. You know, I've been taking these graphic art classes on the side, and they've been really fulfilling. I kind of want to explore that."

"Ooo, graphic art," Sandie says as the elevator dings, and we let the elderly couple off first. "You would be so good at that."

"You think?"

She gives me a *come on* stare. "Wylie, you've loved art ever since I've known you, and you're good at it. This is right up your alley."

"That's what I was thinking. And the classes I've been taking are all digital art, so I'm learning the techniques I need to know. And through the class, our teacher found a contest we could enter."

"What is it?" Sandie asks as we head toward the bar.

"It's a concert T-shirt contest for Hayes Farrow."

"Wait." Sandie grips my arm, stopping us in the middle of the lobby. "THE Hayes Farrow? The singer of *The Black Album*?"

"The one and only," I say. "He thought he'd open the contest to his fans. I know it's a long shot, but my whole class is applying." I let out a deep breath. "I just feel so energized when I'm drawing and designing. When I'm in my business class, I drift off rather than pay attention. I think I want to talk to my dad about maybe leaving school to pursue this full-time."

Sandie winces because she knows my dad well enough to understand how that talk will go. "I'm glad I won't be around when you have that conversation."

"What are you talking about?" I ask. "Did you really think dinner would be just you and me?" I shake my head. "I'm telling my dad about my school news during dinner, and you're there for backup."

"If you weren't wearing that shirt, I'd believe you."

I laugh as we reach the bar. It's a seat-yourself situation with tables, high-tops, and couches scattered throughout the grand space. Deep purple and royal blue cover the seats, while gold-accented tables are scattered throughout to make the setup a less formal but usable space. The tall ceilings allow for ornate chandeliers to hang over the room, giving the space an elegant and moody feel.

"Oh, it's so fancy," Sandie says. "Where should we sit?"

"I was thinking—"

"Sandie?" a male voice says from behind us, turning us around.

"Dale," Sandie says in shock right before she takes off and hugs the man with all her might. "Oh my God, what are you doing here?"

"I'm in town for the night." Dale pushes his hand through his floppy blond hair.

"You are? You should have told me so we could catch up."

Dale's cheeks blush. "I was afraid you might say no."

"Are you kidding?" Sandie says, looking all starry-eyed. Who the hell is Dale? And how come she never told me about this man who seems to have captured my best friend? "I would have said yes."

"Really?" he asks, his brows shooting up to his hairline. Tall and lanky, the man has that almost nerdy look about him but dresses with style in his tight-fitting chinos and button-up shirt with the sleeves rolled. I can see the attraction and why Sandie's blushing with excitement.

"Yes, of course. I've missed you." She runs her hand down his arm. Oh boy, if that isn't a sign of her attraction to him, then I don't know what is.

"I've missed you too," he says.

And then they stare at each other for a solid thirty seconds without saying a word.

It would be cute if my stomach wasn't growling, so I clear my throat and step in. "Hey, Dale," I say. "I'm Wylie, Sandie's best friend."

Dale glances at me, and to his credit, he keeps his eyes on mine, never drifting any farther south where the restraints of fabric are being tested. "Wylie, it's nice to meet you. I heard so much about you when Sandie and I were in a study group together."

I shake his outstretched hand and look over at Sandie. "Wait. Is this D? The guy you talked about constantly?"

Sandie's face heats with embarrassment.

"You talked about me a lot?" Dale asks, looking very pleased with that information.

"All the time," I say, knowing Sandie would deny it. "She even told me about the night that you two stayed late—"

"Okay, that's enough from you," Sandie says, stepping in front of me. "Anyway, are you just here for tonight?"

He nods. "I leave tomorrow."

"Oh." I can feel Sandie's defeat from here.

"Well, good thing I'm here for more than one night," I say. "Because look who just became available for dinner." I nudge Sandie toward Dale.

"You're available?" Dale asks, his expression morphing into utter joy.

"Uh." Sandie glances in my direction, then holds up her finger toward Dale. "Give us a moment." She tugs me a few feet away, and with her back toward Dale, she says, "This night was supposed to be about you and me."

"It was, but now it's about you and Dale."

She shakes her head. "I can't ditch you."

"You're not ditching me when I'm telling you to go. Seriously, Sandie, I'm here another night. We can catch up all day tomorrow and go to the drag show tomorrow night."

She bites on the corner of her mouth and looks over her shoulder at Dale, who now has his hands in his pockets as he waits for us. When she turns back around, she says, "I feel guilty."

"Don't. I can see how excited you are to see him, and it's been a while. You look . . . happy around him."

"I am," she says softly. "We sort of lost touch when he moved, but seeing him now, it almost feels like we were meant to run into each other."

"Perfect, then go have fun, and we'll hang out tomorrow."

"Are you sure?" She winces.

"I promise, I'm good. Go have fun."

She gives it some thought, then reaches out and pulls me into a hug. "You're the best friend ever."

―――――

"HOW DOES THAT TASTE?" the bartender asks me as he leans against the edge of the bar, his arms propping him up.

I take a sip of my dry martini and let the liquid roll across my tastebuds before I swallow. Pleased, I smile up at the bartender. "Perfect."

His eyes momentarily drop to my exposed cleavage before lifting back up to my eyes. "On the house," he says before tapping the bar top and moving toward the end to help another customer.

I should be disgusted with his blatant perusal and offer of a free drink, but it's a pretty good martini. If I've learned anything by my fourth year of college, it's to take a free drink from the bartender when you can.

I spin around on my chair and find Sandie in the corner with Dale. They're both laughing, and her hand is precariously perched on his thigh. I smile over the rim of my glass, excited to see the start of something new. She used to talk about Dale a lot, so her hanging out with him tonight doesn't bother me in the slightest. It actually makes me excited about the possibilities of what tonight could be the start of.

Maybe a fragrant love affair.

Or the beginning of a lifelong coupling.

Or perhaps a rowdy night in the sheets.

Either way, I'm here for it.

"Is this seat taken?" a deep voice asks, startling me away from staring at my friend.

I glance to my right and come face to face with a gorgeous set of greenish-gold eyes framed by dark bushy brows and nearly black lashes. I lean back ever so slightly as I take in the rest of his face.

Strong, carved jaw sprinkled with a coarse five o'clock

shadow. Distinctive cheekbones that are not too pronounced but high enough to offer this man some heavenly bone structure. A thick head of soft brown hair with a singular curl that falls over his forehead. And a pair of lips just full enough to entice anyone to beg for a make out session.

He . . . is . . . hot.

And I know how hot because I've stared at this face many times while visiting my dad in his office at the Agitators arena. This face has been in my fantasies a time or two.

It's none other than Levi Posey, the star defenseman for my dad's hockey team.

And because I've had some pretty naughty thoughts about this man, there is no reason I should be denying him the seat next to me.

None at all.

I cross one leg over the other, wishing I hadn't gone with pants tonight but rather a mini skirt that would show off the definition in my legs from all those nights I've spent on a Pilates reformer. "That seat is all yours," I say before lifting my glass to my lips and taking a soft sip while keeping my eyes on him.

He glances down at my drink, then back up to my eyes. "Dirty martini?" he asks.

"Good guess," I reply, keeping it casual.

He gains the bartender's attention with a concise flick of his hand. "Your finest water."

Of course he orders a water. He might be one of the toughest players on the ice with a terrifying right hook that has knocked out quite a few opponents, and he might also be known as the biggest player on the team, but he's also a rule follower. Therefore, as it's the night before a game . . . he's not drinking.

"Water, huh?" I ask, not wanting to give away that I recognize him. "Really living on the edge."

"I am," he says. "Severely dehydrated. If the clock strikes twelve without me replenishing my body's fluids, I very well might turn into dust."

"Sounds like a Cinderella knockoff story to me," I reply.

"But instead of a glass slipper falling off, it's a jockstrap that no one can fit in besides me." He says that with such pride beaming from ear to ear, I nearly crack a smile, but I hold strong. Can't give away my excitement over sitting next to him just yet.

"Jockstrap?" I ask. "That's an interesting item to choose over something like . . . I don't know, a dress shoe."

"That's because I wear jockstraps," he says.

"For fun?" I ask, feigning confusion.

His brow draws together.

Oh dear me, is the famous hockey player not used to people not recognizing him?

Hilarious.

"No, not for fun," he says. "I play hockey."

"Oh, that's nice," I reply. "In like a middle-aged men's league?"

"Middle-aged?" he nearly shouts as his water is set in front of him. He doesn't even bother looking at it as he stares me down with vicious eyes. "Thirty-one is nowhere near middle-aged, thank you very much. And I play professionally."

I've always heard about Levi Posey being the funniest, the most sensitive, almost like the golden retriever everyone wants in a man, but with a reputation for sleeping around and standing up for his teammates out on the ice. From the minute of conversation we've had, every aspect of that reputation is true.

"Oh, that's cool. Professional hockey, is that usually your pickup line? That you play professional hockey? Bet you look for women to line up at your feet when you mention that."

"No," he says with a slight lift of his chin while he reaches for his water. "I have a different pickup line."

"Uh-huh, and what would that be?"

"Why would I tell you my pickup line? I'm not even sure I want you to hear it. It's pretty strong. I don't need you getting all clingy on me when I'm still assessing you."

"Assessing me?" I ask, amused by his honesty.

"Yes," he replies. "Who's to say that I would even want you?"

I analyze him for a moment. "From the way your gaze is

straining to stay north, I'm pretty sure there's some want coming from your end."

"Straining seems like an intense way to put it."

"Because your eyes are twitching. Go ahead, just take a look. I know you want to."

"I'm better than that."

I chuckle. "You are, are you? So if I were to, I don't know, drag my hand down the center of my chest, you wouldn't follow it?"

"Nope," he says, leaning back and taking a sip of his drink. "I'm not that easy. I like a challenge, and that shirt challenged me from a mile away."

"Is that why you came over here?"

"I came over here because I was thirsty."

"Thirsty for what?" I ask with a smirk as I lean toward him. "Water . . . or something else?"

He casually wets his lips, and it is single-handedly one of the sexiest things I've ever witnessed.

"Maybe a little bit of both." He holds his hand out to me. "I'm Levi."

I take his hand, sliding our palms together and reveling in the feel of how large his hand is compared to mine. A hand that I know handles a hockey stick with precision and grace. A hand that so easily can switch from playing a sport to creating a blood-bath on the ice.

"Nice to meet you, Levi," I answer, then pull away before I find myself running the tips of my fingers over his wrist. It's a seduction technique I've used plenty of times.

"And you are?" he asks, dragging it out.

"Unavailable," I say before taking another sip of my drink.

His brow falls. "Unavailable as in . . . you have a boyfriend, girlfriend, married?"

"Unavailable for someone like you."

"Someone like me?" he asks, sitting taller while pointing at his chest. I can see the spark in his eye, the feeling of being challenged once again pulsing through his veins, hence why I told him I was unavailable. Nothing like spoon-feeding a man in order to get him to fall right where I want him . . . in my bed.

Because, oh my God, a night with Levi Posey would be a dream come true.

"Yes, someone like you."

He fully faces me now so our knees knock together. "And what is so wrong with someone like me?"

"For one, you're drinking water at a bar, which means you're here for one thing and one thing only, to pick up a girl. Second, you refuse to look at my cleavage even though I know you want to. If you were a more confident man, you would have stolen at least three glances by now. And third, you're far too good-looking."

The last reason puts a smile on his face as he leans in closer to me. "Understandable. But I think you're judging me wrongly. Sure, I came down here to hook up. I'm not going to lie about that. I want to fuck tonight, and I see no problem in wanting to find someone compatible. Second, I've glanced at your delicious tits four times. Each time I've looked, you were looking away. To prove it, you're not wearing a bra right now, and I know that not because of the obvious split down your shirt but because both your nipples are pebbling against the thin gold fabric barely being held together by a string." That just made them harder. "And last, can't help that I'm hot, babe. God was generous with this bone structure." He flashes me a devilish smile. "Only question is, are you willing to give me a chance?"

No wonder the man is known as the player on the team. If he addresses all women like this, there's no question they're falling at his feet.

I mull over his proposition for a moment, wanting him to sweat it out before saying, "Maybe we can move over to one of those couches and talk some more."

He devilishly smirks. "I love talking." He stands from his chair and, with one hand, carries his drink. He takes my hand with the other, helping me down from the chair. Together, we weave through the dining area, eyes watching us until we reach a more private couch with a high back tucked into the corner of the room. I take a seat first, and when he sits down next to me, he leaves no room between us.

"Care to tell me your name?" he asks.

"Think you've earned it?"

"I think so," he says. "I got you over here, didn't I?"

"You did." I lean back on one hand, and this time, I catch him giving me a full perusal, his eyes fixed on my chest for a few beats longer. *That's it, take your fill.*

I've always been open about my sexuality. I've never been offended by a man's blatant gaze. I find it empowering that I can create such desire in someone else, *and* I have the choice of whether I want to indulge in that desire. So having Levi give me a possessive once-over only turns me on.

"Does that grant me your name at least?"

"Maybe," I say. "I think I need to know more about you first."

He turns toward me, tucking one leg up against mine so there really is no room between us. "What do you want to know?"

I let my eyes linger on his lips for a beat before I ask, "Was I your first choice when you came down here?"

"Yes," he answers.

"How do I know you're not lying?"

"Because you're a redhead, and redheads make my blood boil in a good, heart-racing way. You also have amazing tits. And when I got closer, I saw how light your eyes were and was captivated. No one else in this room was worth my time compared to you."

"What a line," I scoff as I reach for my drink and take a sip, letting his words hit my soul. Once I swallow, I say, "But it did make me all warm inside."

"That's a start. Tell me, what do you do?"

"Nothing," I answer. "I'm still in school." He pauses, and I can see the panic on his face, so I place my hand on his thigh and add, "Grad school."

"Oh." He nervously laughs. "Okay, that, uh . . . that sits better with my conscience."

"Ten years older than me sits better with me too. I like them older."

"Yeah?" He lifts a brow. "Why's that?"

"More mature," I answer. "I've seen my fair share of idiots my age, and they just don't vibe the way I want them to."

"And how would that be?" he asks.

"Well, I prefer when the man I'm with actually makes me come and doesn't leave it up to me while he's cleaning himself off."

His brow creases together. "Did a guy actually do that to you?"

I hold up two fingers and wiggle them at him. "Twice. I also prefer for the man I'm with to have some meat on his bones, the ability to grow facial hair, and some semblance of an idea of what it means to seduce a woman."

"No problem there," he says as he leans his shoulder against the back of the couch but stays turned toward me. "I once grew a beard so thick that I lost a jellybean in it."

I let out a laugh just loud enough to draw attention from other tables.

"Wow, you sure know how to turn a lady on, lost jellybeans in beards." I shiver. "Really gets me hot."

"I knew you'd appreciate that." He smiles, and it's so incredibly sexy that I find myself leaning toward him. He takes advantage of the lean by placing his hand on my leg and drags his thumb softly up and down my inner thigh. Fuck, I hate that I didn't wear a skirt tonight. His hand on my bare skin would undoubtedly feel sublime.

"What else do you look for in a man?" he asks. "Maybe I can check off more of your boxes."

"Hmm, well, large hands."

He lifts his hand from my thigh and holds it up, then takes my hand and places it right up against his, comparing the size. No contest, his eclipses mine.

"That big enough?"

"It will do." I smirk.

He returns his hand to my leg. "What else?"

"I prefer a large dick."

His brow lifts again because a naughty smile passes over his lips. "Can't whip out my cock for you in public, so you're going to have to take my word for it, but you can look at my feet and make your own assessment."

I bend at the waist and glance at one of his feet . . . one of his extremely large feet.

My mouth goes dry from the thought of how that could translate into so much more.

When I glance back up at him, he says, "Like what you see?"

To throw him a bone, I reply, "I do." And then I twist toward him so his hand on my thigh slides over my hip. "What do you like in a woman?"

"Confidence," he says. "No shame. Humor. And a great pair of killer eyes. Which you have."

"Hmm, I thought you were going to say tits."

"That's just a bonus," he says, wetting his lips again.

"What about in the bedroom?" I ask. "If I were to go up to your room tonight, what would you expect from me?"

"I expect nothing, but I accept everything," he says.

"So . . ." I dance my fingers over the unbuttoned portion of his shirt. "If I were to tell you that I wanted to give you, I don't know, a lap dance as a way to disrobe myself, would you be okay with that?"

"Baby, I would hum music for you if you needed it."

I chuckle. "And if I were to, I don't know . . ." I drag my fingers down the front of his chest to his stomach, where I can feel the definition of his abs against my fingertips. "Want to take you into my mouth, would you let me?"

"I would help you to your knees and offer you a pillow to kneel on."

"Ooo, a gentleman." I move my hand closer to his waistline.

"And if I told you I wanted to come on your cock, would you try to get me to come on your tongue first?"

"Yes," he answers, his eyes looking hazy now, so I move my hand just a bit more south until I come in contact with his hardening cock. His teeth pull over his bottom lip as he stares at me, never telling me to stop, so I dance my fingers over his length.

"But I said I wanted to come on your cock, not your tongue."

"You act as if you've only come once in a night."

"What if I have?" I ask.

"Then you need to spend the night with me, baby, because you aren't coming just once. Guaran-fucking-tee."

My nipples go hard from the thought.

A dull throb erupts between my legs.

And all caution is thrown to the wind as I realize there is no chance in hell I'm not getting off several times tonight. I can tell he wants this, but I know for a fact that I want this more.

My palm smooths over his cock, and he growls under his breath as he moves in close and drags his hand up my arm, to my shoulder, then right to the base of my neck, where he lightly encircles it, claiming me as his right here at this moment.

"You want this, don't you?" he asks.

"I think you know the answer to that, Levi."

"Then tell me your fucking name and come back to my room with me because I'm dying to show you what it's like to be with a real man."

I wet my lips and run my hand over the side of his cheek, feeling the scruff from the day. "Maybe you can just fuck me without knowing my name," I answer.

"What if I fuck you and like it too damn much, then what?"

"You saying this could be more than one night for you? Because this is one night for me."

"I'm saying it would be nice to know who the hell is making me hard as a goddamn stone right now. I think that's only fair."

"Perhaps," I say as I lean in close, leading with my breasts as I drape my arm over his shoulder, looking for a small taste. I let my fingers sift through his hair as I move in until I'm only an inch from his face. My breasts press against his chest, and his hand slides up the back of my shirt as he brings me in that last inch, right before our mouths lock.

Immediately, I part my lips and get lost in the feel of his tongue sliding against mine, of the demand he has for me, of the way he pulls me in just enough that I'm almost sitting on his lap.

You can relinquish a certain amount of control when you're kissing someone else, and right now, I surrender completely to Levi. I let him take over, loving how his tongue artfully tangles with mine. Loving how his hand slowly slides to my ribs so his thumb rests just under my breast. And loving how the scruff of his jaw scrapes against the sensitive skin on my face.

Everything about this kiss is addicting.

Everything about this kiss tells me I made the right decision.

And everything about this kiss leads me to believe this will be the best night of my entire life.

Not wanting to get too out of hand in the middle of the bar, I pull away from the kiss and watch as his eyes slowly open and make contact with mine.

He stares.

Almost unbelieving. Like he can't quite possibly comprehend the kiss we just shared.

I'm right there with him because I can still feel the sparks shooting off between us.

"That was, uh . . . great," he says in shock.

I smile because, yeah, that was great.

That was more than great.

That was addictive.

That was everything I wanted and so much more.

If I wasn't already convinced I'd be spending the night with this man, I am now.

I smooth my hand up his chest, wanting another taste. So I lean in just as something catches the corner of my eye. I glance over Levi's shoulder and spot my dad walking toward the dining room with a few people gathering around him.

Oh shit.

I quickly pull away from Levi. "Uh, I . . . uh, I need to go."

"What?" he asks.

"Yeah, I think, oh yup, that's my phone." I pick up my phone, and I bring it up to my ear. "Hello. Yup, hi. Sure, be there soon. Okay. Bye." I stand from the couch, and Levi quickly stands as well, letting his back face the dining room. "Sorry, got to head out, but it was nice chatting with you."

"Wait, seriously?" he asks. "Is everything okay? Was it something I said?"

"Nope, great kiss." I pat his chest. "Just need to help out a friend, so good luck with the hockey and everything." I start to leave when he grabs my hand, stopping me.

"Wait, I don't even know your name."

"Oh yeah, right . . . well, see ya." And with that, I sneak off toward the back, away from where my dad is talking to who I can only assume are a few fans. I slip behind the bar and out of sight.

I lean against the wall behind me and take a few deep breaths.

Ugh, the biggest cock block of all time. But if my dad caught us kissing, he would have not only killed me . . . but he would have murdered Levi.

⸏⸏⸏

Little less than a year later . . .

I KNOCK on my dad's office door and take a bite of my bologna sandwich. Whoever's bologna this is, it's freaking good. It's my third one this week.

"Come in," my dad's raspy voice says, so I open the door and walk right in, making sure to shut the door behind me. When he looks up at me, he sets his tablet to the side and leans back in his chair. "What the hell are you eating?" he asks in greeting.

"A sandwich. Bologna. Want to try?"

"Christ, no."

I shrug and take a bite. His loss.

You'd think winning last season would have lightened the old man up, but according to the scowl in his brow and the distaste in his expression, nothing is ever good enough for this man. I chalk it up to the new season and the pressure on his shoulders for another win. "You beckoned?"

"Yes, I did." He leans forward now, his chair creaking beneath his large body. His bald head is shinier than ever under these lights, and the muscles in his traps look like they're about to explode out of his shirt from the tension set in his shoulders. "I want to know why I just got a call from your college admissions saying they're returning the check I made out to them for your tuition this semester?"

Crap.

Freaking admissions. They couldn't give me the weekend to figure out what to say to my father? They had to contact him right away?

"They called you, huh?" I ask, going for casual.

"Yes, they fucking called me," Dad nearly roars. "What the fuck is going on, Wylie?"

Here's the thing, when you have a father who has been a single dad for a better part of two decades, he tends to be very cranky, very short-tempered, and very demanding of perfection. I knew he wouldn't take this well, but he's already at level nine out of ten, and ten is when he blows a gasket.

Trust me when I say you don't want to see that happen.

I've seen it, and the fire in his eyes will make your legs quiver with fear.

Clearing my throat, I rest my sandwich on the edge of my dad's desk. "Well, I planned on telling you after your game tonight, but since they called, I guess I'm going to have to let you in on what's happening."

"Damn right, you're going to let me in on what's happening. Tell me what's going on, Wylie. Now."

Yup, he's fuming.

Tread carefully.

Still trying to be casual because maybe my soothing voice will calm him, I say, "You see, I've been doing some thinking for almost a year now, ever since last semester to be precise, and well, I sort of haven't been having much fun at school—"

"School isn't supposed to be fun, Wylie. School is supposed to be educating."

"Yup, hear you on that one, Dad," I say, pointing at him. "Love education, but, uh . . . well, I don't foresee myself continuing down the road I've been studying."

"The road as in business?" he asks.

"Yes."

"And what road would you like to continue down exactly?" he asks, his nostrils flaring—a sure-fire sign that the steam inside him brewing like a tea kettle is ready to spout out of his ears.

Knowing there's no easy way of putting this, I go with the facts. "I'm not finishing my business degree. I'm pursuing independent graphic art instead."

"What?" Dad roars, spittle flying from his mouth as he stares me down. "No, not happening." He shakes his head and picks up his phone. "Miranda, transfer me to the University of Vancouver's admissions."

"Dad." I lean forward to grab the phone from him, but he leans back. "I'm not going back there."

"The fuck you're not," he says. "You have one year left. Finish it out, take your degree, and do something worthwhile."

"This is worthwhile, Dad."

He hangs up the phone with a slam. "Graphic art? You think graphic art is worthwhile? What are you going to do? Dream up logos for the local shipping yard? Jesus Christ, Wylie. This is your future you're talking about, not some random idea that came into your head one lonely night."

Growing frustrated with my dad's ignorance—because the man *does not know me at all*—I say, "It's not a random idea that's come to my mind. I've been going to classes at night for a year and am really good at it. I've been paid a few times."

"Paid a few times? Well, then." Dad wipes his hands and leans back in his chair. "Then, by all means, let me roll out the red carpet. You've been paid 'a few times,' so we might as well start looking into private jets."

My expression falls flat as I stare at the man I hold in high regard. The man who raised me and put me first in every aspect, even over hockey. When my mom left him and said she didn't want to take me with her, he stepped in and gave me a memorable childhood. Is he controlling? Yes. Does he think he can run my life? Yes. But do I love him . . . yes, although he's making it hard at the moment.

"Dad, this means a lot to me, and I think if you just let me show you what I can do, you will believe that I can do something great with this."

"I have no doubt you have talent," he says. "You're my daughter, after all, but that doesn't negate the fact that you're throwing away a stable future."

"A master's in business doesn't provide a stable future. A master's in business is like throwing a coin in a pond and hoping someone makes your wish come true. I don't want a desk job, something that bores me day in and day out, and over the past year, I've come to realize that's exactly what will happen if I continue moving forward with this degree. I don't want to waste my time or your money."

"You've already wasted my money if you cut out a year before you graduate." He runs his hand over his smooth head. "I don't see why you can't just finish the year, graduate, and then pursue whatever it is you want to pursue."

"Because it's a waste of time, Dad. It's a giant waste of my time, and you, out of everyone, know how time is an invaluable commodity. You never get it back. So why would I waste a year of my life to appease someone else?"

"Because I'm your father, and I've paid for your college until now. I've housed you, fed you, taken care of you."

"And I appreciate everything you've done for me, Dad, but I'm twenty-two, and I think I should be able to start making my own decisions, don't you?"

"No," he says flatly, not even considering it.

I sigh heavily. "Well, I don't know what else to say other than I'm not going back to school, so if you want to pay for my classes, by all means, pay for them, but I won't attend."

He does not take too kindly to that because his jaw tenses, then works back and forth as his eyes remain fixed on me.

That look would have scared me right out of my shoes a few years ago. I would have apologized and told my dad I'd do whatever he wanted. But over the past few years, I've grown a thicker skin. I've started to realize what I want—well, at least what I don't want. The direction of my graphic art aspirations is still a little foggy, but I do know I want to be creative.

"Fine," he says while placing his hands on the desk. "If that's what you want, then you can cut out of school." Why do I feel like that's not the end of the conversation? There's no way he's going to let me just quit school, not with the anger boiling inside him.

"Fine?" I ask. "I can pursue graphic art?"

"Yes, of course. If anything, I want you to be happy."

I don't believe that for a second. He has something up his sleeve.

"But . . ."

And there it is.

"Since I paid for your five years of college, I believe you owe me something."

I sigh heavily, knowing it was too good to be true.

"And what do I owe you, Dad?"

He folds his hands together. "Here's the deal. I don't think you're making a smart choice."

"That much is obvious," I say as I fold my arms across my chest.

"Therefore," he continues, "I think you owe me one semester."

"Of school? What's the point—"

"Of working."

26

"Working?" I ask.

"Yes, working. Working a job that you might possibly have to work in order to pay the bills while you attempt to pursue this graphic art thing. I'll call admissions, tell them you're taking a semester off and to expect you back at the beginning of the year. Unless you can prove to me that you can hold a steady job and make headway on your graphic art desires."

"Where's the catch?" I ask.

"There is no catch," he says.

"Dad, come on, there has to be a catch."

"Well, you will have to be financially independent from me."

Boom. *Yep. The catch.*

It's not that I *need* my dad's money. I could survive on my own. I have a few thousand saved from the few jobs I've taken. I could find a job and make a living, prove to him that I don't need his money or a stupid master's in business to make my life work.

I shrug. "That's fine."

"Cut off from me completely," he says. "No housing. No car. No insurance. Nothing."

No housing?

Well, when he puts it like that, I might have to get a pedicure so I can start selling feet pics. Housing in Vancouver is expensive, and I don't have THAT much money saved.

"Dad, it's really expensive to live here in Vancouver."

"Not if you have a well-paying job that you earned through a solid college education." He smiles at me with an *I got you* look. "Don't worry, though," he continues. "I'll give you a week to get on your feet. I won't kick you out immediately, and I'll hook you up with a job that will resemble what you might have to do to make your dreams come true."

"And what sort of job is that?" I ask, knowing full well he's probably setting this up for me to fail.

"What all other struggling creatives do . . . a personal assistant." He smiles, and I swear a gleam beams off his tooth.

I see what he's trying to do. He's trying to scare me. Make me think that I can't do this. That my life will be filled with retrieving coffees and returning clothes while trying to sneak in some personal time to be creative when I get a moment, but little does he know, I'm just as stubborn as he is because if he cuts me off, makes me move out, creating a scenario where I'm bound to fail, it only makes me want to prove him wrong that much more.

So with my chin held high and my confidence brimming with *I can do this*, I lend out my hand and say, "Deal." Surprised, he takes my hand in his and gives it a shake. "Now, who will I be assisting?"

Chapter Two

LEVI

"Who the fuck keeps eating my bologna?" I yell as I toss the empty bologna bag in the trash. "And who leaves the empty deli bag in the fridge? That's fucking rude." I turn toward OC who is sitting at one of the tables in the cafeteria, eating a protein bar. "Is it you?"

His nose crinkles. "Dude, I know better by now not to touch your bologna."

"Please tell me when you say bologna, you're talking about Posey's disgusting sandwiches and not something else?" Silas asks as he walks into the cafeteria and grabs an electrolyte drink.

Silas Taters is one of my very best friends and our right wing. A quick motherfucker, he practically tiptoes across the ice, nearly outskating all our opponents. He was a grumpy asshole for a bit before he met Ollie, who is now the most important person in his life. He lives and breathes to see her, and they're together, thanks to me.

And before you get confused and ask who the other best friends are, let me just give you a quick rundown.

Pacey Lawes is our goalie. Ten out of ten in the stretching department, he can do the splits without cracking his nuts in half. He's probably the most levelheaded out of all of us and is currently engaged to Winnie. They're in love and happy . . . because of me.

Then there's Eli Hornsby. Our other defenseman besides myself. He has the prettiest goddamn face you will ever lay your eyes on, likes green apples and French silk pie, and got Pacey's sister, Penny, pregnant. They had a baby, named him Holden, and now they're living happily ever after and in love . . . because of me.

Rounding it all out is Halsey Holmes. A book nerd, the quiet one, the mysterious center with the speed of a goddamn gazelle, he holds the record for most goals in Agitators history and has the girthiest dick on the team. We're talking a thick motherfucker that scared me once in the shower. He's currently married—got married over the summer—to Blakely, who works for the Agitators and Cane Enterprises. Yeah, both. Blakely is so good that after the wedding, the Agitators front office asked her to do some contract work and gave her office space so she could work both jobs while being close to her husband. Talk about fucking power. She's also Penny's best friend. But Blakely and Halsey are happily married and in love . . . because of me!

Are you seeing a trend here?

All these assholes are head over heels, living in their lover era, because of me.

OC, Oden O'Connor, is the only lonely one left besides yours truly because I haven't had the chance to dig my meaty claws into him yet. But word on the street is he has a thing with one of our athletic trainers. We got drunk one night and shared some secrets. He told me about Grace, and well . . . we don't have to talk about what I told him.

"I have a hell of a lot more respect for bologna than to refer to my dick as the most delicious meaty substance ever formed," I say. "So no, I wasn't talking about something else. I was talking about my fucking bologna. Someone has been eating it."

"You sound like one of those bears from that Goldilocks story," OC says. And then in a deep voice, he carries on, "Someone's been sleeping in my bed. Someone's been eating my bologna."

"If only someone has been sleeping in my bed," I mutter. Been a bit of a drought as of late. I blame these teammates of mine. I've been so busy taking care of their lives that I haven't been able to take care of mine.

But that stops today.

After tonight's game, I'm going out, and I'm going to pick someone up. We are going to fuck. My dick will be happy. And then everything will be right in the world.

"You really should get yourself a girlfriend," Taters says as he kicks back and puts his feet up on one of the tables. I quickly push his feet off.

"Show some respect. Pacey nervously eats his protein bar on that table before games," I chastise.

"Seriously, though, wasn't it last season when OC let the cat out of the bag and told us that you're crushing on some girl? What ever happened with that?"

OC slowly sinks into his chair, knowing full well he broke our drunk-guy code that night. It was in a text thread. He was getting all riled up, probably trying to gain likes since he was the new guy at the time, and blurted it out. He received a stern talking-to after that and was put on probation.

He has yet to be fully trusted again.

"Nothing happened," I answer. "And it's nothing you need to concern yourself with. That is private information that never should have seen the light of day in the group chat."

"Says the guy who butts into everyone else's love lives," says Taters.

"Oh fuck off," I say as I take a seat at the table, bologna sandwich-less. "The only love life I butted in on was Halsey's, but that's because it was low-hanging fruit, and there was no way he was going to pluck it. Other than that, I was a savior to the rest of you. And you're welcome, by the way. I take presents as thank-yous. Expensive watches, fancy shoes, and tailored suits."

"You're delusional," Taters says.

I glance over at the fridge, contemplating what to do. I need a sandwich before my game, but I'm not one to send an SOS to the staff. If this were Taters or Hornsby, they probably would have already sent someone to the store to buy more bologna.

Not me. I'm a gentleman, not a diva.

"It looks like he's thinking about his sandwich," OC says.

"That's because he is. He needs one before every game."

I stare my two teammates down. "It gives me protein and energy," I say. "It makes me skate harder and faster. It gives me comfort and ease. Bologna is the reason I'm able to accurately dig the puck away from our opponent from behind the net. It isn't just any sandwich. It's magic. So excuse me for needing that fucking sandwich." My fists grow tight as I try to take calming breaths and . . . wait. I turn toward OC and Taters and say, "Did one of you motherfuckers take my bologna? Because if you did, it's not funny. So just bring me my bologna, and no one will get hurt."

I hold out my hand, but Taters and OC don't move.

Finally, OC says, "Dude, although it's slightly entertaining watching you spiral over processed meat, I know better than to fuck with your bologna."

"Same," Taters says, holding his hands up in defense. "The whole team knows better."

I slam my fist on the table. "Then who the fuck did it?"

"Posey!" I nearly fly out of my chair at the sound of my coach's voice. I turn to see him standing in the doorway of the cafeteria, looking like he's ready to blow his fist through the wall.

Did he . . . did he take my bologna?

"Coach Wood," I say, straightening up. "Can I help you—"

"My office. Now." He walks away, his bald head glistening under the fluorescent lights in the hallway.

"Fuck," I mutter. "I think my dick just shriveled up."

"If yours didn't, mine sure as hell did," OC says.

"What the hell could that be about?" Taters asks, looking concerned.

"I don't know, but will you come with me and hold my hand?" I ask.

"Fuck, no." Taters shakes his head. "You're on your own."

I glance over at OC, and he shakes his head as well. "Sorry, man. That's a you thing."

"And here I thought you were my friends. My family." I push my chair in and head down the hallway toward my coach's office.

Sure, I might be a thirty-two-year-old man with plenty of life experience under my belt, but that will never change the fact that I still want to weep into my pillow when my coach demands I join him in his office. From college to professional, I've always feared the dreaded office visit because nothing good comes from it.

Nothing.

It means they've found out about something you did, and you have to sit there and get lectured and berated about how you need to be a better example. How you need to be a better representative for the team.

Like, don't fuck your teammate's sister.

That was college.

Don't get wasted the night before a game and sit your bare ass on the coach's car windshield that's covered in snow.

Also college.

Don't run around the locker room naked and towel-whip your teammates in the ass.

That was last season before the playoffs, and to be honest, the zip in the ass propelled us to win the Cup . . . so once again, some thanks would be appreciated.

I probably have two solid years left on the ice, but that doesn't lessen the anxiety ramping up in my chest over what Coach Wood will say to me.

I have this sick and twisted feeling in my stomach about what's going to happen.

I very much want to do anything to please my coach because that's how I was raised. Respect your coach, do what he says, don't fuck up.

Well . . . looks like I've fucked up, and I don't know how.

It's not like I've fucked anyone recently, which is what most of my infractions are, despite not mentioning them above. I fuck the wrong person, and it comes back to bite me in the ass.

The reporter.

The opposing team's social media manager.

The owner's wife.

Oye, that one nearly got me kicked out of the league.

But in my defense, I wasn't aware of these things, and it wasn't until later that I found out my dick was in the wrong pussy.

The very wrong pussy.

But this can't be that. Lately, I've developed a difficult case of blue balls.

So what could it be?

When I reach his door, I give it a knock only for him to yell, "Get your ass in here."

Yup, dick is completely shriveled.

I'm in trouble.

Is this a baby mama situation?

Please no, please no baby mamas. I'm not ready for diapers and bottles. I'm still as immature as a twelve-year-old.

On a shaky breath, I walk into his office and find him sitting in his chair, leaning back, hands crossed over his stomach.

I nervously lift my hand at him in a wave.

"Sit," he says tersely, so I quickly take a seat and look him in the eyes. If I know one thing about Coach Wood, he doesn't like squirrely men. He likes confident players, so even though my innards shiver in fear, I'll still pay him the respect he demands. "Do you remember the time I saved you from making a grave mistake in Washington?"

Ehhh . . . what?

I mean, yes, I do, but that is not the first sentence I expected him to say.

I shift in my chair. "Uh, with that one girl at the bar?" I ask.

He nods. "She was an undercover reporter, and you had no idea. You were about to take her up to your room, and I stopped you."

I nod. "Yes, you really did me a solid there," I say, unsure of where this is going since that was over a year ago.

"I'm glad you see it that way." He leans forward and places his hands on his desk. Looking me dead in the eyes, he says, "I'm going to need you to return the favor."

"Uhh . . . you want me to stop you from taking an under-cover reporter up to your room?"

"No, you moron." He sighs with irritation. "I need you to do me a favor."

"Oh." I nervously chuckle. "Well, that I can do."

"Good." He clasps his hands together. "I need you to teach my daughter a lesson."

"You have a daughter? When did that happen?"

"Twenty-two years ago."

"Huh, interesting." *He has a daughter?* How many years has he been our coach? How the hell did we not know he had a daughter? I cross one leg over the other and casually say, "You know, we don't get to talk much. What is she like? Are you close with her? Do you—"

"Can you shut the fuck up?"

I uncross my leg and sit up straight. "Yup, of course. So . . . you were saying . . ."

"I need you to teach my daughter a lesson."

Confused, I tilt my head to the side and say, "Uh, what kind of lesson, sir? Because I'll be honest with you, education and school really weren't my strong suit. Wasn't really into the whole learning thing or tutoring. Although I do excel at meddling. Perhaps I can offer you some help in that regard."

He pinches the bridge of his nose, clearly growing increasingly more frustrated with me by the second. Too bad for him, I grow more irritating the more nervous I am. "Not an actual lesson. Jesus fuck, Posey, you need to stop getting into fights on the ice." He picks up a pen and clicks it a few times. "I need you to hire my daughter as your personal assistant. I know you don't have one, correct?"

"Correct," I answer. "But how is me hiring your daughter as my personal assistant going to teach her a lesson?"

"Glad you asked." He leans back in his chair now, looking more like a manipulating mastermind than the scary coach who screams at me daily. "My daughter, Wylie, has recently told me she wants to quit school, even though she has one year left in her master's program. She's been taking business classes, setting herself up for a great future, but instead wants to pursue graphic art."

"Ah." I nod, not quite understanding. "And that is a . . . bad thing?"

"Yes, it's a bad thing. Do you really think I want my daughter to be a struggling artist?"

"Well, to be fair," I say, "she does have you as a father, so would she really be struggling?"

His eyes narrow, and I realize that maybe I don't debate him on the welfare of his child but instead go along with whatever plan he has in mind.

"Although." I nervously laugh. "It would be a great life lesson to learn if she sees what kind of hardship it would be to be a struggling artist in a world of capitalism."

That lightens the scowl in his forehead. Despite the many fights on the ice, that was a pretty impressive comeback if I do say so myself.

"Glad you see it that way." He clears his throat. "To keep things short, I told her she could have one semester off to prove to me that she could handle making a life for herself as a graphic artist. If she can't make a life for herself, she must return to school. The caveat is that I've cut her off completely, but I told her I'd offer her a job that she'd probably have to take as a graphic artist to pay the bills. She agreed, which leads me back to you. You are the job. You will pay her minimum wage, and you will be demanding."

"Uh, what now?" I ask, blinking a few times.

"As your assistant, I require you to make her run around town, do illogical tasks, and work at all hours of the day. I want you to make her life a living hell, Posey. Show her that finishing school would be better than being a struggling artist."

"Wow, that sounds great. Quite the lesson to be learned," I say, trying to hide the sarcasm from my voice. "But I have to say, I'm not that high-maintenance."

"Then find a way to be high-maintenance. Have her clean your apartment. Make you meals. Do your shopping, your laundry. For fuck's sake, make her feed you your dinner because you're saving your energy for your games. Be respectful, as this is my daughter, but make her life hell."

"Uh-huh, I see where you're going with this, and wow, what a great plan." I slowly clap for him. "But I'm slightly hesitant because I do have a reputation and—"

"I already have an NDA for her to sign."

I nod, trying to come up with another reason as to why I don't want to be an asshole to my coach's daughter.

"What if I upset her?" I ask. "I don't want her going to you, and you getting pissed at me."

"If you upset her, I'll give you a goddamn bonus. I'll cover any fines you might incur through the season. I'm asking you to upset her."

"Yup, I hear that." I point at my ear. "Just feel uneasy about that aspect of it. I'm a pretty nice dude. Not one to hurt someone's feelings."

"Jesus Christ, Posey," Coach yells. "You beat men up on the ice for a living. I'm asking you to be a little demanding with my daughter. Is that something you really can't fucking handle?"

I quiver from the anger in his voice.

"No, I can." I swallow hard. "For sure I can, but you know, there's also the aspect of paying her. I tend to invest my money, so I'm not sure I can afford—"

"If you can't afford to pay my daughter minimum wage for a semester, then we need to talk about your spending habits."

"Quite right, quite right." I nod, starting to come up short with excuses. I snap my finger and point at him. "You know, I actually enjoy the mundane tasks of life, and I'm not sure I'll be able to give them up. Nothing gives me more joy than picking up a pack of batteries from the corner store because I forgot to write them down on my grocery list. So you know—"

"For fuck's sake, Posey. Are you trying to tell me you can't do me this little favor?" His eyes bore into me, like lasers trying to blow my head off my neck. "Because I would hate to see what happens if you can't."

And this is why I should stop sleeping around. This very reason.

Because people hold it against you at the most inopportune time.

Also, I'm pretty sure Coach Wood doesn't really understand the definition of a favor. It's a simple ask like, oh hey, can you help me move? Or heck, I have an itch on my back, can you get that for me? Or egad, I forgot my underwear, mind if I grab a pair of yours?

Those are favors. This is . . . this is a chore.

This is a task.

This is an objective.

A mission.

A secret operative.

A goddamn developing nightmare that I want nothing to do with.

But that doesn't seem like an option for me.

"Uh, no," I say, tacking on a smile. "I can help you. This won't be a problem at all."

"Good." He picks up a piece of paper and hands it to me.

"What's this?" I ask.

"Ground rules."

"Ground rules?" I ask, staring down at the paper.

"Yes, ground rules." He picks up a piece of paper as well and starts reading. "Rule number one, you are not to become friends with my daughter. You are her boss, and that is it."

"Yup. Understandable. Establishing a—"

"Rule number two." Okay, moving on. "You will pay her minimum wage and offer her no bonuses."

"Bonuses, pffft, who likes those anyway?"

"Rule number three," he continues with a force in his voice. "You will not offer her a place to live."

"Wasn't planning on it. But just so I'm aware, will she be homeless?"

"Rule number four," he booms. Okay, so possibly homeless. Good to know. "There will be no perks to the job. No feeding her. No car service. No transportation. No credit card. She will have to figure all of this out on her own."

"So you want me acting as a ruthless dictator. I haven't practiced such a thing in my life just yet, but I'm up for the task. There's always a time for a first."

"And most importantly, rule number five. Under no circumstances will you have any sort of physical contact with my daughter."

"What do you mean—"

"Fucking her. You will not fuck her, Posey."

"Ahh . . ." I smile. "Well, no worries there. Pretty sure if she looks anything like you, there will be no need for rule number five."

His brow lifts, and I realize what I just said.

"I mean, shit, I didn't mean that. You're actually, wow, you're a good-looking guy, very attractive. The bald thing really accentuates your . . . uh, steely eyes, and the tan you've been able to procure while coaching a winter sport is really impressive. Not to mention your physique, just oof, what a bundle of muscles that are not wrinkly. Some people your age might look wrinkly, but not you. You're firm. Firm in all the right places. So much firmness. Just look at those forearms and the sinew and firmness. Lots of firmness. And you know, just to throw it out there, not that you asked, but if I were a woman, then hell yeah, I would be talking to you about a date, or maybe a kiss or—"

"Shut the fuck up."

"Yup." I nod. "Thank you for that." I bow my head as a courteous thank-you.

"There will be no fucking her. No touching her. Don't even look at her if you can avoid it."

I make a check mark in the air with my finger. "Got it. No plans to go anywhere near your daughter. There will be no touching, no sexual encounters, completely and utterly platonic."

He eyes me suspiciously, then finally says, "Good. Now sign on the line at the bottom."

"You want me to sign this?" I ask.

"Yes, I want you to agree to these terms and sign it."

Jokingly, I flip to the blank back page and then to the front again. "I don't know, sir. I think I might want my lawyer to look this over. Possibly my agent."

"Sign the fucking paper, Posey."

"Yup," I say, nearly jumping out of my seat from his booming voice. I grab a pen off his desk, sign quickly at the bottom, and then hand the paper back over to him. "Should we shake? Hug it out? Grab a whiskey and cheers?"

"Get the fuck out of my office."

"Sooo, that's a no on the celebration?"

"Get out," he yells while pointing at the door.

"Great, yup, I wanted to leave anyway." I stand from my chair and grip the handle to the door right before I pull away and ask, "Uh, when do I meet her?"

"Tonight, after the game. Come to my office."

"Got it. Okay, see you then. Yay for teaching lessons." I raise my fist in celebration.

He just points at the door. I get the hint and leave his office and head down the hallway toward the locker room, feeling like I was just put through the wringer.

So I have an assistant now.

I'd be sort of thrilled if it wasn't the coach's daughter.

Really thrilled if I didn't have this sick feeling that I'm being set up to fail.

Incredibly thrilled if I wasn't the one who had to teach this twenty-two-year-old a lesson on responsibility and career building.

What the hell am I in for?

⸺

"JUST PUT A BUTTERFLY BANDAGE OVER IT," I say as blood drips down the side of my face.

Grace, our trainer, holds a towel to my face. "This needs to be cleaned up. I can't just put a butterfly bandage on it."

"I need to get back out on the ice," I say.

"You're winning by two goals and have one minute left in the game. You're going to the training room. Now move."

Irritated, I take the towel from her, press it against my face myself, then let her guide me back to the training room, fans on either side cheering me on as I leave the game. Surprisingly, this was not from a fight. Instead, it was an elbow to the head. Must have been a hard as shit elbow because I've never broken skin like this before.

Just my luck.

When we reach the training room, Grace tells me to take a seat on one of the benches, so I do as I'm told, sit down, and then pull my jersey up and over my head while Grace gathers the supplies she needs.

She glances over at me and says, "I'd appreciate it if you hold the towel to your head to help with the bleeding and not disrobe yourself."

"Sorry," I mutter as I bring the towel back up to my forehead, right above my eye.

When she comes over with her supplies, she sets them down on the bench and says, "You seem a bit off tonight. Any reason?"

"Off?" I say. "How so?"

"Well, normally, if someone elbowed you in the head, you

would have tossed your gloves and gone after them. You wouldn't have stood there, stunned. I think the fans were just as confused as your teammates. Think they were looking for a Posey Brawl."

"Oh," I say. "I guess I didn't think about it."

"Which means you were thinking about something else. Care to share what that is?"

"Not really," I say because I'm not sure I'm even aware of what's going on.

When I went back to the boys, they asked what Coach Wood wanted, and I told them that his daughter was looking for work and wondered if I needed an assistant. I left it at that. I felt like if I got into the details, they'd ask a lot of questions, and I wasn't up for it.

"Well, if you need someone to talk to about it, I'm here. You know, if it's girl troubles or something like that."

"Thanks, Grace," I say as she starts cleaning my cut. "I do have a question for you."

"Yeah?" she asks as she picks up some gauze. "What is it?"

"Do you happen to know who is eating my bologna?"

She pauses and lifts away from me to look me in the eyes. "That's your question?"

"Yes," I groan. "Someone is eating it, and I didn't get to have my pre-game sandwich today and I think it made me sluggish. I rely on that sandwich."

"Bologna is terrible for you. How many times have we gone over this?"

"Bologna is my savior. Wait . . ." I look at her. "Is it you? Are you taking my bologna away because you think it's bad for me, therefore you're eliminating it from my diet? That's really something we should discuss, Grace, before you start taking my bologna. Don't you think?"

"I'm not taking your freaking bologna, Posey. I might think it's terrible for you, but I understand the importance of rituals. I wouldn't mess with that."

"So then who is taking my bologna?"

"You just got a gash in the head, and that's what you're worried about?" she asks.

"Yes, because I don't get hurt. But I didn't have a bologna sandwich today, so maybe that's the reason."

Grace shakes her head as she finishes. "That's not the reason, but nice try. Okay, you're all set. Do not touch the tape, as you know, and wash your face with a washcloth. See me tomorrow so I can look at it."

I hop off the bench and grab my jersey. "Thanks, Grace."

"Not a problem," she says. "And hey, if you ever need to talk, I'm here."

I offer her a smile and then head into the locker room just as the guys start filtering in, smiles on their faces. We secured the win.

"How's the head?" Eli asks as he walks by me.

"Fine," I answer. "All bandaged up."

"You looked stunned out there on the ice. Everything okay?" he asks.

"Yup. Everything is fine," I answer. "Just have a headache."

"Posey," Coach calls out from the entry of the locker room. "Ten minutes, my office."

Jesus, can't give a guy a goddamn second?

I nod, but he's gone before he even sees me agreeing.

"What's that about?" Eli asks.

"Meeting his daughter, who is going to be my assistant."

"Wood's daughter is going to be your assistant?" Eli asks. "Dude, how did that happen?"

"Wait, you knew he had a daughter?"

"Everyone knows he has a daughter."

"Not everyone," I mumble. "But anyway, he knew I didn't have an assistant, and his daughter was looking for some experience." It's not a total lie. "Could be nice."

"So clearly, you've never met her," he says.

"No." I take off my skates and pads, being careful of my head. "Have you?"

"Yeah. Penny introduced me once." Eli smirks. "Dude, you have your work cut out for you."

"What does that mean?" I ask.

"You'll see." He chuckles, then nods toward the showers. "Better wash up. Wood doesn't like it when you're late."

I eye Eli for a few more seconds, but all he does is smile, so I move toward the showers and clean up. The entire time as I work through the process of trying to de-escalate my adrenaline from the game, I try to come up with a scenario where none of this will be weird and awkward, but the more I think about it, the more I regret agreeing to hire Coach Wood's daughter.

Like . . . really fucking regret it.

And it doesn't help that Hornsby tells me I have my work cut out for me. What the hell does that even mean?

I power through getting dressed, ignoring the chatter in the locker room, and avoiding reporters. I pocket my wallet, phone, and keys and then head toward Coach's office without a single goodbye to my friends. It wouldn't be the first time I snuck out.

When I reach Coach Wood's door, I give it a knock.

"Come in," he says.

I push through the door, half expecting his daughter to be in there, but when I see two empty chairs in front of his desk, I realize it's just me and him again.

He looks up at me from his tablet. "How's the head?"

"Fine," I answer. "Good win today."

"Could have been better," he says. Under Coach Wood's regime, there is always room for improvement. It's why we won last season, and it's why we're on track to win this season.

I take a seat. "Is your daughter here?"

"Does she look like she's here?" he asks.

"No, but I thought I would, I don't know, engage in small talk."

"Posey, does it seem like I'm the kind of guy who wants to engage in small talk?"

"Nope," I answer, rubbing my hands over my thighs.

"She's on her way. And when she gets here, I want to remind you of the rules we went over."

"Trust me." I tap my head. "They're engrained here. I'm here to teach her a valuable lesson about earning an education and nothing more. I don't house her. I don't feed her. We are not friends, and I certainly don't fuck her."

"Correct." He taps away on his iPad. "Because I don't want you fucking this up, I thought it might be easier on you if I send you a list of things for her to do every week on top of her tasks. That way, you don't slip up."

"Oh, shit, yeah, that would be helpful. Nothing too crazy, right? Like . . . getting me adult diapers. Because I know that might seem funny to you, but it's not funny to me."

"I don't have time to joke around, Posey."

"Right," I say while nodding. "That was foolish of me to think you would take advantage of the situation and try to embarrass me." *Or that you have any hint of a sense of humor.*

"If you slip up, I will embarrass you. Keep that in mind."

"No need to worry about me slipping up. I'm as solid as they come. Probably the most trustworthy on your team. Well-respected among the team, I've led the charge in many missions. I have this in the bag."

Just then, there's a knock on the door, and Coach Wood and I sit a little taller.

"Come in," Coach Wood says.

Yes, please come in. Can't wait to start this misery.

I hold my breath as the door cracks open, and a very familiar redhead pokes her head in. With a smile to her father, she says, "Is now a good time?"

"Perfect time," Coach Wood says, his voice a touch lighter than the screaming banshee he is when we're out on the ice.

And even though there is a distinct difference in the softness of Coach Wood when his daughter steps into the room, that is not what makes my heart beat faster.

Or my skin break out in sweat.

Nope, it's Coach Wood's daughter, and it's not just because

45

she's insanely hot with her dark red hair and light gray eyes or her killer curves.

Nope, it's the fact that I know that face. I know that voice. I've touched those legs. I've kissed those lips.

It's the redhead from the bar.

The girl I've been searching high and low for over the better part of a year. The girl who haunts me in my sleep. The girl I think about whenever I consider hooking up with another woman. The one I compare everyone to, who no one ever comes close to matching.

The girl I hired a fucking private investigator to find. That's how goddamn desperate I was.

Wasted money, since all I had to do was ask Coach Wood to meet his daughter.

Because holy shit, she's here.

"Posey," Coach Wood snaps, and I'm quickly tossed out of my reverie.

"Yes, hi." I clear my throat and hold out my hand awkwardly. "I'm Levi Posey, your new boss."

With a devilish smirk on her lips, Wylie—now I know her goddamn name—sits down in the chair next to me and takes my hand in hers. Just like last time, a bolt of electricity shoots up my arm and straight to my cock.

Mother of fuck . . .

"Great to meet you, Levi. I look forward to tending to your every need."

She lets go of my hand and turns to her father, who doesn't seem too pleased.

Maybe it was my staring.

Maybe it was her sexual innuendo.

Maybe because this office now feels like a pressure cooker.

Either way, he looks back and forth between us and says, "Wylie, you understand your job responsibilities, correct?"

"Oh yes, to be at Mr. Posey's beck and call."

"Levi," I croak out. "Levi is fine."

"To keep things professional, I prefer Mr. Posey," Wylie says with a glint in her stormy eye.

Jesus, is it hot in here? Because it feels really hot. Is it just me?

"Posey, you recall what we spoke about with boundaries?" Coach Wood asks, still eyeing me.

"Yes," I squeak. "Yup, all good there." I clear my throat. "Is there a, uh, start time—"

"Tomorrow would be great," Wylie says. "Actually, I'd love to go over what you need from me and your expectations if you're free."

Unsure if that's a smart idea, I glance over at Coach Wood, who gives a slight nod. Since I have the go-ahead, I say, "I'm free. Do we want to grab a—"

"One of the media rooms will be fine for your use," Coach Wood says.

"Yup, I was going to suggest that," I say even though I wasn't. I was going to say grab a drink, but he doesn't need to know that. "We can grab a media room."

"Perfect. Let me snag us a couple of drinks from the cafeteria, and I'll meet you in media room B. Does that work?" Wylie asks.

"Sure," I reply.

She stands from her chair and taps on her dad's desk. "Thanks for the opportunity, Dad. I really appreciate it." And then she's off, skipping right out of his office.

When the door shuts and I start to stand, Coach dangerously points his finger at me while his brow contorts into a valley of crevices. "Listen to me, you fuck," he starts, apparently forgetting his bedside manners for people doing him a favor. "I saw the way you just looked at her, and if you even think about her in any way other than your coach's extremely off-limits daughter, I will personally slice your dick off with a rusty pair of skates. Got it?"

I swallow the lump in my throat and attempt an even smile, but it feels more deranged than welcoming and reassuring. "You won't need to worry about me when it comes to your daughter," I say as fear pulses up my spine. Because holy fuck, he's right.

Wylie isn't the redhead I've been thinking about for a year. Wylie is my coach's daughter.

But not just that.

She is my *scary* coach's daughter.

Meaning, despite the kiss we shared or the way she made me feel that night, she is completely and utterly off limits.

"I'm counting on you," Coach Wood says. "I'll email you tasks for her to complete. Don't fuck this up."

"You can count on me," I say with a fist pump, feeling like a complete asshat.

Coach Wood ignores my enthusiasm and goes back to his tablet, silently excusing me.

Probably best.

I leave his office and make my way down to the media room, where I part the door only to find an empty room. I step inside and take a seat on one of the leather couches. I rub my sweaty palms across my pant legs and try to work this out.

I've been a decent human. I donate time and money to charitable causes. I'm a good teammate and an even better friend. Sure, I've slept around a bit, but every woman has been a more than willing participant. I wouldn't say that's a black mark on my name that would put me in such a position where I need to repay my coach by hiring his daughter—who I've secretly been trying to find for a year—the one and only woman who has actually made me think I want more.

I drag my hand over my face.

What are the fucking chances?

Pretty good apparently.

The door to the media room opens, and Wylie comes in, holding two coffees, each with a cookie resting on top. The door shuts behind her, and she saunters over to me in a pair of jogger pants and a crop top. I try to avoid looking at her exposed stomach, but I'm a guilty fucker as she moves closer. I can't help it. I've never found a woman as attractive to me as she is. She checks all my fucking boxes. Every single one of them.

"Thought you might want a little treat after such a great

win." She hands me the coffee with the cookie on top, then empties her pocket of sugars and creamers. "Not sure how you take your coffee, but I'll learn." Taking a seat, she turns toward me, propping one leg up on the couch just like the night we spent together. "How's your head? Looks like a nasty gash."

Is she really not going to address the giant elephant in the room? I know she knows who I am. There's no way she didn't know who I was that night. And she sure as hell can't fake it now. So I decide to break the silence on the past.

"So we're not going to talk about the first time we met?"

She presses her hand to her chest. "You remember that night?"

I nearly crumple my coffee cup in my hand as I say in a low voice, "Of course I remember that night. I sought you out. I *wanted* you. We kissed. It was phenomenal. You took off before I could even find out your name. You've left me wondering about you for a goddamn year."

"Technically," she says, holding up her finger, "it wasn't a full year, but that's neither here nor there."

"And the reason you didn't tell me your name, was that because of who your dad is?"

"That and protection. How did I know you weren't going to be some creep who took me back to your hotel room to do freaky things to me like tie me down and smell my feet?"

"Does it look like I'm that kind of man?"

She casually shrugs. "Never can be too sure."

"And then you took off, out of nowhere." I lean in even closer and say, "You were palming my dick."

"Was I?" she asks, sipping her coffee. "I can barely remember."

"Well, I fucking remember," I say. "I've remembered almost every goddamn night."

"That's sweet," she says. "And I love this reminiscing, but I truly think we should keep this professional, so if you could not talk about me palming your dick, I would appreciate it."

"Excuse me for trying to wrap my head around all of this.

You knew who I was that night. I had no fucking clue who you were."

"And now you do, so everyone is in the know. Should we talk living arrangements?"

"Uh, what?" I ask.

"As your assistant, I'm assuming you'll need me at all hours, so I'm guessing you'll need me to live with you."

Live with me? Is she fucking insane? I couldn't think of a worse situation. Shacking up with Wylie Wood? Nope. Not when she's off limits. The last thing I need is for her to be walking around my place in nothing but a towel, all wet from her shower.

Nope. Not going to happen.

"Yeah, I don't think I'll need you that much," I say. "Feel free to stay wherever you are."

"I really don't mind," she says. "I want to be the best assistant I can be."

"And I'm sure you'll be the best assistant ever . . . from your place of residence."

Her eyes bore into me, the same fucking eyes as her father, but whereas his are scary . . . hers are mesmerizing.

Oh, fuck me . . .

Chapter Three

WYLIE

He's infuriatingly handsome.

Like stop-you-in-your-tracks, you-have-to-stare handsome.

And the gash above his eye just makes him that much more attractive.

I've pushed that one night to the back of my mind, almost to the point that I've completely forgotten about it until Dad told me I would be working for Levi Posey.

Then it all came flooding back with a vengeance.

The command in his hands.

The teasing but deep tone of his voice.

The way his lips controlled me.

The scruff of his five o'clock shadow.

If it wasn't for spotting my dad across the dining space, I would know exactly what it feels like to have spent the night with Levi Posey.

And from the way my body reacts to him, I'd assume it

wouldn't have been a one-time thing. Nope, I would have kept going back.

So this, this right here, trying to act like that night meant nothing, is uncomfortable to say the least.

Painful actually.

Because even though it's been months, the moment I sat next to him, all I could think about was how much I wanted him still. How much I want a do-over of that night.

But of course, this is my luck. Instead of giving in to temptation, I must avoid it because I need to prove to my dad that a career as a graphic artist is a possibility. That I don't need to rely on him for help.

That I can make it on my own.

And getting mixed up with one of his players is not the way to do that.

But I will admit, if Levi has a bedroom to spare, I won't pass that up either, given I have one week to find a place to live and not much in savings at the moment.

Levi studies me. "Yeah, so I truly think it's best if you just stay where you are, and we can work out an arrangement with dropping things off at my place. Maybe we can fashion some sort of drop box."

And he's adorable.

Adorable when he's clearly reaching for any reason I shouldn't stay with him.

But that won't be acceptable. He's my only hope for housing.

"If I'm honest, I don't currently have a place of residence," I say.

His face softens as he asks, "You don't?"

"Not at the moment. I was going to look for a place tomorrow, but I'm sure you live in a fancy area, right? I'd want to be close to you so I can help you out, but given my salary and savings, I'm not sure I can afford anywhere near you."

He looks away from me and mutters something under his breath.

"What's that?" I ask. "I didn't catch what you said."

He sighs heavily and then presses his fingers to his forehead as if working through a complex equation. After a few seconds of silence, he says, "I have this spare room meant for a nanny. I don't use it. I don't even bother with it, honestly. It has a separate entrance and is just a room with a bathroom. That's it. It's connected to my apartment, and you can use it until you find a place that works for you, but you can't tell your dad."

"Really? I can stay there?" I ask, relief washing through me. I don't care if it's a closet. It's a roof over my head that I don't have to pay for. I will take just about anything.

"Yes." His eyes connect with mine. "But like I said, you can't tell your dad. I'm not fucking kidding about that, okay?"

"I promise. I won't say anything. Thank you, Levi. This is a huge weight off my shoulders. I really appreciate it."

"Sure," he begrudgingly says.

He might not be happy about it, but I am. Sorry to say, that's all that matters to me.

"When can I move in? Tomorrow?"

His eyes flash to mine in surprise. "Uh, if you want."

"That would be great. The sooner, the better."

"But you're not going to tell your dad, right? That I'm housing you?"

I tilt my head, studying him. "I told you I wouldn't. Why are you so adamant about this?"

"Because," he says, sitting taller. "I don't want him thinking I'm, uh, taking advantage or anything." Levi drums his fingers on his coffee cup, looking nervous and twitchy. After a few seconds of silence, he says, "Fuck, I'm just going to level with you, Wylie, okay?"

"That's probably best since I'm going to be your assistant," I reply.

He drags his hand over his face, looking pained. After a few seconds of mulling over his words, he starts with, "I just want to get this out in the open."

"Probably best," I say.

"I think the sooner we say it, the better."

"Could not agree more." I nod in approval.

"So I think if I just say it, then we can—"

"Oh my God, Levi, just say it." I laugh.

His Adam's apple bobs as he nods. "Yeah, so, uh . . . we had an almost night together."

"We did." I can't hide the smirk that appears because he is clearly distraught over this.

"If you hadn't ditched me that evening, I would have taken you back to my room."

"Yup, that's where it was leading."

He slowly nods and then looks me in the eyes. "And, uh, I would have fucked you."

"Yes, and I would have allowed that to happen multiple times."

"Multiple?" he asks, almost looking wounded.

"Oh yes. Multiple."

He presses his fingers to his eyebrow and takes a few seconds to gather himself. When he's ready, he says, "That being said"— he clears his throat—"I'm insanely attracted to you, and I'm not saying that as a pickup line. I'm putting it out there because I'm massively uncomfortable with this setup."

"Okay," I say, not expecting him to be so forthright. But also, oh my God! Levi Posey is insanely attracted to me. *The feeling is mutual.* But has he really given me more thought since our "almost night?" Yes, I've thought about him, but he's a player. He's probably had several *nights* with other women since then.

"And I need you to know that nothing will happen between us. What was in the past is in the past. We need to start on a fresh slate as if we don't know each other."

"Technically, we don't know each other," I say.

"I mean . . . know how, you know, how our lips, uh . . . kiss."

I chuckle. "Ah, that we do know about each other. But it's been long enough, you must have forgotten."

He looks away and once again mumbles something under his breath. It's cute, like he's conversing with the angel and devil on his shoulder.

Wanting to ease his tension, I say, "You don't need to worry about that night. I plan on being the epitome of a professional. This job means something to me, so I don't plan on screwing it up because we had one night where we were very attracted to each other and kissed. Let's just forget about it and move forward. Okay?"

"Yeah, that sounds good," he says.

"Perfect." I yawn as the late night's getting to me. "Well, you must be tired, given you just played a game, and your eye must be hurting, so I'll let you go." I hand him my phone. "Put your number in here so I have a way to get in touch with you and vice versa."

He plugs his number in my phone and sends himself a text. His phone beeps in his pocket, letting me know he has my number. When he hands me back my phone, I stand and say, "What's a good time for me to come over tomorrow to go over all of your needs?"

He stands as well, and I can't help but notice just how much larger he is than me. How much larger he is in person. I've spent the better part of a year watching him skate around the ice and slam men into the boards as if they weigh nothing, but seeing him in person and standing next to him, I realize all those games I watched did not do him justice.

"How about nine in the morning?"

"Nine?" I nearly shout only to realize that's a normal, appropriate time for people to do work things. "I mean, sure, nine sounds great. Can I bring you anything?"

"No, I'm good. I'll text you the address and show you to the nanny hole."

I smile. "Sounds like a sex club, The Nanny Hole."

"It's definitely not a sex club," he scoffs.

"Ooo, seems like you have experience in that area. Have you ever been to one?"

His eyes widen for a second before he shakes his head. "Uh, no."

Ha. I'm going to take that as a yes.

My goodness. Levi Posey enjoying a sex club. That's very interesting.

Intriguing.

And definitely not something I should be thinking about.

Or asking about for that matter.

"Well, if you did, I wouldn't judge you. I've been to a few. They're fun."

He pulls on the back of his neck, the muscles in his forearm straining. "Things I shouldn't know," he says, moving toward the door. "Okay, see you tomorrow at nine. I'll text you my address."

"Sounds good," I say as he disappears out of the room.

Well, I think that went well. As well as it could have gone.

I have a job.

A place to live.

And what seems to be a pretty easygoing boss.

Dad thought this would be a challenge, but it's seeming like anything but that.

Except for the glaringly obvious fact that my new boss is the sexiest man I've ever laid eyes on.

———

"YOU'RE UP EARLY," Dad says as he walks into the kitchen. I'm suckling at a cup of coffee, attempting to wake myself up. My class schedule had been fixed to have lectures later in the day along with some night classes for my graphic art, so this morning's wake up is making me rethink this entire challenge from my dad.

"Just gearing up for my day of work," I say. "Very excited to hit the ground running."

"Should be," Dad says as he moves over to the coffee and pours himself a cup. I made that all for me, but whatever. "Posey has been known to be hard to work with. Hence why he needed an assistant."

I find that hard to believe, but then again, I guess I don't know him the way my dad knows him.

"Well, I'm up for the challenge."

"I hope so." Dad leans against the counter. "I would hate to see you fail."

Ha. I'm calling bullshit on that. I know my dad loves me, but this challenge, this one he's hoping I don't complete? He's hoping more than anything for me to come crawling back to him, but to hell if I'll let that happen.

"Well, no need to worry about that, big guy." I elbow him. "I already have a place to stay, actually. I'm moving in today."

He whips his head around to look at me. "Where?"

"Uptown. It's a sublet," I answer, not wanting to give him all the details, not that he needs them. "Lucked out, actually. I was asking around yesterday, and a friend had this sublet option, and I snatched it up. It's an old nanny housing unit, so it's not much, but hey, it's something, right?"

"Yeah, that's something," he says while running his hand over his jaw.

"Anyway, I should probably head into the shower. I'm meeting Levi at nine to go over my responsibilities and expectations, and I don't want to be late."

"No, you don't. Not sure he would appreciate you being late."

"Which means I need to get going." I set my coffee mug on the counter and stand on my toes to kiss my dad's cheek. "Great game last night."

And then I take off to my bedroom, where I plop down on my comfortable mattress, soaking in the last minutes of a Tempur-Pedic because I doubt the nanny hole will be anything luxurious. I grab my phone and text Sandie.

Wylie: *Are you frothing at the mouth, wondering who my new boss is?*

I texted her yesterday after my conversation with my dad, sharing everything that was going on, and she, for one, couldn't believe my dad was being such a dick. And two, she was dying to know who the player would be.

Sandie: *YES! I thought you were going to text me last night.*

Wylie: *I thought about it, but I didn't want to wake you.*

Sandie: *For that kind of information, I would have risen from the dead.*

Wylie: *LOL. Good to know. So are you ready?*

Sandie: *Yes! Tell me. Stop prolonging it.*

Wylie: *Levi Posey.*

Sandie: *I knew it! I freaking knew it. It had to be him. OMG, did you meet with him yet? Did he recognize you?*

Wylie: *I did meet with him last night, and he recognized me immediately. You should have seen the ghostly pallor of his skin when I walked into the room. And then when we went to one of the media rooms to talk, he brought up that night. Had no problem telling me how attracted he is to me.*

Sandie: *Wow, now that's refreshing. Did you climb on his lap and say thank you, let's have a redo of that night?*

Wylie: *If only. He's very adamant about keeping this professional, which I understand. And I want to do the same. Given my dad's doubt in me, I truly want to show him that I can do this, no matter what obstacles he throws in front of me.*

Sandie: *What a shame. That kind of chemistry should be explored, not suppressed.*

Wylie: *Tell me about it, but I'm not about to risk anything, not when this could be a pathway to get my dad to understand where I'm coming from. That I can do this.*

Sandie: *Understandable. At least tell me he offered up his place to stay.*

Wylie: *He didn't. I asked, and he was very hesitant at first, but then he told me about this nanny bedroom with a separate entry that he never uses. He said I could stay there, but I couldn't tell my dad.*

Sandie: *That's odd. Why wouldn't you be able to tell your dad?*

Wylie: *I don't know, but I took it. I don't care where I live. I just want a place to sleep that's not my dad's place. And it can't be any worse than the dorm we shared our first year.*

Sandie: *True! Nothing is worse than that cockroach-infested nightmare.*

Wylie: *Remember when we spent three hours on my bed, huddled together because there was a cockroach the size of a mouse under your bed, and we were afraid it would attack our feet if we got off the bed?*

Sandie: *That will forever be engrained in my memory. I still shiver just thinking about it. Hopefully, that won't be the case with the nanny room.*

Wylie: *I'm referring to it as the Nanny Hole.*

Sandie: *Sounds like that one club we went to.*

Wylie: *That's what I said to him, and you should have seen the sweat on his temple. I asked him if he's ever been to a club like that, and he said no, but there was guilt written all over his face.*

Sandie: *Did you tell him you love a sex club?*

Wylie: *I told him I had been to a few, and that's when he bolted.*

Sandie: *LOL. I'm guessing that's not something he wanted to know about you.*

Wylie: *That much is obvious. Ugh . . . if only circumstances were different because I'd show that man such a good time.*

Sandie: *Instead, you get to fetch him coffee.*

Wylie: *Maybe I can do it topless.*

Sandie: *I'll give you twenty bucks to do it topless.*

Wylie: *I would do it for five.*

Chapter Four

LEVI

To: Levi Posey
  From: Will Wood
  Subject: Your List
  Don't fuck this up, Posey.
  Aside from regular tasks like social media, retrieving your food, arranging your calendar, and being at your beck and call, here are a few tasks you need to give her this week:
  Hand her a copy of a book. I don't care what book, but give her a copy of it. Tell her you don't like the font it's written in, and have her type it out in a different font. Yes, have her type up the entire book, word for word. Tell her you want it in a week for your away trip to the Northeast.
  Spill something on your floor. Don't care what it is. But make it disgusting. Tell her she needs to clean it up and make it seem like it was never there.
  Ask her to get you ten pounds of Skittles. The Skittles must be divided into colors and placed in separate jars. But you want more reds than any other color. At least half a jar more.
  Have her purchase you fifty number two pencils. Have her sharpen them

just enough so they're pointed but not too much where they're splintering. Use them as a decoration for a day and then have her donate them to a local school, but she must receive a receipt for the donation.

Text her in the middle of the night that you need something, anything. Make her get it for you.

After each task, I expect you to take a picture and inform me that it's been completed. Do not let her off the hook. Don't let her skate by. I want you to make her life a living hell, got it?

And don't forget the rules. Don't forget why you're doing this. And mainly, don't forget that she's completely off limits.

Your worst nightmare if you mess this up,

Coach Wood

⊏══⊐

I SIT on the edge of my couch, fully showered, dressed, and ready for the day as I count down the minutes until Wylie arrives.

Sleep was nonexistent last night, and not because the gash above my eye was throbbing, but because I couldn't fucking believe that Coach Wood's daughter is the woman I've been searching for. She fucking knew who I was and didn't say anything. She played it off like she didn't even know the sport of hockey existed.

And then just ditched me. Why?

I have so many questions and annoyed emotions over the situation that I'm trying to calm myself before she shows up so I don't explode on her. I feel like I'll pace the room angrily at any moment, demanding why she didn't come looking for me when she knew who I was. I know she enjoyed that kiss.

So why did she bolt?

I push my hand through my hair and stand from the couch.

Get it together, man.

Forget about that night. It's in the past.

Because now my coach has me by the balls, and one slip-up could cost me. I wouldn't put it past Coach Wood to fuck with me if I screw this up.

I head toward the kitchen to grab a drink when my phone beeps in my pocket. Maybe it's Wylie, and she's changed her mind. Maybe she decided to go back to school rather than be my assistant. All would be right in the world.

Wouldn't that be fucking great?

I take my phone out of my pocket and see that it's a text from OC.

OC: *So . . . are you going to share with the group how your meeting with the new assistant went?*

And this is exactly why you don't get involved in your friends' lives because then they think they can treat you the same way. My buddies, they're what I like to call incompetent nitwits when it comes to women. Granted, I'm still learning about OC, but from what I can tell about what's going on between him and Grace, he'll fall in the line of incompetency along with the rest.

My phone beeps with more texts.

Here we go . . .

Pacey: *Wait, what assistant?*

Eli: *Coach Wood assigned his daughter to be Posey's assistant.*

Silas: *Wait, you didn't say she would be your assistant, just that she was looking for work.*

Eli: *Oh yeah, full-blown assistant. And let me tell you, she's a piece of work.*

Pacey: *Why don't I know anything?*

Silas: *Because you're always with Winnie. You barely hang out with us now.*

Eli: *Says the guy who's always with Ollie.*

Halsey: *As if you have any room to speak.*

Levi: *None of you have room to speak, you neglectful assholes. You're all in happy, loving relationships because of me.*

OC: *Uh, I'm not happy.*

Levi: *Don't worry, I'll get to you.*

Pacey: *Back to Coach Wood. Why does he want you to hire his daughter?*

Here's the thing, I could tell my boys exactly what's going on in my life, let them know that there's been a girl I've been searching high and low for, that I've been desperate to find her because of one fucking kiss, and she just so happens to be our coach's daughter. And now I have to act like an ass to her because her father wants to prove a point, and somehow I've been placed in the middle or . . .

I can tell them that it's nothing and reveal nothing.

Telling them will lead to constant chatter, relentless text messages, because they'd absolutely LOVE to see me in distress over a woman, and I do not want to subject myself to the impending ridicule.

Therefore, I'm cutting them off.

Yup.

They don't need to know all the details. It's for the best. For my sanity.

Levi: *She needed some experience, and Coach Wood knows I don't have an assistant, so he asked if I'd hire her. I said it wasn't a problem at all, so yeah, I have an assistant now. Please direct all your menial demands to her. Thanks.*

Silas: *Why is Hornsby saying she's a piece of work?*

Eli: *Because she is. I've met her through Penny, and she's just . . . on a different planet.*

I didn't gather that from my impression, but then again, Eli has a child, and maybe said child has sucked all the common sense from him. I've heard of that happening.

Maybe that's why babies look like aliens when they're fresh from the womb . . . mind suckers.

Pacey: *Meaning . . . she's going to give him a hard time? Because that would be amazing.*

Levi: *Why would that be amazing? Have I not been an absolute blessing to all of you?*

OC: *I have yet to witness the blessing personally so . . .*

Levi: *I said I would get to you. Patience, you fuck.*

Halsey: *I wouldn't consider what you did to me a blessing. I could have figured out a way to be with Blakely without all the fanfare.*

Eli: *And Penny and I would have gotten together either way because Pacey made us live together.*

Pacey: *And I beg to see how you did anything to get me together with Winnie.*

Silas: *Not to mention, your texting nearly scared Ollie away.*

Levi: *Wow, I've never seen such a sad bunch of ungrateful motherfuckers in my life. If I have to recap . . . *clears throat* Pacey, you're with Winnie because I didn't make the first move. You're welcome. Hornsby, if it weren't for me, you'd still be texting Penny that you're eating an apple. You're welcome. Taters, don't even get me fucking started. The reason you got tit pics from Ollie was because of me, and you know it. You're welcome. Holmes, I stepped it up for you, lied, decorated your apartment, and practically placed Blakely on your ginormous dick. You are fucking welcome. Now, if you don't mind, I have to train my new assistant. Go back to your happy lives.*

OC: *Uh . . . what do you want me to do?*

Levi: *Write me a synopsis of the history between you and Grace. Have it in my locker in a week. If you want happiness, don't skip out on the details.*

With that, I shove my phone in my pocket and pick up the email from Coach Wood that's on my island counter. I look over the list a few more times, shaking my head at how stupid this all is. I'm an easy target for Coach Wood because he knows I'm a people pleaser. He knows I'll do just about anything asked of me. Not to mention, he has me by the balls because sure, he helped me out with that one reporter, but that wasn't the only night he's helped me out. There have been many others when he's pounded on my door just to get a clinger out of my hotel room. So yeah, he has me in a rough fucking spot.

I fold the paper in half just as there's a knock on my door. In a panic, I slip the paper between the pages of one of my coffee table books—get rid of the evidence—and then move to the entryway.

Well, here we fucking go.

Keep it professional.

Don't stare at her.

Don't drool.

And keep it together unlike your nimrod friends who have no idea how to act around a woman.

Shoulders back, I open the door and feel my stomach immediately turn warm from the sight of Wylie.

Fuck me, she's so hot.

The epitome of what I look for in a woman. Gorgeous face with those steely gray eyes, the lightest smattering of freckles across her nose and cheeks, and she has bow-shaped lips that glisten under the lights of my entryway. Her dark red hair is silky smooth and long, enticing me to wrap it around my fist to see what kind of hold I can have on her. And her curvy and sensual body is out of this world.

Today, she's wearing high-waisted wide-leg jeans, a black shirt tucked into the waist, and a blazer with the sleeves rolled up to her elbows. She's professional but also casual at the same time. Her hair is down and straightened over her shoulders, and her eyes are highlighted by a thick coat of mascara.

What I wouldn't give to grab her by the neck, pull her in close, and finish the night we shared.

"Hello, Mr. Posey," Wylie says, knocking me out of my thoughts. "Is now still good?"

"Yeah," I say, but don't invite her in just yet. "But listen, you've got to cut it out with that Mr. Posey shit. It makes me feel ancient."

"Well . . . aren't you?" She smirks, and goddammit, it takes me back to that night when I was tasting those lips and looking for so much more.

"Ancient?" I shriek. "I'm not ancient. I don't even have gray hair . . . or hair on my balls." Her eyes widen, and I realize what I said. "I mean . . . not like in a prepubescent kind of way, like the testes haven't dropped yet, because they have. They've dropped. I was just referring to my manscaping." I pull on the back of my neck. "Have you heard of manscaping? Uh, well, I have nice balls because of how I take care of them and lotion them. Not that you needed to know that, but old men don't usually manscape. They just let the hairs run wild, and that's not the case here because I'm neither old nor ancient. So, to conclude, call me Levi, I have nice balls, and I manscape."

Her smile is so bright as she says, "Don't forget the lotioning."

"Right." I nod awkwardly. "The lotioning."

She helps herself in and says, "And I meant in hockey years, you're old."

Ahh, yes, well, that makes more sense.

Trying to recover, I say, "Well, that just means I get to retire early on a mountain of cash."

Ignoring my comment, she walks past me, and because I'm desperate and pathetic, I attempt to check out her ass, but her blazer covers it. That's probably for the best. I shouldn't be checking anything out.

She glances around my apartment, taking in the subtle decorations I purposely used to create a cohesive and well-put-together theme for my apartment. A theme I like to call electric thunder. I know what you're thinking—how does one decorate with the theme electric thunder in mind?

Well, it's a combination of dark, moody colors, pops of unsuspecting accent hues, and not too much texture where you think, whoa, my eyes are offended.

Unlike Halsey, who lived in a jail cell before Blakely came along, I have taste and a keen eye for interior design.

I have a personal Instagram account no one knows about, and I follow some of my favorite profiles, like Pottery Barn, Rejuvenation, and especially Joanna Gaines—I like her decorating style. Very neutral design style while she's moved away from some of the farmhouse trends and taken a more modern aesthetic. I also follow a few baking accounts. One of my favorites is of a Turkish lady who makes the best bread-inspired recipes. When she punches that dough after it rises . . . fuck me, it's chef's kiss!

But back to my apartment. I went for the whole dark cigar-room vibe even though I don't smoke cigars—see, electric thunder. Blacks and gunmetal grays span the walls and in tasteful accents while camel-colored leather furniture takes center stage. An oversized area rug adds a cozy feel, tasteful art decorates the walls, and cream-colored curtains add a touch of lightness to the space.

"This is really nice," she says. "I half expected to walk into a bachelor pad, but this is a man's apartment. Like a man's man."

"Thank you," I say, smoothing my palms together. "I'd consider myself a man's man."

"You clearly have the lotioned balls to prove it," she jokes while gesturing to my crotch.

Heh.

Yeah . . .

Glad we can bring that full circle.

I pull on the back of my neck. "I go through a lot of lotion."

Not something she needs to know.

"I can imagine." Her eyes meet mine. "Any special type? Perhaps a burnt mahogany scent. Make that sack extra manly."

Christ. *Change the subject, man.*

"Just regular," I answer while clearing my throat. "Anyway, I, uh, I take great pride in my apartment."

"I see that. You should. It's really nice in here." Her eyes fall to the coffee table in my living room, where I have three books stacked with a candle on top. "Do you even read those books?"

"Nope," I say. "It's all part of the design and feel of the apartment."

"Ah, so you're trying to portray intelligence when, in reality, there's very little intelligence in this apartment?"

"Pretty mu—" I pause, thinking about it. "Uh, no. There's intelligence in this apartment."

She turns toward me and smiles. "Well, there must be intelligence if you're wise enough to pair a camel-colored couch with a gunmetal-gray wall."

"Some might say brave," I say.

"Very brave." She pats my chest, and I let out the breath I was holding in one giant swoop. Her eyes meet mine as she says, "You know, I'm just trying to lighten the mood. Make conversation. No need to hold your breath . . . or your tongue. I know this is awkward for both of us, and I don't want it to be awkward."

It's awkward, all right.

It's never *not* going to be awkward.

But I'm not going to say that to her.

"I'm not awkward. Are you awkward? Because I feel fine. Great actually. Rip-roaring and ready to go."

Her smile grows wider. "Oh yes, I'm rip-roaring and ready to go as well."

"Great." I stuff my hands in my pockets and rock on my heels. "Because I think if we keep everything super professional, we can make the most of this situation. Possibly excel as the best boss/assistant relationship."

"Wouldn't that just be fantastic," she says. "Imagine the accolades we could win by not being awkward but rather rip-roaring professionals. People around us might be so impressed that they write to the Foreign Press. Tell them there needs to be an award made just for us."

I know she's being sarcastic.

I know she's trying to lighten the mood.

But, Jesus fuck . . . I'd be fucking thrilled to win an award documenting my excellence in professionalism and managerial skills.

"What would the trophy look like?" I ask, feeling myself drift off in thought.

"Maybe a statue of a man with a woman at his feet, clutching his leg and looking for direction."

I glance her way and scratch my jaw. "Uh, not exactly what I was thinking."

She chuckles and places her purse on the coffee table, then pulls out a notebook and a pen. "Maybe we can brainstorm later, but for now, why don't you show me around and tell me what I can do for you."

Right, what she can do for me.

Focus, Posey.

If you want to mentally win the award, you have to act like the boss who'd win it.

But for the record, I'd like it to be known that everything I'm going to ask her to do are tasks I can do for myself. Things I've been doing for years with no problem. I want it to be noted that any wild or obscene shit I tell Wylie to do should not be held against me.

I'm merely a pawn in the battle between Coach Wood and his daughter.

And despite being a man's man with perfectly manscaped and lotioned balls, I clearly have no idea how to say . . . no.

"Well, as you can see, this is my apartment." I stretch out my arms as if showing off the place . . . even though she's been here for the past few minutes.

She presses her hand to her chest. "Is it? Wow, I had no idea."

"Cheeky," I say as I continue. "This is the main living space, which is, uh . . . off limits for you. So no lounging around on this camel-colored couch." I point at the couch. "And, uh, no watching TV on this gigantic screen. And, uh . . . no, uh, no rolling around on the area rug."

"Ooo, really? I was really hoping to get my rolling done in here, but I can find a new place." She makes a note in her notebook, then looks up at me. "Where should I do my morning staring? Should I keep that to my own space, or am I allowed to come in here and stare at the wall?"

I work my jaw to the side, seeing how easy it is for her to make fun of me. "Your own space will suffice."

"Noted." She marks something on her notepad again.

"But you are allowed in here for certain reasons."

"Like restocking the lotion," she offers.

"Yes," I say tersely. "And cleaning, restocking the groceries, and delivering whatever I might need. Other than that, you must stay in your own space."

"Got it. Don't bother Mr. Posey."

"Levi," I say.

"Don't bother Levi. Shouldn't be a problem. I can manage whatever space you offer up. Like I said, it's a real help."

"Sure, yeah. Should I show you that space now?"

"That would be great. That way I know what I'm working with."

I gesture toward the open-concept kitchen, and we both walk that way.

I hate this.

I hate how uncomfortable this is. Clearly, she's trying to be grateful for the opportunity, and I'm preparing to rain down hell on her day. It's the last fucking thing I want to do, yet here I am, about to introduce her to a hole in the wall that she can sleep in despite my lavish apartment.

And you're probably wondering, did I spruce it up? Did I make it as inviting as I did when Blakely was moving into Halsey's place? The answer is no. I didn't even wipe down one cobweb. Not even sure what the hell is going on in the hole because the door hasn't been opened in years. But I kept it untouched to help dissociate myself. Makes me feel like I'm taking on the boss role rather than the caretaker.

"The entrance to your room is right back here," I say, leading her past the open kitchen, past the pantry off to the left, and down a narrow hallway toward a door at the very end. "Not sure the condition of the place because I've never used it, so, I'm sorry in advance." I open the door and switch on a light, highlighting the small room, less than two hundred square feet. There's a twin bed off to the right with no mattress—huh, she's going to need one of those—and a nightstand with one dilapidated drawer. There's one overhead light in the room, one of those traditional boob lights that every tract home has installed in a hallway. Just past the bed is a door leading to the bathroom, where you can wash your hands and sit on the toilet at the same time. I know this because I joked about it when I first viewed the apartment. There's also a stand-up shower that I couldn't really fit in, but she will do just fine. A separate entrance from the outside is at the other end of the room.

It's much bleaker than I remember.

Maybe a touch spooky.

And definitely not up to my man-boy standards.

"Oh wow, this is bigger than I thought it was going to be," she says, moving into the space with hopeful eyes, which feels surprising. Her father is a world-class coach. She grew up with money and has lived on the higher end of life, yet she can be positive about the space I'm presenting her? How?

"I can, uh, get you a mattress." I point at the empty bed.

"No need." She waves me off. "We actually have one in the spare bedroom at my dad's house that I can grab."

"Okay, and sorry about this nightstand," I say as I reach down and tug the drawer open only for it to fall to the ground with a crash. "Shit, sorry." I bend down to pick it up just as a furry critter skitters over my hand and across the floor.

Mother.

Of.

God.

The world stops spinning as the skin on my knuckles tingles with the sensation of clammy, claw feet. I stare down at my hand and then to the right, where the furry critter scurries around the baseboard of the tiny bedroom.

"Oh . . . my . . . fuck," I scream like a man whose nuts just got lassoed off before levitating off the floor and right on top of the slats of the bed. "Mouse," I squeal. "There's a fucking mouse in here." I point at it as it runs back and forth. "A rodent. Right there. Holy fuck, a rodent."

Wylie turns toward the mouse just as it scurries toward me again and under the bed.

"Ahhhh, it's under me," I scream as I attempt to leap off the bed, but unfortunately, the bed can't handle my weight, and the slat I'm standing on buckles together in a snap and my foot lands on the ground with a resounding squish.

I still.

My blood goes cold.

And I look up at Wylie, who is now wincing.

Please fuck . . . no.

Nope.

No.

Breathing heavily, I rest my hand against the exposed brick wall next to me as I very quietly and calmly say, "Is . . . is it under my foot?"

She shifts uncomfortably and cringes. "That would be a yes."

I slowly nod, reality puncturing me.

"The whole thing?"

"Yes. Your very large foot carries quite the radial stomp."

I gulp.

"Would you say it's . . . dead?"

She glances down at my foot, then back up at me. "I would be surprised if it's not."

"Okay." I swallow my building saliva. "Okay, everything will be okay." I remain still, unmoving. "I'm, uh, I'm going to need some privacy."

"If you need to scream in private, I'm going to hear it, so you might as well just do it now."

"Right." I take a deep breath right before a full-on shiver takes over my body from the tips of my toes to the roots of the hair on top of my head and I let out an ear-piercing squeal that echoes through the quaint space. "Ahhhhhhhhhhhhhhhhhhhhh!"

When I'm done, Wylie takes a step forward. "Want me to help you out of your shoe?"

"I just, uh, I need a second."

"Right, understandable." She crosses her arms at her chest and looks around. "While we wait, I'll tell you that this space will be perfect. I don't need much." She sticks her head in the bathroom, and for a moment, I catch her nose scrunching up in disgust. "Yup, lovely. It will be great."

Foot still squishing the mouse, I say, "It's a touch small."

She pops her head back out and says, "It's free, so it works." She glances down at my foot, then back up at me, clearly noticing I'm not ready yet to address what's under my foot. All I have to say is thank fuck I'm wearing shoes. "I assume you want me using this entrance here rather than moving through your apartment."

"Yeah, that would be preferred."

"Not a problem." She sighs. "You ready?"

I squeeze my hands into fists. "I fear what you might hear when I lift my foot."

"If you're afraid I might judge you, fear not, I judged you when you said you lotioned your balls."

I press my fingers to my forehead. "Yeah, that's fair."

"So how about this. As my first act as your new assistant, I will hold your shoe down while you slip your foot out. Then you can just walk back into your apartment. I'll take care of the remnants and wash your shoe."

"Burn," I say.

"Huh?"

"Burn my shoe. I'll never be able to wear these again."

She smirks. "Mouse traps as footwear. I don't think that ever caught on as a popular fashion choice, so I can understand that. How about I donate them? The death history of the shoe will remain with us, but the shoes can live on."

"I don't care what you do with the shoe, but it can't go back into my closet."

"Consider it taken care of."

━━━

"OH, look at all these baking supplies." She looks through my kitchen cabinets, making herself at home while I remain shaken and stunned from rodent death by the size fourteen shoe incident. *I squealed in front of her. I broke the bed. I killed a fucking rodent with my foot.* The boys will NEVER hear about that. "What, uh . . . what's going on here? Do you like to bake?"

"I do," I say, trying to forget about the mouse I murdered. "When it strikes me, I like to have the basics on hand."

"And what do you like to bake the most?"

"Bready items," I answer.

"Like . . ."

I shrug. "Like a cranberry orange bread or a pastry. Just carbs."

"Well, maybe if I do a good job as your assistant, you'll bake me something one day." She shuts the cabinet door.

Bake something for her? Hell, I would like to bake *with her*.

Both of us wearing nothing but aprons.

Me behind her as she sifts flour only to boop her nose with a little bit of it.

We'd chuckle.

I'd get hard.

And then I'd fuck her on the counter.

"Or you don't have to," she says. "Don't want to overstep."

"Huh?" I ask, being pulled out of my thoughts. "Uh, no, I can bake you something."

She pats my chest and smirks. "Don't let me pressure you." And then she moves into the living room. "Do you have any plants I need to take care of?"

If only.

I think about Sherman . . . original Sherman. Long story short, Halsey had a bonsai tree. It was decapitated, and I tried to bring it back to life without him knowing because I felt bonded to it, but I did not succeed. And it wasn't from a lack of me trying every trick in the book. His trunk was snapped as if his neck had been broken in half, and there was no saving him. I buried him alone in the park just outside of my apartment building in the middle of the night with a headlamp and a gardening shovel. I said a few well wishes and let him compost into the ground.

Devastating.

"No plants," I say.

"Would you like a plant? Perhaps a ficus tree in the corner might add the green you lack in your living space."

"You think I'm lacking green?" I ask. "I have some green right over there." I point at my fake plant on the shelf.

"But that's fake." She scrunches her nose in this cute way. "You want some life in the apartment. I know Joanna Gaines is huge on having real plants around the home."

I gasp as my hand presses to my chest. "You follow Joanna?"

She softly smiles. "Do you?"

"How could I not?" I reply. "That couch is from the Magnolia brand."

She glances at my couch, then back at me. "You know, I thought I recognized it. Great taste, Mr. Posey."

"Hey." I point at her. "What did I say about that shit? Just call me Levi or Posey."

"Oh, I could never call you Posey. That feels very bro-like. What about Mr. Levi?"

"What about just Levi and leave it at that?"

"Fine, but just remember, I'm the one trying to be professional here. You are my boss, after all."

Don't fucking remind me.

"I can still be your boss and be Levi at the same time."

She shrugs and then writes on her notepad. "Buy a ficus."

"What kind of ficus are we talking about? Because I honestly really like the looks of a fiddle leaf fig tree but haven't had the time or energy to really look for one."

"Oh, I can find you a nice one. Would you like a pot for it or a basket? Personally, I think a basket would add some nice texture to the space. We can put the tree over there in the corner where it will get some sunlight but also add an element to the space that softens it a little more, especially with the woven pot."

I nod, envisioning the fiddle leaf fig tree. Fuck yeah, that would look amazing.

A piece of my design puzzle I haven't been able to fulfill.

"Yeah, I think that'll be nice."

"Perfect. I'll get right on that. Shall you show me the rest of the space?"

"Sure," I say, thinking that maybe this assistant thing won't be as bad as I thought. First, she takes care of the mouse—RIP, you mangy rodent—and now my very own fiddle leaf fig tree. Wow. I won't let her know how excited I am about the prospect of having one. And in a fucking basket . . . talk about living the good life. My apartment will be unmatched compared to the other guys. Halsey might have a bonsai tree, but I'll have a giant, and I mean leaves taking up the apartment space giant, fiddle leaf fig plant that will fill my apartment with oxygen and goodness.

None of them will have that.

None.

I internally cackle, knowing once again I'll have a leg up on my nimrod friends.

I lead her to my office, which is more like a den. I had some sliding French quarter black-framed barn doors installed in case I ever wanted to shut them, but given that I'm the only one here, they're more for show than use.

"This is my office. I usually answer emails here in the morning while drinking my coffee. So if you ever need me to look at something or adjust my calendar, you can leave Post-it notes along my desk."

"Okay. Do you need my email so you can send me access to your calendar?"

"Yeah, just text it to me, and I'll introduce you to everyone I work with."

"Do you want to have morning meetings? I can bring you coffee, and we can discuss the day."

"Uh . . . you don't have to do that," I say even though the thought of her delivering me coffee in the morning, and then sitting cross-legged on my desk has its charms.

"Not a problem. Just here to make your life easier."

"Thanks." I move her down the hall. "This is the spare guest room that no one ever uses." She pokes her head in, and I know she spots the comfy bed and the large, decorated, cozy space. I feel guilt in my gut, knowing she has to move into the cold, brick-exposed dungeon where I just squished a mouse where she's supposed to sleep. Lucky her. "I, uh . . . I just feel like if you're in this room—"

"You don't need to explain," she says. "I get it. We have to keep things separate. I'm seriously grateful for the space you've given me. Dead mouse and all." I cringe, the feel of it under my foot still throbbing in my toes. "Also, I love what you did with the throw pillows and the comforter. Did you design the bedding yourself?"

At least she's good at changing the subject. And has a good eye for style. *Good taste in designers. Clothes . . .*

"I did." I stick my hands in my pockets and puff my chest with pride. "Spent a lot of time in West Elm, trying to figure out what I liked."

"You did a fantastic job . . . Levi." Fuck, that sounds good rolling off her tongue. "You really have an eye for design and colors."

"Thank you," I reply, letting the compliment go straight to my head.

It's not very often I receive the praise I deserve. Lord knows my fucking friends don't offer it up. I know the fans love me and shower me with accolades, but that's hockey. What about the other parts of my life? Like my decorating sense. My baking. My ability to create love connections. What about the shit that really matters? Hockey is a game—okay, my job and livelihood—but I'm talking about life here.

After just a few minutes with Wylie, she has me feeling like the king of the mountain. Wait until she tries my coffee cake— what fucking dreams are made of. She's going to be writing sonnets in my name. Shimmying her tits in satisfaction, moaning all over this goddamn apartment from the perfect ratio of yellow cake to crumble topping.

"And is this your bedroom down here?" she asks, moving down the hallway.

"Uh, yeah, but you don't have to—"

She opens my bedroom door, revealing the pitch-black room. It's such a contrast to the rest of the apartment. Of course, I still have the dark tones, but instead of lightening up the space with soft cream tones and camel colors, I kept everything black—from the furniture to the walls to the curtains and the bedding. Not an ounce of color.

"Wow," she says as she moves around my mid-century modern canopy bed. Her fingers draw along the dark wood up to the strategically placed hooks. Her eyes flash mischievously to mine. "Seems to me like someone enjoys a little kink in their lives."

A little . . . okay.

Ignoring her statement, I say, "Not much you need to do in here."

"I'd say, seems like the room carries its own agenda." She drags her hand over the velvet comforter. "Soft." She sits on the edge of my bed and crosses one leg over the other, testing the bounciness of the mattress. "Not too firm, not too soft. The perfect balance for better . . . thrusting."

For the love of God, don't say thrusting while you're on my bed.

I can barely take the image of her propped up on my mattress, let alone her running her hands over my hooks or testing out my mattress.

"I assume I'm going to be doing laundry for you." She hops off my bed and moves to my closet. "Oh, an in-closet washer and dryer. This will make it easy. Is there a certain way you want me to fold your clothes? Your underwear?"

"Uh, you don't have to do that," I say.

"I insist." She winks. "Anything to make your life easier."

She keeps saying that, but at the moment, she's making things harder . . . if you know what I mean.

"And not that I was looking too much, but you did an impeccable job organizing your closet. Seems like someone has been paying attention to how to be efficient with space."

"It bodes well for you that you're noticing things others don't. My friends seem to find my details in organizing pointless. I, on the other hand, find it soothing and valuable, especially when packing for an away trip."

"Oh yes, I can see how that would be beneficial. Very smart, Levi."

If I was wearing a suit, I'd be proudly gripping the lapels right now.

"Speaking of packing, that's something I can do for you. Just give me a list, and I'll throw everything together for you. We can even do a test run before your away trip so you feel comfortable with what I'm packing."

"Yeah, that could be a good idea. I do hate packing even though I'm efficient with my organizing."

She winks at me. "Very efficient. If you have time, we can go over that right now since we're done with the tour."

"Yeah, I think we can do that."

She follows me into the closet, and I grab my suitcase.

"Oh," she says. "I assumed you'd like a rollie bag."

"Technically, I do," I answer. "But now that social media has picked up and they're using pictures and videos of us entering and leaving the arenas as well as on and off the planes, I saw one video of me with a rollie bag and nearly died of embarrassment. Now, it's this handheld bag. Stylish and masculine."

"That's probably the most ridiculous thing I've ever heard, but I get it." She removes her blazer, leaving her in jeans and what I can only assume is a body suit from how skintight the damn thing is. With the blazer off, I'm reminded of just how voluptuous—to put it nicely—she is up top. "But also, I can see what you mean because my dad uses a rollie bag and looks like a total dweeb even though it's matte black and what he considers to be cool. I, on the other hand, find it lame." She examines my bag. "This is nice, though. Surprised you don't have a luxury designer bag."

"That's because I care about animals."

"Oh? Tell me more." She opens the bag and looks inside, only to pull out my packing cubes. She holds them close to her heart in approval and smiles.

"You'll be hard-pressed to find a luxury brand that doesn't use fur, leather, down, exotic animal hair, the list goes on. And I'm not into torturing and hurting animals for fashion. So I found this duffel bag by Peak Design that has a sleek look but is also one hundred percent carbon neutral. I save my image and the earth at the same time."

She chuckles. "Huh, who would have known the beast on the ice has a heart for animals?"

"There's a lot people don't know about me. Also, if I'm going on an away trip that's more than just one game, we go for the Patagonia." I pull down my Patagonia duffel bag, which is larger. "This one is more of a bitch to carry, but once again, it's better than the rollie."

"Can't you . . . have like the equipment boys roll your suitcase to your hotel room? I know that's what my dad does."

"I . . ." I pause and scratch the back of my head. "You know, I've never thought about that."

She laughs and lays out the black packing cubes. "And that's why I'm here." She then pulls out her notepad and writes something at the top. "Okay, tell me everything you need."

"Clothes," I say.

"Yes, but what kind of clothes are we talking about? Comfies? Suits? Casual wear? Do you have pajamas I need to worry about, or do you sleep naked?" She cutely wiggles her brows.

"Naked at home, but in hotels, I sleep in boxer briefs because something about laying my dick to rest on anything other than my sheets makes me feel disgusting."

"Laying your dick to rest makes it sound like you're putting it to sleep, you know . . . death."

"If my dick dies, I die," I say.

"Typical man." She rolls her eyes. "Okay, so extra underwear. What about spare clothes? You need a suit for game day. What do you like to wear when it's not game day or you're traveling?"

"I'll take care of my airplane outfit because I have to wear it there, but just some comfy sweatsuits, joggers, or long-sleeved T-shirts that go together. And a suit with a matching top and shoes. I'll wear a watch, but if you can make sure that every outfit has shoes, that would be awesome."

She writes it all down. "What about toiletries?"

"I can send you a list of things."

"Great. And then we have chargers. Computers. Gaming system for the plane."

"I'll pack all of that in my backpack."

"Great." She checks that off her list. "What about condoms?"

I nearly choke on my own saliva. "What?" I ask.

"Condoms. You'll need them, right? Or . . . oh . . . do you go bareback? You know, that's risky with all the venereal diseases floating around. I'd suggest we wrap you up."

Clearing my throat, I say, "I always wrap up."

"What a great practice to take part in," she says. "Good job taking care of yourself and the woman."

"Uh, thank you?"

"You're welcome. Now, where are they?"

"Where are what?" I ask.

"The condoms, Levi. I know you'll want them on your away trips, and I want to be able to pack them for you." *She does?* She stands from the closet and moves over to my nightstand, then opens it up before I can stop her. Her eyes widen with a smile as she looks up at me. "Man alive," she says while revealing a well-organized drawer of silk ties, eye masks, vibrators . . . and condoms. She reaches into the drawer and pulls out my Orgaster Neo G-spot vibrator. "Do you use this? You don't have holes, well, unless . . ."

I snatch it from her hand and accidentally press the on button in the process, causing the vibrator to start in my hand, which inevitably leads me to drop it on the floor.

We both look down as it jingle-jangles across the hardwood and right up against my foot, almost nudging me in a suggestive way to use it.

"Quite the vibration," she says as the vibrator's buzzing fills the silence. "Feels strong yet not too powerful where it could cause your innards to turn inward."

I look up at her. "Is that a thing?"

She shrugs. "Feels like it could be. Is that supposed to hit the G-spot?"

I glance down at the flat side that is, in fact, supposed to massage the G-spot. It's currently massaging the tip of my toe.

"Yes," I answer.

"Fascinating. And that piece on the end there, is that for the clit?"

"The one that is currently sucking my pinky toe?" I ask.

"Yes, that one."

"Yeah," I answer. "That's for the clit."

"And how does it feel against your toe?" She taps her chin, studying me for my reaction.

"Humiliating," I answer.

"Honestly, I'm surprised you've let it suck on your toe for this long. By now, I would have grabbed it, turned it off, and stuffed it back in my drawer."

"That would have been the intelligent reaction," I reply as I stick my hands in my pockets and let the vibrator rumble against the floor.

"So . . ." she says, "we're just going to let this happen? That thing is going to suck your toe, and I'm supposed to act like it's not and just have a normal conversation with you about your packing needs?"

"Not really sure how else to move on."

"You could . . . oh, I don't know, pick up the vibrator."

"I think the moment has passed," I reply.

"I disagree. I don't think there's ever a moment when you can't remove a clit sucker off your toe. I think the window is always open for something like that," she replies.

"But we've talked about it too much. It feels weird."

"I'd assume getting your toe sucked by a vibrator in front of your new assistant would be even weirder, but I guess to each their own." She stares at me.

I stare at her.

She shifts.

I pull on the back of my neck.

The vibrator rumbles.

She clasps her hands tighter against the notebook.

I nervously press my lips together.

And we continue to look at each other until she says, "Oh, for fuck's sake." She bends at the waist, yanks the vibrator off my toe, turns it off, and then puts it back in the nightstand where it will never be removed ever again.

She lets out a heavy breath. "There. I did it for you."

With the tip of my toe, I shut the drawer and look her in the eyes. "That drawer is private."

"You don't say?" She chuckles and then gives me a slow once-over. "You know, I never would have guessed you're a man of kink, although the hooks in your bed were a dead giveaway. Still . . . getting your toe sucked?"

I point at her. "I didn't enjoy that. I just didn't know how to react to the situation."

"So you let the clit sucker continue to do its work?"

I drag my hand over my forehead. "You know, let's get back to packing. Let's leave it at I can pack my own condoms."

"Fair enough." She goes back to her notebook, and with her poised pen, she asks, "What about the vibrators? Are you going to pack those on your own as well?"

Jesus.

Christus.

———

"BEFORE I LEAVE FOR PRACTICE, I was hoping you could help me with a few things," I say as I take a seat at my kitchen island.

We just went through a lot of things. I set her up with contact information for everyone she'll communicate with. I gave her access to my social media, made her sign an NDA and a code of conduct so she didn't make a fool of me on social media, told her what I expected, and showed her how I like my shirts folded. That was my own addition. I thought it was clever and demanding.

"Of course. Anything you need. Let me know. I'm here to serve."

"Yeah, let's not put it that way," I say as I smooth my hand over my thigh. I grab my phone and look through the email that

Coach Wood sent me, the one I printed out. "So there's this book I've been wanting to read—"

"Oh? Want me to pick it up from the store for you?"

"Not really, I already have it," I say. "But I don't like the font they used, so could you please type it up for me?" I hold back the wince because this is easily the douchiest thing I've ever said or asked for. I've had my douche moments and slip-ups—texting *Oye my dick* to Ollie, acting as Silas, that was one of them—but this, this tops them all.

"You want me to type up the book in a different font? Like the whole book?"

"Yup," I say. My leg quivers with instant regret. "Uh, in Arial font please. Something about it is soothing to the eye and easier for me to read."

"Okay, uh . . . I could get you a Kindle or something. You could change the font that way."

"Oh, this isn't on Kindle."

"It's not?" she asks. "What book is it?"

Yeah, Posey, what book is it?

If I were Halsey, I'd have a stack of books to choose from. But I'm not the group bookworm. I'm the kinky one—not that any of them know that. The only books I have are stuffed in my nightstand on how to properly tie a woman, and I'm not about to have her type up one of those.

That's when my eyes land on the coffee table books.

Perfect.

"That one," I say, pointing at the book on the top that I believe is about Vermont.

She glances at it, then back at me. "Is that a book about Vermont?"

"Yup," I say. "Very passionate about the state. Did a fourth-grade report about it, and well, I just love me some maple syrup and changing leaves. Would love to know more about that sliver of heaven. So yeah, if you could type that up for me, I'd appreciate it."

"Uh, sure. Can I give it to you in chapters? Might take me a while."

"Installments will work," I say even though I know that's not what Coach Wood asked for.

"Also, I have this stain," I say, lifting one of my placemats that I doused in barbecue sauce this morning. To hell if I was about to stain my rug or carpet not knowing her stain defense techniques. A placemat is easy to let go of if she royally fucks it up. And it's not like Coach Wood will be able to tell the difference from the picture I took of the stain. At least I hope he won't.

"Oh, that is quite the stain. Looks like you smeared barbecue sauce all over your placemat." Yup, pretty much.

"I can be a clumsy eater," I say. "Think you could get this stain out? I have an attachment to this placemat. I eat best when using it."

Her brows raise in question, and I don't blame her. That's something one of my idiot friends would say, not me. I don't say stupid shit. I correct stupid shit. *Except when I'm nervous or I'm put in an uncomfortable position. Like making myself look like an absolute dick.*

"Well, have no fear. I'll take care of the stain, and you can eat your best once again."

"Thank you," I say while putting the placemat down. "I also have two other things that are meticulous but necessary. You know, superstitions and all."

"Oh, I know all about them." She leans a little forward and whispers, "Did you know that my dad has to do the sign of the cross over his underwear before he puts it on every game day?"

Oh fuck, that's amazing.

I hold back my snort, but it makes my eyes water. I try to blink away the tears of amusement, but God, that's great intel.

Coach Wood, blessing his fucking underwear. If hiring Wylie as my assistant means I get special snippets about Coach Wood to make him less . . . scary, then this was one of my best decisions.

Blessing his fucking underwear. *mentally shakes head* That will be shared with the boys.

"Oh yeah, blessing the underwear, I totally get it," I say even though I don't. What does blessing your crotch have anything to do with the game? The man must think very highly of his penis —like it has magical powers on how the game plays out. To each their own, I guess.

"So what can I do to help you with your superstitions?" she asks.

I clear my throat and hope she doesn't judge me for this. "Well, now that school is in session, it reminds me of my elementary days when we would go back-to-school shopping."

"Yes, I know what you mean. Nothing smells better than a new box of crayons." She smiles up at me.

"That and number two pencils," I say, hating myself and Coach Wood. "I like them so much that I like to fill the apartment with them."

She shifts and stares at me quizzically. "What do you mean?"

"Well, I just think they're nice to have, you know, around the house, on display."

"Ohh-kay. So do you want me to get you some pencils?"

"Yes," I say, feeling like an idiot. "Fifty."

"Fifty?" Her eyes widen.

"Yes, fifty. And I'd like them to be sharpened. But not with a motorized sharpener. I don't like the burnt smell that it gives off when you sharpen a pencil. I'd like them to be sharpened manually and placed in a vase."

She slowly nods. "And where do you want this vase placed?"

"Uh, dining room table, like flowers."

She glances back at the dining room table with nothing on it, the one space I've yet to decorate, mainly because it's a forgotten space. I never use it. The only reason I have the table is for . . . well . . . extracurricular activities, hence the hidden hooks underneath for, well, you know, restraining someone.

"So you want fifty manually sharpened number two pencils placed in a vase on the dining room table?"

"That would be correct."

She writes it down on her pad as she says, "Feels like *You've Got Mail*."

"Huh?" I ask.

"You know, when Tom Hanks says he'd send Meg Ryan a bouquet of newly sharpened pencils if he knew her name and address since she loves New York in the fall." I stare at her, and she shakes her head, continuing to write on her notepad. "Never mind. Anything else?"

"Skittles," I say.

"Skittles," she says flatly. "Do you want some?"

"Yes—"

"And let me guess, you want them sorted by color with a certain ratio?"

Shocked that she'd guess that, I nod. "Yes. Fifty percent red, the rest I don't care."

She winks. "Red is my favorite too." She writes down a note. "Anything else?"

"Uh, I think that's it for now. I'll have Blakely send you my social media clips so you can start working on posts, and I'll get Penny involved with you on the calendar stuff. I have it so they just input my events on the calendar, but now you can approve them and prepare me for what I have going on every week."

"Sounds great." She smiles brightly. "And as for moving in, am I allowed to paint? Hang things?"

"Yeah, whatever you want to make it comfy."

"Okay, great. If you don't mind, I'd like to take part of the day to set up my space, so I'm free for you moving forward."

"Yeah, that works," I say.

"Great." She holds out her hand, and weirdly, I take it. She gives it a good shake. "It's a pleasure to work for you, Mr. Posey." I lift a brow, which causes her to laugh. "I mean, Levi." She winks and then heads back through the kitchen toward her hole in the wall.

I lean against the counter and let out a deep breath.

I can do this.

I will probably barely even see her.

And in the meantime—because I cannot *ever* fuck my hot-as-hell assistant, who I want more than my next Cup win—I have to find someone to fuck. I *need* to get this raw and exasperating energy out of me.

———

LEVI: *I'm unwell.*

Eli: *Is it the bologna? Dude, we don't want to hear about it.*

Halsey: *I told you not to eat that shit.*

Pacey: *Remember when he got sick in Banff from eating five sandwiches within two hours?*

Silas: *Remember when I got sick just hearing him say he devoured the whole package of bologna while doing it?*

Levi: *This has nothing to do with my precious bologna. Stop hating on it, you fucks.*

OC: *You know, we really shouldn't be food shaming.*

Eli: *OC, you have some brown on your nose.*

Silas: *Yeah, dude. If you're sucking up because you're looking for love help, just act like you don't want it. He'll insert himself then.*

Levi: *PAY ATTENTION TO ME! I'm unwell because I stepped on a mouse and killed it today. I can still feel the squish.*

Pacey: *Why the hell did you step on a mouse?*

Silas: *Ew, were you wearing a shoe?*

Eli: *I don't understand why you feel like you need to share this with us.*

Halsey: *That's . . . gross.*

OC: *Guess I'll be the only one who asks . . . are you okay, Posey?*

Levi: *No. Mentally distraught. Thank you, OC, for being my only friend. Also, yes, I was wearing shoes, and it was an accident.*

Silas: *Seriously, OC, chill, man.*

Levi: *Does anyone care about the mouse? Or me?*

Pacey: **deadpans* Yes, we care so much. We hope everything is okay with your life.*

Eli: *Sending you well wishes and sorrows.*

Silas: *Prayers for the mouse.*

OC: *May he rest in peace . . .*

Halsey: *Moment of silence.*

Levi: *Thanks, guys, that means a lot. Now that we've celebrated a mousy life of living among the dust and baseboards, let's move on to more important things. Coach blesses his underwear before every game. The sign of the cross right over the crotch. I'll never be able to look at him the same.*

Eli: *That's what you should have started out with. Holy shit.*

Silas: *Did you hear this from your new assistant?*

Levi: *Directly from her, without even asking. It was handed to me on a silver platter.*

Eli: *You know, this new assistant thing might be a great idea. Can you find out if he squeals when he's excited as well?*

Pacey: *What kind of question is that? You know he barely smiles.*

Eli: *But maybe when he's alone, he squeals.*

Halsey: *Do you want him to squeal?*

Silas: *Better question . . . do you want to make him squeal?*

Eli: *Yes *deadpans* I want to make our coach squeal.*

Pacey: *As the brother of your future wife, I'm going to say I'm not happy about this.*

Silas: *You know, I never thought of you as someone who likes to make a man squeal in delight, but now that I think about it . . .*

OC: *What the hell am I reading?*

Levi: *Eli wants to bless Coach Wood's underwear for him.*

Eli: *Oh fuck off, all of you.*

OC: *Maybe he wants to eat an apple while he blesses the underwear. (See what I did there?)*

Pacey: *Bringing it full circle. I approve.*

Silas: *Clever.*

Halsey: *I think I need to leave this group chat.*

Levi: *You're slowly becoming my favorite with every passing day, OC.*

Eli: *You must have low standards, then.*

OC: *Ouch, quite the burn, but it doesn't quite compare to the burn you feel in your loins over wanting to make Coach Wood squeal.*

Silas: *Oh shit.*

Halsey: *Okay, that was good.*
Pacey: *I snorted on Winnie. She's not happy.*
Levi: *Appreciate the use of loins.*

Chapter Five

WYLIE

"Do you think he'll be mad that I'm here?" Sandie asks as she takes in my new dwelling.

"No," I say. "I have my own entrance. It's not like I traipsed you around his apartment. I can have people over to my closet."

"You know, I think your walk-in closet at your dad's house is bigger than this."

"Oh, it one hundred percent is, but that just means I need to make this space cozy." I set down my bags of decor.

After Levi and I parted ways, I picked up some cleaning supplies with bleach—despite not liking to use bleach products, but given the circumstances—and I scrubbed the floor of my bedroom, in particular where the mouse was massacred.

I then went around all the baseboards, furniture, bathroom, and every single crevice and scrubbed them with a bristle brush until I was fully satisfied with the cleanliness. I followed this up with painting the only wall that doesn't have exposed brick a very dark gray, almost black. Some people might scoff at the idea of painting a small space a dark color, but for me, a dark aesthetic creates true comfort. It's why I love Levi's apartment so much.

I tried not to drool too much over the hardwood floors, or the perfectly placed furniture, or his bedroom . . .

Oh my God, his bedroom.

Sin happens in there. The moment I walked in, I felt it— despite the awkward length of time he allowed a vibrator with a clit sucker to cling to his toe.

"I know we didn't really address it, but . . . the mouse," Sandie says.

I hold up my hand. "Trust me when I say I looked in every crevice and searched high and low for any opening that rodents could climb through. We are safe here."

"And from the powerful bleach smell in here, I can tell you cleaned."

I nod. "My hands feel raw."

"At least you can rest easy tonight, and we don't have to worry about stepping on anything."

I shake my head and chuckle, still remembering the look of horror on Levi's face when he realized what had happened. "No, we're good." I take a seat on the mattress that Sandie helped me bring up the stairs and say, "But before we get started, I need to get something off my chest."

Looking confused, Sandie sits beside me. "Okay, what's going on? Did something happen?"

Did something happen? Of course something happened.

Minus the mouse and the vibrator and the weird tasks Levi asked me to take care of, I could not stop feeling this heavy, electric draw toward him.

Like my body was being pulled in by some cosmic force, and if I don't talk about it, I think I might scream.

"Yes, something happened." I look her in the eyes. "I am crushing so hard on Levi Posey, and I know you know this. I know you've seen me fawn over the man for a long time, but being here, being next to him, seeing the way he tries to inconspicuously check me out. It's driving me nuts. I know I can't do anything about these feelings. It's almost as if my dad knew I liked this man and decided to torture me by putting me in a situation where I can't have him."

"Even if you weren't in this position, you wouldn't be able to have him. Hence why you bolted that one night. You know your dad would kill you if you hooked up or went out with any of his players, so how is this any different?"

"Because . . ." I bite on the corner of my lip. "I have to be near him now. I know what his apartment smells like. I have to fold his underwear and see his collection of magnum condoms."

"Magnum?" Sandie's brow lifts.

"Yes." I let out a deep sigh. "And I know I shouldn't be talking about this, but oh my God, Sandie, his bedroom is designed for two things: sleeping and fucking. He has a four-poster bed with hooks, and in his nightstand are toys and ties, and God, just looking at it made my nipples hard. He doesn't portray this dark, sinister man in real life. Sure, you see a part of that on the ice, but normally he's goofing off with his friends in interviews and being a jokester. I never would have guessed that he has a secret kink. If I had to pick one of them to have a secret kink, I would have guessed Silas Taters. He gives the vibe of tying someone up and fucking them until they can't take it anymore. Not Levi Posey."

Sandie slowly nods. "I see and hear everything you're saying, but I just want to make sure you understand that no matter what, you can't do anything with him. If you want to prove your dad wrong, you need to keep to yourself, even if he does seem to let his eyes wander."

"I know," I say with a heavy sigh. "But I just had to tell you that because it's been eating away at me. He's so hot, Sandie. So freaking hot."

She chuckles. "I know. It's what you say every time you see him."

"Because it's true." I lean back against the wall and stare up at the ceiling. "But I'm determined to prove to my dad that I can do this, that I can provide for myself and do what will make me happiest in life."

"Good, hold on to that determination when you see Posey with his shirt off for the first time."

I roll my head to the side to look at my friend. "Think that'll happen?"

"Most likely. I can't imagine it not happening. You're going to be in and out of his apartment. I bet you'll see more than you're ready to see."

I rub my hands together. "One can only hope."

Sandie pushes at my shoulder, laughing. "You're so freaking horny. Oh my God, Wylie."

I chuckle. "Easy for you to say. You're the one who's in a happy relationship and can have sex anytime you want. I either have to do it myself or try to find someone out on the streets to do it for me."

"Can you please not find someone on the streets? Standards, Wylie."

"At this point, it's been months, and I have no standards. None at all."

Blushing, she says, "You haven't been to that club you like to go to?"

I shake my head. "No, they raised the rates, and I just don't have a way to pay for it. Especially not now. It's fine. I can concentrate on my job and sharpening pencils and dividing up Skittles."

"Ah, the joys of being an assistant." She hops off my bed and starts pulling bedding out of my bags. "Seems odd that Posey would have you do such menial tasks. He doesn't seem like that kind of man."

"I thought the same thing," I say. "Very odd. The whole rewriting of the book thing was really weird."

Together, we make my bed with the deep green sheets I purchased as well as the emerald-green velvet comforter I found and fell in love with. I splurged just a little on some bedroom necessities, but that's because this place is a hellhole. If I'm going to live here, I will make sure I'm comfortable. Luckily, I had some money saved from some designs I've done for a few small businesses, so I dipped into the pot for some serenity.

Now that I feel the comforter and see it in this space, I'm not mad at myself at all. I'm actually patting myself on the back.

"Maybe he's secretly very particular but doesn't show his diva tendencies in public," Sandie says as she eyes my nightstand. "Also, am I putting this in the hallway outside?"

"Yes." I chuckle. "And then if you want to start making the one we purchased, I will love you forever."

"Why did I know you were going to make me build that?"

"Because you're better at using tools than I am."

She shakes her head but gets to work by moving the drawerless nightstand out to the hallway. Maybe I'll get a plant for it or something, make use of it somehow. While she builds the nightstand, I work on hanging and steaming curtains.

We went to Room In Order for organizational ideas and found great space-saving ways to store my clothes and utilize the height of the space. I think we're going to make it work.

"So what are you going to do first? Start rewriting the book?" Sandie asks as she looks over the instructions.

"Uh, no, I think I'll start small and work up to the book. He seemed really into the sharpened pencils, so I'll work on that tonight, perhaps. Then the Skittles and the stain. I think I can bang those out tomorrow morning and possibly work on some social media posts during lunch. I also have to go shopping for him. I think if I complete a few of the things that will give him instant gratification, I can show him I'm working hard, and slowly tackle the harder tasks."

"Probably smart. At night, will you be working on your art?"

"Yes," I say. "That's why I got that lap desk, so I can hang out here on my bed and field any requests."

"Do you have any prospects?"

I steam the black curtains I purchased and shake my head. "No, but I want to enter some competitions, and I'm also working on updating my portfolio. Now that I don't have to worry about classes and telling my dad, I can contemplate how I want to handle this career change."

"I think that's smart." She glances over her shoulder at me. "I'm proud of you, Wylie. I know this was a tough decision, but following your heart is what will bring you joy."

"Thank you," I say. "I just truly hope my dad can see it that way. He'll see how I can make a life of this by giving me this opportunity."

"He will. I know he will." She smiles at me. "Just keep your mouth, hands, and vagina to yourself."

I let out a loud laugh. "Yes . . . Mom."

I STAND in the middle of my room, exhausted, sweaty, and ready to plant my face into my pillow, but oh my God, I'm so glad I stayed up late to finish setting up.

I found a plush area rug that we placed partially under my bed and then rolled out to cover most of the floor. It feels like I'm walking on a cloud rather than the old, scuffed-up hardwood floors. I took some duct tape to the splintered bed slat and patched that up. We hung the curtains higher than the window, making the room's space look larger and grander. The emerald-tone bedding looks luxurious, and we added some greenery with a potted Monstera plant. I built a movable rack for clothing and a small black cube shelf that fits perfectly next to the door for my undergarments. Sweatshirts and T-shirts are in bins under my bed, which we propped up with risers. And in the bathroom, I used the space the best I could by building one of those over-the-toilet shelves as well as using storage shelves under the sink. It's tight in there, but it works.

And now that I'm fully moved in and ready to start this new chapter in my life, I don't think I've ever been more hopeful.

Smiling to myself, I crash onto my bed, ready to go to sleep when my phone rings. I glance over at the nightstand and see my dad calling.

Sighing, I pick it up and answer. "Hey, Dad."

"It's late, Wylie."

"You're the one who called me," I say. "Also, nice hello."

"Why aren't you home?"

Smiling, I say, "I moved out, Dad."

"What?" he asks.

"I told you I found a place. I moved out today. I'm currently at the new place and, before you ask, there is one window, and I put up a bar so no one can open it. I also have my Addalock in my door as well as the doorjamb. No one is getting in, and the only one getting out is me."

He's silent for a second before he says, "I knew you were moving, but I thought you would actually give me more than just a quick heads up." Almost sounds like he's regretful.

"You gave me one week to find housing, Dad. What did you expect me to do? Wait until the last minute? No, I'm serious about this. I want you to know that I can do this. That I can live on my own, support myself without your help, and make this dream of mine a reality."

He's quiet again, and then he finally clears his throat. "Well, glad to hear it. Have you met with Posey? Been advised of your responsibilities?"

"Yes," I answer. "Met with him this morning. Between you and me, there are some odd things he wants done. Almost feels like he's trying to make things difficult for me. You wouldn't have anything to do with that, would you?" I thought about it earlier when I was working with Sandie. The tasks he laid out—like the barbecue stain—seem so odd, like they were purposely given to me to keep me busy. Sandie brought up the idea that maybe my dad was telling him to make things difficult.

"Do you really think I have time to come up with idiotic tasks for you to do? What Posey asks you to do is up to him. He might have odd requests, given he hasn't had an assistant before. As long as you're earning a wage and you're learning what life will be like for you if you leave school, I'm okay with it."

I take a look around my apartment and realize if this is what life will be like if I leave school, then I'm not doing too bad. Nope, I could totally manage this. And that's what my dad doesn't realize. He didn't raise a fool. I have a good grasp of common sense. He provided me with a wonderful roof over my head and anything I could have wanted growing up, and while I'm grateful, it's all material things.

What I really want is to feel satisfied and happy. Like I'm doing something that fills my heart with joy, not irritation.

And I don't think he realizes that. He's too far into his career to remember where he started. I'm sure his parents scoffed at the idea of him wanting to be a head coach, but look at him now. We all have to start somewhere, and if that means working a nonsense job to get to where I want to be, then so be it.

"Well, I'm doing pretty good right now. I'm comfortable. Safe. Happy. And at night, I plan on working on my artwork. I know it's probably not what you want to hear, but I think I can handle this."

"Good to know," he says, sounding angry about my happiness.

God, if only he'd understand.

"Well, I'm exhausted, and I have to wake up early to get a jumpstart on things. I should go. Thanks for checking on me, Dad. I love you."

He sighs. "I love you, Wylie. Be safe."

"I will. Night, Dad."

"Night."

I hang up the phone and set it down on the nightstand.

I slip under the covers of my freshly made bed and sink into the comfortable mattress.

You got this, Wylie.

You can do this.

You can prove to him that you can handle this on your own.

I let out a deep breath, close my eyes, and allow my mind to drift to the designs I want to work on. To my plans of starting my own business. I have a checklist of everything I need to do to make that happen, a checklist I unfortunately learned from school—hate saying that because it just shows that my dad is right about a few things—and then there are—

Ding.

My eyes flash open, and I glance at my lit-up phone screen. A text from Levi.

I turn on my side and open the text.

Levi: *Hopefully, you're not asleep yet. I forgot I need something from the store. Think you can run out and get it?*

Is he serious right now?

Sitting up, I type him back.

Wylie: *I'm awake. What do you need?*

Barely awake, but it's fine. If he wants something, I'll grab it even though I'm ready to pass out.

Levi: *You can drive, right?*

Wylie: *Yes.*

Levi: *Great. There's a bakery that stays open twenty-four hours. They have the best bagels ever, and they're most fresh at one in the morning. It's their first batch for the morning. Can you grab me a dozen everything bagels?*

I stare at the text, blinking a few times.

Wylie: *Wouldn't the second batch be fresher for you? Since you're going to sleep? I can grab them first thing in the morning.*

Levi: *They use different water for the second batch. Trust me, these are way better. Put them on the card I gave you to use. Thanks.*

Is this seriously happening? He wants me to get out of bed and grab him bagels that he won't eat for hours?

A part of me wants to go to sleep, wake up a little earlier than he does, purchase the second batch, and see if he can even tell, but with my luck, he'll wake up at five and be looking for his bagels with none to eat.

Reluctantly, I slide out of bed, put on my shoes, and text him back.

Wylie: *Send me the address, and I'll grab those bagels for you.*

Levi: *You're awesome. Thanks. It's Port Hole Bagels.*

I pull up Google Maps on my phone and look up Port Hole Bagels, only to find that it's a forty-five-minute drive from here.

Mouth agape, I text him back.

Wylie: Is this the address?

I attach the address to the text.

Levi: Yup. That's the one. Why, is that a problem?

Yes!

I want to sleep.

I'm tired. I don't want to drive forty-five minutes one way just to grab stupid bagels because he thinks the water is different at one in the morning than four o'clock. But this is what Dad was talking about, right? Earning my way through life, suffering as an artist at a job just to make money.

Guess I better grab some coffee because I have a drive to make.

Wylie: Not a problem at all. What do you want me to do with the bagels when I get back?

Levi: Just stick them in the freezer.

Doesn't that negate the fact that they won't be fresh anymore?

My nostrils flare as I type him back.

Wylie: But they won't be fresh anymore.

Levi: In my mind, they will be. Thanks.

"Jesus Christ," I mutter as I throw on my sweatshirt and grab my car keys. No wonder he didn't have an assistant before this. He probably couldn't keep anyone at the job long enough to buy the one-in-the-morning everything bagels.

Lucky for him, it will take a lot more than one-in-the-morning bagels, barbecue stains, and manually sharpened pencils to break me.

———

LEVI: *Can you come to the kitchen? I need to speak with you.*

Blurry-eyed and barely able to hold my body upright thanks to a closed bridge that added twenty minutes to my drive—both ways—I'm hardly holding on to my sanity as I pull my hair back into a sleek ponytail.

Wylie: Be right there.

I stare at myself in the mirror, not even bothering with makeup because I don't have it in me. And I don't care enough for him to see me makeup-free to even consider one coat of mascara. Nope, maybe my makeup-free face will scare him away, and he'll never ask me to grab one-in-the-morning bagels again.

Slippers on, I move down the hallway toward the kitchen and try to muster a happy face when he comes into view.

"Good morning," I say.

He turns around, looking so good in a fitted long-sleeved Under Armor shirt that clings to his thick, barrel chest and carved arms. His hair is still wet, clearly fresh from the shower, and instead of shaving, he's left the scruff on his face to make him that much more enticing.

Ughhhh, why does he have to look so good in the morning?

And smell so good.

And why do I want to curl into his side and let him hold me? What I wouldn't give for a solid snuggle session right now where I can pass out in his large arms, and he slowly runs his hand over my hair, calming me to a deep slumber.

Instead, here I stand, his wench, ready to be at his beck and call.

"Morning," he says in a deep timbre that his nighttime visitors are probably privileged to hear. Like he hasn't warmed up his vocal cords enough just yet, so he has this rasp that makes him exponentially more attractive. "Thanks for the bagels."

"Did you make one?" I ask.

He shakes his head. "Nah, I'll get something at the arena. Just going to have a protein shake this morning. Could you grab that for me? I'm headed in for a meeting and don't have time."

He's not eating one of the freaking bagels I got him last night?

Doesn't he know that I had to drink two boiling hot cups of coffee to make it through that drive? That I had to listen to a playlist called *Don't Fall Asleep* the entire way that was put together by some psychopath on Spotify that consists of horrific animal noises and loud screeching? I nearly drove myself mad.

And he's not going to have a bagel?

HE'S NOT GOING TO HAVE A FREAKING BAGEL?

What was the point of it all, then?

Just to be a dick?

"A protein shake, of course," I reply with a sweet smile—at least I hope it's sweet. It could be a bit on the snarly side. "Want me to grab the ingredients to make you one, or do you want me to pick you one up?"

"Pick me one up. I'll text you the details. I'll order it, and you can just grab it and bring it to the arena."

"Sure, that works."

"Also"—he picks up a book from the counter—"don't forget about this. Vermont is calling my name."

"Ah, yes." I take the book and hold it against my chest. "Can't wait to learn some facts about Vermont myself. You know, if you're chomping at the bit to learn something about the beautiful state also known as one of the biggest maple providers in the country, then I can send you some YouTube videos. Something to watch while you're getting treatment."

"I prefer to read," he says.

Just not in a font other than Arial, right? Jesus Christ.

"Okay, well, the option is there. I've found quite a few travel blogs that do wonderful jobs. None of that shaky camera work, you know?"

"I'll think about it." He pockets his phone and his wallet. "Well, I'm off. I'll text you. See you at the arena."

"See you there," I say with a wave.

He's about to leave when he turns toward me. "Oh, and don't forget about the fiddle leaf fig tree. I'm looking forward to seeing what you choose."

"Yup, it's on the list," I say.

"Great." He offers me a delicious smile before taking off and leaving me alone in his apartment.

I set the book down on the counter, lean against the cold marble, and let out a deep breath. "You're fine," I say as irritation claws up the back of my neck. "This is life just testing you.

No need to get frustrated and upset. So what if he didn't eat a bagel after everything you went through to get them? Not a big deal at all. And sure, you're exhausted, and the last thing you want to do is get back in your car to pick up a smoothie. Everything will be okay because you're strong, and you're not going to let your dad win."

I take a few calming breaths and ensure that I'm not going to freak out on him before I grab the book again and head to my bedroom, just as I get a text from him with his order and where to pick it up. I quickly look the address up on Google Maps, praying that it isn't far, and lucky for me, it's between here and the arena. It seems like an easy pickup for him, but that's fine. While I'm out, I can grab the Skittles and stain remover.

See how that works? Thinking on the positive side.

Sure, would I have wanted him to eat one of the bagels I drove to get him? Yes, that would have been nice, but when he does decide to eat one, I know he'll be able to taste that different water. At least that's what I try to tell myself.

Everything will be just fine.

Chapter Six

LEVI

"What did you make her do last night?" Coach Wood asks, staring down at me.

Yup, this is my early morning meeting. A recap on my first day with Wylie. And when I say the last thing I wanted to do was wake up early and come to this meeting, I mean it. I stayed up all fucking night, my stomach churning from the errand I sent Wylie on. It wasn't until I heard her put the bagels in the freezer that I could actually shut my eyes. Even at that, though, I probably got an hour of sleep.

Guilt consumed me.

So much guilt that I actually felt nauseous at one point and sat on the edge of my bed with a trash can in hand.

Yeah, this guy, hovering over a trash can, ready to puke.

Probably not the image you want of me, right? Well, fuck, I don't want it either. It's humiliating. That's not the man I am. That's something Eli would do.

Or perhaps Pacey.

I don't throw up.

Yet, there I was last night, ready to hurl over making Wylie run the stupidest errand ever.

Fucking different water. I don't even know if that's a thing. I was flying by the seat of my pants on that one. I actually got the idea by looking up stupid tasks personal assistants had to do. It was a Buzzfeed article providing outrageous stories from assistants. I couldn't believe the amount of insane tasks humans make other humans do.

But because my coach has my balls in a vise grip, I don't have much choice.

I shift in my seat and try to conjure up the image of Coach Wood blessing his underwear this morning so he seems less intimidating. If it wasn't for the throbbing vein in his bald head drawing my attention, the underwear blessing might have worked.

"I had her grab me bagels from a place forty-five minutes away . . . at one in the morning."

Coach Wood smiles. *Sick bastard.* "Did she do it?"

"She did, and then . . . well, I didn't have one of the bagels this morning." Not because I was being an ass, but because I didn't think I could bring myself to even look at the bagels. That's how guilty I felt.

Coach lets out a short but deep chuckle. "Made her get bagels at one in the morning and didn't even eat one. What a fucking dick."

Nerves shoot up my arms as I say, "That's what you wanted, though, right? You wanted me to be a dick?"

"Yes. That's perfect. There's no doubt in my mind that she was cursing your name this morning."

Great, just what I want.

Although, I would prefer the cursing to be in the context of, "Oh God, Levi, oh fuck . . ."

But we all know that's not going to happen.

"Yeah, she seemed pretty tired. Felt kind of bad."

The smile fades from his face as he stares me down. "Don't

feel bad for her. Don't feel anything for her. This is a job. This isn't personal. You do the job, and you move on. Don't feel any sort of emotion toward my daughter, understood?"

I gulp. "Yup. No emotion. Completely emotionless. No need to worry about emotions with me. I don't even know what they are. I'm an empty—"

"Shut up."

"Right. Yup." I grip the chair's arms, trying to keep calm.

"What else have you done? Has she started on the rewrite of the book?"

"Yes, I gave it to her this morning. Presented her with the stain to get out. Told her about the pencils and the Skittles. She has also been assigned my social media, calendar, fan mail, and all of that admin stuff. On top of that, she's getting me food, stocking up, and I think I'll have her food prep for me as well. Oh, and I tasked her with getting me a plant."

"A plant?"

I nod. "To add more life to my apartment. You see, there's a certain balance you need when it comes to your living space . . ." My voice fades when I see his jaw tense.

He doesn't want to hear about living space balance, you moron.

"Let me guess, you want me to shut up?" I ask.

He shifts in his seat and folds his hands together. "Keep her fucking busy. Run her ragged. Make her regret she ever took this position. I'll put together another list and email it to you. Continue to be demanding. I talked to her last night, and her hopes seemed high. I didn't like it."

Why? Doesn't he want his daughter to be happy?

I don't understand this entire ruse.

If I had a child, I'd want what's best for them, and what's best for them is their happiness. *Why doesn't Coach Wood want that?*

Maybe he's unaware of what happiness is. He's just an old crotch of a man with beefy shoulders and a bald head.

Perhaps he needs a little love in his life. Maybe I'm the one to help him find that love. My success rate is at one hundred percent right now, so I could help him find a lady friend—or man friend if that's where he's headed. Who knows. I've never gotten that personal with him. Either way, I'm the key to him finding love, and I'm up for the challenge.

"You know, Coach Wood, have you ever considered dating?"

He points at his door and yells, "Get the fuck out."

I wince as I scurry out of my chair. "Sure . . . yup."

I duck out of his office. "I'm going to take that as a no on the dating thing."

His loss.

I head down the hallway toward the locker room just as I receive a text. I pull out my phone and see that it's from Wylie.

Wylie: *Here with your smoothie. Where should I meet you?*

Levi: *I'll come to you. Where are you?*

Wylie: *Third level, going to meet with Blakely who caught me in the hallway.*

Levi: *Be right there.*

I pocket my phone and head toward the elevators, where I find Eli as well.

"Hey man, you're here early," Eli says.

"Yeah, had to meet with Coach."

"About what?" Eli asks.

"Uh . . . payment for his daughter," I answer. "He wanted to make sure I was being fair."

"Oh, sure," he says, buying it . . . thankfully.

"What are you up to?" I ask.

"Just dropped off Holden. Penny has breakfast, so I was going to eat with her in her office."

Holden is Penny and Eli's baby boy. We have full-time daycare here in the arena, so they're able to do what they need to do for their jobs while visiting Holden throughout the day. I know they love the convenience. Especially Eli, who likes to visit between practices, warm-ups, and training sessions.

The elevator opens, and we both walk in. He pushes the button for the third floor, where Penny and Blakely work. "How's the new assistant anyway?"

"It's been a day," I say. "Not even a full day. It's fine. Nothing special."

"So she hasn't given you any problems?"

"No," I say. "Why would she give me problems? You make it seem like she's difficult, and I haven't seen anything to indicate that."

"Not difficult. She's just strong-willed is all. She knows what she likes, and when she likes it, she goes after it. And I know you . . ."

"What about me?" I ask.

The doors part, and we step off the elevator. "Dude, you like to fuck. She's an attractive girl. I could see something there."

Little does he know.

There's more than just something.

There's a fucking semi-truck full of lust.

"Yeah, but she's Coach Wood's daughter. Do you really think I'd get even close to that?"

"I mean . . . I could see it. You let your dick do the thinking a lot. I've had to get you out of a few mishaps."

Everyone seems to remember the little favors they've done for me here and there, but heaven forbid they give me any fucking credit for the ginormous favors I've done for them—found them love.

"Trust me when I say nothing will be happening between us. First of all, she's fucking young, like ten years younger."

"Silas is ten years older than Ollie."

"Yeah, and there are times when she calls him granddad. Do you really think I want that for my life?"

Eli chuckles. "No."

"And second. If I even think about going near her, Coach Wood will find out somehow and chop off my dick, douse it in gold, and then keep it as a trophy on his desk as a prized possession."

Eli nods. "Yup, that pretty much sums it up."

"Oh, there you are," Penny says as she spots us in the hall-way. "How did Holden do?" She takes Eli by the hand, and he leans down and kisses her. I look away because I'm so fucking hard up at this point that a light peck on the cheek could get me revved up and ready.

"He did great," Eli says in his sweet voice made only for Penny.

"Wonderful. Ready for breakfast?"

He wiggles his brows. "More than ready."

Looks like Penny is on the menu.

They take off and slip into her office without even having the decency of saying goodbye. Fucking rude. They shut the door behind them with a click of the lock. Yup, it's a do-not-disturb situation over there.

I head down the hallway and poke my head in Blakely's office. She's sitting across from Wylie, and Wylie's back is toward me. For a second, I take in the long slope of her neck and the poise in her shoulders as she speaks with Blakely.

This morning, when she walked into the kitchen, makeup-free, I had to keep myself from getting close, tugging her into my chest, and lifting her onto the counter so I could personally count every freckle on her cheeks. It was a monumental feat, and when I remained stoic and in place, I inwardly said I'd reward myself later for such strength.

Even now, though, I feel the pull with her a few feet away.

My body wants to gravitate toward her like Eli gravitated toward Penny. And I'm sure if Halsey was here right now, he'd be doing the same with—

"Hey, can I interrupt?"

Speak of the devil.

Blakely looks up at the doorframe and catches me and Halsey standing there, but whereas I'm empty-handed, looking for my protein shake, Halsey has a box of donuts for his wife.

Wow, I look like a real fucking asshole.

"Did you bring me donuts?" Blakely asks as she stands from her chair.

"I did," Halsey says as he walks into the office.

And painfully, I watch as they meet in the middle. Blakely

slides her hand up Halsey's chest as he wraps his free arm around her waist, and they kiss.

These motherfuckers. All around me, they're in love because of me. Rubbing it in my goddamn face while I'm over here living a fucking nightmare of blue balls and semi-hard-ons with no relief. Not to mention, a live-in assistant who I can't fuck. A girl so fucking hot, so fucking perfect for me that the night I met her, I wept myself to sleep from not being able to bury myself between her legs.

How is this fair?

"Oh, here is your protein shake, Mr. Posey," Wylie says as she hands me my shake.

"You make her call you Mr. Posey?" Halsey asks with a disgusted look.

"No," I say and then glance down at Wylie, who now has a coat of mascara on her lashes, making her light gray eyes stand out even more. "We went over this. You can call me Levi."

"Ooo, Levi, that seems so personal," Blakely says while her arm is still wrapped around Halsey.

"She didn't want to call me Posey. I didn't want her to call me Mr. Posey. So we settled on Levi."

"I don't know anyone who calls you that," Blakely says.

"Only when he's in trouble," Halsey says.

When it comes to Wylie Wood, I'm in a whole lot of trouble.

"I didn't want to seem disrespectful at work," Wylie says.

"Call me Levi at all times. There's no need to be fancy around these guys."

"What does that mean?" Blakely asks. "Are we not upper crust enough for you?"

"Not even a little." I take my protein shake from Wylie. "Thanks for this."

"Do you really have her fetching you drinks, Posey?" Halsey asks. "You're better than that, dude."

Yeah, I fucking know!

If it were up to me, Wylie would be sitting pretty in my guest room, playing around with her art while casually making social media posts for me. But thanks to her dictator father, I have no choice but to have her fetch me things. If the way her dad pulled me into the office today isn't an indication of the tightrope he has me on, I don't know what is.

"I don't mind," Wylie says. "I'm here to help Levi with whatever he needs. Which, by the way, when you get a chance, will you send me access to all the team photos and video clips?" she asks Blakely.

"Yes, I'll talk to the team and get you a login this morning."

"That's amazing. Thank you."

"Not a problem," Blakely says. "There are some clips of Posey I've never used, but they're solid gold. Have fun."

"Just don't embarrass me," I say, wanting to clarify that.

"You embarrass yourself on your own terms," Halsey says. Look at this motherfucker, coming out of his shell now that he's found happiness. He wouldn't have even said two words to Wylie a year ago, but now he's making jokes at my expense.

See what I'm talking about? Ungrateful friends.

"And with that, I'm taking off. You coming, Wylie? Lord knows these two want to share a donut *Lady and the Tramp* style."

"Nothing wrong with that," Blakely says as she leans into Halsey.

Rolling my eyes, I leave the office with Wylie trailing. Once we're down the hallway, she says, "They're really cute together. They got married this past summer, right? I think I remember seeing a picture from their wedding."

"Yeah. This summer. It was an intimate wedding in Banff."

Halsey and Blakely kept the guest list to a minimum and celebrated the wedding at Silas's cabin in the Canadian Rockies, where they said their vows in the backyard. Silas's private chef catered the event.

I offered up the great idea to have bologna sliders as an appetizer, but they didn't take the suggestion, nor did they listen to me about bringing Sherman—their bonsai tree—to the wedding, which I thought was flat-out irreverent. That tree was one of the main reasons—besides me—that they got together. Because of those two huge misses in their event planning, I knocked their wedding score a full point. They didn't care when I told them.

Fucking rude.

"So you're close with Halsey, right? And from what I can tell, Eli Hornsby. And perhaps Silas Taters?"

"Yeah. And Pacey Lawes. Oden O'Connor is in the mix now too, as well as Ian Rivers, but with his injury that still has him out, I'm not sure he's going to return. He seems to keep having complications."

"And Oden is new to the team from last season?"

I nod and press the elevator button. "Yes. Surprised you even have to ask, given who your father is."

"Shockingly, we don't talk hockey, like ever. Anything I know is from what I've seen. He's sort of closed off when it comes to the job. When he's home, he asks me how school is going and talks to me about the future. That's about it."

Sounds pretty sad.

"But he's never really been a talker," she adds, probably to make him seem like less of an ass.

She doesn't need to pretend. I know the type of man he is. One sneer will make any private part shrivel up.

"Not much of a talker? You don't say," I joke, which makes her smile.

"Yeah, he's always kept to himself." The elevator doors open, and we head down the hallway, but I stop right before the locker room to keep talking to her.

"Was he like that when you were growing up too?"

"Yes," she answers. "He never talks about my mom, ever. He acts like she doesn't even exist. He doesn't talk about his feelings. Doesn't talk about the wins or the losses. After you guys won everything last year and I congratulated him, he just nodded and kissed the top of my head. That night, we had dinner in front of the TV and watched *Miracle*. It's the one movie we've both loved over time. I tried to get him into *The Mighty Ducks* franchise, but he wasn't having any of it."

"What?" I ask, shocked. "Not a fan of Gordon Bombay?"

"Not even a little. Nor was he a fan of the flying V."

"Oh bullshit," I say. "We have a very similar play to the flying V. Maybe he's a secret fan, and you don't know it. He doesn't want to tell you out of fear of people thinking he's copying Gordon." I take a sip of my protein smoothie, enjoying the chocolate peanut butter flavor that floats over my tongue. So fucking good.

"Ooo, you know, I never thought about that," she says. "What if he's a secret fan? Perhaps he has an homage to him in his closet, behind some coats. After blessing his underwear, he says a prayer to the great Bombay before taking off."

I let out a loud laugh. "Fuck, that would be amazing." I take another sip of my smoothie. "Thanks for this, by the way. I know you were out late last night and the last thing you wanted to do was grab me something else for breakfast. I really appreciate it."

"Of course." She smiles that beautiful smile up at me. "That's why I'm here."

And then she leans against the wall, staring up at me, those stunning eyes sucking me in, making me want to reach out and touch her face, stroke her cheek, pull her in close.

If things were different and she met me in my kitchen, I would have scooped her up and carried her to the couch.

I would have held her and played with her hair while I talked to her about the day ahead.

She would have laughed at some joke I said.

I would have kissed the tip of her nose.

And then, when I slid my hand under her shirt, she would have—

"Posey!" Coach Wood yells from down the hallway, puckering my balls into a sunflower seed.

Jesus Christ.

I turn just in time to catch the fury in his eyes. "Yes, hey, hello. Howdy, uh . . . what's up, Coach?" I try to act as casual as possible despite just daydreaming about his daughter.

"What the hell are you doing? Get in the locker room."

"Right, yup, just finishing up some tasks over here." I turn back to Wylie. "So get that stain out. Thanks."

"Not a problem." She smirks. "Good luck tonight. I'll be watching."

"Uh-huh. Sure." I swallow hard, feeling Coach Wood staring me down. "Okay. Bye."

I move away from her and head into the locker room where Coach Wood stands, staring me down. I offer him a nervous smile and scoot past him, clenching my ass the entire time.

Yup, having a great fucking time.

———

"HEARD you made your new assistant fetch you a smoothie this morning," Pacey says as he pulls his socks up. "You really going to be *that* boss?"

I look over at Halsey, who's happily in his own little world, texting Blakely, I assume. So now he's just going to tell everyone my business, then not participate in the discussion?

He's changed, and I'm not sure I like it.

"It's called helping your employee fulfill their job responsibilities."

"It's called being a douche," Silas says. "Get your own damn smoothie, man."

"She wants stuff to do." I will defend myself here. "There's nothing wrong with giving her tasks so she feels like she's aiding in the success of my life."

"Is that how you're really going to put it?" Eli says. "The success of your life?"

"I think it has a nice ring," OC says.

All the boys turn toward OC, who sheepishly picks up his socks and puts them on.

"Dude, just tell us what the hell is going on with Grace so we don't have to watch you pathetically suck up to Posey all the time," Silas says. "You're starting to lose our respect."

"Don't listen to them," I say to OC. "You just write up that synopsis for me, and we'll figure out what to do. Trust me when I say these morons have no idea how to handle a budding relationship."

"Not this again," Eli says with a groan. "If you're so good, then why the fuck aren't you with someone?"

"Great point," Pacey says. "Explain to us why you aren't the master of your own heart."

Silas presses his palm to his chest. "That's a nice way to put it, man."

Pacey nods. "Thanks, it felt like it had a nice ring to it. Something in one of Halsey's books."

Halsey doesn't even look up from his phone, where he's smiling largely now.

I can see that the honeymoon phase hasn't passed yet.

"I don't even think he's been with anyone in a while," Silas adds. "I haven't seen Posey with a girl in, I don't know . . . a few months."

"Unless he's been hooking up at home," Eli says.

Pacey shakes his head. "No, you can always tell when Posey is backed up. He gets this tic in his jaw whenever he sees us around our girls."

My jaw ticks right at that moment, and Eli points it out. "You mean that tic right there, where it pops out like a heartbeat?"

"That exact one," Pacey says.

"Can you stop looking at my jaw, you perverts," I say. "Staring at a man's jaw is like staring at a pair of tits, and I don't appreciate the ogling." I press both of my hands to my jaw.

"Not the same thing." Eli shakes his head.

"Not even a little," Silas adds.

"Not even close."

OC holds up his finger. "You know, I actually think a man's jaw—"

"Shut up," Silas, Pacey, and Eli say at the same time, and OC clams right up.

I turn to him and say, "Don't let them treat you like that. You go ahead and compliment me. I'll be sure to add it to the running tally of reasons I like you and why I'll help you with your love life."

"Jesus Christ," Silas says on a groan. "Yeah, have fun, OC, working with a real wizard. The guy has zero credentials. No love of his own. No girlfriend. Not even a recent one-night stand."

"You don't fucking know that," I shout, losing my cool. We can thank the makeup-free face of Wylie Wood this morning for that and the restricted access to her.

"From the sounds of the outburst," Pacey says, "we do."

"Seems odd, though," Eli says. "Being that he's the guy who always has a girl with him, even secretly. What has changed?"

I look over at Silas, who now studies me, his hand to his chin. "You know, ever since last year, it seems like he's paid more attention to us and less attention to himself, and then there was that girl he was crushing on that OC told us about."

"I, uh . . . I was lying," OC says. "I didn't say anything. I was drunk. Medicated. Mistaken. Anything you heard from me was a fabrication."

Silas just rolls his eyes and looks back at me. "He's hiding something. All of this tension, all of this backup, it has to do with that girl." I look down at my skates, and that's all Silas needs. He snaps his fingers. "That's it. He's going through girl troubles, and he won't tell us."

"Is he really?" Pacey asks.

"That can't be right," Eli says while bending at the waist to try to look me in the eyes. "Are you having girl troubles?"

"No," I growl as I stand. "I'm not having girl troubles. I'm having . . . fuck, I'm having bologna withdrawals." I grip my hair, ready to lie right through my teeth because I can't fathom telling them anything else. "I'm trying to quit cold turkey because Grace said it wasn't good for me. So yeah, I'm crushing. You're right. I'm crushing hard on lady bologna, so if you all don't mind, I'd prefer for you to leave me the fuck alone so I can deal with my anxiety and heartache in private."

With that, I stomp toward the bathroom, locking myself in a

stall and leaving the tension, anger, irritation, and frustration to bottle up in my shoulders.

It's not going to be a good game tonight.

I know it already.

Sending well wishes to the opposing players . . .

"YOU SEEM TENSE," Eli says over the roar of the crowd while I squirt some water into my mouth.

"Not tense," I reply, eyeing Vladmir Popov out on the ice. He's been fucking with me all night, and when our line is called in, I'm going to do something about it.

"Uh-huh. You have a snarl in your lip. What's going on?"

"Nothing," I say as I slam my water down and grip my stick tightly.

"Yeah, I'm not going to take that as a response. What's going on?"

"Dude, we're in the middle of a fucking game. This isn't a therapy session," I snap, just waiting for the moment we're called out on the ice.

"Yeah, and I'm afraid you'll do something stupid if we don't discuss it."

"I'm not going to do something—"

"Change it up," Coach Wood yells, and I'm off the bench and out on the ice in seconds. I spot Vladmir, who has the puck, and I charge after him with one thing on my mind.

Slamming him into the boards.

I sprint toward him, only hearing Eli briefly in the background, and with his back toward me, I slam into Vladmir, sending him right into the boards and freeing the puck to toss it down to Holmes.

"Fuck," Vladmir shouts as he pushes off the plexiglass and then turns toward me. Immediately, he drops his stick, wraps his arm around my neck, and starts punching me in the ribs.

Perfect. Just what I wanted.

A way to release my frustration.

The crowd erupts, and whistles are blown as I spin out of his grasp just enough to cock my arm back and clock him in the head, sending him down to the ice. I free my gloves, ready to take this further, when I'm grabbed from behind by one of my teammates, stopping me from getting out the rest of my aggression and pent-up irritation.

I'm sent straight to the penalty box with a five-minute penalty, leaving the team short-handed, but thankfully, Vladmir is serving as well because he started the fight.

"Think you needed that therapy session," Eli says as he skates past.

Yeah, maybe, but at least I got one good punch in before it was broken up.

Of course the fans love it. They erupt around me, calling out my name and cheering for me. Sometimes I wonder if they're fans of my hockey skills or my right hook. I think some more for my right hook. Regardless, it was fucking satisfying.

I glance over at Vladmir, who spits out a chunk of blood. *Maybe stop slashing me with your stick, and I won't slam you into the boards next time, you fuck.*

I lean back and let out a deep breath. That's when I catch Coach Wood out of the corner of my eye. His arms are crossed, and he's staring me down.

Can't tell if he's pleased with what I did or angry.

Either way, I'm probably going to hear about it.

———

I PUSH my hand through my hair as I move toward the apartment elevator and push the up button.

We suffered a loss tonight. Not because of my penalty, but because we couldn't pull together any goals. It was a zero-one game. We were all off, and of course Coach Wood let us hear it while throwing a chair across the locker room.

If anyone needs a therapy session, I think it's that dude. *Talk about blue balls. He needs to get laid.* No one talked to each other. Halsey was pissed at himself for not scoring at least one goal. Silas was off as well with his passes, making it harder for Halsey to score. And OC seemed to be somewhere else. It was the first time we didn't work together. And that's bound to happen. You can't be perfect every game, but you can sure as hell learn from it.

My phone dings with a text as the elevator door opens, and I press the button for my floor.

Eli: *Want to have that therapy session now?*

This guy. Christ. He's been more involved in my life in the past few days than ever before. He has a lady and a baby. He needs to focus on them, not me.

Levi: *Seriously, I'm good, dude.*

Eli: *You sure? Because it seems like all this pent-up aggression you had tonight could be directed toward the new change in your life. Perhaps the hot redhead who's working for you?*

Levi: *If you think I'm angry because I can't fuck her, you couldn't be more wrong.*

Eli: *I didn't say it. You did.*

Clever fuck.

Levi: *Just some built-up aggression. Nothing you need to worry about.*

Eli: *I do need to worry about it. You're my second half out there on the ice. We'll be off if your head isn't in the right spot. Lawes worked his ass off tonight, blocking shots left and right. We have to do a better job.*

Levi: *I know. But I promise, it was just an off day. It will be better next game. We'll get the dub.*

Eli: *Okay, but promise you'll talk to me if you need to.*

Levi: *Promise.*

Yeah, I don't mean that. No chance in hell am I going to bring this up to the guys. Nope. They give the worst advice. I've lived through it. They're lucky they had me to get them through their girl problems. Nope, I can solve this on my own.

I unlock my door and move into my apartment, flipping on the light only to find Wylie sitting at the island, waiting for me.

"Jesus Christ," I say, hand to heart. "Fuck, what are you doing here sitting in the dark?"

"Sorry. Didn't mean to scare you. I was working on your placemat stain and then got tired and started doing social media. It turned dark, and before I realized it, you arrived home. I hope you don't mind that I was in here. I know you said it's not a hang-out space. But I needed the room and counter for the stain."

"It's fine," I say, shutting the door behind me. *Compose yourself, Posey. Be cool. Steady.*

"Sorry about the loss. Also, saw that you got in a brawl. Did you get hurt?"

"No." I set down my keys and wallet on my console table, then take off my shoes. "Vlad punched me in my padding, but I got him in the face."

"So he's the one who got hurt?"

"That seems to always be the case." I move over toward her and glance down at the placemat. The stain is now larger than it was before, spread out and only partially faded. I don't believe she's made it better but worse.

"Yeah, don't look at that," she says as she takes the placemat away and sets it on her lap. "I was trying to go for a non-toxic chemical route, but it seems that won't do the trick. I'll do more research and see how to remove this. In the meantime, please direct your attention to the corner of the room to meet your new fiddle leaf fig tree."

Oh, fuck yeah.

The time has come.

Dreams are coming true after a shit of a day.

Come to Papa . . .

I turn toward the corner of the living room, expecting to see a well-nourished, thriving fiddle leaf fig, but to my dismay, a small pot sits on the floor with three leaves sprouting from it instead.

My brow pinches together. "What's that?"

"I know what you must be thinking." She gets off her stool

and walks over to the plant. "It's small now, but with lots of love and devotion to its growth, this fiddle leaf fig will soon be a blooming fiend taking over this very space."

Those three leaves will need a lot more than some love and devotion.

She got me the Charlie Brown version of a fiddle leaf fig tree, not the monstrous, girthy log of a tree I expected.

"It's incredibly small," I say. "Especially for the space. I was thinking of something that would be bigger, more . . . mature."

"And I thought that too, but Cahutta at the nursery said it would feel more satisfying to build a connection with a plant at such a young stage in its journey and watch it flourish throughout its life and yours."

"Cahutta?" I ask with a quirked brow.

"Yes, he was amazing. I spent about an hour and a half just walking through the nursery with him, talking about different plants. He offered to meet up with me later to go over the intricacies of taking care of a fiddle leaf fig, but I told him I was busy. Gave him my number, though, so he could call later and fill me in."

Well, Cahutta is fucking dead.

"Call later? Wylie, you realize he was hitting on you, right?"

She pauses and thinks about it. "God, you think so?"

"Uh, yeah. Who the fuck spends that much time talking about a plant?"

"I just thought he was being nice. Huh." She taps her chin. "Well, I hope he was. This girl could use a wild night." She clears her throat and picks up the minuscule plant. I swear, it's smaller than Sherman. And here I was, about to brag about my giant tree in my apartment, and this is what I have to work with? Christ. "I think we should set him on the coffee table for now. Don't need him getting trampled."

"Yeah, don't want that," I say while grabbing the back of my neck. What a disappointment.

And to add salt to the wound, apparently, she's fishing for a wild night.

Step into my bedroom, and I'll give you exactly what you're looking for.

"I'm sorry it's not bigger. I can see your disappointment. I can go back and talk to Cahutta, let him know we're looking for something more mature and not necessarily a human/plant bonding experience."

"Nope, this works," I say, not wanting her to go back to that nursery. Fucking Cahutta. Last thing I need is for her to speak to some romanticizing plant man who she brings back to her nanny hole.

"Are you sure? I don't mind going back."

"No, don't. Let's just focus on the tasks you need to complete. Because I have more. And you need to pack for me."

"Don't worry, I already did that. You're all set to go." She wiggles her eyebrows. "Even took it upon myself to pack you some condoms and a vibrator, in case you wanted to go solo." Jesus. "Wasn't sure how many condoms you'd need. I figured one a night because I wasn't sure how long you could go—"

"All night," I say, that irritation clawing up me once again. "I can go all fucking night."

With a surprised expression, she says, "Oh, good for you. With your age, I wasn't sure what your stamina was like."

"I'm not *that* goddamn old," I say in a snappier tone, which of course only makes her smile more. Seems like my pain is her pleasure.

"Well, either way. I can add more if you'd like."

"Don't plan on fucking anyone while I'm away," I say as I move down toward my bedroom to find my suitcase on the bed with the packing cubes spread out and full.

"Don't plan on fucking anyone?" she asks. "I don't think that's a very good decision."

"Why not?" I ask.

"Well, not to point out the obvious, but it seems like you're very tense at the moment. Your shoulders are practically kissing your ears. Whenever I see that much tension in a man, I know they need to let loose."

"I'm fine."

"Ehhh, once again, not to overstep here, but I care to disagree. Maybe there's something I can do to help."

Uh, yeah, there is.

Take your shirt off.

Take your pants off.

Disrobe everything and get on your fucking knees.

Let me wrap your hair around my fist and guide that sweet mouth over my cock.

Let me fuck your mouth until you gag.

That's what you can fucking do.

"I'm fine," I say, turning away from her. I look at all the packing cubes and sift through them. "Why did you pack so many boxer briefs?" Focus on something else other than her plump and pouty lips.

"Because you can never have enough underwear. Plus you like to sleep in them, so I figured you would want to have extras on hand."

Smart. Didn't think about that.

I pick up a matching sweatsuit. "What's this?"

"A sweatsuit," she replies.

"I see that, but why did you pack it?"

"Because I thought you could use a style update." How dare she. My style is impeccable. "I was going through your social media videos, and some of the casual outfits you wear lack some modern Gen Z appeal."

Is she talking about tucking my sweatpants into my tube socks? Because I fucking refuse.

REFUSE!

"That's because I'm a millennial," I say.

"Yes, I know. It's obvious." Uh, pardon me? "I thought I'd spice it up a bit. Give you something to wear that the kids can relate to. Also, how do you feel about a bolo tie?"

"Not a fan," I say.

"Oof, good thing I asked," she says as she reaches into one of the packing cubes and pulls it out.

Where the hell did she even get that?

"You know, maybe I should just pack myself."

"No," she says quickly. "I can handle it." She places her hand on my arm, and I nearly come. Yeah, you read that correctly. COME! "This is what we call a teachable lesson. I've learned to pack lots of condoms because you can go all night, bravo to you, and no bolo tie. See, making mental notes now. But look at what else I packed. I think I did a great job with the rest. Your toiletry bag is in the bathroom ready to go, but I left out your toothbrush because you still need to use that as well as your deodorant and cologne, which I might have sniffed. It smells good, in case you were wondering. From the lady's perspective, great choice."

Pheromones will do that.

"Thanks," I say. Feeling awkward—*again*—I move into the bathroom and check out the toiletry bag, which seems to be all packed up correctly.

"See, I can do this. Just give me a chance. I know working with an assistant might be weird, but this is my first time, and I'm still learning. I promise I can do this for you."

I can see the desperation in her eyes, hear it in her voice, and it makes me feel that much worse because I know that she wants this to prove to her dad that she can handle everything. Meanwhile, I'm in an epic battle of keeping my hands to myself and trying to sabotage her simultaneously by being her dad's puppet. Guilt consumes me all over again.

"Yeah, you did a great job with the toiletry bag," I say and move back into the bedroom, wanting to make her feel better. "And yeah, this sweatsuit outfit might look good." I look through the cubes and see the vibrator that she chose, a simple flat-faced one that works great against my balls. "And my favorite vibrator," I say. "Good job."

"That's your favorite?" she asks. "Interesting. I thought it might be, but I was just guessing. And I know what you're thinking. Is it weird that I know what vibrator my male boss might like? The answer is no. I think personal assistants have to get on up there." She motions her hands in an upward motion. "Really know everything about their boss to make sure to please them as best as possible. So I'm glad I know about your condoms and vibrators. Aren't you glad?"

Oh yeah, really fucking glad. It makes me so goddamn happy.

Especially since I'm not allowed to use any of it on you.

Couldn't be happier.

"Yeah, I guess so," I reply uncomfortably.

"Okay, so this was a great learning moment." She clasps her hands together. "I also set up your backpack in your office, but I wasn't sure what you needed."

I walk out of the bedroom and into the office, where I see a few Post-it notes from her on my desk.

The first reads a social media schedule that she must have written down for both of us.

The second one is a note that just says highlighters.

The third is one name: Patty Ford.

Confused, I point at the Post-it and say, "What's this?"

She glances down, and then I watch her cheeks blush as she picks it up and crumples it in her hand. "Uh, nothing. Just a note to myself that I forgot to pick up. Oh, and here's my highlighter one. Sorry about that. I wasn't working here if you were wondering. I was just writing you a note and realized I forgot to grab my two notes."

"Not a problem," I reply, wanting to know who the hell Patty Ford is. I make a mental note to look it up when she leaves.

"Anyway, I have everything ready to go in your backpack and added some snacks. I know you get them from the team, but just in case you get hungry."

"Great. Thanks." I turn toward her and say, "Good job, Wylie."

With pride, she puffs her gorgeous chest. "Thank you." She follows that with a yawn and says, "Well, if that's all, I need to get to bed. I'm exhausted."

Actually, I could use you in the bedroom for a moment. Won't take too long. Just need to suck on your tits is all.

"Yeah, sure." I shift on my feet. "That's it."

"Great. Well, good luck on your away trip. Text me if you need anything, and I'll keep working hard over here on your behalf." She smiles brightly. "Good night . . . *Mr. Posey*."

I roll my eyes, causing her to laugh. "Good night, *Miss Wood*."

"Ooo." She pretends to shiver. "I like the sound of that." Chuckling, she takes off, and I follow her into the kitchen, listening for the click of her door before I turn out all the lights and head into my bedroom, where I quickly get ready for bed.

I'll pack the cubes in my suitcase in the morning, so I set them to the side and strip out of my clothes to nothing before slipping under my sheets. I open my Google search on my phone and type in the name Patty Ford.

Maybe it's a long-lost friend or maybe a travel blogger. Maybe someone she . . .

The Google results pop up, and all of them are X-rated.

No fucking way.

I click on the website under Patty Ford, and I'm immediately met with a hot brunette with huge tits and a curvy ass.

The banner picture on the website is of who I'm going to assume is Patty, completely naked and on her knees. Her hand and arm cover all the important parts, but fuck, is she hot. I scroll down and find videos of her masturbating and live sessions where you can get off with her.

Holy shit.

I wet my lips and explore the website a little more, feeling myself go hard with every picture and video I come across.

And sure, she's hot.

But what's really getting me hard is the idea that Wylie was interested in this website as well.

And there could be two reasons why: for her own personal pleasure, or for research. Either way, I fucking like it a lot.

I settle into my pillow and run my hand down my stomach, ready to grip my cock just as a text appears on my phone.

Fuck.

Talk about a cock block and an instant way to deflate things.

Coach Wood: *Make her get bagels again tonight.*

My stomach clenches, and I squeeze my eyes shut.

Fuck. That's the last thing I want to ask her to do, especially since I didn't eat any of them today.

Levi: *But she already got some, and I didn't eat any.*

Coach Wood: *Does it look like I care, Posey? Make her get the bagels again.*

Jesus Christ, why is he being such a dick?

Coach Wood: *Don't let me down, Posey.*

Yeah, hearing you loud and clear, you ass.

Levi: *Okay.*

Groaning inwardly and completely out of the mood now, I pull up my text thread with Wylie.

If she didn't think I was an asshole before, she sure as hell is going to think it now.

Chapter Seven

WYLIE

"I love you, but you look terrible," Sandie says as she sits on my bed and stares at my useless body.

"I feel terrible." I let out a yawn and sip some of the coffee that Sandie so nicely brought me.

"I can't believe he made you get the bagels again. And he didn't eat any. What the hell is that about? Is he stocking up to have a bagel party?"

"I have no idea. But if he asks me to get more tonight, I'm grabbing them from the local grocery store and passing them off as the good water bagels."

Sandie chuckles. "I hope that you do."

"And you know what? I went on Yelp to see if there was hype around these bagels, and there was some, but nothing spoke about the good water or the one-in-the-morning session. I think it's all in his head."

"Could very much be in his head. You know how athletes are. They're all sorts of superstitious. Next time you're near the bagel place, you should just buy two dozen and put them in my freezer so when he asks, you just have to drive to my place and grab them."

"Oh . . . wow, I should have thought about that sooner."

She pats my leg. "Blame it on the sleep deprivation."

"I will, but yeah, next time I'm over there, I'm buying extra bagels and freezing them at your place. And guess what? I'm going to buy the bad water ones."

"That will teach him," she says on a laugh. "He make you do anything else crazy?"

"Not really. He seemed not to like my packing but then quickly said that he did like it and told me what a great job I was doing. It was a weird change of tone. Like he wants to be this tough guy but then pulls back for a moment. He's hard to read. And oh my God, I didn't tell you this, but when we were in his office, he saw a Post-it note I left for myself. And I have no doubt he looked up what was on the Post-it note."

"What was on it?" Sandie asks.

"Patty Ford."

"The girl I told you about?" Sandie asks.

"Yup, I wrote down the name because I didn't want to forget, and then, bam, he saw it."

Sandie shrugs. "If anything, he should be appreciative."

I chuckle. "I guess that's one way to look at it. I'm helping in all aspects of his life."

"Did you see her logo contest, though?" Sandie asks.

"I did, and I started thinking up ideas last night on my drive to Port Hole Bagels and back. I think I'm going to draw some things up and see what you like best. It has to be sexy but not obvious."

"And it would be great work because she's offering a hefty prize for the winner. Maybe you can write in the entry form that you're a woman entrepreneur like she is."

"Ooo, good idea. She could appreciate that. Yeah, I think I'll draw some things tonight or maybe tomorrow. I still have so many tasks to do on Levi's list. I thought I'd be able to get more done, but between being sleep-deprived and having to drive around everywhere, I haven't been able to do everything I want to. I still need to do the pencils and the Skittles. And then this stupid book," I say, lifting the Vermont book. "Tell me when I'll find the time for this?"

Sandie takes the book from me and flips through the pages. "Do you really think he has a love for Vermont?"

"I don't know. He's an odd one, Sandie. You should have heard Halsey yesterday morning when he saw that I went out and got Levi his protein smoothie. He gave him shit for it, and Levi had the guiltiest look on his face."

"I don't know much about him, but he always seemed chill to me from all the online interactions . . . that you've shown me."

I shrug. Yeah, I've shown her a lot.

"Still, this rewriting thing is so weird." She flips open the first page, and a piece of paper falls out of it.

"What's that?" I ask.

"Probably instructions on how he wants the book typed up exactly." We both laugh, and she flips open the page. I watch her eyes scan over it before her jaw drops, and her wide eyes look up at me.

"What?" I ask.

"Oh my God, Wylie."

"What?" I say again, scooting closer. "Is it a diary entry or something?"

She shakes her head. "It's an email from your father."

"What?" I shout as I take the paper from her and start reading.

To: Levi Posey

From: Will Wood

Subject: Your List

Don't fuck this up, Posey.

Aside from regular tasks like social media, retrieving your food, arranging your calendar, and being at your beck and call, here are a few tasks you need to give her this week:

Hand her a copy of a book. I don't care what book, but give her a copy of it. Tell her you don't like the font it's written in, and have her type it out in a different font. Yes, have her type up the entire book, word for word. Tell her you want it in a week for your away trip to the Northeast.

Spill something on your floor. Don't care what it is. But make it disgusting. Tell her she needs to clean it up and make it seem like it was never there.

Ask her to get you ten pounds of Skittles. The Skittles must be divided into colors and placed in separate jars. But you want more reds than any other color. At least half a jar more.

Have her purchase you fifty number two pencils. Have her sharpen them just enough so they're pointed but not too much where they're splintering. Use them as a decoration for a day and then have her donate them to a local school, but she must receive a receipt of the donation.

Text her in the middle of the night that you need something, anything. Make her get it for you.

After each task, I expect you to take a picture and inform me that it's been completed. Do not let her off the hook. Don't let her skate by. I want you to make her life a living hell, got it?

And don't forget the rules. Don't forget why you're doing this. And mainly, don't forget that she's completely off limits.

My eyes slowly lift as anger sears through me.

"You have got to be fucking kidding me." I hop out of bed, all of my exhaustion fleeing as red-hot rage and adrenaline pulse through me. "Is this real?" I shake the paper at Sandie.

"It looks real to me." She grabs it and scans the paper. "It's printed out like a real email. Is that your dad's real email?"

I snatch the paper again, looking over the email a few times. My eyes feel wild at the moment. When I realize that it is, my entire body breaks out into an angry sweat. "It is." I toss the paper to the floor and start pacing the length of my tiny hole of a bedroom. "I can't believe this."

"What part can't you believe?"

"All of it." I toss my hands up in the air. "This is all a joke to him. To my dad. He's not giving me a chance to prove to him that I can handle this. He's trying to make me fail. That's so . . . that's so fucked up."

"It is," Sandie says softly. "I'm sorry, Wylie. You deserve better."

"I do deserve better," I reply. Hands on my hips, I stare down at the printed email as realization falls over me. "And he's helping my dad."

"Levi?" she asks.

I nod. "Yes. He's helping him." I look up at her. "All this insane shit that he's made me do. The bagels. The writing of the goddamn book. The stain. The pencils. That's all because of my dad's direction. Direction that Levi is taking. Why would he listen to my dad? Why would he be a part of this?"

"Well, according to the email, it seems as though there's a reason he's doing this." She picks up the paper and reads, *"Remember why you're doing this.* Maybe . . . I don't know . . . maybe he knew who you were that night and is pissed that you took off and is now trying to get back at you."

I whip around to look at Sandie. "There's no way he knew who I was, unless . . . do you think my dad saw us and confronted Levi after? Maybe Dad has been holding this over his head, and they've come together to get me back."

"That seems very calculated," Sandie says. "But also, slightly plausible."

"Wow." I shake my head as I cross my arms and sit back down on the bed. "I can't fucking believe this. Here I thought I was actually getting a chance to do something different with my life, and it turns out it's all a freaking setup. A setup to try to get me to do something I don't want to do."

"And I think we all know that you don't do things you don't want to do."

"That's correct." *Not to mention that my dad doesn't care whether I fail or succeed. Why? Why would he do that?* What parent deliberately sets up their only child to feel bad about herself? I lean against the headboard, feeling so incredibly hurt. So angry. So horrified at the fact that my dad thinks this is all a game. This isn't a game. This is my life. And it's about time he realizes he can't control me anymore.

I run my tongue over my teeth, my mind whirling.

"Do you want to talk about what's going on in your head? Because I can see you thinking over there, and I don't want you to spiral."

"It just sucks," I say, my throat growing tight. "He's never trusted me to make smart decisions for my life. He's always controlled me. What school I went to. What I majored in. The people I hung out with. And now this. It's just him tightening his grasp on me, and I'm done. I don't want to be his puppet anymore. The leading player in his game."

"Then don't be."

I shake my head. "I'm not going to." I pull my legs into my chest. "And here I thought Levi was feeling bad about the things he was making me do. I thought I saw a shred of doubt in his eyes."

"Maybe you did. Maybe he's not fully in on this plan. I mean, the email does seem pretty threatening. Maybe he didn't have a choice."

"There's always a choice," I say as I hug my knees and work my jaw to the side, a thought coming into my head.

Sandie notices. "What's the evil look on your face for?"

"There's no evil look."

"Uh, yeah, there is. You went from sad to conniving in seconds."

"I was just thinking, if they can play, why can't I?"

"Oh boy, what do you mean by that?"

I sit up taller. "Well, I don't want to give this up. This place to live, this job, because it is money and gives me the opportunity to do what I want to do. I will admit that it's a pretty decent setup so I can get my feet on the ground and get myself established. But what if . . . what if I had fun with it?"

"Like get the wrong bagels?"

"That, but so much more." Excitement pulses through me as an idea formulates in my head. "There's chemistry between Levi and me. It's obvious from the way I catch him checking me out and blatantly obvious from the night we first met. Also, he's told me he finds me incredibly attractive, so what if I use that to my advantage to torture him?"

"Oh dear God," Sandie says as I snatch the email from her.

"Look, right here at the bottom, it says, don't fuck her. My dad distinctly warned Levi against such behavior, so what if I make it impossible for him not to fuck me?"

Sandie rubs her temples. "You know, I think we could go a different direction. I think we could have a constructive conversation with your father and then with Levi and let them know you're disappointed in both of them."

I shake my head. "No, they want to battle? Well, this is war now. My dad wants to teach me a lesson? Well, I'm going to teach him one. That lesson being don't mess with me." Feeling empowered, I continue, "I'm going to prove to him that despite his negativity and lack of belief in me, I can make a career out of what brings me joy. And Levi, well, he's going to learn the hard way that I'm not one to mess with either. He's going to learn very quickly what he's missing out on by helping my dad."

Sandie slowly nods. "And you're not up for a conversation?"

"Sure, is that the adult thing to do? Probably, but what will it actually accomplish? I tried having a conversation with my dad before all of this, and this is where we ended up. It's not going to do anything. I have to show him with action."

"And Posey?" she asks.

"He made me get bagels at one in the morning, two nights in a row, and didn't even eat them. Payback is a bitch."

She shrugs. "Yeah, that sucks. What exactly does payback entail?"

"Erotic torture," I say, staring at the wall.

She laughs. "I think that's a first I've heard for payback. Erotic torture, okay, tell me what that entails."

"Ohhh, I don't think you're ready for this," I say, feeling slightly crazed.

"I'm ready," she says, rubbing her hands together. "Lay it on me."

Leaning forward, I paint her a picture. "Erotic torture is the apex of blue ball-ism."

"Did you make up that word?"

"Perhaps," I reply. "Erotic torture is a fine art, a master class in corrupting unsuspecting cocks."

"Ehh, are you okay?" she asks.

"Never been better," I say as my eyes go wild. "Envision this . . . me, no bra, just a tank top, walking around his space, flirting with him, touching him, resting my hardened nipple on his forearm. Driving him so crazy with need, with lust, that he'll walk around with a constant hard-on. He wakes up with one, works out with one, plays his games with one. Hard-on after hard-on after hard-on. And no amount of dingo dangling with it will the hard-on become flaccid. He will be hard for the ages." I move my hand across the sky, staring up at the ceiling.

Sandie is silent for a second. "A few comments. Dingo dangling is a first for me. I'm not sure where that came from, but it will never leave my head. Ever. Second, using the word flaccid, was that by choice?"

"Dingo dangling was a fly-by-the-seat-of-my-pants terminology," I say. "And flaccid, yes, that was by choice. Nothing is sadder than a flaccid dick."

Sandie slightly nods. "Agreed, and hey, this plan, it seems like fun, but what happens when he cracks? Because I have a feeling he will."

"Then I win . . . in multiple ways." I wink.

"And the end goal?"

I smile at my friend. "To show these men that women are not their puppets."

"And what are we?" she asks.

"Strong, confident, smart, and in no need for a penis to dictate our future." I raise my fist to the sky, feeling drunk off power.

"Well, if that's the case, then I'm all in. What can I do to help?"

I stare at my friend and smile. "I need to borrow some of your shirts."

"Why? They're way too small for your chest size."

I smile at her. "Exactly."

━━

LEVI: *I know this might sound crazy, but can you get more bagels tonight?*

I stare down at his text, my teeth grinding together as I read his request over and over. The freaking audacity. Oh, he'll be getting his bagels. He'll have so many bagels he won't know what to do with them.

Wylie: *Not a problem. Same count and type?*

Levi: *Yeah, and can you freeze them?*

Wylie: *Not a problem. I don't know how much room is left in the freezer, but I'll shift some things around.*

Levi: *Thank you.*

Wylie: *Anything for you . . . Mr. Posey. And good luck tonight.*

Levi: *It's Levi. And thanks.*

━━

WYLIE: *Anything I can help you with today? Your pencils have been sharpened and are beautifully displayed on the dining room table. Skittles have been sorted and are waiting for consumption. I'm almost done with the book, and I must say, Vermont is such an interesting state. I can't wait to discuss it with you over a bagel when you get back. Oh, and I took it upon myself to fold all your underwear a certain way to fit better in your dresser.*

Levi: *Wow, you've been busy. Thanks. The underwear sounds interesting. Can't wait to see what you've done with it. And as for other tasks, yeah, do you think you could pull all my laundry out of my drawers and rewash it all, fold it, and put it away? I love walking into my closet and smelling fresh clothes when I get home.*

Wylie: *I know the smell you're referring to. Delicious. Sure thing. Want me to add some fabric softener? I saw that you don't have any.*

Levi: That would be awesome. Thanks. And how did that stain come out?

Wylie: Perfect, looks brand new. Get ready to do your best eating.

Levi: Wow, I'm impressed.

Wylie: Also went shopping for you, so food is stocked up. I've also been learning to make that protein smoothie you like so much, and I think I've nailed it. I'll make it for you when you get back.

Levi: Great. Thanks.

Wylie: Okay, safe travels. See you later tonight.

Levi: Yeah, see you tonight.

"WHAT ARE YOU DOING RIGHT NOW?" Sandie asks over the phone.

"Spraying Levi's clothes."

"What?" Sandie asks on a chuckle.

"He asked me to rewash all of his clothes, and there was no way I was going to do that, so I picked up some fabric spray, and I'm giving them a spray down to avoid extra work."

"Ooo, smart."

"Thank you. Also stocked up on grocery store bagels and froze those. The fucker won't even know the difference. And I did what you said to do with the book, wrote the first few pages and then just copy and pasted shit from the internet and formatted it. Doubt he'll even read it."

"Did you bind it together like a book?"

"Yup, he's going to think I'm a magician."

Sandie laughs. "And the placemat?"

"Found it at West Elm. Bought three on sale, just in case he tries to pull another stain stunt."

"You are my hero."

"Thank you, I try. Oh, and because I half-fisted all of my tasks, I was able to sit on his comfy couch today and work on that entry for Patty Ford."

"How did it come out?" she asks as I open his underwear drawer and spray the fabric down.

"I think okay. I took a screenshot of her and did a silhouette of her body. Still working in the right lettering, but I think it could be a viable option. I want to make a few options, some sexy ones and some discreet ones."

"I think that's smart. When's the boss supposed to be home?"

"Anytime now."

"What are you wearing?"

Smirking to myself, I say, "A pair of loose-fitting sweatpants being held up single-handedly by my hips and your Mickey Mouse shirt."

"Oh my God, Wylie." She laughs. "That shirt is short on me. What the hell does it look like on you?"

"A toddler's shirt. I had a very hard time getting it over my breasts. Most of my stomach is showing, not wearing a bra, and I plan on playing with my nipples right before he gets home so they're hard as stones."

"You're evil, but also, I'm interested to see how long he can hold out. I'm invested."

"I'm interested to see as well," I say.

"And when he gives in, will you give in too?"

"You know, I thought about that, and I don't know. I'd have to see how it is at the time."

"I think that's fair," she says. "But also for your sake, I hope you give in. I know how much you've wanted him."

"That was before I found out he was in cahoots with my father. Now . . . now I'm seeking revenge."

"No, you're seeking erotic torture."

We both laugh. "He has no idea what's coming for him." I hear some fumbling at the front door, so I whisper, "Oh shit, I think he's here. Talk later."

"Bye," she says as I quickly toss the fabric spray under his bed, making a mental note to collect it later.

Before I walk out into the living room, I play with my nipples quickly, making them poke against the fabric of the shirt.

Perfect.

Feeling good, I strut out of his bedroom and down the hall where I get my first glance at him.

He's wearing the sweatsuit I picked out for him, and his hair looks like he's been running his hand through it for the better portion of the flight. He's left the scruff on his jaw, and there's some light bruising around his eyes where he got hit in the head the other day. And to my demise, he looks so fucking good that it pains me to have to conduct erotic torture on him . . . because I think it's going to be just as torturous on me.

Stepping in closer, I say, "Welcome home." He glances to the side, and immediately, his eyes fall to my breasts.

Classic.

I could read this man like a book.

He wets his lips before his eyes slowly move up to my face. "Uh, hey," he says before looking away.

"How was the flight?" I walk up to him, letting my breasts skim across his arm before I take his bag from his hand to set it down.

He shivers from the touch and steps back. "It was, uh . . . it was good."

"That's great to hear." I smooth my hand over his arm.

"Yeah," he squeaks. "Great flight. Just great. All around great." He backs up to the kitchen island chairs. "Really, uh, great."

I smirk at him. "Sounds like it was great." I wink and then add, "I'm guessing it's better to fly home when you win than when you lose. I'm sure my dad is a nightmare to be with on a flight after a loss."

His eyes fall to my chest again before he glances away. "He, uh, he doesn't really say much for a win or a loss."

I take a step closer. "And here I thought he raged. Well, anyway, welcome home. Let me show you what I've done." I take his hand, which he seems surprised by, and lead him to the dining room table, where his pencils are set up. I pick up the vase and say, "What do you think? Perfectly sharpened, right?"

His eyes remain fixed on me for a moment as if he's trying to study me, and then he looks back down at the pencils. "Wow, yeah, those look sharpened." He pulls on the back of his neck, looking so uncomfortable. Just the way I want him.

"Sniff one."

"Huh?" he asks.

I take his hand in mine again, force him to grab one of the pencils, and bring it up to his nose. "Sniff it like a flower. I know how much you love the smell."

"Sure, yeah. Love a good sniff." He leans close to the pencil and takes a short but quick sniff. His eyebrows shoot up as he says, "Woodsy. That's nice."

"That's what I thought when I smelled it," I say as I press my hand to his chest. His eyes fall to my hand and dart back up to me. "It was a pleasure sharpening those for you, Levi."

His eyes widen slightly as he sets the pencil back in the vase. "Good to know." He takes a step back from me and sticks his hands in his pockets, clearly trying to keep his distance.

Inwardly smiling, I turn away from him and bend at the waist, making sure to stick my ass out as I put the vase back down, giving him a great view. When I glance over my shoulder, I catch him checking me out. Yup, this is going to be so much fun.

"And then here are your Skittles," I say, showing them off at the kitchen counter. "I hope I did it right. Was this what you were looking for?" I stand behind the containers, my breasts right at the same eye level. I watch his eyes scan the Skittles but mainly remain on my chest.

"Yeah," he murmurs. "Exactly what I was looking for."

And thank God my nipples are still hard because what a show for him right now.

"Great." I walk around the island and take his hand again. I pick up his bag and guide him toward his bedroom.

"Uh, what are you doing?" he asks.

"Unpacking your bag for you. And I think I should get that sweatsuit into the wash. I saved a light load so I could add your travel clothes into the washer and dryer when you got home. Oh, and I ordered some dinner for you. Steak and potatoes. Not sure if that's your meal of choice, but figured I'd give it a try. Should be here soon."

I set his bag down on the bed and sit him next to it. "Do you want to get undressed so I can take those clothes?"

"In front of you?" he asks on a gulp.

I chuckle. "You can if you want, but if you're shy about your body, you can change in the bathroom and hand me your sweatsuit."

"I'm not shy, just . . . don't want to be creepy is all."

"Remember what I said, Levi." I place my hand on his shoulder and lean into him. Our noses are mere inches from touching. "This is not your typical boss/assistant relationship. We are going to get intimate with each other."

"We . . . we are?" he asks as I grip the hem of his sweatshirt and pull it up and over his head. To my surprise, he's not wearing a shirt under it, and dear God in heaven . . .

Oh fuck me, he's so hot.

Ughhh, look at his chest.

It's so thick, so large. So broad. He's a big man but packed with muscle. His pecs protrude off his chest, flat but muscular. His shoulders and arms are shapely, carved and rock hard like made from stone. And then he has a set of abs I really wasn't expecting at all. They're not nearly as defined as what I've seen on some of his other teammates, but this man is also a bruiser. He's dense and built on protein and weight.

And of course because he's a brawny, sexy man, there's the lightest smattering of chest hair across his pecs that he keeps well trimmed. I'm far too tempted to drag my fingers over the stubble.

Looking away, I say, "Not that kind of intimate." I try to laugh it off. *Maybe this erotic torture will be harder than I thought.* Especially with the ripped body this man's working with. "Do you need me to take off your sweats too, or can you handle that? I can get on my knees and remove them for you."

"No," he says loudly. "I can, uh, I can do that." But he doesn't move.

"Well, are you going to remove them?"

"Yup." He slowly nods but still doesn't move.

"Okay, but do you realize you say you're going to remove them, yet you haven't removed them?"

"Yeah, I know."

"So see where I'm confused. Because if you need help, I have no problem taking your clothes off for you. I can slip my hands right under the waistline and—"

"I got it," he says quickly and then stands from the bed and pushes his sweats down, leaving him in his black boxer briefs.

He holds the sweats out to me, but my eyes land on the bulge between his legs, the very large bulge.

He's half hard. He has to be.

If he's not, then sleeping with him is going to be a no, thank you. If that's flaccid Posey penis, then it's not fitting in me, that's for damn sure.

"I'm, uh . . . I'm sorry about . . ." He gestures toward his crotch.

"Why apologize?" I say with another wink. "It's hot." And as I turn away from him with sweats in hand, my legs quiver with yearning. I toss the sweats in the closet where the washer and dryer are and then open his bag to pull out his dirty laundry. "Did you happen to use any of the condoms I packed you?" I ask as he stands next to me. From the corner of my eye, I catch just how muscular his thighs are, and for some reason, it's a huge turn-on for me. Like stick a watermelon between those thighs, and he's cracking it open on one pulse.

"Uh, no," he says.

"Oh, that's sad. Couldn't find a willing participant?" I ask.

"Didn't look for one."

"No?" I reply as I gather his dirty laundry and take it to the closet. "Why not?"

"Distracted," he says from his bedroom, still just standing there. "Uh, you know, I think I might take a shower."

"Good idea, get that plane off you."

"Yeah, sure."

I hear him move into the bathroom and click the door shut. I shove the laundry in the washer and then grab my phone.

Wylie: *He's frazzled, Sandie. He has stared at my breasts at least a half dozen times since he's come home.*

Luckily, Sandie is quick to text me back.

Sandie: *Excellent. *Insert evil laugh* What's he doing now?*

Wylie: *Taking a shower.*

Sandie: *Seems to me like you need to walk in there and ask him a question.*

Wylie: *OMG, should I?*

Sandie: *If we're conducting erotic torture, then yes, you need to walk in there while he's soaping up.*

Wylie: *And this is why we're friends. I'll report back.*

I pocket my phone, and with some mustered-up courage, I open the bathroom door.

"Uh, hello?" he asks.

"Hey, just me," I say casually, helping myself in.

"Can I help you?" he asks, his back toward me. The shower is foggy so I can't see anything other than his silhouette. Shame. I was hoping to see a little ass at least.

"Just came in to grab your underwear. I assume you want this washed as well."

"Sure," he says in a tense voice.

"Oh, and I checked on the food. Should be here in the next twenty minutes."

"Yup, that's great."

"I can set it up on your favored placemat if you want. Dining room or kitchen island?"

"Kitchen island is fine," he answers, not moving.

"Sounds good. Can I get you anything else?"

"Just some privacy," he says through clenched teeth.

"Oh." I laugh. "Sorry about that." I grab his underwear and head toward the door. "Enjoy your shower."

And then I leave, smiling brightly to myself. Yup, this is going to be a lot of fun.

⸻

"OOO, YOU SMELL AMAZING," I say as I walk by a freshly showered Levi, who is now wearing a pair of shorts and a simple heather gray T-shirt with an Agitators logo on the front. The sleeves strain around his biceps and chest while the torso clings to his muscled body. I lean into him. "Is that your soap or cologne?"

He clears his throat as he takes a seat at the island. "Soap."

"Wow. It's amazing," I say as I let my hand drag over the contours of his back before I move to the fridge to grab him a drink. "Would you like a soda?"

He's silent for a second, and when I look over my shoulder, his eyes revert from my ass to me. "You, uh, you don't have to serve me, Wylie."

"Oh, I don't mind. I'll grab you a Diet Coke." I grab one for myself as well and take a seat next to him at the island, but I angle my body to face him and rest my feet on the rung of his chair. "Here you go." I slide the soda over to him, not really giving him any space from me. "Hope you don't mind if I eat here with you. I hate when my little bedroom smells like food. Stinks up my clothes. Also, we can catch up."

"Sure, yeah, you can eat here."

"Great." I pull the food out of the paper bag and say, "Hope you don't mind that I got myself a salad. I can pay you back later. Just thought it would be easier."

"You don't have to pay me back, Wylie."

"Oh, I'm not going to be a freeloader. I'll pay you back . . . somehow." I wink, and he quickly looks away as he picks up his fork and knife, ready to eat. "How was the trip? Do anything fun? We already know that you didn't do anybody fun, but perhaps you did something else while you were away?"

He shakes his head. "Just hockey."

"Not even a fun meal with the guys?"

He shakes his head again as he opens his container and stabs one of his potatoes with a fork rather aggressively. "All the guys went straight to their rooms. OC met up with a friend, so I was kind of on my own."

"What were the guys doing in their rooms?"

"Calling their girls."

"Oh," I say as I pop open my steak salad. "Like frisky FaceTimes?"

"Pretty much," he says on a sigh, then cuts into his steak, which cuts like butter.

"You say that as if it makes you sad. Do you wish you were FaceTiming someone?"

He looks over at me and says, "Sometimes, yeah."

"Well, you can always FaceTime me," I say. And then for the hell of it, I shimmy at him and say, "I could make it fun for you."

He glances down at my bouncing breasts and then back at his steak. "You sure as hell could."

"Ooo, I take that as you're interested. You know, topless Face-Times will come at a surcharge, but I'll make it worth it." I joke around, but from the tension in his shoulders, he's anything *but* in a joking mood, which means I'm doing my job.

Not so fun being played around with, is it, Levi?

When he makes no attempt at a comment, I say, "Well, if interested, we can add it to my duties. Shimmy for boss. I actually have some pretty great lingerie. I have this one set that ties together like a bow in the front. With one tug, it's hello breasts."

The grip on his fork tightens as he says, "Yeah, we're not crossing that line, remember?"

"I know, but just putting it out there, though." I run my hand over his back. "You seem so tense, like you need someone to loosen you up. I can't have my boss unhappy." I run my hands over his shoulders. "Ooo, you're really tense. Everything is all bunched up here. Do you need me to massage you? Because I can. I used to give out massages all the time in college."

"What kind of massages?" he asks when he glances my way.

"All kinds . . ." I wiggle my brows. "Obviously not for money, but the few guys I dated loved my hand—"

He bounds out of his chair, startling me back as he grips his forehead in distress. He turns in a few circles, almost confused as to what he should do next. After a few seconds, he says, "You know, maybe we should change the subject."

"Oh, why? Did I say something bad?" I act innocent even though I'm the furthest thing from it.

"No . . . I mean, yes . . . ugh, not really." He pinches his brow. "Fuck, I'm sorry. I'm just distracted."

"Anything I can help you get off your mind?" I say as I puff my chest out just a touch more.

His eyes take the bait, and I catch him wet his lips right before he starts shaking his head, almost as if he needs to convince himself. "No. Nope. Nothing you can do. I can, uh, I can handle it myself."

"Why are you so jittery?" I ask.

"Because." He pushes his hand through his hair. "Just . . . fuck, I wasn't expecting you to be here when I got home, so I'm a little jumpy is all."

"Oh, okay. Well, I can leave." I stand from my chair. "I don't want to make you uncomfortable."

"You're not. You're fine." He mumbles. "Fuck, you're so fine." He drags both hands over his face, and I can see the strain in his body. I can see his will coming close to snapping. When his eyes open again, they land on my breasts, and I know my nipples are hard because I'm turned on. Turned on from having this much control over a man. I've barely done anything, and he's squirming. There's something so empowering about that.

"Well, how about I just take my salad and give you some space. I'll be back in an hour to change the laundry."

"I can do that," he says quickly. "I can change it out."

"Are you sure? I don't mind coming back."

He shakes his head. "Just take the night off. You've done a lot."

"Okay, if you insist." I start to gather my dinner when I

remember the book. "Oh, almost forgot." I walk over to his living room and pull the bound book I made of Vermont for him. "Here's everything typed up and put in Arial font. I added some pictures just to make it interesting for you. I hope you enjoy it."

He stares down at the book, dumbfounded, then back at me. "You put it in binding?"

"I'm efficient, Levi," I say as I poke his chest. "Ooo, that's strong. I probably shouldn't say this, but you have an amazing body. I noticed when I took your sweatshirt off. Too bad for the girls who missed out the other night, right? Oh, by the way, if you want, I can handle any type of dating profile you want to put together. I can swipe left or right for you, choose girls I think you might like."

"Yeah, not interested in dating at the moment."

"Right," I say, booping him on the nose. "Only fucking. Well, I can put that in the profile. Looking for one-night stands."

Once again, he shakes his head. "Not necessary."

"Okay, well, the option is there. Now I'm going to take my salad back to my room, despite not liking eating in there. I've been working on a design for a contest. Have you ever heard of Patty Ford?"

His eyes widen a little as his cheeks flush.

Oh, he so looked her up. I like that he did.

My only question is, did he get off to her?

I hope so . . . because I know I did.

"Uh, no, who is she?"

Such a liar. *Adorable.*

"An erotic entertainer. And I know what you're thinking, that's a fancy way to say porn star, but she doesn't do it with other people. She is more about trying to have a one-on-one experience with the fans. Sort of like an OnlyFans account, but she's designed her own website so she takes all the money. Brilliant if you ask me. Well, she's looking for a new logo, and I decided to enter the contest. I've been working on some designs and want to finalize them tonight. Studying her has been fun. There's something about her that just gets me so hot."

His cheeks redden even more. "Uh, really?" he asks.

"Oh, yeah. I must have gotten off three times already just working on this logo."

He pulls on his neck, the strain in his chest and forearms evident. "Cool, yeah, I'll, uh, I'll check her out."

"You should. There's this one video where she tells you what to do, could be for a man or woman. And as she talks to you, she starts stripping. Oh my God, it's so hot. A must watch. I was throbbing by the time I allowed my fingers to finish myself off." I smile brightly at his tortured expression. "All right, I'll leave you to it. Let me know if you need anything, oh . . . before I leave, are you going to need bagels tonight that you won't be eating?"

He slowly shakes his head. "No. I think I'm good."

"Great. Okay, have a good night."

And with that, I'm out of his apartment feeling fully satisfied with myself.

Chapter Eight

LEVI

This is what modern-day hell would be.

This right here.

Sharing a living space—not sure how that happened when I specifically told her to stick to her room—with a girl who apparently doesn't own any bras. Oh wait, no, that's not correct. She does own bras, but they tie into a bow in the front and with one tug . . . breasts. Pretty sure that's how she put it.

This is day two of being back from my trip, and this morning, she walked into the kitchen in nothing but a threadbare tank top. I saw the definition of her nipples and had to retreat to my bedroom where I took some calming breaths and attempted to subdue the blue balls that are squeezing me to death.

I refuse to masturbate to the image of her in my head. Absolutely refuse because the moment I do it, is the moment I lose all control. I have to keep her out of my mind.

That's how I found myself alone in my hotel room the other night, playing Phase 10 on my phone and swearing at an online player who I didn't know. Player4756. The motherfucker kept skipping me. Several times, I almost chucked my phone against the wall.

Luckily for me, I could take out some of my pent-up aggression on the ice, and it did me well because it was a shutout game for us. No one was getting by me, and certainly not Eli, either. It was a much better showing than before, and Coach even complimented me, which he never does. Sure, his compliment was a nod of approval, but still, I counted it.

But now that I'm back home, it's like she's trying to make me hard every chance she gets.

And it's working.

Last night, I was hard while eating steak.

I went to bed hard.

I woke up so fucking hard.

And now as I sit here in my living room, staring at the tiny fiddle leaf fig tree she got for me, my balls ache, wanting relief.

"Hey, you in here?" I hear her call out from the kitchen.

Here we go. How is she going to torture me now?

I lean back on the couch and say, "Living room."

"Oh, hey." She steps up, and when I look to the side, I find her wet with a towel barely wrapped around her body.

Fuck.

Me.

"What are you doing?" I ask, averting my eyes.

"Sorry, I tried calling you, but you weren't answering."

"Oh, my phone is in my room," I groan because fuck me, she's wet.

She's in a towel, and she's wet.

"Well, I ran out of soap, and I was wondering if I could borrow some of yours. And I know what you're thinking, I'm making this up because I was saying how great you smelled last night and I want to smell the same. And whereas a part of that is true, I don't have any soap and need some."

Keeping my eyes averted, I say, "Yeah, you can borrow some."

"Awesome. Thank you. Is it okay if I just finish in your shower since I'm already naked and wet?"

"Finish?" I gulp.

Do you need help finishing?

Because I know a few ways I can get you off in that shower.

"Yeah, finish showering."

Oh fuck, duh.

Jesus Christ, man. You are way too horny to be having these conversations.

"Oh yeah, sure. Showering. Can't, uh, can't just walk away from the water without soaping up, and since you don't have soap, how can you soap up?"

She cutely tilts her head to the side, her towel dipping just a centimeter. "Are you okay?"

"Yes," I say quickly. "Fine. Really just doing fantastic. Are you . . . uh, are you okay? Not that I care if you are because you're my assistant and I shouldn't be asking you that kind of stuff, but are you okay?"

"Why shouldn't you care if I'm okay?"

"Did I say that?" I nervously laugh. "I meant that I care, I care about your well-being but not like . . . you know, other things."

"Actually, I don't know. What are you talking about?"

Yeah, Posey, what the hell are you talking about?

Can't be sure.

I'm distracted.

Her breasts are ready to pop out of that towel. There's nothing but terrycloth between us, and I can't stop myself from getting hard.

Pathetic and creepy, I get it!

You don't have to tell me.

I wish I could smack my dick into shape, but out of fear I might come from a whisper of a breeze, I couldn't possibly punish it for being out of control.

"You know . . ." I tug on my hair. "I think I'm tired. Sleep-deprived and jet-lagged are not a good combo. So to sum up this conversation, you can use my soap, finish off in my shower, and I care if you're fine."

Her gleamingly beautiful smile nearly makes me weep. "Good to know. And thank you. I really appreciate it."

With that, she takes off down the hallway, and my eyes trail her, watching the towel climb up against the bubble of her ass just as she disappears into my room.

I drag my hands over my face and groan into my palms.

I won't last this. There is no fucking way.

And did she have to say naked and wet? I mean, it was obvious, but she didn't have to point it out.

I don't think I can keep this inside me. I have to tell someone. I need someone to bounce ideas off and combat this internal hell I'm living in.

I consider going into my room to grab my phone, but knowing her, she left the bathroom door wide open. She doesn't seem to have any issues with privacy. She just lets it all out.

So instead of doing anything, I just sit here, twiddling my fingers and taking calming breaths. I was so desperate to get over this aching feeling inside me that I watched a twenty-minute video on YouTube on how to combat horniness through meditation.

I take deep breaths, envisioning a peaceful meadow, waves of green bristling against the wind. Puffy clouds against a bright blue sky. And Wylie, running toward me, her tits bouncing against her threadbare tank top tempting the elasticity of the fabric.

Annnnnnd . . . I'm hard all over.

I pick up a throw pillow, place it against my face, and scream into it, only to lower the pillow and find Wylie standing there, drying her hair while wearing one of my hockey shirts.

Mother.

Of.

God.

"Are you okay?" she asks.

No.

I'm not.

I want to fuck you.

I want to bury myself between your legs.

I want to live there for days on end, making you come on my tongue over and over again just so I can watch you writhe against the mattress.

I want to feel you squeeze my cock.

I want to feel your slick pussy, bare, with nothing between us.

I want to hear you cry out my name until your voice is hoarse.

I want to be rid of this ache that's holding my dick hostage.

I FUCKING WANT YOU!

I tack on a smile, painfully aware of my desperation. "Yup, everything is great."

"Okay because it looked like you were screaming into a pillow."

"Stubbed my toe," I reply. "Got me good."

"Ooo, I hate when that happens. You okay?"

"Yeah, I'm good."

"Because I can take care of it for you if you want. Ice it. Massage. Suck on it . . ." She winks, and I nearly choke on my own saliva. *Suck. On. It. Yes, I fucking want you to suck on it—it being my cock that is weeping for you.*

I nervously laugh. "Uh, not needed. I'll survive."

She clutches her chest. "You're so brave. By the way, I hope it's okay that I'm wearing one of your shirts. I thought it would be better than a wet towel."

I prefer the wet towel.

Actually, if I'm taking requests, no clothes would be best. And if you want, you can sit on my lap to air dry if you need to.

"Yeah, totally cool."

"Great because I might keep it. You have like twenty of these in your closet, and it's the perfect nighttime shirt." She moves over to the living room and takes a seat next to me. Okay, so she's sitting down, that's what's happening. Be cool, man. "Have you looked through the social media posts I've made? People are loving them."

"I haven't. I'll be sure to look through them." I keep my eyes forward and not on the way her tits sway against the loose fabric of my shirt.

"Some of your female fans are using the hashtag, Pretty Posey." She props her head on her hand while leaning against the back of the couch and asks, "Were you aware that you're pretty?"

"Uh, I prefer handsome, but sure, I do tend to look at myself in the mirror and think, wow, you're a good-looking man."

She laughs. "How often? Every time you look in the mirror?"

I rub my palms on my thighs, still looking straight ahead. "I average about once a day."

"You know, it's good to have confidence. As long as that confidence doesn't turn into cockiness."

"Cockiness isn't bad," I reply while I pretend to pick a piece of lint off my shirt. Anything to avoid looking at her.

"Maybe on the ice, but when dealing with women, it's bad. It's kind of a turnoff."

That piques my interest, so I turn toward her. "You'd rather have a blubbering mess trying to hit on you than a guy who's sure of himself?"

She smiles broadly at me, probably because I'm finally looking at her rather than avoiding her like . . . well . . . a blubbering mess. "I think there's a fine line." She drags her finger on my forearm and says, "I think it's good to have a man who's confident but doesn't think a woman is beneath him, like she's lucky to breathe the same air as him."

Chills pulse up my arm from her touch. "Uh-huh. Yup."

I have no other response because my mouth is salivating.

Actually salivating.

In any other circumstances, I'd be turned fully toward her, my hand on her thigh, my thumb rubbing along her smooth skin, moving higher and higher. I'd lean into her, touch her hair, stare at her lips, and get lost in her eyes. I'd make a fucking move, tell her how goddamn beautiful she is, how she steals my breath when she enters the room.

But lucky for me, she's completely and totally off limits. So off limits that if I were to even think about touching her, I might get my dick skated off by her father.

I remain stiff—in all areas—salivating over a touch of a finger.

"You remember that night we first met?" she asks.

Uh, like it was fucking two hours ago. That night plays in my head every time I shut my eyes for bed. I think about it. Dream about it. Wish about it. That night fucking haunts me.

"Uh, yeah. I believe so," I say casually.

"You seemed different from how you are now. Like the confidence I was talking about."

That's because my dick didn't have a muzzle on it like it does now.

"Oh, really?" I laugh nervously. "Well, you know, people change."

"They do, but I think it's something else. Are you scared of me?"

"Ha!" I bellow. "You? Scared of you?" I shake my head. "No, no, no. Nope. Not scared of you. Not even a little. Definitely not scared. Nope. No scaries over here."

Now, am I scared of your father?

Yes.

My nipples have inverted just thinking about him seeing us like this side by side on my couch, and nothing is even happening. Well, besides my growing affection for this woman. Oh, did I say affection? I meant erection.

My growing erection.

"Hmm, but you're so jumpy. Is there anything that I'm doing to make you so jumpy?"

She squeezes in closer, her breast rubbing up against my arm, the distinctive feel of her hard nipple right there on my bicep, poking my sensitive skin. The smell of her shampoo combined with the scent of my masculine soap has my head swirling with debauchery, and when her hand lands on my thigh with concern, I feel the telltale sign of my dick press against the fabric of my pants.

Alert. Alert.

Warning. Warning.

Bad thoughts are occurring.

Sexual thoughts.

Aching urges are taking over.

Hands are ready to cup breasts.

The mouth is ready to suckle.

The dick is ready to pulse between her legs . . .

Posey, you're going to do something bad if you don't remove yourself right this instant.

Out of self-preservation, I fly off the couch, letting her fall into the spot I was just occupying as I shout, "Bologna."

"Huh?" she asks, sitting back.

"B-bologna." I keep my hands placed in front of my aching cock to block her view of my obvious bulge. "Did you, uh, did you get me bologna? At the store. Did you secure the bologna?"

"Um, yes," she says with a quizzical tone. "The bologna has been secured."

"Are you sure? Because it's important. The bologna is important, Wylie."

Her brow pinches together. "Yes, I'm sure. The bologna has been purchased and properly placed in the fridge." She studies me for a moment. "Is everything okay, Levi?"

No.

Everything is not okay.

I have a raging hard-on, I'm fumbling around like a jackass, and I'm pretty sure tonight I'm going to whimper myself to sleep from the thought of the tip of your nipple on the sensitive flesh of my bulging bicep.

But instead of vocalizing my innermost thoughts, I nod. "Just love bologna is all, and someone has been eating my bologna at the arena, so I want to make sure I have some on hand because I like to eat a sandwich before every game. Kind of a tradition, and I really like the way it tastes, makes me feel like I'm gearing up for a takedown. Like a beast. A man beast. A man beast on the ice. That should be my new hashtag." I nervously laugh. "Man beast on the ice, powered by bologna. And without that bologna, I'm no good. Just wreckage out there with no purpose. Garbage. Trash. Some might say an abomination in skates. So I just want to make sure the bologna is there. So I can be the best man bologna beast out there, you know?" I nervously laugh again, and it comes out more like a giggle which, in return, makes me want to take my own skate to my dick.

"Bologna makes you feel manly?" she asks almost with a sneer.

"Very," I say. "Like I have a lot of muscles. And with great muscles comes great responsibility, Wylie."

What the fuck am I saying?

Just shut the fuck up, man.

"Hmm, I wouldn't have put you in the category of being built on bologna, but okay. And also, your bologna at the arena, the one in the cafeteria? That was yours?"

What the hell does she mean . . . that was yours?

My heart's beating wildly as I stare down at her. "What do you mean when you ask, that was yours?"

She crosses one beautiful leg over the other and casually says, "Well, I saw it in the cafeteria, and I thought it was up for grabs. I made myself a few sandwiches. I'm sorry, I didn't know it was yours."

The world stands still as I blink a few times, my brain catching up with her words, processing them, sitting deep in the wrinkles of my cranium, stirring and festering . . . and dipping me right into a frenzied tailspin as my ears boil and my pulse pounds through my veins.

She can't be . . .

No.

There's no fucking way.

"Hold on . . ." I take a deep breath, trying to make sure my voice doesn't come out shaky. "You . . . you like bologna sandwiches?"

"Love them," she answers with a smile.

Mother.

Of.

Fuck.

This is the worst-case scenario out of all scenarios.

This . . . this is blasphemy.

This is bullshit.

This can't be the world I'm living in.

No, this is a nightmare. Someone punch me. Poke me. Stick a chopstick right up my dick hole.

Pull me away from this disaster I'm living because, oh my fucking God, the girl of my absolute dreams, the one that's been persistent in my mind for a year, the girl who could do no wrong, she likes bologna.

No, not like . . . loves.

LOVES!

Actual tears spring to my eyes as panic races through me.

I'm going to lose it. I have two choices, ask her to open her mouth so I can fuck it, right here, right now—possibly while she eats a bologna sandwich—or just run.

Run as far away as I can run.

I choose the latter.

"Excuse me," I say as I bow my head in dismissal and sprint down the hallway straight to my bedroom, where I slam the door and fling myself onto the bed.

I grab my pillow, bury my head against it, and scream again, muffling myself better this time.

After a few kicks to the mattress, punches, and "why mes," I snatch my phone from the nightstand and pull up a text thread.

Can't do this alone. Nope.

Need help.

Now.

Because . . . fuck me, she likes bologna.

She loves it.

I've never met another soul who likes bologna. And lo and behold, the woman of my dreams has been stealing my goddamn deli meat right from under me. How did I not know? How did I not see her? How did I not sniff out the evidence like a goddamn bloodhound searching the trail?

I've lost my touch.

A curvy woman with red hair has blinded me.

And now, with my dick standing at full mast, I realize one thing. There is no way in hell I'm going to make it through this assignment without reinforcements.

It pains me, but I need help.

Levi: *URGENT. CODE RED. DEFCON 1. PLEASE JESUS, HELP ME! I don't care what you're doing, drop everything and meet me at Café Peppermint in fifteen minutes. Drinks and snacks are on me. Tell NO ONE!*

I set my phone down and take a few deep breaths as my cock strains against my pants.

Whispering meadows.

Babbling brooks.

Woodland creatures.

Deep breaths . . . that's it.

Fluttering branches.

Cotton-candy skies.

Wylie eating bologna.

No. No. No.

Focus.

Bunny with cotton tail.

Wild berries in brilliant hues of red.

Singsonging birds with white chests.

Chests . . .

Tits.

Wylie's tits bouncing.

NO!

No bouncing tits in the meadow.

Tits not allowed.

Or nipples.

Or any breasts.

Just woodland creatures that talk and sing little ditties like . . .

we are the woodland creatures of whispering pines. We like to sing and dance to help the boner decline . . .

"We are the woodland creatures—"

Knock. Knock.

I shoot up off my bed as Wylie says, "Uh, everything okay in here?"

"Peachy!" I squeak out. "Grand. On the up and up. No help needed."

"Are you sure? Because it seems like something's bothering you."

You!

You are bothering me, you beautiful, magnificent, bologna-eating wench.

"Nope. Everything is wonderful. Loving life." I offer her a thumbs-up even though I'm pretty sure she wasn't born with X-ray vision and can't see me. "Life is a ball of fun."

I stand from the bed and stare down at my tented joggers. This is not going to do. I can't go to Café Peppermint with my dick leading the way. They'll never let me return. So I grab a pair of jeans from my closet and slip off my joggers, say a quick hello to my erection—*looking painful, my guy*—and slip my jeans on, sliding my dick carefully against the more restrictive fabric.

"Are you sure you don't need anything?" she asks.

For the love of God, woman, leave me alone!

I stare down at my dick and how it's protruding against the jeans. Fuck.

I glance around my closet, looking for something, anything to help cover up, and that's when I see one of my dress shirts. Untucked, it will cover up just enough.

So I tear my current shirt off and slip a black dress shirt on. I fluff it over my dick, then look at myself in the floor-length mirror. I turn to the side, then the other side.

Yup, I think that works.

"Levi?"

"Yup, hey, hello. Just changing."

"Oh, are you leaving?"

"Going out," I shout and slip on my tennis shoes because I don't care right now. I don't care what I look like.

Well . . . I kind of care. I don't need people recognizing me. So I grab a bucket hat and toss that on my head, followed by a pair of sunglasses, and for the hell of it, I wrap a scarf around my neck and up to my chin.

There.

Unrecognizable.

Knowing I'll be able to walk around undetected, I proudly step out of my closet and straight to my door, opening it to find Wylie on the other side, worrying her lip.

When her eyes meet mine, the worried expression morphs into humor.

"What . . . what are you doing?"

I adjust my sunglasses and say, "It's called going incognito."

"You think you'll go undetected walking around like that?"

"Yes. People won't notice me."

"They're going to notice the six-foot-four man walking around with a scarf around his neck."

"Not the people I'm walking by."

"Oh-kay," she says, giving me a once-over. "At least tuck your shirt in." She reaches for the hem of my shirt, but I booty blast the air, backing that ass up so quick and folding over at the waist.

"Penis," I shout.

"Huh?"

"Uh, don't touch my penis."

She stands back. "I wasn't going to. I was going to suggest tucking your shirt in."

I stand taller, prouder.

I flip my scarf over my shoulder, and with my chin held high, I say, "And I suggest you don't touch my penis."

"Okay, suggestion received, but I wasn't going to touch it."

"As long as we've made that clear." Shoulders back, I walk past her—painfully—and head for the door.

"Are you sure nothing's wrong?" Her hand touches my back, and it feels like lava scalding my skin.

"Everything's fine," I yelp and hop away from her, my dick nearly acting like a pogo stick for me. "Just fine."

"Levi, you can talk to me." She corners me in the entryway, her hand caressing my arm. *My cock's trying to dig a hole through the fabric of my jeans.* It's a wonder it hasn't popped through and knocked Wylie on the ovaries, saying "Let me in, let me in. Please let me play with your skinny, skin, skin."

"I know I can talk to you. You're a great listener."

She studies me for a second and asks, "Was it the bologna?" She steps in just close enough that her breast rubs against my arm. "I can get different—"

Her nipple caresses my arm hair . . .

"It's not the bologna," I yelp. "The bologna is delicious. Top-notch. I fucking love bologna." And with that, I grab my keys and wallet and bolt out of the apartment, slamming the door behind me.

⸻

"THANK YOU ALL FOR BEING HERE." I rest my hands on the table. "I know you have busy lives, and I want you to know I value your time—"

"Just tell us what's going on," Ollie says, her arms folded across her chest.

"And it better be good," Penny adds. "Because Eli was just getting out of the shower."

"Halsey and I were just about to go to bed," Blakely says. "I think you know what that means."

I nod just as Winnie says, "Hold on, ladies, before we get irritated with him, let's hear him out. He wouldn't pull us all out of our homes for something stupid." She gestures toward me. "Tell us what's going on."

I clear my throat and say, "I have a boner."

"Oh my God." Ollie tosses her hands up in the air and stands.

"Jesus Christ, Posey." Penny stands as well.

"You're disgusting." Blakely scoots her chair out, and I hold my hands out to stop them.

"Wait," I say in a panic. "Just listen."

"I stood up for you," Winnie says, looking offended. "And you open with I have a boner? Come on, man."

"I'm sorry, but . . . fuck, it hurts bad."

Penny turns to Blakely and says, "I told you this would be stupid, but you were like, ohhhh, let's give him a chance. It's Posey, whatever DEFCON 1 means to him, means a leisurely stroll to us. Come on, let's go."

"No, wait, please don't go," I say, standing and slightly bending over because the boner is still very much present. "I promise, this is worth your time." The server with our drinks walks over at just that moment. "And see, look, drinks. And treats. You don't want to abandon drinks and treats, do you?"

Blakely and Penny exchange looks. Winnie wets her lips. And Ollie sits down.

"Fine, but this better be good," Ollie says, acting like her man, Silas, the grump. Seems as though couples do start to act like each other, which means I hope Mrs. Holmes offers sympathy like Halsey usually does.

They all take their seats. I divvy out their drinks and treats, and watch them settle in.

Once all their eyes are on me, and they seem semi-satisfied with the blueberry coffee cake that's been passed around, I say, "I have a boner."

"Mother of God," Penny whispers.

"And it won't go away," I continue.

"That's what emergency rooms are for," Blakely says.

"It's not an emergency room kind of thing. This is a mental thing. You see, I'm in quite the situation, and I called upon you four because I believe you are my best bet at figuring this all out."

"You didn't think to text the men who brought us into this situation?" Penny asks. "You know, your teammates, your friends?"

"Why would I ask them for help? They're completely inept

when it comes to love. And before you all start defending them, I'll have you know I'm the backbone of your relationships. The reason you were able to find peace and love with the humans you share a life with now is because of me." I point at my chest. "Without me, you would all be single or with someone else."

"What do you mean?" Winnie asks.

I sigh heavily and run through the list. I point at Winnie and say, "I didn't hit on you and take the spotlight. You're welcome." I point at Ollie and say, "Oye my dick, that was from me. You're welcome." I point at Penny next. "I helped Eli move from 'I just ate an apple' to actual conversation. You're welcome." Finally, I point at Blakely and say, "Don't even get me started on the marathon I ran for the two of you. You're welcome."

They're silent for a second, all looking at each other before Winnie says, "You not hitting on me was not a favor."

"Trust me." I wiggle my eyebrows at her. "It was. But we're not going to get into that. Let's just say, I value your opinion over theirs."

Ollie nods. "I can accept that. Also, to be fair, oye my dick was a huge turnoff."

I lean in and hold my finger up while saying, "But it made you push harder. Therefore, I moved things along." I curtly bow. "You're welcome."

"You're a moron," she says.

I nod. "Yes, yes, I'm aware of my moronic tendencies. See how I can admit that?"

"You're so brave," Penny says, voice full of sarcasm.

I press my hand to my heart. "Thank you. Now, back to my boner."

"Can you not start with the boner again?" Blakely asks. "It's making it hard for me to eat my coffee cake."

"Do you know what's hard?" I ask with a quizzical brow.

"Dear Jesus, Posey, just tell us what's going on," Penny shouts.

"Right." I take a deep breath and say, "I want to fuck my coach's daughter."

They all still, staring blankly at me.

Finally, Blakely leans toward Penny and says, "See, I told you it would be good."

Penny lifts her drink to her mouth. "You were right. I apologize."

"What do you mean you want to fuck her?" Winnie asks.

"I think it means he wants to stick his penis inside of her holes, right?" Ollie asks.

"Precisely. In every hole, just to be clear. All holes she's offering up," I say.

"We don't need the details." Penny holds up her hand. "But tell us how this happened and how you came to this conclusion of wanting all her holes."

"It started about a year ago," I say. "I was trolling the lobby, looking for my next conquest." All the girls roll their eyes. "When I came upon a redhead with the body of a goddess. Now, I need to preface this by saying I'm obsessed with redheads. There's something about them that gets my dick spiking up like a turkey thermometer."

"Ew," Blakely says. "Can you not say shit like that?"

"I would appreciate that as well." Winnie holds up her hand. "I don't need the visuals."

"None of us do," Penny adds.

"Noted. Trying to paint a picture, but fine," I say. "Anyway, we had an amazing night. We talked, she rubbed my penis through my jeans, we kissed . . ."

"You know, I do love rubbing Silas's penis through his jeans," Ollie says.

"I like a good jean rub, too," Blakely says.

"I made Pacey come once while doing that." Winnie beams.

"Eck, that's my brother," Penny complains.

Winnie shrugs. "What? He really liked it."

I clear my throat. "Ladies, focus." They all bring their attention back to me, so I continue. "The kiss was . . . well, it was life-changing. I felt it all the way down to the tip of my penis."

"Please, Posey," Penny groans.

"It was magical." I sum it up. "But then, out of nowhere,

she bolted. And when I say we were about to go up to my hotel room, we were. We were seconds away from banging out our lust for each other, and she was a willing participant. But she bolted. I never got her name or where she was from. She was a mystery. I spent a year looking for her—and came up short— until Coach Wood pulled me into his office and told me he needed me to hire his daughter as my assistant. Long story short, I said sure because I owe him big time, and lo and behold, his daughter walks in, and it's the redhead from the bar."

"Ooo, this is good," Penny says while taking a bite of her coffee cake.

"What a twist," Winnie says.

"Kind of funny you were looking for her for so long, and she was in the arena all along," Blakely says.

"I can't even think about that," I say with a shake of my head. "Anyway, she's now my assistant, and Coach Wood told me if I even look at her, he's going to kill me, meaning she's completely off limits."

"Ahh." Ollie nods, understanding. "Hence the forever boner."

"Exactly." I point at Ollie.

"But can I ask something?" Winnie says. "We understand the boner now, but care to explain the bucket hat, sunglasses, and scarf? You look like the leading lady of a movie from the 1920s."

Ha, I almost forgot I was wearing all of this.

"I didn't want anyone noticing me as I walked around with a boner in my jeans."

"Do you really still have one?" Blakely asks with a cringe to her nose.

"It's a semi," I reply.

Blakely makes a gagging expression.

"Hey," I say. "That's offensive. I'll have you know, I have a nice penis. It might not be pierced like Silas's or a girthy cannon like Halsey's, or a baby maker like Eli's or . . . whatever Pacey has, but it's nice."

"Pacey has a wonderful penis." Winnie smiles to the group as if she just offered up a great show-and-tell item.

"Not something his sister needs to hear," Penny says, causing Winnie to laugh.

Cutting in, I say, "For the record, my penis is amazing. There's something secret about it that people don't know, and I also have perfectly shaped balls. Bare balls. Hairless."

They all study me, looks of confusion in their eyes.

Finally, Penny speaks up. "Going to skip over the hairless situation and ask. What do you mean there's something secret about your penis?"

"Yeah, that's confusing because now my mind is racing," Ollie says. "Like . . . what kind of things are happening down there? Does a little man pop out of your penis when the lady comes, offering a congratulations to everyone involved?"

"That's ridiculous. Of course not," I say, but then think about what that little man might look like. Maybe he's holding a pot of gold.

"Oh my God, he's thinking about the little man," Penny says.

"Am not," I say petulantly even though I think he would have a pot of gold, but we'll keep that between us.

"Then what is it?" Blakely asks.

"I'd prefer not to share."

"You open our conversation with you have a boner, but you aren't going to share what's special about your penis?" Penny asks. "Make that make sense."

"Some things are private, and I prefer to keep that private."

Winnie leans forward to address all the women. "I bet he comes glitter."

"Ooo, now that's a trick," Ollie says. "Is that what it is? Do you have glitter cum?"

"You know, under certain light, it does sparkle." I tap my chin.

"Mother of God, I'm going to leave and tell Eli what's going on if you don't clue us in," Penny says with the patience of a saint . . .

Please note the sarcasm.

"Fine, but this is in the circle of trust. We say nothing to the men in your lives. I'm serious, they can't find out about anything we're talking about because they won't be helpful and will probably make the situation worse. The last thing I need is for one of them to say something around Coach Wood. Can I trust you all?"

They nod their heads, seeming genuine.

"Thank you." I take a sip of my coffee and adjust my sunglasses. "My penis is tattooed."

"What?" they all say together.

"How do the boys not know?" Blakely asks.

"You obviously see each other's things in the shower, right?" Winnie cutely asks.

"We do, but my tattoo is on the underside."

"Seriously?" Ollie asks. I nod, and she leans back in her chair, her eyes giving me a once-over. "Well, Levi Posey, you just got increasingly hotter in my eyes."

"Thank you," I reply with a smirk.

"Did you have to get hard for that?" Blakely asks.

"Yup."

"And one prick of the needle didn't deflate it?" Penny asks.

I shake my head. "Kind of thrive on pain."

"Makes sense," Winnie says. "Since you're the bruiser of the team." It's true. Sometimes, I just want to be punched in the face. I like the adrenaline.

Is that healthy?

No, but it's who I am.

"Wow, a tattooed penis. Never would have guessed the guy who eats bologna likes a tattooed dick." Penny shakes her head.

"There are a lot of things you don't know about me," I say. "But we can learn more about each other later. Right now, I'm dealing with a crisis. Remember, the coach's daughter?"

"Right," Penny says. "So what has you hard all the time?"

"To sum it up, Coach Wood is forcing me to give her ridiculous tasks. I hate making her do things, but I have to report back to him, so I don't have a choice. And of course he kicked her out of his house, and she was looking for a place to stay, so I offered her the nanny bedroom in my apartment, which is a hole, and I hate that she lives there when I have a perfectly good guest room, but Coach Wood said she couldn't stay with me, so I'm breaking the rules, but I couldn't let her not have a place to live, but now that she lives with me, well . . . she's walking around the apartment in tight T-shirts with no bras, and wearing my shirts, and wet towels, and nipples on my bicep, and touching, and her smile, and she smells so good, and holy fuck my brain is about to explode."

Blakely presses her hand to my shoulder. "Deep breaths, Posey."

"Deep breaths don't work!" I practically shout. "Meadows don't work. Or cotton-candy skies. All I see are her breasts day in and day out, bouncing toward me. I want them in my mouth. I want to play with them. Fuck them. Watch them unravel from her present bra!"

"Okay, okay," Penny says in a calming voice. "I can see that you're getting yourself worked up. Let's not draw attention to the lady in the bucket hat and scarf." She glances around the café. Yep, people are looking toward us.

Right, trying to keep it incognito.

On a sad and heavy sigh, I say, "I just . . . I want her."

"We can tell," Winnie says.

I look up at all of them and say, "And I swear on my left nut that she's fucking with my head on purpose. She knows how much I want her but can't have her."

"Why do you say that?" Blakely asks.

"Because she's always in my apartment now. She's walking around wearing practically nothing. She's touching me. She's getting close but not intimate, and it's driving me nuts. And worst of all . . ." I take a deep breath, lower my sunglasses to the tip of my nose, and say, "She loves bologna."

A collective gasp falls over the group, all the women with slack jaws and blinking eyes.

"Oh dear God," Winnie whispers, leaning back.

"Fuck," Ollie says.

"Well, that's . . . wow." Penny shakes her head.

"Did not see that coming," Blakely adds. "Now I understand the boner."

"It all makes sense," Ollie says.

"See? Do you see what I'm dealing with? And I don't know how to handle it. I refuse to take care of the boner because I know I'll picture her, and the minute I picture her, it will make my need for her ten times worse."

"Wait, you're not jacking off?" Penny asks.

I shake my head. "My perfectly shaped balls are a midnight blue at this point."

"Posey." Ollie leans in and places her hand on the table. "Dude, you have to take care of the boner, even if you picture her. You can't be this backed up and function intelligently."

"She's right," Penny says. "After I gave birth to Holden, Eli said he wouldn't do anything sexual because I couldn't do anything for at least six weeks. After two weeks, he was dazed, confused, and didn't know how to put shoes on anymore. I decided to take care of it for him. I hate to admit it, but you have to jerk off to get through this."

"But . . . I'm going to envision her."

"Then live through your fantasies," Ollie says. "But for the love of God, take care of it."

"And if you need to, maybe watch some porn. That might distract you," Winnie says.

I roll my teeth over my bottom lip. "Okay, but what do I do in the meantime? This feeling I have for her, it's not going to go away."

"Have you told her that she's making you hard?" Blakely asks. "A little communication might help."

"I don't want to sound like an asshole who can't keep it together if she goes braless."

"But you are the asshole who can't keep it together when she goes braless," Penny says.

"I know, but she doesn't need to know that."

"Maybe set ground rules again," Winnie says. "And honestly, you can just say, hey, I appreciate everything you're doing, but I have to say, you're really hot and making me hard when you walk around without a bra. I don't want to be a creep, but I thought you should know."

"That's a nice way to put it," Ollie says. "I'd put on a bra even though I hate them."

"Yeah, I'd strap up too," Blakely says. "I think that's a great way to approach it."

I look at Penny, the mother of the group. She sips her coffee and then says, "I approve."

"Okay." I nod and let out a deep breath. "Then I shall tell her she's making me hard."

"Great." Penny looks around. "Are we done here?"

Chapter Nine

WYLIE

Sandie: I can't believe he added a scarf to the outfit.

Wylie: It took everything in me not to burst out in laughter.

Sandie: Oh girl, erotic torture is in full swing.

Wylie: Yup. He has no idea how to handle it, and I'm loving every second of it.

Knock. Knock.

I look at my door and then down at my shirtless self. God, imagine what he would do if I told him to come in right now. He might pass out.

Not wanting to do that, I grab the shirt I borrowed from him last night and throw it over my head while I prop myself up in bed.

"Come in," I call out.

The door opens, and Levi steps into the room wearing a pair of jeans and a long-sleeved fitted black shirt, with his hair styled in a messy way.

When his large body consumes the small space, I get a whiff

of his masculine, woodsy cologne and nearly melt right there on my bed.

I might be making it hard on him, but he sure as hell is making it hard on me too.

"Good morning," I say in a cheery voice. "Can I help you? Did I forget something?"

He shakes his head and looks around the space. "It, uh, it looks great in here. Very cozy."

"Oh, thank you," I say. "I'm very happy with it and very grateful you offered me the space."

"Not a problem." He stuffs his hands in his pockets and rocks on his heels.

"Can I help you with something?" I ask.

"Yeah, I kind of wanted to talk to you about something."

"Sure." I pat the end of the bed. "Have a seat."

He glances at the bed, back at me, and then at the bed again. "You know, I think it would be best if I stay standing."

"Not a problem," I say. "What's going on?"

"Well, this is a little awkward, but I wanted to be honest with you."

"Oh," I say as I lift the blankets off me and shimmy out of the bed to a standing position. "Am I not doing my job the way you want me to?" I move in close to him, and he moves back, bumping into my wall.

"Uh, no, you're doing great work. Keep it up."

"Okay, then what is it?"

"You see," he says, sounding slightly jittery. "The fact of the matter is, you're sort of . . . kind of . . . you know, with every-thing happening and the past well—"

"Levi, what's going on?"

"You're making me hard," he says in one fell swoop.

"Oh." I attempt to hold back my smile, and it feels nearly impossible. "I'm sorry. I didn't realize."

"Yeah, I'm sure you didn't. And yes, this is incredibly unpro-fessional of me, but I wanted you to know. That's what's happening."

"Well, thank you for telling me. I'm guessing from the way you're backing away from me, you don't appreciate being hard."

"Not particularly. Granted, I love that my dick can get excited. It makes me feel alive. But when it comes to you, it's forbidden, so I really shouldn't be getting hard, you know?"

I nod. *Sadly.* "I know what you mean. My dad was very explicit when it came to any sexual behavior with any of his players."

"See? You know."

"I do." I cross my arms over my chest, lifting my breasts while doing so, and I watch his eyes bounce from my face, down to my torso, and then back up. The man is impossible. "Can I ask you, is there anything in particular that's making you hard?"

"Yup," he answers. "And I don't want this to sound chauvinistic, but the no bra situation is just about destroying me."

"Oh." I chuckle. "I'm sorry. It's just more comfortable that way."

"I get it," he says. "I've seen my fair share of bras being torn off after a long day. But maybe we can leave it on when walking around my apartment?"

"Sure, that's not a problem." I reach out and touch his arm. "I'm so sorry I've been making you uncomfortable."

He swats my hand away and says, "Not uncomfortable, just . . . you know . . . aroused."

"Which leads to discomfort. I get it. I'll do better."

"Thank you." He sighs in relief. "Fuck." He pushes his hand through his hair. "I thought this was going to be a tough conversation. Thanks for being so cool about it."

"Not a problem. Anything you need or want to talk about, I'm here for you, Mr. Posey. We're in this together."

He eyes me, and I chuckle. "None of that mister shit."

"Just teasing." I nudge him with my foot. "Also, I'm very flattered that a man of your stature and attractiveness would be turned on by me. Makes me feel good."

"Yeah, well, hard not to be turned on by you."

I smirk. "Stop, you're going to make my nipples hard, and we don't want that."

"Yeah, we don't," he says in a haze as his eyes float to my chest.

"Levi."

"Huh?" His eyes snap up.

"Maybe you should leave since, you know, you're getting all dazed."

"Right, yeah. I should go." He reaches into his back pocket. "By the way, here is a list of things I need done. Think you can do them today? Game tonight, then we leave tomorrow for a few days. I need some suits and new shoes, some snacks for the plane, and a refill on my vitamins. It's all written down."

He hands me the list, and I don't bother looking at it.

"Not a problem. I can get this done for you. Are you headed over to the arena soon?"

"Shortly."

"Can I grab a ride with you?" I ask. "I left my car there yesterday."

"Oh, yeah, sure."

"Great, give me like fifteen. I'll be ready."

"Sounds good."

He takes off, and when my bedroom door is shut, I run over to my phone.

Wylie: *He just came to my bedroom. Told me I'm making him hard by going braless.*

I move into my bathroom, where I start the shower. It takes far too long for the water to warm up.

Sandie: *Oh, didn't see that coming. So he asked you to put a bra on?*

Wylie: *Yup. You know what that means?*

Sandie: *Oh, I do . . .*

Wylie: *Time for the ultimate push-up bra to take the reins.*

Sandie: *Poor, poor Posey. Should have stuck with the braless attire.*

LEVI

"LET'S PRACTICE OUR BOX BREATHING," Yogi Carl says.

"Fuck you and your box breathing," I mutter, exiting YouTube just as I hear Wylie head down the hallway.

I sit up from where I'm leaning on the island counter just in time to see her enter the kitchen . . .

Fuck.

Me.

I'm . . . fucked.

"Hey, thanks for waiting," she says casually as she moves toward the fridge, my hungry eyes eating up every last inch of her.

Wearing a pair of wide-leg jeans that rest low on her hips, she's paired them with a deep V-neck, forest-green sweater and some sort of magical underwire. Her breasts are screaming to pop past the cashmere.

Well, she's wearing a bra, that's for damn sure.

A bra that's making me sweat.

I actually have sweat on my upper lip as I stare at her.

At the way her curved hips hold up her jeans, the way they cling to her heart-shaped ass. The slight hourglass figure of her torso and the slenderness of her shoulders. And then her perfectly pulled together cleavage that's begging me to touch, to play with.

Why does the universe hate me?

"Everything okay?" she asks.

"Uh . . . yeah. Just a second, left something in my bedroom." Before I can wait for a response, I jog back to my bedroom, shut the door, and start typing on my phone.

Levi: *RED ALERT. RED ALERT. I NEED MY LABIA LADIES!*

Penny: *Ew, you are not calling us that.*

Blakely: *Think of a better name, or we're not helping.*

Ollie: *Agreed. A much better name.*

Winnie: **Snorts**

Levi: *I'M IN DISTRESS! That's the first thing that came to mind.*

Penny: *You know, if we're going to be a part of this, we should really brainstorm a good name.*

Blakely: *I like the idea of using the term queen. Because that's what we are, right? Queens.*

Ollie: *Ooo, I second the queen idea.*

Winnie: *I'm also on board with queen.*

Levi: *Fine, my Quibbling Queens.*

Penny: *Try again.*

Levi: *Quintessential Queens.*

Ollie: *Too long.*

Levi: *Quirky Queens.*

Winnie: *You're getting worse.*

Levi: *Uhh . . . Queefing Queens?*

Penny: *You're going to be dead to us in mere seconds.*

Levi: *I'm sorry! Like I said before, I'M IN DISTRESS!*

Blakely: *You know, it doesn't have to start with a Q.*

Levi: *For the love of God, just help me. Work on the name later.*

Penny: **looks at nails and sighs* Fine. How can we be of service to you?*

Levi: *I told her about getting hard, and she understood completely. I told her to put on a bra. And she did.*

Ollie: *Wow, this really is a red alert. She listened. The horror.*

Winnie: *It is for a man. They don't understand what listening is.*

Blakely: *Ha, good one.*

Winnie: *Thank you, it just came to me.*

Levi: *The listening isn't the problem. It's the kind of bra she's wearing now that's the problem.*

Penny: *Uh-oh. Is it a push-up bra?*

Levi: *Pretty sure she's wearing titanium steel under her breasts, they're so propped up. And she's wearing a deep V-cut sweater. I know you don't want details, but my dick is screaming right now.*

Blakely: *Ugh, God, is this what the men's group text is like?*

Penny: *Pretty much. Just disgusting.*

Winnie: *Could you imagine us saying something like that? Oh, his pecs were bouncing so much, my clit was screaming.*

Ollie: *His bulge, oh his bulge. *drapes hand over forehead* My nipples were leaking they were so turned on.*

Penny: *The cake on that man. I nearly fainted into my own vagina from how turned on I was.*

Blakely: *Fainting into the vagina, that's on point with what they'd say.*

Levi: *Can you really bend that far?*

Penny: *Posey! Focus!*

Levi: *You're the ones talking about screaming clits and leaking nipples. Christ.*

Winnie: *Okay, let's reel it in. Here are the facts. You told her you're turned on and to put on a bra. She listened and doubled down and put on the atomic bomb of all bras.*

Levi: *You think she doubled down?*

Penny: *One thousand percent. This is a classic case of double downing.*

Ollie: *What is double downing?*

Winnie: *Where she was trying to accomplish a task, was caught, so she doubled down on said task to try to accomplish it further. Can't imagine what a triple down would be.*

Levi: *Oh fuck, is that an option?*

Penny: *Triple down would be shirtless. Guaranteed.*

Blakely: *Ooo, or accidental tit pic text. "Ooops, didn't mean to send that to you."*

Levi: *I won't survive a triple down. I know I won't. How do I prevent the triple down?*

Penny: *Pretend the double down doesn't affect you.*

Levi: *But I'm hard!*

Ollie: *Then take a freaking Xanax, for fuck's sake. Honestly, how can you be that hard all the time? Did you not play with yourself last night?*

Levi: *I was too nervous to touch it. I didn't want it to explode. The skin was really tight.*

Blakely: *vomits**

Winnie: *Dear God, Posey.*

Ollie: *Why am I a part of this again?*

Penny: *I'm going to need a lot more than a subpar cup of coffee and coffee cake to deal with this.*

Levi: *Subpar? Café Peppermint is anything but subpar. It's like being transported into a Lovemark movie with the quirky shop owner and everything.*

Penny: *I'm leaving now. Just . . . hold it together while we think about why she's double downing. Okay?*

Levi: *You'll do that? You'll brainstorm?*

Ollie: *If it means you're not talking about your penis skin being tight anymore, then yes.*

WYLIE

WYLIE: *The bra is working. He ran to his bedroom.*

Sandie: *He had no idea what was coming for him. Did he stare?*

Wylie: *His eyes practically fell out of his head.*

Sandie: *I've never been more proud.*

Wylie: *Thank you. Also, did you get the email I sent you last night with the designs?*

Sandie: *Yes, going to open them up when I'm not at work.*

Wylie: *Smart. Let me know what you think.*

Sandie: *Will do.*

"Are you ready?" Levi says, returning to the living space with the fakest smile I've ever seen.

"Yup. Have everything you need?"

"Yes. I, uh, I forgot to put deodorant on. What a stinky situation that would have been." He nervously laughs, and it's really cute.

"Oof, good thing you caught it. My dad hates stink."

"He's told us that. It's why we have multiple equipment

managers." He gestures toward the front door, and I open it, stepping out first.

"I'm sure they're not paid enough to handle your equipment."

"They're not," he says while locking his door.

We both head to the elevator, where he presses the down button.

"You know, this building is an interesting find. Modern but also historic."

I catch him lift his eyes from my chest as the elevator doors open. "Yeah, I wasn't sure I'd like it at first because it doesn't offer the same level of privacy that other buildings do, but the residents are really chill, and I like the parking situation. Plus, the layouts are much bigger. My unit is meant for a family of four, but I converted the one room into my office."

"You did a great job. I love your place."

"Thank you," he says as the doors part to the parking garage. "The black Tesla right over there."

"Oh, that's right. You and the boys all have one."

"Can't remember who started it, but we all followed."

He unlocks the car and, to my surprise, walks over to my door and opens it for me. I can tell the minute he realizes what he's doing because he backs away from the door as if it's on fire and stumbles to get away.

I inwardly chuckle as he rounds the front of the car and gets in on his side. When he's settled, I say, "Thank you for taking me in. My friend Sandie picked me up from work, so we just left my car. I thought I'd be able to catch a ride, so I'm glad it all worked out."

"Yeah, not a problem." He clears his throat and puts his hand on my headrest, turns his body, and starts backing out of his car space, which I think is funny because he has a giant screen in front of him, showing him if there are any cars.

Either way, I like that he put his hand on the headrest. If only he'd put his hand on my thigh next.

"Are you excited about the game tonight? You're playing the Freeze, right? Kind of a big rivalry."

"Yeah, should be an interesting game."

"I dated a guy who the Freeze drafted."

"Who?" His head snaps to look at me.

"He doesn't play with them anymore, so no need to get defensive."

"I wasn't getting defensive," he says as his grip on the steering wheel loosens.

Uh-huh, not defensive at all.

"His name is Rocco Allen."

"Hmm." Levi thinks about it. "Can't say I know who that is."

"Well, he hasn't made an impact on the hockey scene like you, so I'm not surprised you don't know who he is."

"You think I've made an impact in hockey?"

Turning on the charm, I say, "Oh my God, yes. Are you kidding me? You're one of the best defensemen in the game. I remember my dad talking about you once, saying how impressed he was with your footwork while under pressure, especially for being such a large man."

"Huh, never heard him say anything nice about me before."

"Really? He's said a few things."

"Was this before or after he's blessed his underwear?" Levi shoots me a smirk, and it's the most gorgeous expression I've ever seen.

"After, most definitely after."

"Hmm, maybe I should give him some holy water for Christmas."

"You do that. Let me know how it turns out for you."

He laughs. "Probably not well."

"I can guarantee you it won't go over well."

"Was he always this cranky and unpleasant while growing up? And I say that under strict boss-assistant confidentiality."

I pat his shoulder. "Don't worry, I won't be repeating anything we talk about to him. As long as you can promise me the same."

"I don't think he wants to hear about my sore toe, let alone what we talk about."

"Good," I say. "And yes, he's always been like this. His smiles are rare. Even rarer when he's in a good mood. I don't know, he's just always been . . . grumpy."

"Was that hard to live with?"

"At times, yes. Living with someone who gets angry at the drop of a hat is stressful. But I guess I just started to ignore it. There comes a time when you just think, they will always be angry, it's not me, it's them, and you move on."

"Shit, that sucks," he says. "I'm sorry you had to deal with that growing up. Doesn't seem too fair."

"We all have our shortcomings. At least he cared about me. Some parents are angry and don't care. That would be a terrible situation to be in."

"True."

I turn toward him and push his floppy hair back. I immediately notice the goosebumps on his forearm, and I think another great win for me. "What about you? Did you have a pretty decent childhood?"

"Yup," he says. "Really low-key. Played hockey from a young age and pretty much focused on that. My parents knew my passion. They helped me grow it along with my skill, and I skipped out on all the troublemaking in order to accomplish my goal."

"So then how did you become a ladies' man?"

He chuckles. "I thought that was a secret."

"It's not, but nice try."

"Well, throughout high school, I was a beanpole. It wasn't until I reached college that I started lifting more. I grew into my skin and sprouted in a different way. I started getting attention from the opposite sex, and then at twenty, I lost my virginity."

"No way," I say, utterly surprised. "You lost your virginity at twenty? That's so hard to believe. Not that it's a bad thing, but given your reputation, I would have thought it was sooner."

He shakes his head. "Not when all you do is play hockey. I

had no time for anything else growing up. But when college came along, that was a different story. And I started to realize how easy it was to talk to women."

"Talk to women, that's a nice way of putting it."

He chuckles. "Well, either way, that's how it went down."

"Have you ever thought about settling down?"

"Not really," he says. "But only because I haven't found the right person."

"Ever had a girlfriend?"

"Awfully intimate questions for an assistant," he says, seeming more relaxed than ever. This feels like the same Levi Posey I first met in the hotel. Smooth in conversation, smirking. Flirting. He seems like he's in his element.

Which of course makes me like him that much more.

"As your assistant, I think it's my duty to know all things about you, including relationships. You know, in case some lady claims to be your ex, begging for access to you."

"I see. And what if some lady does try to gain access to me? What would you do?"

"Shut her down. My dad is a hockey coach, and he's taught me a thing or two about fighting."

He chuckles. "That's kind of hot. So an assistant and a bodyguard, looks like I'm getting a bargain."

"You are, so tell me . . . anyone I need to look out for?"

He shakes his head. "Nope. Never really been in a relationship long enough to cause drama."

"Have you been in one at all?"

"Um, not really. Never called this one girl my girlfriend. More like, I saw her a few times, went out on a few dates, and then we went our separate ways."

"Did she end things, or did you? Just trying to gauge if it's a you problem or a them problem."

"I ended it," he says as the arena comes into view. Another thing I love is how close he lives to the arena, but still has a piece of history with his older building. "Just wasn't interested. Wasn't invested. Didn't want to waste her time."

"Think you could ever find someone to settle down with?"

"Maybe," he says. "Probably after I retire. I don't think too much about it now."

"Not even with all of your boys now tied up in relationships?"

"The only thing annoying about that is they don't hang out as much."

"That's so sad. Well, if you ever need someone to hang out with, I can be there for you . . . bra and all."

His eyes flash toward my chest, then back up to my face. "Yeah, I can see that."

LEVI

LEVI: *I did it, I ignored the double down. I ended up driving her into the arena, and we had a really good conversation. I felt normal, and what we talked about, well . . . loads of things. It made me like her even more, but not just physically. Emotionally, and that doesn't happen with me very often.*

Penny: *I don't know what we should do. Should we clap for him?*

Ollie: *I think we need to.*

Blakely: *The fact that he was able to drive the atomic bomb of tits without crashing . . . that deserves an applause.*

Winnie: *We are so proud of you, Posey.*

Levi: *Thanks, ladies. I feel good.*

Penny: *So then, are we done with this?*

Levi: *Oh no, not even close. This was just a breath of air. I'm sure something will come up where I'll require your assistance. I'm going to need you on standby at all times.*

Blakely: *It's funny that you thought we were done, Penny.*

Penny: *High hopes, I guess.*

Ollie: *We still need to figure out why she double downed.*

Winnie: *I have a theory. Do we think she's into S&M? Maybe she's a domme and wants to control him with her breasts.*

Penny: *Huh, that's an interesting theory.*

Ollie: *Maybe this assistant thing is all a ruse, and she and her dad are working together to assist her in finding a sub since it's been so hard, and Coach Wood saw weakness in you.*

Blakely: *Ooo, I like that. I could see Posey as subservient. I mean, he said he thrives on pain.*

Winnie: *That's right, he did. Well, I'm more convinced now than ever.*

Levi: *There's no way she's a fucking domme. Trust me, I would know.*

Penny: *Uh, what now? Care to elaborate on that?*

Blakely: **Leans in**

Ollie: *Are we getting a little hint at Posey's sex life?*

Winnie: *The tattoo, now this hint. Is Posey a kinky fella?*

Levi: *Keep working on the double down. I'm reporting back after warm-ups.*

I set my phone down and look up to see Eli, Silas, Pacey, and Halsey all staring down at me. "Uh . . . what's up, guys?"

"Who the hell are you texting?" Silas asks, gesturing to my phone.

"No one in particular, why?" I tuck my phone away in my bag just in case one of the girls text back.

"Because you've been buried in your phone since the minute you got in the locker room," Pacey says.

"So? So were you guys. You're always buried in your phones."

"No, we weren't. We were discussing the different William Sonoma bread in a bag flavorings," Eli says. "And from someone who loves a pumpkin flavor, you sure as hell were silent when Halsey said the pumpkin crumble one was shit."

I sneer at Halsey. "Your palate is undignified."

"Says the guy who eats bologna daily," Halsey says.

I stand from the bench and move past them, heading out of the locker room and toward the ice for some warm-ups. "First of all, the bologna I get isn't just any old Oscar Mayer bologna; this is refined bologna from a deli. The finest in the land. And second of all, there have been articles about how people who like bologna are more intelligent than non-bologna lovers."

"Where did you see those articles?" Pacey asks, following me.

"On the internet."

"Show them to us," Silas says.

"We're about to warm up, I can't." We walk down the tunnel, and just before I head out on the ice, they all stop me by forming a wall before I can enter the rink.

"What is going on with you?" Pacey asks. "You're acting weird, you barely talk to us, and you have shifty eyes."

"I don't have shifty eyes," I say, but then I catch myself looking to the side out of fear that Coach Wood is lurking.

"Yes, you do," Silas says, pointing at my face. "You just shifted. It's like you're waiting for someone to pop out at you."

I grip my stick tightly. "You never know with social media these days. This TikTok craze has made us all vulnerable. Anything for views, that's their motto, even if it's at the expense of scaring the piss out of us."

Eli scratches the back of his neck. "You know, Penny was showing me some scare videos the other day."

"See," I say. "So pardon me for being prepared. You suckers are going to be the ones who are caught, and don't come crying to me when your scared face becomes a meme for the internet to mock."

I try to move forward again, but Pacey stops me once more. "That's not it. There's something else going on, and you're not telling us what it is."

I sigh heavily. "You're right. Something is going on." Pressing my lips together, I look between my friends and on a pained expression, I say, "I have a serious case of blue balls. Think one of you can take care of it for me?"

"Jesus Christ," Silas says as he turns and moves toward the ice.

"Is that a no?" I call out as Eli and Pacey follow closely. They don't bother looking back.

And that's how it's done. Distract and deflect.

As if I would tell them what's going on. No fucking way.

They'd tease me relentlessly because being the intelligent man I am, I know that payback is a bitch. And what I teased them about will only come back with a vengeance.

They'd also be too loud and fucking obnoxious about something meant to be discreet. They have no filter and, within an hour, no doubt Coach Wood would find out about my crush and have me hanging by the balls in his office like a freshly butchered lamb leg.

Keeping them in the quiet, in the unknown, is the best decision.

Happy with myself, I head down the hallway behind them, smirking just as I hear my name. I look over to see Wylie, waving me down, her low-hanging shirt doing nothing to conceal her tits from the chilly arena air.

Either she has nipples of steel or that bra holds the girls up but doesn't conceal because she's clearly cold, if you catch my drift.

Being the lust-sick asshole that I am, a fleeting thought of holding her close to warm her up passes through my mind before it's quickly squashed with reality.

Not going to happen, man.

"Hey, Levi, can I talk to you for a second?" Wylie says, waving me down.

"Sure. What's up?" I ask as I skate over to her.

"Sorry to bother you," she says as a few of the guys skate by us, skating annoyingly close so I have to move right in front of her.

"It's fine, what's up?"

She touches the front of my jersey, adjusting it against my pads. It's very intimate, something a girlfriend would do. *Not my assistant.* From an outsider looking in, you'd think that she's anything but my assistant, especially with her top being at my eye level and the way my eyes keep drifting down.

I know I talk about it a lot, but seriously, she's so achingly hot.

"Your suits. Did you want me to get new ones for you, or get your current ones dry-cleaned?"

"A new suit," I say. "Did I not put my measurements down?"

She shakes her head. "No."

"Oh, sorry about that."

She plays with the collar of my jersey, and I want to ask her what the hell she's doing, but I get distracted by her gorgeous eyes instead.

Those stormy gray eyes.

"Not a problem," she says, pulling me back into the present. "Should I just take one of your current suits in and have them match it?"

I swallow and wet my lips. God, what I wouldn't give to fuck her on the bench right now. It's always been a fantasy of mine. The bench, the locker room, and on the ice. A chilly feat, but I'd be up for the challenge.

"Levi?"

"Huh? Oh, uh, yeah, that would be best."

"Okay, thanks. Don't want your suits to be too tight in the crotch, right?" She winks.

You keep hanging out with me, and they'll always be tight in the crotch.

"Yeah, definitely don't want that." I stare into her mesmerizing eyes, comparing them to the iciness of the ice. A foggy morning. A pair of newly sharpened—

"Posey!" Coach yells, scaring the living daylights out of me. "What the hell are you doing?"

Mother of fuck, I think I just piddled.

I turn toward Coach Wood, who looks like he's about to shove his clipboard up my ass. "She had a question," I say, pushing away from her. "It was urgent."

Coach Wood glances at Wylie. "Did you get your answer?"

"Yes," she says.

"Then I suggest you leave."

Unfazed by her dad's harsh tone, she walks up to him, places her hand on his chest, and kisses his cheek before twiddling her fingers at me and taking off.

Well, fuck, that didn't look good.

I nervously smile at him and start to skate away when he says, "Get your ass over here."

Yup, didn't think I was going to get away with that.

I skate back to the bench and say, "What's up, Coach?"

He leans in and talks in a very dark, very scary voice. "Tell me right fucking now, is there anything going on between you and my daughter?"

"No," I say so quickly that I repeat myself just in case he didn't hear. "No. Nope. Nothing. Nada. Nothing at all. I swear."

"Then why the hell did it look like there is?"

"I, uh, I don't know. But I promise, nothing's going on. I wouldn't cross that line. I told you I wouldn't, and I haven't."

His expression softens as he leans back now. "Did you give her the list I gave you?"

"Yes, that's what she had a question about. We didn't really get to talk about it all too much, so I messed up and forgot to give her suit measurements."

"Are you sending her to the shop downtown?"

"Yes," I answer.

"Good." He eyes me up and down. "You haven't been updating me."

"Sorry, just trying to focus on the game."

"Then get the fuck away from me and focus."

"Yup. Got it."

I take off and skate toward the boys, where they're all stretching. When I join them, Eli whispers, "So . . . nothing going on with her?"

I sigh and start stretching my inner thighs. "Nothing."

Chapter Ten

WYLIE

"Is he going to be mad that I'm in here?" Sandie asks as we watch the game on Levi's large-screen TV rather than my computer in my tiny bedroom.

"He won't even know." I scrunch down on the couch and lean my head back against the cushion. "Ugh, wearing that bra was absolute torture today. Sure my boobs looked great, but that was so uncomfortable."

"Beauty is pain."

"More like horniness is pain."

Sandie chuckles. "But it worked, right?"

"Right. Not sure what else I can put him through. When I was talking to him while he was out on the ice, I was playing with his jersey, and he didn't tell me to stop. It felt . . . real."

"Real?" Sandie asks with a raise of her brow. "I thought we were trying to teach him a lesson."

"We are." I curl under my blanket. "But I don't know, even

190

with all of the running around I had to do today, I just felt like it was nice to help him out."

"Those tasks aren't from him. Those are from your dad. What's happening to you?"

I look over at Sandie as the game goes to commercial. "Okay, don't judge me, but we had a moment this morning in the car. He wasn't fumbling around all nervous, and he was the same man I met at the hotel. He was charming and smooth and intriguing. He asked me questions, and it just felt like . . . like that night."

"But you remember what you're supposed to be doing, right?"

"Yes." I sigh heavily. "It was just nice for a second, you know?"

"Yes, but we have a goal. That goal is to prove to your dad that you can be self-sufficient, that you don't need his help, his career directives, or anything to make it on your own. You can't get caught up in 'moments' with Levi."

"You're right." I nod. "You're very right. Ugh, I'm sorry. I'll be better."

"Don't apologize to me. Apologize to your future self who's reaching for the stars."

I chuckle. "Okay, Sandie, don't be lame."

"Lame? I'm inspiring."

"Okay, Miss Inspiring, tell me what you thought of the logos."

"I'm surprised it took you this long to ask."

"I was trying to be patient. But guess what, my patience is up. Do you think they're good?"

"I do," she says, but I can hear a but coming along. "They are great, but . . ."

"And there it is." I chuckle. "Let me have it. How can I improve?"

"I liked the silhouettes that you made. I thought they looked like her, and they were sexy, but I think you could do better with the font. It felt either thriller or old-school romance, and there's nothing wrong with that, but I think she needs something more modern."

I nod. "For me, font is the hardest. I hate that part of the job. I just don't feel I have a solid grasp on what works."

"That's okay, it will take time. I was showing Dale your designs, and do you know what he said he does when he's deciding on fonts? He'll go to Creative Market and look through all the fonts and how the artist pairs them with designs. He was telling me that you can get a strong feel for how they imagined their font being used."

"Oh, that's a good idea. I'll do that tonight."

"And maybe offer her up some new colors for her brand. I know she's into black and pink, but maybe show her something else. So keep to her branding but offer her something unorthodox." *Unorthodox. That's exactly what I should do. I'm strong at creating things outside of the box.*

"Good idea. Thank you, Sandie."

"You know I'm here for you. Have you been working on anything else?"

"I've been waffling between opening up an Etsy shop or not. I know exposure would be good, but a lot of time and energy and ad spending goes into it. I'm sort of leaning more on UpWork at the moment and interviewing for side jobs."

"Yeah, I'd focus on UpWork and continuing to update your profile, making sure you have the most up-to-date designs. Once you score a few jobs from there, then hopefully word of mouth will pick up the rest. And I'll keep an eye out for any job contests I see floating around. Just want to be clear, but you want to stay freelance?"

"Yeah. I know that's riskier, but I like the idea of being able to do a variety of jobs rather than one particular thing. Like there's a girl in one of my classes and she got a job working for a triathlon company. It is great money and has benefits, but she said all she does is photoshop triathletes and put them against a banner. She hates that there is no creativity involved. I don't want to be stuck like that. I'd rather continue this assistant farce and build up my portfolio than take a job remotely related to design just because it pays well. If I'm going to do this, I'm going to do it right."

"I think that's really smart. And you'll get there, but it definitely won't happen overnight."

"I know that." I sigh. "I don't think my dad thinks I know that, though." I glance at the TV, where I catch Levi slamming someone into the boards right before he shoots the puck behind the net and right to Eli, who flicks it down the ice to OC. "He probably assumes that I'm living in some fairy-tale land where I'll find success overnight with one job. But I know what it means to work hard. I've worked hard at maintaining a relationship with him my entire life. And sure, that isn't job experience, but it's tenacity and goal setting. It's made me realize that nothing comes for free, even my father's love." *I'm not sure I'll ever forget those words he wrote to Levi, though. How can a father be so blasé about how his daughter is treated?* I've dealt with his gruff exterior for over two decades. But to *insist* that Levi make my life a living hell . . .

Do not let her off the hook. Don't let her skate by. I want you to make her life a living hell, got it?

I can't deny that stings. That's not unconditional love. In fact, I doubt I've ever had that.

Sandie's expression softens. "He loves you, Wylie. You know this."

My eyes well up with tears as I stare at the TV, the camera zooming in on my father yelling at the players to change lines. "I just wish it wasn't a conditional love."

⌶

SANDIE LEFT, and with another Agitators win under their belt, I retreated back to my bedroom after making sure to leave no trace of us hanging out in Levi's apartment. While in bed, I started looking through different fonts on Creative Market. Dale was right. There's a vision each artist has when they create their font, and it's interesting to see what kind of vision they had in mind.

Some fonts I would have assumed could be more on the thriller side, but they pair them in a soft background with natural tones, which totally works. Strangely.

It has my brain thinking differently.

Today felt mindless as I ran through task after task. Trying to find Levi a new suit, buying him more underwear, picking out some macaroons from a certain shop that he apparently loves. Makes me wonder, are the macaroons for him or is he going to give them to my father later?

And with every task that I checked off the list, I grew more and more frustrated, especially after Sandie left. I spent a solid hour sorting out pretzels for his snacks because he only wanted whole pretzels, no broken pieces. It was annoying and stupid and just made me realize how infuriating the entire situation is.

It's not like I told my dad that it's my life's calling to be a stripper, and I'm giving up everything for it. I want to work in graphic design, a booming profession in today's online market-ing. Yet he wants me to be some boring executive who doesn't enjoy life because it's safe.

Well, nothing is safe.

Not even those jobs. At least with this, I can hopefully deter-mine my own destiny. As long as my designs don't suck and people love my perspective and aesthetic.

Since I left my bedroom door open, I hear the moment Levi gets home. It's later than before, and I'm not sure if it's because he is avoiding me or if he put in a quick leg workout after the game—some of the guys do that. Either way, I'm surprised how long it took him to get home.

But instead of going to see him right at the moment, I have another plan.

Is it diabolical?

Maybe.

But like Sandie said, I can't let up. I have to keep pushing forward.

It felt like talking to Levi from a year ago during the drive into the arena today, and I got lost in it. In him. And a part of me longed for that moment to carry on, for him to be that guy, not my dad's puppet.

I need to remember that I'm trying to prove a point to two men, and one of them just got home.

I set my iPad down and move to the floor-length mirror. I'm wearing one of my lingerie sets, but it's more . . . casual. It's a silky black camisole top with thin straps and lace around the low neckline. The matching shorts—if you want to call them that— have slits that rise to my hips and of course, naturally, I'm not wearing a bra or underwear. I know he told me to, but it's clear as day that I'm ready for bed. Makeup is off, hair is up in a messy bun, and I'm wearing my fuzzy slippers as well.

The plan is to walk into his bedroom right before he goes to bed, in this outfit, and ask him a few packing questions. Hopefully the outfit will get him worked up.

We shall see.

I brush my teeth, wanting to give the full effect of bed readiness and, for the hell of it, I put on my blue light glasses that I'll wear when I have to stare at my screen for a long period.

Yup, this looks perfect.

Satisfied, I move down my dark hallway toward the kitchen, pausing to listen. I don't hear him moving around in the bathroom, so he must be in bed.

Time to strike.

Carefully, I tiptoe down the hallway to his bedroom, not wanting to make a sound but wanting to be a full surprise. And as I inch closer, I start to hear something coming from the other side of his door.

A woman's voice.

Oh God.

I still.

A sweat breaks out over my skin.

And my heart hammers because . . . *he brought someone home with him.*

My stomach churns at the thought of him being with any other woman than me. And I know that's ridiculous, I know. I have no claim over him, but still, I don't like the thought of someone else being with him when I'm carrying this crush heavy on my chest. And sure, I know I pack him condoms and tease him about hooking up when he's out of town, but I do that so when he does pull out a condom, he thinks of me.

Slightly manipulative, perhaps, but let's remember who the master manipulator is . . . him. Need I remind you of the bagel runs?

Needing to find out if he's with someone else, I move in closer to his bedroom, my breath held as I lean toward his door to listen intently.

I don't hear him.

I just hear a woman.

A woman telling him what to do . . .

And then it clicks.

Holy shit, he's watching a Patty Ford video.

I cover my mouth with my hand, trying to hold back my pure joy from the thought of him fondling himself on the other side of this door. My body heats up, a dull throb pulses between my legs, and my mouth goes dry. It's so incredibly hot that he's touching himself.

So freaking hot that I lean more toward the door . . . aching to hear him.

I want to hear him groan.

I want to hear his hand moving over his cock.

Hell, I want to see the way he stares at the phone intently, listening to everything Patty Ford has to say.

The urge to see him grows strong, and for an instant, the thought of walking in on him flashes through my mind.

What would he do?

Would he scramble to hide himself?

Would he just look up at me while he strokes himself?

Would he ask me to join in?

My pulse pounds heavily in my ears as questions creep up my spine.

What would happen if I actually walked in? I could pass it

off as ignorance. I could apologize profusely. I could lean into him, pressing my hard nipples against his arm while showing him my favorite videos of hers.

Oh God, that last thought, that last idea. Yes, I want that. I want to be on his bed, with him naked, enticing him. Telling him how I like to masturbate when I watch her videos.

I want him to know.

I want him to break out in a sweat.

I want him thinking of me when he watches her.

And before I can stop myself, before I can convince myself this might not be the best decision, I push down the door handle and walk in.

Immediately my eyes land on Levi, who is propped up on his bed, his back to the headboard, his dick covered by his blankets, but his hand slowly working under the sheets. His other hand holds the phone as he stares down at it intently.

So.

Fucking.

Hot.

Bare up top, his chest muscles flex as his teeth pull on the corner of his lip. His bicep flexes with every stroke as the sinew in his forearm fires off with every motion up and down his length.

Mmmm, I want him.

I want him bad.

I want to trade places with him. I want to be the one that strokes him, licks him, sucks him. I want to be the one telling him what to do. I want to be the one he's fantasizing about.

I could stand here all day, watching him, but given our situation, I know I need to make myself known, so I say, "Oh gosh, I'm sorry."

He scrambles under the sheet, fumbling with the phone.

"Fucking hell," he cries out as his wide eyes find me. He tries to find his phone in the mess of the sheets, but is so concerned with covering his dick, that he can't find it, so Patty Ford's voice rings through the quiet room.

"That's it, just like that. Oh God, I love when you touch yourself."

"Fuck," he says, his hand moving over the sheets, blindly looking for the phone that I actually spot on the edge of the bed.

I walk up to him, and his eyes grow wider as I approach. He takes in my lingerie set, his tongue wetting his lips, clearly interested in what he sees—*exactly what I wanted*.

I pick up his phone and then look up at him with a smile. "I love Patty Ford. I come the hardest when watching her videos." I turn the phone toward me and stare down at the seductress. "I love this video," I say as I move closer to him and sit on the edge of his bed . . . right next to him.

He's stiff, unmoving—fairly sure he's still in shock—so when I lean in, he doesn't even flinch.

"She has the best boobs ever, and they're real. There's nothing fake about them. And I love her movements. They're not overly sexualized, but they aren't jagged either. She knows exactly what she's doing with her hands and how her fingers glide over her nipples, pulling against the hard nub. God, I love her."

I glance over my shoulder at Levi. His eyes are heady now, the shock gone. In its place, lust.

Definite lust.

The kind of lust that will make me turn toward him, straddle his lap, and take what I've wanted for a long time.

After a few seconds of staring at each other, he whispers, "What are you doing here?"

"Had some questions," I say as I turn more toward him.

I watch his eyes move from my face, down my neck, and to my breasts. His hand is still under the sheets, probably gripping his cock in a death grip.

"Wylie?"

"Yes?" I ask, feeling breathless.

"You . . . you're, uh . . ."

I smirk and take a chance by bringing my hand to his chest, letting my nails run along his chest hair. His eyes stay fixed on mine, and when he doesn't tell me to stop, I set his phone down and completely turn toward him.

"Were you trying to tell me something?" I ask as my finger circles his nipple.

His head tilts back against the headboard, and the strain in his neck turns me on even more. From the corner of my eye, I catch him moving his hand along his covered cock, and I'm so tempted to pull down the sheet, to watch him touch himself.

"Fuck." He breathes heavily just as Patty's voice continues.

"Like that, oh fuck, my pussy is so wet knowing you're touching yourself."

My thoughts exactly.

"Levi?"

"Hmm?" he says as my fingers glide down his abdomen.

"You were saying something."

He lazily nods and pulls on his lip before saying, "You're . . . you . . . fuck, that top you're wearing."

I smile, knowing I have him right where I want him.

"You like it?" I ask as I puff my chest out.

"A whole fucking lot," he says.

"It's so comfortable. I love sleeping in it because it feels amazing against my skin. I love how the silky fabric rubs against my nipples, too." I trail my fingers farther south, right above where the sheet is.

His hand moves under the covers, and I know for a fact that Patty Ford is no longer part of his thoughts anymore. It's me.

All me.

From the way he's looking at my tits.

The way he's wetting his lips.

He's one temptation away from giving in.

So, with my other hand, I drag my nails along my collarbone, watching his eyes trail my movement. Slowly I glide them down my chest to my breast, where I lightly run my nails across my nipples, a moan slipping past my lips.

He sucks in a sharp breath and then, to my dismay, looks away.

His expression is pained as he mumbles, "Fuck." Then he releases his cock and lets out a deep breath. Keeping his eyes fixated in front of him and not on me, he says, "I think you should leave."

Hope crashes around me. In some made-up land, I envisioned him asking me to take my shirt off.

"Okay, I'm sorry. I didn't mean to interrupt," I say, wanting to stay casual, even though my entire body is burning. "I just wanted to make sure you were ready for your trip tomorrow."

He wets his lips once again, his eyes now connecting with mine. "You need to leave," he says tersely.

I glance down at his lap—at the sheet tenting between us—and then back up at him. "Are you going to come?"

His jaw clenches together, and he says, "Once again, you need to leave."

Seeing the strain in his neck, in his sexy chest, in his shoulders, I decide to push him just a touch more. "If it makes you feel any better, I'm so wet."

His head falls back against the headboard again, and he takes a few deep breaths. I watch his chest heave, the air filling his lungs and then leaving. "Wylie, I don't need details. I need you to leave."

"Okay," I say as I stand. His eyes land on me again, and for the hell of it, I lean forward, letting my top fall forward, giving him an epic view of my chest, which of course he takes full advantage of. I watch as his gaze floats over my breasts, the way he stares, the hunger in his expression. I leave the phone on his nightstand and then stand back up. "Didn't mean to interrupt. Should I ask you the questions tomorrow?"

"Yes," he says in a strained voice.

"Okay, see you in the morning." I turn to walk away and then add, "Also, you won't be the only one getting off tonight."

And with that, I leave his room and head straight for my vibrator.

LEVI

THE MOMENT my bedroom door shuts, I sink into my mattress and start jerking off at a rapid pace. Precum covers my hand as I drag it over my length.

I knew the moment I got home tonight, I had to find release. I didn't care how, but I needed it. I pulled up a Patty Ford video, shut my eyes, and envisioned Wylie as Patty talked. I was hard and ready to come in fucking seconds.

My balls had started to tighten the moment I spotted Wylie in my bedroom. It was as if I conjured her in my mind and brought her in here. And fuck did she look so mouth-wateringly good. I don't know what she was wearing, all I know is that if there was a uniform requirement for her job, I'd pick that. I'd pick that all day, every day.

And every time I'd see her in it, I'd pin her against the wall or the cabinet, or the couch, and I'd pull down the front so I could suck on her tits—those fucking gorgeous tits—and I'd play with her nipples and . . .

"Oh . . . fuck," I groan as I squeeze my cock, my orgasm right on the edge. I hold the base tightly, prolonging the feeling of walking on the edge, waiting to be pushed over.

Hearing her talk about Patty and how she gets turned on, hearing her say she's wet . . . *fuck me.*

The way her fingers ran over my chest. Almost to my dick.

The dip in her shirt where I almost caught sight of those hardened nipples.

Fuck, she's so goddamn hot.

I let go of the base of my cock and then pump hard, up and down, over and over until my cock swells and I come all up the front of my stomach, groaning the entire time.

"Fuck . . . oh fuck."

Jesus Christ, it's been too fucking long.

I let go of my cock and stare up at the ceiling, finding my

breath. What's she doing? Is she getting off right now? Did she slip out of her clothes and into her bed naked? Is she fingering herself? Is she using a toy?

And why the hell did she come over here in the middle of the night? Just to fuck with me?

She has to be fucking with me.

There's no other reason.

The only question is, why?

Why is she trying to entice me? Why is she risking her job when we both said we'd keep things platonic? There has to be an explanation, and I need to know why.

I move into the bathroom and clean myself up.

Then I pull on a pair of gray sweatpants, my dick still half hard as I calm down, and then move through the apartment with one thing on my mind . . . her.

I feel frenzied.

Out of my mind.

Ready to fucking lose my shit with the electricity bouncing through me.

Call it adrenaline left over from the game.

Call it seeing her in that night set.

Whatever it is, it's propelling me straight to her door where I stand for a second.

I listen closely and hear nothing, so I take a chance and turn the doorknob, pushing the door open.

She didn't knock.

Why should I?

When I walk into her bedroom and look to the right at her bed, instead of being startled at seeing me, she almost looks like she was expecting me.

She's under her covers, both hands covered up with the faint sound of a vibrator sounding through the room.

Her teeth pull on her bottom lip as she looks up at me.

And just like that, I get hard all over again.

And because I'm in some sort of weird fucking world where

time stands still now, I don't move. I stare. And she doesn't move as her eyes connect with mine.

I can see it, right there in her pupils, she wants me here.

She was hoping I'd come.

She wants me to see this, and fuck, do I want to watch.

I know I should leave.

I know I shouldn't be here.

Coach Wood would freak the fuck out, but I'm torn.

I'm out of control.

My will is slipping, and I can't seem to stop myself.

And because she's fucking with me, she doesn't stop. She doesn't turn off the vibrator. She shifts on her bed so she's turned more toward me with one leg propped up under the sheets. The shift causes the blankets to fall dangerously close to revealing her naked breasts.

Fuck.

Me.

"Oh, fuck, Levi. Your body. So fucking hot. You're . . . ohhhh . . . fuck," she moans as she moves her hand. "Oh God . . ."

My mouth goes dry.

My pulse picks up.

And my cock swells all over again as her eyes squeeze shut and her mouth parts open.

"Fuck, oh God. Oh, I'm . . . I'm coming," she says right before her moan fills the air, and her body convulses under the sheet.

My skin prickles as I watch her come.

Not only did I fuck up by being in here but the sound of her orgasming is never, ever going to leave my brain.

Ever.

After a few seconds of her catching her breath, she switches off the vibrator, tosses it to the side, and gathers the blankets up around her neck as she props her head on her hand. "Can I help you . . . Mr. Posey?"

Fuck . . . yes.

With one flick of those covers, I could be on top of her. I

could be burying my face between her legs. I could be showing her just how much I want her.

But I can't.

I know I can't.

I realize I can't.

This is not some game. This is my livelihood.

This is my ass on the line.

I might be a horny motherfucker with the taste for one woman, but that doesn't mean I can just toss the promises I made. *I do not break my promises.* Some would say I'm loyal to a T. The Agitators *is* my job, and I won't fuck that up.

Can't fuck that up.

Despite her eyes falling to my crotch, I take a step back, ignoring the droop in her shoulders.

With my eyes set on her, I say, "Tonight, you crossed a line, Wylie. Don't cross it again."

And with that, I push through her door, slamming it as I stride toward my room.

Fuck, I hated that.

I hated everything about it.

———

WYLIE

OKAY, so I pushed him a touch too far last night.

I get that.

I own up to it.

But for the record, just to be petty, he liked it.

He liked everything about me walking in on him.

Him walking in on me.

And of course, the finale.

I saw it in his hazy eyes and tented sweatpants.

And sure, did I cross the line? Of course, but to be fair, this was the goal, right? To push him as far as he can go? And, well, I did that last night.

I'm just glad I didn't drag my sheets down like I wanted to. With him staring at me last night, I was seconds away from inviting him into my bed. And from the way his sweatpants clung to his bulge, I know he would have taken me up on the opportunity.

But once again, maybe it was too far. Talking about Patty Ford's nipples while his hand was on his cock, yeah, that was crossing the line.

Coming in front of him, very much crossing the line.

The good thing is, the mission is accomplished, right? Teaching him a lesson and all. Now, where the hell do I go from here?

I'm supposed to talk to him this morning about his trip and what I should be doing for him while he's gone. Do I go in all casual, as if nothing happened last night?

Do I ride in with a handful of apologies?

Do I drop down to my knees and ask for forgiveness . . . and maybe something else?

Or do I bend over and tell him to punish me for my bad behavior?

I smile to myself as I pull my sweater over my head. I can only imagine what he'd do if I bent over in front of him.

Chuckling, I slip on my slippers just as my phone buzzes on my nightstand. Thinking it might be Levi, I reach for it quickly.

I sigh heavily and answer.

"Hey, Dad."

"Wylie, what was that yesterday?"

"I'm great, Dad. Thanks for asking. How are you?" I ask with a roll of my eyes.

"I don't have time for pleasantries. I repeat, what was that yesterday?"

"You should always have time for me," I reply.

I can hear his growl through the phone. "Wylie, I have a busy day of packing and getting ready for tomorrow's game. I don't have much time for anything, so answer my question."

"Well, I don't understand your question, so how can I answer it?" I say as I sit on my bed.

"Yesterday, with Posey, you seemed . . . intimate. What was that?"

"It was me asking him a question," I say. "There was nothing intimate about it besides how close he was standing, but that's because it was loud out on the ice."

"You were touching him."

"Because he had something on his jersey. As his assistant, I need to make sure he looks the best that he can look."

"So nothing is going on between the two of you? Because if there is, I can guarantee you right now, everything that we agreed upon will be revoked. This job will be taken away, you will owe me tuition payments, and you are on your own. I'll not be fucked with. My players are off limits. You know that."

Grinding my teeth together, I say, "Is that your true opinion about me, Dad? That I would just throw everything away, my chance at proving you wrong about me and my career path, over some guy?"

"I don't know, Wylie. It seems to me like you're throwing a lot away recently."

I twist my lips to the side, trying not to lash out at him—*because it won't do anything.* I've done it before, where I've yelled, trying to get my point across, but that only resulted in an angry father who doesn't understand me. Someone who tells me that I'm disrespecting him by raising my voice.

So I hold back my temper and calmly say, "Nothing is going on between me and Levi. Absolutely nothing. I'm just doing my job and doing my job well. Now, if you'll excuse me, I need to get back to work." Without saying goodbye, I hang up on him and toss my phone on my bed.

I press my hands into my face and let out a disgruntled growl of frustration. And for the millionth time in my life, I ask the same questions that I'm sure I'll never get answers to.

Why?

Why did my mom have to leave him?

Why did she have to leave me with him?

It's not fair.

My entire life I've felt like I've had to walk on eggshells around him, judge his mood, and try to fall in line to avoid making his mood worse. He says he loves me, but this isn't love. This isn't how a parent should treat their child. I've watched Sandie with her parents, how they treat her. Parents are supposed to be loving and supportive.

And sure, yes, I've been messing around with Levi because I'm irritated with him for being a part of this master plan my dad constructed, but would I have crossed that line with him . . .

Maybe.

Now, will I?

No.

Fuck, no.

That's a big fucking no and all because my dad thinks I have no willpower. That he believes instead of doing a job, I'm over here just fucking one of his players.

Well, my dad can fuck right off.

I stand and wipe at my watery eyes.

It's fine, you're fine, everything is fine.

I take a few deep breaths, straighten my shoulders, and then head down the hallway toward the kitchen to meet up with Levi.

This phone call was a good wake-up call. Last night was as well. He told me not to cross the line, so I won't. I'm done messing with him. Now it's time to focus on what really matters, and that's making something of myself.

Not for my dad . . . but for me.

When I enter the kitchen, Levi is at the island with one of the many bagels I've purchased for him. He paired it with eggs to make a sandwich, and I'm grateful he's eating it. So grateful that it nearly makes me cry. I feel like I've been put through the wringer of emotions this past week, so to see him eat that bagel, one that I've lost sleep over, well, it does something to me.

"Morning." He studies me for a second before asking, "Are you okay?"

"Fine." I wipe at my eyes and move toward the fridge, where I grab a strawberry banana Naked Juice. I purchased some the other day, thinking that Levi might like them, but instead, I've been the single consumer.

"It doesn't look like you're fine," he says.

I shut the fridge door and turn toward him. "How about we just talk about what you need from me and answer those questions from last night?"

He pushes away from the counter, looking confused as he sets his bagel sandwich down. "Whoa, why are you mad at me? I'm the one you disrupted last night."

"I don't care about what happened last night, Levi. I just want to get started on my day, okay?"

His brow creases as he wipes his fingers on his napkin. "Consider me confused because it seems like you're mad at me, and I have no idea why. Is it because I didn't knock on your door? Well, you didn't fucking knock either."

"Not everything has to do with you," I say. "This isn't about last night. Last night was stupid and a mistake, and yes, I crossed the line. I'm sorry, it won't happen again. Now, can we talk about your suit?"

He doesn't answer right away, but he does study me. I can see he wants to press and get to the bottom of my mood change, but thankfully, he moves past it. "Sure, what about my suit?"

Perfect. Revert to work. *That's what you're here for anyway.*

"Because you have such specific measurements, I wasn't able to pick you up the blue velvet you wanted, but I did order it. Instead, I packed you a navy-blue suit for your trip, along with a maroon one and a black one. I paired them all with shirts, but no tie because I know you don't enjoy wearing a tie. They also have matching shoes to go with them. You can wear the same shoes for the maroon and black. I packed navy-blue loafers for the blue suit. The macaroons you wanted are in the fridge, don't forget them. I waited in a thirty-minute line just to order them. Your high-maintenance pretzels have been sorted, social media is ready to go for the rest of the week, and Blakely is sending me your game day shots so I can use them as well. I packed your backpack, but it's up to you to put any snacks you might want, including the pretzels. While you're gone, I'll work on the list you gave me, but is there anything else you need before I leave?"

He stares at me, blankly. Almost shocked from the laundry list I just read out to him. If I'm honest, I'm impressed with myself. Proud of how I've adapted from college student to working as an assistant. Dad may never be proud of me—*I'm still learning to accept that*—but I can be proud of myself.

"Well?" I ask, crossing my arms now.

"Uh, no, I think that's it."

"Great, well I'm going to head out. Email or text. Good luck this week."

And with that, I turn away from him and head down the hallway where I shut my door, flop on my bed . . . and cry.

LEVI

"WHAT DO YOU HAVE THERE?" Halsey asks as he sits down next to me. "I didn't think you read."

"I don't," I say as I stare down at the book of Vermont that Wylie typed up for me. When I was packing my bag—after getting the rundown from her—I decided to include the book of Vermont out of guilt. She did work hard on it, so I might as well try to read it.

"Are you planning a trip to Vermont?" Halsey asks.

"Nope," I say, looking down at the book and the bridge image she chose for the cover.

"Okay, then what's with the book?"

I look up at Halsey and say, "Can't a fucking guy just want to read a book without getting the tenth degree from another man?"

Halsey blinks a few times. "Uh, a guy can read a book, but you looked tense so that's why I came over here. The others volunteered me because there was a book in front of you, and they were worried."

I glance toward the back of the airplane, where Pacey, Hornsby, Taters, and OC are all craning their necks to see what's happening.

"Tell them I'm fine, and I don't need them worrying about me." I reach into my backpack and pull out my Tupperware of unbroken pretzels.

"Well, it seems like—"

"I said I'm fine," I say tersely, startling Halsey.

He holds up his hands. "Okay, if you think you're fine, then you're fine. But you know, if you want to talk about anything, we're here for you."

"Thank you, Danny Tanner, now please be gone. I need to read my book." I shoo him with my hand and then open to the first page.

Halsey scoots away and I'm left in peace with some fine literature.

The first thing I'd like to note about this book is that the Arial font is quite pleasing to the eye, so I'm not mad about that.

I kind of wish there were more pictures, but I made her rewrite the whole thing so how *can* I be mad about that?

I flip through the first few pages, taking it in. How did she type all this in a few days? She must have magic Mavis Beacon fingers that fly across the keyboard at 100 words per minute. I mean look at this, all lined up and . . .

I glance down at the words.

Wait a second.

I flip to the first page and read the first paragraph, then flip back to the page I was just at. It's the same. The same paragraph. I flip through some more pages, and lo and behold, it's the same thing. Over and over again.

"Son of a bitch," I mutter as I slam the Vermont book shut. And here I was, ready to educate myself on the country's maple candy capital.

How dare she?

Why would she do that?

She knew I'd read it.

Or did she . . .

I pull out my phone and because I'm hooked up to the Wi-Fi on the plane, I can send text messages, so I go to the queens.

Levi: *Red alert! A lot has happened in the last twenty-four hours, and I need my ladies.*

I pop a few pretzels in my mouth and wait for a response while I sift through the book. At least she had the decency to change up the pictures, but . . . oh my God. I bring the book closer. One of the pictures has a watermark on it from Shutterstock. She didn't even have the decency to pay for the freaking picture.

The audacity.

My phone buzzes with a text.

Winnie: *The queens are here, or at least I am. What's going on?*

Levi: *So many things. Let's start with how she walked in on me last night while I was pleasuring myself.*

Ollie: *That's hot.*

Blakely: *OMG, did she see your tattooed wiener?*

Penny: *Ew, did she see your O face?*

Levi: *For the record, I have a nice O face. I saw it in a mirror once and congratulated myself on a dignified and respectable way to experience an orgasm. Second, no, she did not see my wiener, everything was covered up. And third, it was really fucking hot and the minute she left I came on my stomach.*

Penny: *The coming on the stomach is not a detail we needed.*

Ollie: *I love it when Silas comes on his stomach, seeing it across his abs. Yes, chef's kiss.*

Blakely: **raises hand* I like it too.*

Winnie: *I shall not say if I like it or not since my man's sister is in this text thread.*

Penny: *Thank you, Winnie. And yes, I like it as well, but I don't want to picture Posey with cum on his stomach.*

Levi: *What is your problem with me? You have some sort of aversion to thinking of me in a sexual way. Is it the bologna?*

Penny: *Yes, and because you're just . . . Posey.*

Winnie: *Perfect way to describe him.*

Ollie: *I second that.*

Blakely: *Third.*

Levi: *Not sure if I should be happy about that or not. But either way, back to the topic at hand. She walked in on me, then I got pissed, walked in on her, and then told her she'd crossed the line and left.*

Ollie: *Hold on, when you say walked in on her . . . what does that mean?*

Winnie: *Was about to ask the same thing.*

Levi: *She was getting off as well.*

Winnie: *Wow, what a night.*

Blakely: *Did you see anything?*

Levi: *She was covered by her bedding as well, but she did actually come while I was there.*

Penny: *Oh my God, she finished in front of you? I think I might like this girl.*

Winnie: *Bold choice.*

Ollie: *I'm getting horny.*

Blakely: *When are you not horny, Ollie?*

Ollie: *Never. I'm horny all the time.*

Winnie: *Same. I never knew sex until Pacey came along—sorry, Penny.*

Penny: *It's fine. I'm just going to pretend you're not with my brother and leave it at that. Congrats on the amazing sex.*

Winnie: *Thank you, he's so good with his tongue.*

Penny: *I said congrats, I didn't ask for details.*

Ollie: *Let's talk more about tongues.*

Levi: *CAN WE FOCUS ON ME! I saw her come last night. I can't get her moan out of my head.*

Blakely: *Right, we're here to support bologna boy. What did you do after she came?*

Levi: *Laid down the hammer.*

Ollie: *The hammer being your penis?*

Penny: *Great question.*

Levi: *No, not my penis, a metaphorical hammer. Told her she crossed the line. And then this morning, she was a bit cold and standoffish. She actually looked upset, like she was going to cry. I was worried that I'd hurt her feelings, and I've been stewing about it all goddamn morning. Then I found something . . .*

Penny: *^^^ See that pause, ladies? He uses that for the drama.*

Winnie: *I was going to say, it's quite dramatic. Just tell us, why did you have to use the ellipses?*

Levi: *It's better that way.*

Ollie: *It's more annoying. Just tell us what you found.*

Levi: *Well, I was eating my pretzels, about to read the book about Vermont that she typed up for me, when I noticed that what she'd typed was the same few paragraphs, over and over and over again.*

Ollie: *Wow, and here I thought he'd admit she stuffed one of her thongs in his backpack.*

Winnie: *Or maybe a picture of her, a nudey.*

Blakely: *Or even sprayed his clothes with her perfume.*

Penny: *Something other than a book about Vermont.*

Blakely: *You were right about the ups and downs of dealing with him. Never seen anything like it before.*

Penny: *Should have been there when he was trying to get you and Halsey together. Epic meltdowns. A total drama queen.*

Ollie: *Silas told me all about it. He was so irritated one night with the text messages that I had to pacify him with my boob in his mouth.*

Winnie: *I let Pacey motorboat me when he's upset.*

Penny: *I massage Eli's balls.*

Levi: *For the love of God, please, stay focused. This is important.*

Penny: *Right, the book. *rolls eyes* What's so important about the book?*

Levi: *You don't get it. I asked her to type this up.*

Penny: *And . . .*

Blakely: *Is that supposed to give us chills?*

Levi: *It was one of the tasks I gave her.*

Ollie: *Soo . . .*

Levi: *And she didn't do it properly.*

Blakely: *The actual horror . . .*

Winnie: *Wait, ladies, I think he's trying to say that she didn't do the task properly, which means she didn't take it seriously, which means . . . maybe she knows that he wasn't taking his boss duties seriously.*

Levi: *Winnie, you're my new favorite.*

Ollie: *Uh, that seems a little hasty, don't you think?*

Penny: *Do you really want to be his favorite?*

Ollie: *Just nice to be considered.*

Winnie: *I accept Queen Bee Number One as my title. Thank you.*

Blakely: *Hold on, if she didn't take it seriously because she thought that you didn't take your boss duties seriously, do you think that's why she double downed?*

Levi: *Wait, what do you mean?*

Blakely: *Hear me out. So you asked her to retype this book for God knows what reason and if she was acting as a real assistant who didn't want to get fired, then she would have seriously typed up the whole thing. But given that she didn't, that she just made the task look complete, do you think she knows something that you know?*

Winnie: *Gah! Do you think she knows that her dad's behind this?*

Blakely: *That's exactly what I'm thinking.*

Penny: *And if she knows about her dad's involvement, then that would mean she knows that there should be no fooling around, which is why she double downed.*

Levi: *Wait, I'm lost.*

Ollie: *So am I.*

Blakely: *Let me put it to you straight. She knows that her dad put you in charge of making her life hell. Which means she's going to try to make your life hell in return, and how can she do that? By flaunting herself in front of you. She knows that she's off limits.*

Levi: *HOLY SHIT! You think that's what she's doing?*

Penny: *The braless walk around . . .*

Blakely: *The push-up bra . . .*

Winnie: *The walking in on you while you're coming on your stomach.*

Levi: *note* *I was not coming on my stomach when she was in the room. I was in her room when she was coming. Thank you.*

Ollie: *OMG, you guys are right. This is the classic double down with a vengeance. She knows about you and her dad working together, and she's getting back at you by torturing you with her eroticness.*

Penny: *Whispers* *Erotic torture.*

Levi: *What the hell is erotic torture?*

Ollie: *Oh, you poor, poor man.*

Winnie: *Even I know what erotic torture is. You stand no chance.*

Blakely: *I think it's time we just throw in the towel now.*

Levi: *Hey! You can't throw in the towel. I need you!*

Winnie: *He's right. We can't dump him when he's in the middle of erotic torture.*

Ollie: *I say just give in.*

Penny: *But what if Coach Wood finds out? That won't be good.*

Levi: *No, it won't, therefore, we need to figure out what to do. I will say this, she came into the kitchen this morning, apologized for crossing the line, and was also decently dressed. It almost felt like she was throwing in the towel.*

Blakely: *I wouldn't trust it.*

Ollie: *Neither would I. Erotic torture could strike at any time, especially if she double downed. You're working with a mistress of sex here.*

Winnie: *For sure a mistress of sex. She has wild ways . . . beware!*

Levi: *Okay, now I'm scared. How the hell do I battle the mistress of sex, the erotic torture lady?*

Blakely: *Great question. Anyone?*

Penny: *Thinking.*

Ollie: *Well, we could . . . uh . . .*

Winnie: *There's the . . . uh . . .*

Blakely: *You know, we could . . . well, no, that won't work.*

Penny: *thinks*

Levi: *This is not helpful!*

Winnie: *What about this, this is going to sound like a* Friends *episode, but she doesn't know that you know she knows, which means . . .*

Levi: *Hold on a second . . . to quote* Friends, *the messer becomes the messee?*

Winnie: *Precisely, and I think we all know the only way to battle erotic torture . . .*

Penny: *A wet blanket?*

Ollie: *Deflated noodle? Also known as a flaccid penis?*

Blakely: *No . . . with . . . *whispers* erotic torture.*

Winnie: *Precisely. We fight fire with fire.*

Levi: *Wait, you want me to battle with my penis?*

Blakely: *Penis, pecs, ass, muscles, I'm sure you have them.*

Winnie: *The perfectly shaped balls you've proudly mentioned.*

Penny: *You guys, this doesn't seem like a good idea. We're talking about Posey here. Do you really think he can go into war, an erotic war, with wielding just his body as a weapon?*

Ollie: *I have to admit, I'm a little nervous about this tactic.*

Winnie: *I have confidence in him.*

Levi: *I appreciate the confidence, but do we not remember the torture I've been through the last week? How the hell do you expect me to fight temptation with well . . . temptation? Seems like a recipe for my penis to easily slide inside of her main hole.*

Blakely: *I TOLD YOU NEVER TO USE THAT TERM AGAIN!*

Ollie: *You make it hard to help you, Posey.*

Penny: *Hold on, ladies. Posey, don't you want revenge? Don't you want to show her who has the upper hand? You do, right?*

Levi: *I don't know. Her nipples sort of have the upper hand at the moment.*

Winnie: *For the love of God, Posey, man up! Do you like losing? Because that's what's going to happen here. You're going to lose! Are you a loser?*

Blakely: *Are you?*

Levi: *I'm not. I'm a winner.*

Blakely: *Then buck up and semi-seduce her!*

Penny: *I'm not fully on board with this plan, but I can see the benefit of trying to beat her at her own game. Because she won't go the whole way with you, what happens if you come at her with the same playbook?*

Ollie: *The more I think about it, the more I think this could work.*

Winnie: *See! This is the way to win.*

Levi: *Okay, so I beat her at her own game. How do I even start doing that without looking obvious? I've been pretty frank about not crossing that line, especially after last night.*

Winnie: *Ease her in. Start simple. You're on an away trip. Strike up conversation. Get to know her better. Act like you're working, but you're really flirting.*

Blakely: *And then when you get back, you serve her your penis on a platter for dinner.*

Ollie: *I love when Silas does that.*

Penny: *What kind of sex life do you have?*

Ollie: *One that involves choking.*

Levi: *I'm going to leave now. Thanks, queens.*

Winnie: *Remember, ease her in.*

Blakely: *Then platter.*

Penny: *No platter, no nudity. Just shirtless seduction.*

Ollie: *Then choke her!*

WYLIE

I THOUGHT about watching the game tonight but decided not to. After everything that happened this morning with my dad, I didn't want to see his face. And then with Levi, well, I don't know. I feel embarrassed now.

Embarrassed over what my dad thinks of me.

What he saw at the arena.

Embarrassed of almost crying in front of Levi.

Of coming in front of him.

Of my behavior.

I basically lost track of everything, and now . . . now I almost feel lost.

I move my Apple pencil over my screen, working out some minor detail changes for Patty Ford's logo, but I'm not feeling the font or the colors I'm choosing. Everything just seems off, so before I can annoy myself too much, I turn off my screen and set my iPad and pencil to the side. I can work on it some more tomorrow.

All ready for bed, I pick up my phone to mindlessly scroll through social media just as it buzzes in my hand. It's a Face-Time from Levi.

Uh-oh, what could he want now?

Sitting up in my bed, I adjust my bun on the top of my head and then hold the phone in front of me as I answer it.

His face comes on screen, and he looks fresh from the shower with wet hair and a slightly red face.

"Hey," I say. "Uh, how's it going?"

He smiles. "Good. Catch the game?"

"No," I reply, feeling weird since we haven't talked on the phone like this before. And with how we last ended things . . . "I was catching up on some work. Did you win?"

"Smashed them."

"Oh . . . uh, congrats."

"Thank you. So, I wanted to call you and thank you for the pretzels. I appreciate the hard work you put into those."

"Oh, you're welcome," I reply.

"I actually am really grateful for everything you've done this past week. I know I haven't been the easiest to work for."

"You haven't been too bad, well, besides your good water bagels."

He smirks, and just the light turn up of his lips has my stomach bouncing with desire. "They were worth it. Best bagels ever. Which reminds me, feel free to help yourself to the stash. You should be able to enjoy them as well."

"Careful what you say. I might eat them all."

"Just means more morning trips for you."

I tap my chin. "Hmm, decisions, decisions."

He chuckles, and it's an earthy sound straight from his barrel-like chest. "I do want to thank you, though, so I sent you a gift card to your email. Did you get it?"

"Uh, I haven't checked," I say.

"Go ahead and look." Really confused by this change in behavior and the lightness in his eyes, I swipe out of our chat and go to my email, where I find a gift card from him to get a massage.

"You're sending me to get a massage?"

"Tomorrow," he says. "I booked an appointment for you and everything. Told them it's all on me. Get what you want. But you have to be there around nine thirty. Hope that's okay."

"Yeah, I mean, I don't have anything going on other than regular work." I stare at him for a few seconds. "Levi, you didn't have to do that."

"I know, but I just wanted to show you that I appreciate you."

"Well, thank you. That'll be really nice."

"You're welcome." He smiles, and ugh, it makes me feel even more guilty for what I've put him through.

And because my guilt takes over, I say, "And I'm sorry if I've been difficult or unsatisfactory. Just been going through some things, and I don't think I handled it well."

"You've been great," he says. "More than great. No need to apologize, but I do need to ask you something."

"Okay," I say. "What is it?"

"Today, in the kitchen, were you crying?"

I glance away from looking at his handsome face and tug on the corner of my lip. Why is it so easy for him to read me? He barely knows me, and it's like he can already see past my defenses. That connection is there, just like the first night we met.

"You were, weren't you?" he presses.

"It's nothing you need to concern yourself with," I say, looking back at him. "And I mean that. Don't bother asking me because I won't say anything."

"Okay," he says. "If that's the case, did your day improve?"

"Uh, yeah. It was okay."

"Cool, yeah, my day was pretty good, thanks for asking."

I smile. "Wasn't aware we were gabbing."

"Don't you think you should gab with your boss? I am your only co-worker, after all."

"I guess you are." I shift to be more comfortable as I stare at Levi's face. "How was your day?"

"Like I said, pretty good. Considered going down to the bar after the game tonight but wasn't feeling it."

"No?" I ask, feeling grateful that he's not trying to pick someone up, but I guess, rather talking to me. "Why not?"

"Thought I'd give that Patty Ford girl another go-around since I was interrupted last time."

"Why, Levi, isn't that a little too intimate for a boss-assistant relationship?" I tease.

"According to you and the vibrator you packed me for my travels, nothing is too intimate. The more we know about each other, the better. You know . . . so you can meet all my needs." The way he says that in such a dark voice sends a shiver right up my spine.

If I was still trying to drive him nuts with erotic torture, I might playfully talk about his needs being met, but I keep it clean. "Aw, you do listen to me."

"I listen to everything you say."

"Not everything," I reply. "When I tell you that waking up at one in the morning to retrieve bagels is not my idea of fun, you seem to keep telling me it might happen again."

"Which reminds me, I'm going to need more bagels."

I stare blankly at him, and he laughs.

"Fine, I'll eat the ones we have before I make you grab more."

"That's a good boy, Levi."

His grin nearly melts me right into the spring coils of my mattress. "So which Patty Ford video is your favorite?"

"Looking for ideas on how to get off?" I ask.

"You're my assistant. Shouldn't you be helping me make decisions?"

"I suppose so." I playfully tap my chin. "Well, personally, I like it when she's fully clothed and slowly takes her clothes off, one by one. There's this one outfit she wears, it's an oversized button-up blouse with a tight mini skirt and these high boots. As she's undressing, she tells you exactly where to touch yourself, and she uses all parts of the body."

He wets his lips. "Yeah, that's hot."

"You'll enjoy yourself."

"Thanks for the tip."

"That's what I'm here for." *Also, I'm so glad you're not going down to the bar.* The thought of him hooking up makes my stomach sour. I know I can't have him, and I know he's not mine, but I hate the idea of him touching another woman. At least not right now.

What am I thinking? I'll never be able to have Levi as anything other than my temporary boss. And that's . . . well, that's fucking sad. Every moment I spend with *this* Levi makes me like him more. It's not as if I'm ready for marriage or want to *settle down*, per se—*I'm only twenty-two*—but I genuinely like this man. He ticks so many boxes. Good humor, kind, sexy, fun to chat with . . . *real.*

He yawns. "Okay, time to release this adrenaline."

"Is that why you usually pick someone up at the bar?" I ask, not wanting him to hang up yet.

"Yeah." He pushes his hand through his hair. "I'm usually buzzing after a game, and it's a great way to blow off steam."

"So is that a regular activity for you then? Just so I'm aware not to bother you after a game."

"Yes, it's a regular occurrence. So, unless you want to walk in on me again, I'd probably stay away. Although it seemed like you were ready for a show."

My cheeks heat. "No, I mean . . . I was, uh, no, I wasn't ready for a show."

He laughs. "Are you sure? You seemed to linger."

"Was just making conversation."

"While I was holding my hard dick?"

"Is that, uh, not an appropriate time to converse?" I lightly chuckle.

He grins. "Not so much, Wylie."

"Oh, okay. Noted."

He chuckles some more, and God, I love that sound. I love how easy it is to talk with him. This is the Levi that I almost spent the night with. There's something about him that's changed, and it's making me want him so much more.

Which means one thing: I'm glad I put the brakes on the erotic torture because I'm not sure I could hold out. One once-over from him, and I'm pretty sure I'd be pushing him down on the couch and settling on his lap.

"Question for you," I say.

"What's that?" He plays with the ends of his hair, his bicep flexing with every twist and pull of the short strands.

"Should I expect you to bring a woman back to your place? Just want to know since you like to get that adrenaline out."

Please say no. Please say no.

"Why?" he asks and grins even wider. "Jealous, Wylie?"

"What? No," I say quickly. "Just, you know, wanting to see if I need to account for, uh, more bagels or something like that."

"It's rare if I bring someone back to my place."

"That's surprising, given the toys and bed you have."

He wets his lips, and his eyes become hazy as he says, "Didn't say I *never* bring women back, it's just rare. And the women I do bring back have signed an NDA, everything we do is consensual, and we have the same sort of pleasure in mind."

Dear God.

I squeeze my legs together from what he could possibly mean by that.

Hell, I know what he means.

I've seen the ties.

I've seen the toys.

I've seen the hooks and the blindfolds.

"How, uh, how do you know she's someone who has that same mindset?"

"Usually meet her at the club," he says casually.

"The club?" I ask, confused.

He slowly nods. "The sex club, Wylie."

"Right, oh yeah, sure, of course. Yup, that makes sense." Sweat forms on my upper lip. "Well, I'm sure you have a lot of fun with those women. They're adventurous."

"They are." From the way his lips tilt up, I know he can sense how uncomfortable I am.

"Anyway, I'll let you get to your release. Enjoy."

He winks.

Freaking winks.

"I will. Night, Wylie."

"Good night." I gulp.

Chapter Eleven

LEVI

"Wow, look who it is," Silas says as I show up for breakfast in the team conference room. A buffet of protein, carbs, snacks and drinks the team nutritionist has approved is lined up for us to eat. "I'm surprised you're gracing us with your presence."

I pick up a plate and ignore him.

Last night, they all wanted to grab a quick drink at the bar, but I skipped out and opted to call Wylie instead. They were not pleased. Claimed they haven't hung out with me in a while. Well, whose fucking fault is that? Theirs. I've been available, but they're the ones who always sprint up to their rooms after games —I think we all know why—so I gave them a taste of their own medicine, and it looks like it's bitter.

"Are you going to ignore us?" Pacey asks as he picks up a plate as well and follows me down the line of food.

"What makes you think I'm ignoring you?" I ask as I plop some eggs and a pile of bacon on my plate. One time, our nutritionist, Tony, had some cooked bologna as a treat for me . . .

God, that was my best day. I haven't seen it since, which makes me want to ask him about it and see if he'll make me some more.

"Uh, you ditched us last night."

"So," I say as I grab a protein smoothie at the end of the buffet and sit at the table where Silas, Eli, and Halsey are already sitting. "You guys ditch me every night."

"I don't," OC says as he picks up a plate and follows Pacey. "I'm there for you, man."

"You ditched me the other night."

"For a friend I haven't seen in a while," he defends. "Normally, I'm there for you, stroking your ego, telling you what a beautifully strong man you are."

"Jesus Christ, this guy," Silas says. "Sucking up to Posey because you think he's going to help you with your love problems?"

"No," OC says and then winces at me. "Maybe a little."

"I told you," I say. "All in good time."

"Is that because you're trying to figure out your own love life?" Eli asks as he takes a bite of a floppy piece of bacon.

There are two types of people in the world. People who let a piece of bacon slap their chin after biting into it, and people who like their bacon to turn into dust in their mouth after one bite.

The floppy-bacon chin-slappers, those are the people you need to look out for. They're the freaks. The wild ones. The type of person who thinks it's funny to say things like . . . "Oh, long time no see" even though they saw you five minutes ago. I'd suggest detaching yourself from that type of person. They're unsavory, untrustworthy, and loose cannons.

Unfortunately for me, it's too late to detach from Hornsby.

But save yourselves!

"I don't have a love life," I say while I pick up my piece of crispy and erect bacon. No flaccid meat on my plate, that's for damn sure.

"I don't believe it," Pacey says as he takes a seat next to me. "You're hiding something. It's obvious."

"Maybe it has something to do with his new assistant," Silas says with a conspiratory glance in my direction. A glance slightly incriminating. Like he knows something. I'm going to have to check in with the Quibbling Queens—name not finalized—to see if they've been speaking to their men.

"Nothing is going on there, and also, keep your fucking voice down because everyone knows who my new assistant is, and the last fucking thing I need is gossip to be spread about Coach Wood's daughter. He'd have my dick in a vise so fast, I wouldn't even know he tore my pants down."

"The imagery on that," Eli says while shaking his head. "Fuck."

"Yeah, not sure Coach Wood is the one to pull pants down," Pacey says. "I think it would be more of a stare that would scare your pants right off your body. Like a Darth Vader, Kylo Ren-type move. One lift of his hands and blamo, pants are off."

Silas nods. "Yeah, that feels right. Can't see him taking the time to unbutton your pants only to yank them to your ankles."

"I've seen him fumble with his pen before," OC says. "Not sure the dexterity is there to make a smooth transition on the pants."

"You saw him fumble his pen?" Eli asks, horror on his face. "Did he know you saw that?"

"No." OC shakes his head. "Fuck, imagine if he did? I wouldn't have eyes. He would have popped them out with an old one-two jab-jab to the eye sockets. I'd be eyeless."

"It would be unfortunate," Pacey says. "But it would serve you right for catching him in such a vulnerable state."

"You're all idiots," Halsey says while shaking his head. "You've let Posey fuck with your heads."

"What the hell is that supposed to mean?" I ask, offended because frankly, this conversation is right up my alley.

Dexterous fingers.

Pulling pants down.

Fumbling of pens.

Eye sockets.

The only thing this is missing is maybe a little live-action reenactment.

"It means you're all talking fucking nonsense." Halsey takes a sip of his coffee while leaning back in his chair.

"Well, excuse us," I say. "Apologies for not being able to have hoity-toity conversations about whatever nonsensical fiction you're currently consuming."

"We don't have to talk about books," Halsey says. "But we certainly don't have to talk about Coach Wood pulling our pants down. For fuck's sake."

"I don't know, seems charming," Eli says just as Coach Wood walks into the conference room. And just like that, we all straighten up and start focusing on our food.

We might talk a big talk, but there's no way in hell any of us would ever say what we said in front of Coach Wood. No fucking chance.

I can feel his eyes on me the moment he starts looking around, but instead of looking up, I take great interest in the fluffiness of my eggs. What do they do to make them so fluffy? Is it more milk? Cottage cheese perhaps? Maybe they—

"Posey!"

Yup, saw that coming.

I look up at Coach Wood who has his arms crossed, staring daggers at me.

"Hey, Coach," I say. "Good morning. What a great shave job this morning. Very smooth."

"Shut up and come here."

Not accepting compliments. Okay.

Although, if another man told me I did a nice shave job, I'd offer a thank you, but it just seems we were raised differently. Someone never taught him to express gratitude for compliments.

I approach him, but he turns on his heel and walks out of the conference room. Seems like he wants me to follow him, so I do.

When we are out in the hall, he brings me to the corner and says, "What's the update on my daughter?"

I place my hands in my jogger pockets and ask, "Uh, what do you mean?"

"Are you making her life hell? Because it seems as though she's having no problem working for you and advancing in her artwork."

"Oh, uh . . . are we mad about the artwork thing?"

"Yes," he rages.

I wince. "Okay, just wanted to make sure. So, uh, to be honest, I'm having a hard time coming up with tasks to give her. And the ones you give me, she seems to be able to do quickly. I don't know what to tell you. She's efficient."

"I don't want her being efficient. I want her to realize that her life would be better with a solid education and a stable job. You are not doing that."

I scratch the back of my neck. "Well, can I just put it out there that maybe I wasn't the right guy for this? You know, Silas is more of an asshole than I am. He might be the one you're looking for."

"I don't want Silas in on this. I need someone who is unattached to a woman who softens him. I thought you were tough. Hard."

Well, I'm hard, that's for damn sure, but I don't think that's the version of hard he's talking about. And I sure as hell know he wouldn't want me to tell him that either.

"What do you want me to do? Make her fly here just so she can tie my shoes?"

That sparks a thought in his head, and I see the evil look in his eye.

Uh-oh, that was the wrong thing to say. "Yes. I do."

"Wait, what?" I ask. "You want me to fly her here?"

"Yes. I want her attached to your hip. Everywhere you go, she goes. I want her running around constantly. If we're on the ice practicing, she's watching you. If we're out to eat, she's there dabbing your face with a napkin. If we're flying, she's in the back, writing handwritten notes to your fans. She needs to be glued to you."

Well, isn't that fun?

"Um, okay. And where do you want her to stay? In my hotel room?"

His eyes darken, and he takes a step forward, invading my space. "Do you think I want her to stay in your hotel room?"

"Well, you said like glue. I assumed that's what you'd want."

He pauses for a moment and looks off to the side. He scratches the side of his cheek and then says, "Can you keep your dick to yourself?"

"I mean, he is a wild man, but he knows his limits."

"A simple yes would suffice."

"Then yes," I say.

He studies me for a short second before he curtly nods. "Yes. I want her to stay in your room."

The minute he says it, I instantly regret the suggestion because . . . how the fuck am I supposed to find relief if she's in my fucking room? Probably don't want to hear about it, but still suffering from some hard dick scenarios over here.

I clear my throat and say, "Well, that might be a great idea and all, but there's usually only one bed in my room so . . ."

"Make her sleep on the floor."

Oh, for fuck's sake.

"Coach Wood, with all due respect, I'm all for asking her to do just about anything, but sleeping on the floor is out of the question. I can be an asshole, but I'm not comfortable with that."

"But you're comfortable sharing a room with her?"

I let out a frustrated sigh. "Honestly? No. I said that just to, I don't know, be a dick. But I'd prefer, for you know . . . manly release's sake, for her not to be there."

He cringes. "You're disgusting."

"Oh come on, everyone fucking does it. Even you," I say, gesturing to him.

He doesn't move.

Doesn't even flinch.

Huh, maybe he doesn't.

Nervously, I shift. "From the look in your eyes, I'm going to guess you haven't touched your penis in over a decade."

His nostrils flare. "Do you really want to be talking about my penis?"

"Not really, but I tend to ramble when presented with uncomfortable situations like this one." He's silent, so I continue, "Do you watch porn?"

"Shut. The. Fuck. Up," he growls.

"My pleasure." I clamp my mouth shut.

Coach Wood pinches his brow, clearly feeling the effects of dealing with me. Don't blame him. Sometimes I can hardly stand myself, and this is one of those moments. "She needs to be in your room. She needs to be turned off by the constant need for her assistance from you."

I scratch my forehead. "I see what you're trying to do here, but I'm not making her sleep on the floor, and I sure as hell don't want to sleep on the floor. I know you want to prove something to your daughter, but not at the expense of your best d-man's back."

"Then get her a cot."

"Won't that be tight?" His eyes rage, and I shrink just a centimeter. "On better thought, yes, what a great idea. A cot. Why didn't I think of that?"

"Much better." He rubs his hands together, looking like a maniacal mastermind rather than a loving father. "Now, get her out here, and I'll come up with a list of things for you to tell her to do."

"Sounds like a plan," I say. I hate every bit of this.

She's going to see right through all of it.

She already knows her dad is behind this, so what the hell is going to happen now? How is she going to act? Do I still fight fire with fire?

"Call her."

"Huh?" I ask, looking up at Coach Wood.

"Call her right now, tell her you need her here on the next flight. And to bring some of those bagels."

My nostrils flare. I never should have told him about the goddamn bagels. After all of this is said and done, I'll never be able to look at another bagel the same.

I pull my phone out of my pocket and press on her name to call. I hold the phone up to my ear and hope and pray he doesn't ask me to put the conversation on speaker.

It rings twice, and then she answers, "Hey, there," she says casually.

"Uh, hey, Wylie." Coach Wood studies me carefully. "So, change of plans. It looks like I will need you to come out to New York."

"Oh, really?" she asks, confused.

"Yup, seems as though I need you here to help me. Guess I've become dependent on your help."

"Okay, uh, do you want me there today? Don't you come home in a few days?"

"We do, but since this is a longer away trip, I'm just finding that I need you here." Coach Wood mouths *bagels*, so I add, "And, uh, I could really use some more of those bagels."

"Levi," she says in a teasing tone, and I really hope he can't hear her. "You can't be serious."

"Yeah, so if you can book your flight and bring the bagels, that would be great." And just to add something for Coach Wood's approval, I say, "And when you're at the airport, if you can find a book on Maine, I'd appreciate it, but remember the font."

"Wait, really?"

"Yup, thanks. See you soon." And then I hang up. I pocket my phone and smile at Coach Wood. "All done."

He nods in approval. "Maine?" he asks.

"Oh, the first book I made her rewrite was about Vermont, so, you know, stuck with the New England theme."

"Are you going to make her rewrite this one?"

"Do you want me to?" I ask.

He nods. "Yes, yes, I do."

"Great," I say, knowing damn well I won't get the full book.

"If that's all, I'm very interested in eating the cold eggs on my plate now."

"Get the fuck out of here," he says before turning away and moving past the conference room and down the hall.

I let out a large breath and know there's only one group of people I want to talk to about this . . .

———

PENNY: *Let me get this straight, he doesn't want you fucking his daughter, but he's now requiring her to sleep in your hotel room with you?*

Levi: *That would be correct.*

Ollie: *Why are men so confusing?*

Blakely: *Halsey isn't confusing. He's perfect.*

Winnie: *Pacey is pretty perfect too.*

Penny: *Eli can be an idiot a lot of the time.*

Ollie: *Silas is stubborn and only wants things done his way, which doesn't settle well with me sometimes. That's why I give him a lot of hell, and he ends up spanking me. It's a win-win for everyone.*

Levi: *That's great and all, but can we get back to me? She knows this will all be a ploy from her dad, so how do I handle this? Do I still fight fire with fire? An epic battle between penis and vagina, who will weep first?*

Blakely: *Ew, can we not have genitals weeping please?*

Winnie: *Why can I picture a weeping penis so well?*

Ollie: *You know, I see it too. All droopy and sad, the balls dangling in depression.*

Penny: *The wrinkles wrinkling even more from the sadness.*

Blakely: *So many wrinkles.*

Levi: *I can see now why Halsey gets so frustrated in group texts. You queens aren't focusing. What the hell do I do?*

Penny: *How did last night go when you called her? Were you naked?*

Blakely: *I was wondering the same thing. Did you strip for her?*

Winnie: *Did she like the massage?*

Levi: *The massage was supposed to be today, but she'll miss it now that she has to fly here.*

Penny: *Ooo, what a wonderful opportunity for erotic torture.*

Blakely: *I think I know where you're going with this, and I couldn't agree more.*

Ollie: *Oily massage performed by Posey? Yup, this is erotic torture all right.*

Levi: *You want me to massage her? You do realize how hard that's going to make me, right? And since she's staying in my room, I can't really take care of the hardness.*

Penny: *Sure you can. Are you scared to come in front of her?*

Levi: *Penny, you know I love you and your ideas, but that is inappropriate. No way am I going to jack off in my bed while she's sleeping on a cot next to me.*

Ollie: *Although it would be really hot.*

Winnie: *Weird, but hot.*

Blakely: *What if she started feeling herself up at the same time. A mutual masturbation. Maybe that's what you guys could call it. Instead of a work meeting, it's mutual masturbation time.*

Levi: *Jesus Christ. If I wanted such ridiculous advice, I would have asked my teammates. I expect better from you.*

Penny: *Please note that it's been a few days away from our men. We're not thinking clearly.*

Ollie: *She's right. Silas and I tried to have phone sex last night, and for some reason, it was more frustrating than satisfying. His phone kept falling, and the video kept pausing. It was a nightmare.*

Blakely: *Halsey and I seemed to manage. I just think a mutual masturbation party seems like fun.*

Winnie: *I think we need to remember what we're doing here. She knows about her father's plan to make life difficult. In return, she has tried to make your life difficult, which we have learned she was successful at. To counteract her play, we chose to battle with the same fire. Which means . . .*

Levi: *I massage her?*

Winnie: *Correct.*

Penny: *Winnie is right. You walk around the hotel room practically naked. You massage her. You ask her to massage you. When you're moving around the room, you touch her back, her hip, anywhere you can.*

Ollie: *Have a half-hardy and motion toward your bulge.*

Blakely: *You walk around in a towel, water dripping down your chest.*

Penny: *You make sexual innuendos that would get her hot.*

Winnie: *Compliment her. Tell her how pretty she is.*

Levi: *This feels a lot like I'm trying to woo her, not erotic torture her.*

Penny: *There's a fine line. You must walk carefully because going too far would be like placing your penis on her pillow. But not going far enough would be like, hey, let's play Go Fish.*

Levi: *Those are very different ends of the spectrum.*

Winnie: *Find the happy medium. You came to us for help. So this is the chance to do so.*

Levi: *And if I get hard?*

Blakely: *Show her first . . .*

Penny: *Then take a shower.*

I GLANCE at the text from Wylie that I received when I was in the middle of our game.

Wylie: *Arrived at the hotel. Watching the game at the bar.*

We're riding in the bus after a tough loss. That's not sitting well with Pacey since he let three goals go by, meaning he's in a shit mood. I'm in a shit mood because they never should have even had a shot at scoring through me and Eli. And now I have to try to put on a performance for my assistant who can see right through me.

Not to mention, the fucking list that Coach Wood sent me right before the game that put me in the worst of moods. Idiotic tasks that are a pointless waste of time. This is stupid. Really fucking stupid and I almost went up to him after the game to tell him that, but he wasn't in a position to speak to anyone. I think he hates a loss more than we do, and I'm sure if I approached him about his daughter, he'd really have something to say about it.

But this one item on the list, it's fucking terrible.

He wants me to ask Wylie to help me pick someone up at the hotel bar.

That's . . . that's not cool with me.

For one, I don't need help.

Also, I don't want to pick someone else up.

And last, what the hell am I supposed to do if I pick someone up? Do I bring her back to the hotel and tell her not to mind my assistant in the cot next to my bed?

Jesus Christ.

I drag my hand over my face just as we arrive at the hotel. Solemnly, we all start climbing off the bus in silence. No one heads toward the lobby as we make our way through the back entrance because we all know the last thing we should be doing is hanging out at the bar.

I text Wylie to meet me at my room.

A bunch of us pile into a service elevator, and we ride up together to our floor.

When we arrive, I just nod at my teammates and walk over to my room, where I open it with my key card. A cot has been placed next to the window, off to the side, and I let out a heavy sigh.

This is so fucking stupid.

Really fucking stupid.

I toss my key card on the dresser and kick my shoes off just as there's a knock on my door.

Here we go.

I open the door and find a smiling Wylie on the other side. "Sorry about the loss," she says as I step aside, letting her in.

"Yeah, it was a shitty night," I reply as she stops in the hallway of the hotel room, her rollie bag right behind her.

"Um, what is that?" she asks, pointing at the cot.

"Your bed," I say while shutting the door behind her. I take off my suit jacket and hang it in the closet.

"What do you mean, my bed?" When I turn toward her, I see the concern in her brow. "We're sharing a hotel room? I'm sorry for assuming, but . . . I don't get my own room?"

"No," I answer. "I want you close in case I need anything." Then I start unbuttoning my dress shirt and catch her eyes following my fingers from button to button. Her eyes grow intense as I pull out the tucked-in ends.

When I turn away from her, she says, "What kind of things are you talking about?"

"Just anything," I say as I shed out of my shirt and then move farther into the room where I hear her draw closer.

"You . . . you have a bruise on your side."

"Yeah, I tripped and fell in the training room, ran into the corner of a table."

"Does it hurt?"

"Sore, but it's fine," I say as I turn toward her. Her eyes once again scan my chest and it takes everything in me not to pull her into my body and then toss her on the bed to make use of those greedy, hungry eyes of hers.

Then she just stands there and watches me move around the room. Finally after a few seconds, I turn toward her and say, "Get comfortable, Wylie."

She bites on the corner of her lip and says, "I didn't pack with the idea that I'd be sharing a room with you."

I take her bag from her and prop it up on the luggage rack I'm not using. Then I move by her and like Penny said . . . I drag my hand across her stomach as I go by and ask, "Oh yeah, what did you pack for?"

I feel her sharp intake of breath before I walk into the bathroom and line my toothbrush with toothpaste.

"Umm, I packed for being alone, meaning, I don't have work-appropriate pajamas and after everything that happened."

"It's fine," I say. "I won't be looking."

Lies, but whatever to placate her.

"Okay, well, if it's easier, I can just get my own room."

"Nope," I answer with a mouthful of toothpaste. "This is easiest."

I can see her contemplate that, probably thinking, yeah, easy for me, not for her.

When I spit out my toothpaste, I say, "Just going to go to the bathroom quick and then you can take over." I shut the door and take care of business, the entire time wondering how the hell I'm going to get through whatever outfit she wears tonight.

Just fight fire with fire. That's all.

After washing my hands, I move out of the bathroom, and she moves in with toiletries and clothes held close to her chest.

When she shuts the door, I slip out of my pants and socks and then move toward the bed, where I get under the covers. I send a quick text to the queens.

Levi: *She's in my hotel room. Do I massage?*

Luckily and surprisingly, they text right back.

Penny: *Yes. For sure.*

Winnie: *It will be a nice gesture, and it will be sexual.*

Blakely: *Use lotion and straddle her thighs so she can feel your dick when it goes hard because we know it will.*

Ollie: *Don't forget an accidental side boob graze.*

Penny: *For sure, the side boob.*

Winnie: *Love a good side boob.*

Blakely: *Side boob for the win.*

Ollie: *I go feral for side boob.*

Levi: *Will she think it's accidental?*

Penny: *Who cares. Get that tit, Posey!*

Winnie: *Either way, everyone wins.*

Ollie: *If she is offended by the side boob graze, then she's not the girl for us.*

Blakely: *If she turns over from the side boob graze and shows her tits, you better end the night with one of her nipples in your mouth.*

Penny: *NO! We are not going all the way, remember?*

Levi: *What if I can't help it?*

Ollie: *She's right, we can't go all the way. This is torture, not satisfaction. If she turns over, tell her great tits and then get off her.*

Winnie: *The great tits comment will make her feel nice while you ghost her for the rest of the night. She'll be thinking, at least he said I have great tits.*

Penny: *Something for her to hold on to while she questions everything she ever did.*

Levi: *This sounds . . . mean.*

Blakely: *Did she or did she not walk in on you while you were coming on your stomach?*

Levi: *She didn't! There was no active cum.*

The door to the bathroom unlocks, and I quickly set my phone down and stare at the ceiling. I know I told her I wouldn't look, but as she enters the room, I glance over at her and the rolled-up flannel shorts she's wearing, along with the white tank top that does nothing to hide the shape of her breasts.

"What's wrong with those pajamas?" I ask.

She glances over at me as she sets her dirty but folded clothes by her bag.

"Just . . . the no bra thing."

"I'll survive," I say and then sit up. "Now lie down on the edge of the bed."

She pauses and stares at me quizzically. "Huh? I thought I was sleeping on the cot."

"You are," I say as I get out of bed, and her eyes take me all in. I walk over to the bathroom and snag the free lotion. "But you missed your massage today, and I'm going to make sure you get one."

Her unconvinced eyes meet mine as she asks, "You're going to give me a massage?"

"Yeah. Problem with that?" I hold up my hand and say, "Look at how big my palm is, how long my fingers are. I can't imagine you'd get a better massage from someone with smaller hands."

"Probably not," she says. "But isn't that crossing the line?"

"I'm not going to do anything inappropriate. Just ease the tension in your shoulders." I shrug. "It's fine if you don't want one, but the offer is there." I set the lotion down on the dresser and move toward the bed again while she stands in the middle of the room contemplating.

After a few seconds, she says, "This is so weird."

"What is?" I ask as I pick up my phone and see a text from the queens. I ignore it and go on TikTok, looking for highlights of the game.

"This whole thing. I didn't think I'd see you for a few days, and now I'm here, sharing a room with you, and you're offering to give me a massage. It just seems so odd."

"Well, that's what happens when you're a bologna lover. You shoot for the unexpected. By the way, did you grab a book about Maine?"

"All they had was Washington state. But I grabbed it anyway."

"Eh, I'll give it a try." When she stands there still, I glance over my phone and ask, "Are you going to get on your cot, or do you plan on running away in the middle of the night?"

Her teeth pull on her bottom lip as she says, "Well, I was looking forward to the massage."

Ha, she can't resist. I fucking love it.

"Then lie down," I say. "Promise, it'll be worth it."

Still slightly hesitant, she takes a seat on the bed but doesn't lie down. "You know, actually, I think I should just go to bed."

"Up to you," I say as I set down the lotion one more time.

"Yeah, I mean, it might be weird, you're paying me and all . . . unless . . ." Her eyes meet mine. "Are you asking because it will help release some of your adrenaline?"

Look at her looking for a way for this to be okay in her head. Here I am, ready to go, and she's trying to justify it.

"I'm asking because I feel bad that you didn't get your massage today, and I want to make it up to you, but if I make you uncomfortable, I get it."

"You don't," she says. "But I'm just trying to, you know, not cross that line."

"I get it. You can keep your shirt on if you want."

Her eyes widen. "You were going to have me take my shirt off?"

"That's usually what happens with massages."

"But I'm not wearing a bra."

I smirk at her. "I wasn't planning on giving your tits a rubdown, Wylie. That would cost you extra." I nod at the mattress. "Just lie down."

She chews on it for a second but then gives in and lies down on the bed.

I grab one of the flatter pillows to rest her head on, and then I ask, "Can I move your shirt up?"

"Um, I can just take it off, but can you turn around?"

"Sure," I answer as I turn away and hear her take her shirt off.

Deep breaths, man. Don't be the fucking creep with a boner over a girl taking her shirt off.

"Ready," she says.

When I face her, I'm greeted by the sight of her silky skin, ready to be touched.

Keep it together, Posey.

I squeeze some lotion on my hands, rub it together, and then place my hands on her shoulders.

She flinches with a squeak. "Oh my God, your hands are cold."

I chuckle softly. "Sorry." I bring them up to my mouth and warm them up for a second before I move them back down to her back. "That better?"

"Yes, thank you."

I lightly run my thumbs along her spine and across her shoulder blades, making little circles to tie up any of the knots she might have accumulated.

"I'm trying not to moan here, but God, that feels good."

And there's the first stir of arousal.

I knew this would happen.

She didn't even moan. She just talked about it.

And the girls thought this would be a good idea. Christ.

This is why I should help myself out and only myself out. Going to anyone else for advice is like asking a damp cloth for its opinion on how to handle a frisky, sexy assistant. It has no idea, it's a fucking damp cloth!

"Everything okay?" she asks.

"Huh?" I glance down at her as my hands continue to work over her back.

"You went silent on me."

"Oh, uh, just giving you the full experience."

She laughs. "You can talk, Levi. You don't have to be quiet."

"Are you sure? Oh shit, I didn't even turn on music."

"Do not turn on music. Seriously, you don't even need to do this. Bosses usually don't go full-service massage for their assistants."

"Clearly, they aren't winning boss of the year, then." I move my hands down to her lower back, where I press into the spot right above her ass.

"Oh fuck," she says, her hands crawling up to the pillow where she grips it. "Sorry, really sore there."

"Your lower back?" I ask.

"Yeah, I twist when I sleep and tend to lay on my stomach, which strains my lower back. I try not to, but it's how I feel the most comfortable."

"I get it," I say. "I like lying on my stomach too. Never on my back, I feel so exposed."

"Me too," she says as I work my hands back up her spine to her shoulders and neck. "I also feel like if I'm on my back, my eyes don't fully close. If I wake up on my back, my eyes feel dry. When my dad sleeps on his back, his eyes remain partially open."

I pause and lean to the side to look her in the face. "You're fucking with me."

She shakes her head. "Nope. Guaranteed, if you went to his hotel room right now, he'd be passed out on his back with his eyes partially open. It's some serial killer-type sleeping."

"Jesus." I shiver. "I don't know if that makes him less scary or scarier."

"Maybe a little of both."

I trail my hands down to her lower back again, where I knead her spine and the dimples just above her ass. Wylie Wood is perfect in just about every way. Her legs aren't super skinny, giving her a great plump ass that looks amazing in her shorts.

Her waist is a touch narrower than her hips, showing off an

hourglass figure, and then there's her top half that I think I've talked about a whole fucking lot.

Her hair is my undoing, her eyes are soul-searing, and the freckles on her freshly washed face make me fucking weak in the knees. The only negative about this woman is the fact that her father is Coach Wood, the underwear blesser, who sleeps with his eyes partially open and is a scary-as-shit ogre.

"How is the pressure?" I ask.

"Amazing," she says. "I'd love to know if any other bosses do this for their assistants."

"The answer would probably be no," I say as I make circles with my thumbs over the base of her spine, feeling the tension in her muscles. "Is your mattress in the nanny hole okay?"

"Yeah, it's comfortable," she answers. "Why?"

"Because your muscles are just tense is all."

"Like I said, I think it's because I sleep on my stomach."

"Yeah, okay."

I spend the next few minutes working my hands over her back, over her shoulders, against her neck. She groans and shifts and melts farther and farther into the mattress, her relaxation taking over, and I can't help but feel a slight hint of pride that she's that comfortable with me. That I can relax her to the point of . . . hold on . . .

Leaning forward just a little to look at her face, I notice that, yup . . . she's sleeping.

Well, there goes the side boob graze. Can't do it now. If I did it when she was sleeping, that would make me the ultimate pervert, and I already feel pretty low about myself. I don't need to add pervert into the mix.

I move off the bed and assess the situation. I don't want to wake her up. That seems cruel since she must be exhausted from all the shit I've made her do. And I can't move her myself because, well, she's not wearing a shirt, and therefore, I'd be moving around a topless girl, which would give me that pervert mark I'm trying to avoid.

Fuck.

I look over at the cot and then back at the king-sized bed where she's sleeping diagonally. There's no way I'd fit on that. And I know climbing into bed with her, with her shirt off, will be a big red flag as a boss.

It looks like I'm going to sleep on the goddamn cot.

Grumbling in annoyance, I find one of the spare blankets kept in the closet, and I drape it over her before I take my phone and charger to the cot. The entire thing creaks under my large body when I sit on it.

I swear to God if I end up folded in half in the morning because this thing has buckled under me, I'm going to have some choice words for the Queens.

Which makes me think . . .

I lie down on the cot, immediately noticing that my calf muscle to my foot is hanging off the end. *I'm far too big for this fucking thing.*

Could I wake her up? Yeah.

Do I want to wake her up and say, "Excuse me, ma'am, but you seem to have fallen asleep topless on my bed, and I'm going to need you to move it on over to the cot."

Not going to happen.

I type out a disgruntled text.

Levi: *I say this with respect, but you ladies have failed me, and I'm not so sure I can continue this journey with you. I fear your advice is not even a step above what I'd get from the men.*

I send it knowing the minute they see the text, they're going to respond. At least I would. When I was helping desperate Halsey with his love for Blakely, the number of times he told me to fuck off with advice, it cut deep.

And look at him now. He's lucky I hung around.

My phone buzzes in my hand, and the first text is from Penny —who I consider the leader, although, I'd never say that in fear that she'd assume too much power.

Penny: *Excuse me? Did you really just come into this thread to insult us?*

Levi: *I'm just speaking the truth.*

Ollie: *Well, the truth hurts.*

Levi: *Maybe give better advice.*

Blakely: *Whoa, where did all this hostility come from? A few days ago, we were queens, and now we're a step above the boys? I need an explanation.*

Winnie: *Sometimes I think my advice isn't that much better than Pacey's.*

Penny: *Winnie, pull yourself together. Of course your advice is better than Pacey's.*

Ollie: *I think before we start doubting ourselves, we need to have the man in this group explain himself.*

Levi: *"Massage her, touch her boob, it will be great." < - - that's what you said. Well guess what? I did massage her, but she fell asleep topless on my bed, and I can't move her because that would mean I touched her breasts, and if I touch her breasts, I'll get hard, not to mention, advance to pervert levels. So now I have to sleep on her cot, and because this cot was made for no bigger than a tween girl, my legs are hanging off the end. All because of you.*

Penny: *Hold on a second. She fell asleep?*

Levi: *Yeah. To my fucking luck, she fell asleep diagonally, so I can't even slip into the bed if I want to.*

Ollie: *Why did she fall asleep?*

Levi: *Because I have magical hands that not just handle a hockey stick, but will massage all your worries away. Should have known the kind of powers I possess.*

Winnie: *Pacey has great hands. And a great penis. God, I love his penis.*

Penny: *Winnie, babe, I know you're missing him, but remember, the sister is in this text thread.*

Winnie: *Sorry. I just miss his dick.*

Ollie: *I miss Silas and his piercings. God, I love it when he tells me to ride them.*

Blakely: *I miss Halsey's tongue. And his chest. I love playing with his nipples.*

Levi: *Really not interested in hearing about the above. Also, side note, Halsey does have great nipples.*

Blakely: *Have you touched them? Very responsive.*

Levi: *Can't say that I have but will be sure to accidentally graze them in the showers and see what happens.*

Winnie: *Ooo, graze Pacey's nipples too! I bet they harden like little pebbles.*

Ollie: *While you're at it, poke Silas's stomach. His nipples will shrivel up quickly. I do it all the time. I laugh about it, but he hates that I do it.*

Levi: *Any place on the stomach, or is there a certain spot?*

Penny: *Uh, hello! We're being blamed for someone else's faults. Focus, ladies.*

Blakely: *She's right. We gave you the goods, and you messed it up.*

Levi: *Hold on a goddamn second. I did not mess it up. I laid her down, even got her topless, and started massaging. I did it in my boxer briefs.*

Penny: *Wait, she shouldn't have fallen asleep. She should be buzzing with erotic torture at the moment. Did you not touch the side boob?*

Levi: *She fell asleep before I could even make a move to the side boob.*

Ollie: *Was she really tired?*

Winnie: *How long were you massaging her before she fell asleep?*

Levi: *I don't know, maybe like twenty minutes?*

Penny: *Twenty minutes and you still didn't touch the side boob? Oh my God, Posey, you weren't supposed to be a massage therapist, rubbing her worries away. You were supposed to diddle her orgasm button.*

Ollie: *Yeah . . . this is on you.*

Blakely: *Twenty minutes of just . . . massage. Woof, Posey.*

Levi: *What the hell was I supposed to do? The minute she lay down, start groping her? I wanted to warm her up a bit.*

Penny: *Warm her up for a minute and then start caressing all the places you shouldn't be caressing.*

Winnie: *I'm upset about this. Truly.*

Blakely: *Me too. This jackass comes in here thinking he can blame us when he's setting up to earn his massage license.*

Ollie: *It's insulting. I think we should just drop him out of the group. Clearly, he can't take instruction well and then to turn it around and blame us. Typical man.*

Penny: *All in favor of voting Posey out. Say aye.*

Winnie: *Aye!*

Blakely: *Aye.*

Ollie: *Aye.*

Levi: *WAIT! Don't vote me out. I'm sorry! I never should have blamed you. I see where I went wrong and take full responsibility for my mistakes. Please, please don't leave me out here alone with no direction. I'm in over my head, and I need you.*

Penny: **stares down at your pitiful self* I don't know, queens, what do you think?*

Ollie: *I appreciate the ability he has to quickly admit when he's wrong.*

Winnie: *It would have been nice if he called himself pathetic in the apology.*

Blakely: *I agree with that. An insult to himself would have been the icing on the cake.*

Levi: *I'm a pathetic little man. Please don't leave me. < - - that better?*

Winnie: *Much.*

Penny: *We shall take the night to think about this apology. But this is your one and only warning. We're the key to your success. Never forget that.*

Ollie: *Never!*

Winnie: **points finger at you* Never.*

Blakely: **Huffs**

Levi: *Thank you, Queens. Thank you.*

Chapter Twelve

WYLIE

The smell of fresh soap floats through the air as the tiniest sliver of light shines down on my face. Slowly, I open my eyes as there's a clunk sound followed by a "fuck" coming from the other room.

Where the hell am I?

A scratchy, uncomfortable blanket rubs against my bare back as I shift up, and that's when I realize I'm topless.

I quickly lie back down on the bed and take in my surroundings.

Hotel room.

Bed.

Topless.

Oh God. The massage last night.

Did I fall asleep?

I look around and see that the bed I'm lying on has been untouched. I glance behind me and notice the cot has been slept in.

No.

No. No. No.

He slept on the cot last night? This is humiliating.

I quickly sit up and find my tank top that's on the bed as well. I slip it over my head and then push my hair out of my face as I stand. Unsure of what to do, I move around in circles for a second just as the bathroom door opens, flooding the room in light.

Levi steps out in a low-slung towel, droplets of water dripping down his impressive chest, all the way to the deep V in his hips and the smallest patch of hair just above his pubic bone. His pecs flex and bounce when he stops, noticing me just standing in the middle of the room, and when our eyes meet, the slightest of smirks crosses his lips.

"Morning," he says while moving around me, his fresh soap scent making me feel delirious.

"G-good morning," I offer while I push my hair behind my ear. "Um, I'm sorry about last night."

"What are you sorry about?" he asks as he dips into his suit-case and pulls out a pair of briefs.

"Falling asleep while you massaged me."

He turns his back toward me, and then, to my utter shock, he releases his towel, baring his tight, sculpted rear end to me.

Mother of God.

Two things happen simultaneously.

My legs clench together from the sight of such a perfect rear end and my eyes squeeze shut in horror.

Oh my God, that's his bare ass.

His bare ass that I want to touch.

Rub.

Bite.

And he just so freely offered it up to me.

Why? Why would he do such a thing?

He turns around and picks up his towel, his playful eyes landing on me. "Don't sweat it. I've fallen asleep while getting massaged before." He walks by me, and in passing, he tips my chin up, only for his forearm to graze against my breast, causing my nipples to go hard.

Trying to gain control of the way my body's buzzing, I say, "But you slept on the cot."

"Yeah, that wasn't ideal," he says from the bathroom. "But I survived. Probably a good thing. I needed the punishment after such a shit game." He pops out of the bathroom, grasping the lotion we used last night. He holds it out to me and says, "Think you can lotion my shoulder blades for me? They've been feeling dry, and it's hard to reach them."

"Oh, uh, sure," I say as I walk up to his towering body. I take the lotion from him, squirt it in my hand, and then place my hand on his warm back. His muscles jolt under my touch, and I have to take a few calming breaths to avoid getting excited over the fact I'm touching him.

No, not just touching him, but rubbing him.

Would he be mad if I rubbed him all over? Down his chest, to his stomach . . . under his briefs?

Maybe he wants me to lotion his legs too.

Possibly a full-body experience?

I'm not opposed.

"Thanks. Sometimes in the winter with wearing all the protective gear, my shoulders and back can get super dry. I usually ask one of the boys to help me, but they hate it."

"Well, I'll rub lotion on you anytime, anywhere you want," I say, the words sounding far too desperate. *Or maybe that's just how I feel.* I have honestly never been this close to a man so well built. I've *seen* pictures of men like this, but right now, I'm touching one.

"And that's why you're a good assistant," he says when I finish up, sad that I don't get to touch him anymore. When he turns around, he smiles down at me, and for a moment, I feel like he's going to reach out and touch me, cup my face, and bring me in close to his chest. Maybe tell me how much he wants a repeat of our first night. "Think you can grab me some coffee?"

Poof. Just like that, I'm knocked right out of the fantasy and back to reality.

"Umm, yes," I say, blinking a few times. "What kind of coffee do you want?"

"The boys were talking about a place about twenty minutes away. Do you mind? I can't go out, or else I'll be taunted, and after last night, I'm not in the mood."

"Yeah, I can do that. Just let me take a quick shower—"

"Yeah, you don't have time for that," he says. "We leave in an hour and a half and still have to pack. Grabbing the coffee will take you at least fifty minutes, so you should probably get going now."

"Right, okay," I say. "Let me just grab a sweatshirt to put over my shirt and go to the bathroom."

"Tick-tock, Wylie."

My easygoing attitude quickly flashes to annoyance, but he doesn't seem to care as he takes a seat on the bed, kicks his feet up, wearing nothing but his briefs, and picks up the book I got him about Washington. "Pictures are great in this."

Right. You're his assistant.

Don't get caught up in him.

Or the tasks.

Or the irritation.

Get the job done and work on yourself.

TO SAY my morning was chaotic is an understatement.

After I sprinted across town to get some coffee that was average at best, I flew into his room with him still in his briefs, but this time on his phone watching highlights. He thanked me for the coffee and then told me that I had to pack for him and we were leaving in fifteen minutes.

So I took the quickest shower of my life, packed myself, and then packed him while he slowly dressed into one of the sweatsuits I got him.

And do you know what's really annoying about that?

He looked fucking good in it.

Like, really good. The sweatshirt didn't cover his butt, so his high and tight rear end was shapely represented by the sweatpants. And since the sweatpants were a jogger fit, his ankles showed against the white of his shoes, which hit me hard for some reason.

It was hot.

Very hot.

So hot that I grew incredibly irritated with him and stopped talking while I finished packing.

In silence, we walked to the player bus, and I climbed on, sitting in the front with the staff, where I stared out the window. I thought about texting Sandie, but I didn't want to get into what happened last night.

Why did he even want to massage me? Because he felt bad? Well, he didn't have to take matters into his own hands. And why did I say yes? Because I'm desperate for the man? Because I wanted to feel his strong hands on my skin? Because I was possibly hoping that it would have turned into so much more?

That's probably the reason.

And I know better than that. It can't turn into anything. I can't get distracted, and that's exactly what's going on.

I've put the logo design for Patty Ford on hold despite the entry form closing soon. I can't seem to find the right font for what I need, and instead, I've been sketching on my iPad in Procreate, just having fun and playing with the techniques I've learned in my classes. I really enjoy just . . . drawing.

It kept me busy while on the plane ride to Chicago as well.

Dad is in the front with all the coaches and staff, probably discussing tomorrow's game. Levi and his friends are toward the middle, a lot of them playing games on their Nintendo Switches —something that will always be funny to me—and a few people are toward the back like Halsey Holmes, who is quietly reading to himself.

I am in the row that's right in front of the bathroom, which is always pleasant, especially when the backup goalie, Torres, decided to spend a solid twenty minutes in there. When he left, he offered me a wink as he walked back to his seat, a stench trailing him.

Disgusting.

"Would you like anything to drink?" the flight attendant asks after she's served everyone else.

"I'm good. Thank you, though."

"Are you sure?"

I nod. "Yeah."

"Well, if you need anything, just ask."

"Thank you," I say, but she doesn't move away, so I look back up at her. "Everything okay?" I ask.

"Are you the coach's daughter?"

"Yes," I say, straightening up.

She nods and looks toward the front of the airplane.

"Is everything okay with him?" I ask, confused.

"Oh yes, sorry, don't mean to worry you. I was just wondering, do you know if he's seeing anyone?"

My expression falls flat as I look up the aisle at my father's bald and shiny head. It's no secret that he's claimed as one of the hotties in the hockey coaching world. He stays in great shape, has that grumpy façade that women tend to like, and he dresses very well, thanks to the stylist he hired a few years back after a magazine shoot he did.

But this, this feels a bit much for me.

"Uh, not that I know of," I say. "Then again, he doesn't talk to me about that stuff."

She nods. "Okay, well, thanks for letting me know, and I'm sorry if I made you uncomfortable. I just felt like, I don't know, there was some flirting, and I thought about giving him my number."

"Flirting?" I scoff, my eyes feeling like they're about to fall out of my face. There is no way Will Wood was flirting. Unless she considers a snarl to his lip flirting, which, in that case, he's flirting twenty-four seven. "My dad was flirting with you?"

"Well, it felt like it. He was touching my hand."

"What?" I nearly shout, drawing the attention of a few people around me, so I lower my voice. "He touched your hand?"

"Is that uncommon?"

I set my iPad down and say, "To be fair . . . uh, what's your name?"

"Giselle."

"Giselle, nice to meet you, but to be fair, I'm not even sure my dad has a sex drive at this point. Unless I don't know anything, I think he's been celibate for nearly my entire life. The man doesn't know what touching is."

She smiles softly. "Hmm, okay. Well, it seems like maybe he does because this isn't the first time it's happened."

I sit taller in my seat. "Excuse me? He's touched you before?"

"Several times and they were always subtle, but this last time just felt like something was there so I was going to slip my number on a napkin. Think that's too much?"

"I mean . . ." I blink a few times. "If you think there's something there, might as well go for it, but don't be alarmed if he doesn't call you."

"I won't take offense." She smiles. "Thank you. I know this was probably awkward, but I just wanted to make sure he was free game before I slipped my number to him. A few flight attendants don't care about that and will hand out their numbers to players, but I never want to be that person."

"Really?" I ask.

"Oh, yeah."

Feeling curious, I ask, "Anyone in particular?"

She looks up the aisle and says, "Uh, a few here and there, but they mainly go to Levi Posey."

Figured that's what her answer would be.

"Ah, my boss," I say.

"Levi is your boss?"

I nod. "I'm his assistant."

"Wow, well, Jessica handed him her number today, so be prepared for that."

"Jessica, the blonde up front?" I ask.

Giselle nods. "Yes, she's had her eye on him for a while and finally got the nerve to hand over her number."

"Did he take it?" I ask.

"Oh yeah. Thanked her with a wink. She's more than excited about the possibility of what might happen."

"I'm sure," I say as a sour feeling fills my gut. "I'll be sure to help her any way that I can." I smile.

"Ooo, I'll be sure to tell her that. Thanks again for the chat. You're really cool . . . uh, what's your name?"

"Wylie," I reply.

"Such a cute name. Well, it was nice meeting you, Wylie."

"You too, Giselle, and who knows, maybe you'll be my new stepmom one day."

She pauses for a moment, then lets out a nervous laugh. "Wouldn't that be something?"

"I like presents on my birthday and Christmas, plus cards on holidays with cash. Don't disappoint me."

She chuckles again and stands taller. "We'll see, Wylie." And with that, she takes off down the aisle, the sway in her ass drawing the attention of some of the men on the plane.

Well, that was . . . not what I expected.

I stare out the window, the puffy clouds passing by as I think about a lady handing my dad her number. Do I care if my dad dates someone? Absolutely not. I honestly think he should. Maybe he wouldn't be so irritable all the time. And maybe he does have fun outside of being home. Then again, he takes hockey so seriously that he doesn't even like it when his players hook up on away trips, so why would he do it himself?

The thought of my dad being a flirt makes me almost dry-heave. I can't imagine it. I can't imagine him being any other way than stern with a pinch in his brow. But who knows, maybe he just saves that demeanor for little old, lucky me.

And then there's Jessica making a move on Levi.

I get it. He has a reputation. Besides some of the newer guys with less playing time, he's one of the only single guys on the team. Easy target. Makes amazing money, has the accolades, has all the charm and good looks—I should know because I fell for it.

But it irks me.

It irks me that he'd take her number. *Nothing can happen between us. Ever.* And just look at her. Ugh.

Tall and skinny with gorgeous blond hair. She's nothing like me. She's the kind of girl with poise and confidence, someone you take home to your parents who then charms them with her smooth handshake and adorable, hoity laugh that gathers the attention of all around. She's the kind of girl who listens in bed, who will do anything to pleasure her man, even if it means giving up her right to an orgasm. She's polished and probably has a twelve-step skincare routine at night and in the morning. She's the girl with the put-together apartment made for grown-ups . . . she's . . . well, she's who my dad would be proud of.

She's the kind of woman I could see with Levi. She'd hold her head high while they walked down some red carpet together. She'd smile for the camera when they visited the local children's hospital. She'd wave to fans while in the stands, watching her man play, and she'd do it with a princess wave. Everyone would fawn over her.

There would be T-shirts made.

Team Jessica.

Go Jessica's Man.

I'm here for the Jessica content.

"Whatcha doin'?"

I nearly leap out of my seat at Levi's voice, startling me away from the clouds and back into reality.

"My God," I say, clutching my chest and looking up at him. "Why didn't you announce yourself?"

"I did," he says with a smirk that I know Jessica will fall head over heels for. "That's why I asked, whatcha doin'?"

"That's not announcing yourself."

"It's not?" he asks as he takes a seat on the armrest of the chair across from me. His large body takes up all the space in the aisle, so it feels like he's practically sitting on my lap. "Should I have made a trumpet sound and then said, 'presenting, the hottest d-man in the league, Sir Levi Posey'?"

I tilt my head against the headrest. "Yes, that would have been preferred."

"Noted for next time." He nods at me. "What are you doing?"

"Uh, drawing, why? What are you doing? Looking for more bagels? Unfortunately, I'm willing to do a lot for you, but parachuting out of an airplane for bagels is not one of them."

He chuckles and shakes his head. "Nah, just came back to see how you were doing."

"Fine," I say, feeling suspicious. I study him for a second. "It seems like you want something."

He shakes his head. "Can't a boss just check on his employee?"

"Yes, but you have this look about you like you're up to something."

"Stop being so skeptical. I'm up to nothing." He crosses his legs at his ankles and taps my iPad. "Working on those logos?"

I shake my head. "No, I was getting frustrated, so I was just drawing."

"What were you drawing?"

I jut my chin out. "Nothing of your concern."

His brows rise. "Nothing of my concern? Well, now you have me intrigued. What could possibly not be of my concern? What are you hiding in there?" Leaning in close, he asks, "Fantasy pics possibly?"

"What do you mean fantasy pics?" I ask.

"You know, maybe some naked drawings of your go-to girl, Patty. Maybe some of your favorite boss . . ." He wiggles his brow.

"I did not draw you." Although I did do a rough sketch the other day, and the guy turned out to look like Levi, but that's not anything he needs to know.

"Shame, I think I'd be a pretty good drawing subject."

I cross my arms at my chest. "Oh yeah, what makes you think that?" I ask.

"Well, for one"—he holds up one finger—"I'm built like a god. I'm handsome and firm, tight in all the right places, which is great experience in drawing for you."

"Very fond of ourselves, aren't we?" I ask.

He winks. "Very. Second, I know how to sit still. I'm pretty good at it. I've been sitting still almost this entire flight until I came back here to see what you were doing."

"Wow, that is very impressive."

"Tell me about it. And last, I'm easy to please. Set me up with a pose that shows off my junk in a beautiful way, hand me a bologna sandwich, and I'm good to go for at least an hour."

Trying not to show just how idiotically charming he is, I say, "And what exactly would that pose be?"

"Isn't it obvious?"

I shake my head, the movement causing my hair to fall in my face. I reach up to push it behind my ear, but Levi beats me to it.

He lightly moves my hair across my cheeks, his fingers skimming the sensitive flesh, and then behind my ear. Stunned, I look up at him as a wave of goosebumps erupts on my body.

Leaning in slightly, he says, "We'd acquire a stool. I'd strip down to nothing, and then I'd prop one leg up on the stool as if it was a rock and I was claiming what's mine. My balls and dick would proudly be on display. If I were erect or not would be up to you. Either way, my package would be handsome to draw."

I clear my throat. "Wow, that's quite the image. What, uh, what would I do with this drawing?"

"Give it to me of course so I can hang it above my fireplace. Is there really any other way to honor the masterpiece?"

"How do you know it would be a masterpiece?" I ask. "What if I make your dick too small and your balls too large?"

"Nothing is too large."

"Two soccer balls dangling between your legs isn't too large?" I ask.

"Never."

I chuckle and shake my head. "What a load of crap."

"Art is interpretation, Wylie. If you choose to draw two soccer balls or two dingleberries, that's up to you. It's up to me to decipher that choice and analyze it."

"Well, I guess it's a good thing I don't plan on drawing you, so we don't have to leave you to decipher anything."

He sighs. "Shame, I was looking forward to soccer ball testicles."

I shrug. "I guess you can't have it all."

He smiles at me. "I guess not."

"Mr. Posey?" We both turn to see Jessica standing in the aisleway. "Is there anything I can offer you? We land in about thirty minutes, and I just want to make sure you're comfortable."

Does he look uncomfortable, Jessica?

Does he look like he needs you to offer anything?

Does he seem to be pained in any way?

The answer is no, no . . . and no. So begone.

"I'm good, but thanks, Jessica. I appreciate it."

"Of course, anytime." And with that, she walks down the aisle and tends to some of the other players.

Levi brings his attention back to me, and I can't help myself when I say, "Are you going to call her?"

He lifts one brow in a quizzical way. "How do you know I have her number?"

"The other flight attendant, Giselle, told me when she asked if my dad was single."

"She wants to go out with Coach Wood?" he whispers and looks toward the front of the plane. "In all the years he's been my coach, I don't think I've ever seen him even look at a woman."

"I haven't seen him glance at a woman either since my mom left either. I think he's dead inside when it comes to romance."

"What did you say to Giselle?" he asks, more invested in this than I thought he'd be.

"She could go for it, but I wasn't giving her a lot of hope."

Glancing toward the front of the plane again, he asks, "Does he even understand what a date is?"

"At this point, I think he considers the term date more of something he eats to help with constipation rather than an opportunity for conversation and a meal."

Levi lets out a roar of a laugh, and the sound travels through me, all the way down to my toes, warming me up.

"Please tell me he eats dates for constipation."

"Are you really interested in my dad's bowel movements?"

"Oddly, yes. Anything to give me that edge when he's yelling at me, spittle flying off his lips and right onto my eyeball."

"Has that happened?" I ask.

"Several times. So give me the goods. Does he have a secret stash of dates when he has a sicky belly of poop?"

I flinch in disgust. "Please, don't refer to it as that."

He chuckles. "Well . . ."

I twist my lips to the side, pretending to give it some thought, then I lean closer to him and say, "He has a date every morning and night to stay regular."

"Is this before or after he blesses his underwear?"

I grin. "Before."

"Good to know." He nods.

"What about Jessica?" I ask, bringing it back to the conversation he clearly avoided.

"What about her?"

"You going to call her?"

He rubs his hand along his jaw and shakes his head. "Not my type."

"Jessica's not your type?" I ask, flabbergasted. "I feel like she's everyone's type."

"Not mine," he says.

"Is that so? Then what is your type?" I ask.

He stands and sticks his hands in his pockets. He looks down at me and says, "I'm staring at it." With that, he heads back toward the middle of the plane, leaving me in utter disarray.

Because who says that and walks away?

Levi Posey, that's who.

———

"SO, couldn't splurge for the extra room again?" I ask as I stare at the cot in his hotel room.

"Told you I need you close in case I need anything."

When we arrived in Chicago, we went straight to the arena. Dad wanted to carve some time out for them to warm up their legs, get some motion into them, and visit with the trainers for any treatment needed. Levi was there longer than I expected, which gave me time to catch up on his social media. Once I began posting, I realized just how much work it is to keep up with all the comments and responses. I don't comment on them, but I like to see what people are saying so I can continue giving them the Levi content they want.

He also had me run a few errands, like grabbing him some bologna for the game tomorrow and for a snack today.

I watched him stuff a sandwich in his mouth with three bites. It was equally impressive and disgusting.

He sets his suitcase to the side and takes a look at his watch. "Fuck, I'm hungry. Want to grab something to eat?"

"Uh, I mean, yes, but do you want to eat with your assistant? Not with your guys?"

"They're all doing other things." He takes a step forward and tugs on my hand. "You're not going to make me eat alone, are you?"

My mouth goes dry.

"When you say it like that, it looks like we're going to dinner."

"Good decision." Once again, he pushes some hair behind my ear. "Let's go."

I swallow down the nerves scattering through me and grab my wallet and phone from my bag, and together, we head down the elevator to the hotel restaurant.

While we wait for a table, he says, "Feels full circle, doesn't it?"

I look up at him. "Are you referring to the first night we met?"

"Yup." He reaches up and twists a strand of my hair around his finger. "Although, I doubt you'll be palming my dick tonight."

I nearly choke on my own saliva as the hostess comes back. With two menus in hand, she directs us toward a two-person table right next to a fireplace.

Very romantic.

Very intimate.

Very *not* what I was hoping for.

I'm trying to keep this professional.

I'm trying to make sure I keep my hands to myself.

But it's as if something has switched in his head.

The touches.

The comments.

The dripping-wet body in a barely-there towel.

It's almost as if the roles have reversed, and he's taunting me.

Levi pulls my chair out before he takes his seat. We're facing each other with the fire on the right, brimming with flames and casting a glow on us as the hostess sets down our menus.

"Jared will be with you shortly."

"Thank you," Levi says, scanning the menu. "Hmm, I'm in the mood for a burger. What about you?" He glances up at me, and I find myself staring, confused that he can be so casual about this.

Glancing down at the menu, I try to rid my thoughts and not be awkward about this. "Umm, I'm kind of feeling a pasta dish."

"Interesting. I thought you'd get a burger as well."

"Why's that?" I ask. "Think I like copying you, and I don't have a mind of my own?" I use a teasing tone so he doesn't think I'm serious.

"No, just seems like you like a lot of meat in your mouth."

My jaw falls open as I stare at him blankly.

He chuckles. "Burger meat, Wylie."

"That is so not what you meant, and you know it."

He smirks. "Take it as you will."

"Well, for your information, I like carbs, so therefore, it will be a pasta dish for me. This primavera looks good."

He scratches the side of his head. "Or do I want tacos? I love a taco in my mouth."

"There aren't tacos . . ." I pause and look up at his grinning face. "Why are you the way that you are?" I ask.

"Why do I like tacos? Well—"

I hold up my hand to stop him. "I meant . . . never mind." I shake my head.

"Do you not like tacos?"

"No, I like tacos," I say, "but I know tacos aren't really what you're talking about."

He leans back in his chair. "And what exactly am I talking about?"

"You're talking about the vagina—"

"Uh, I can come back."

I'm startled as our server steps up to our table, ready to take our order. My cheeks flame with embarrassment as Levi says, "Oh no, I think we're ready. The lady will have the pasta primavera, and I'll take the tacos."

"Great. And to drink?"

Levi looks at me, but I'm still embarrassed about the vagina comment, so he says, "Water for both. Thank you."

"Not a problem. I'll put that right in."

When the server leaves, Levi says, "Not sure where your mind is at, but I was really talking about the tacos."

"I didn't see tacos on the menu, and you knew he was coming up behind me, didn't you? You made me say vagina to him."

"Technically, it wasn't to him. And it could have been worse. You could have said pussy. At least you used the scientific term. The classy version."

I cross my arms over my chest. "I don't think there's any classy way to refer to the female genitalia."

"Not true, you just said it. Female genitalia. Wow, nothing makes me harder than calling a delicious pussy the female genitalia. Talk about a turn-on."

"Delicious?" I ask, brows raised.

"Oh yeah, love eating a good pussy."

Dear God in heaven.

I squeeze my legs together as I clear my throat. "Well, that's new information."

"One of my favorite things to eat," he continues. "If it was on the menu, I would have ordered it." Then he looks at me with those devilish eyes and says, "Maybe for dessert." He winks, and I quickly rise from the table. His eyes track my jerky movements.

"I, uh, I need to make a phone call." Before he can respond, I move toward the back corner of the restaurant, where I hide away from Levi and pull out my phone. Quickly, I dial up Sandie and hope she answers.

On the third ring, she does.

"Hey, how's it going?" she asks.

"Not good," I hiss into the phone.

"Uh, okay, what's going on?"

"He's different," I say.

"I assume we're talking about Levi. How is he different?"

I look past the corner, over at our table where he's sitting casually, staring right at me.

I squeak out a sound before I move out of sight again. "He's . . . he's sexually charged," I answer.

"Describe how he's sexually charged."

"Well, besides the fact that his entire demeanor went from she's off limits to I'm pushing her hair behind her ear now, he's walking around in a towel, all wet from the shower, telling me that I'm his type when there's a woman more suited to him serving him drinks on the airplane, and now he just offered up my vagina for dessert."

"He really said that? That he was going to eat you for dessert?" she asks, shocked.

"Well, not blatantly, but in a roundabout way, yes. And then there's just little things, like, oh, he gave me a massage! And he touches me and twirls my hair. I feel like he's flipped the switch, and he's the one doing erotic torture, not me."

She's silent for a second and then says, "Maybe he is."

"Huh?"

She gasps. "Maybe . . . maybe he knows you know."

"What are you talking about?" I ask as I look past the corner again. This time, Levi twiddles his fingers at me in a wave.

I quickly hide again, squeezing my eyes shut.

"Maybe he knows that you know about the agreement he has with your dad."

I pause and think about it. Consider his transformation. He was skittish, adamant about keeping things platonic and then, all of a sudden, he switched his behavior. A complete one-eighty.

I mean, hell, we're sharing a hotel room in case he needs me in the middle of the night to do God knows what.

It wouldn't be too hard to get me a hotel room. I could easily tend to his every need from another room. And since I've been here, I really haven't done anything.

So maybe . . .

Maybe Sandie is right.

"You really think he knows?" I ask.

"No idea. It's a hunch, though. Did you give him any indication that you know?"

"No, but I did stop the erotic torture, and shortly after that, he picked it up." I press my hand to my forehead. "Do you think he knows about the erotic torture somehow and just decided to play me at my own game?"

"Possibly. Does it feel like he's playing the erotic torture game?"

"I mean . . ." I think about it, tugging on the corner of my lip. "Not as blatant as I was at times, but yeah, it feels like he's trying to turn me on or at least get me to slip somehow."

"Then I bet he knows. How could he not? He was so adamant about not crossing the line with you and keeping all zippers zipped up and all nipples stuffed away. I bet he knows and is playing you at your own game."

I grumble under my breath. "Of course." I rest my head against the wall. "Of course he freaking knows. Why else would he be pulling this stunt?"

"Well, also maybe because he finds you attractive."

"He's said that, I know, but to risk that attraction?" I shake my head even though she can't see me. "No, he's playing the game."

"And what game is that? Because I know I've been a part of this from the beginning, but I'm still confused. What the hell is going on?"

"The *who is going to break first* game," I say.

"And when you say break, you mean . . ."

"Give in to the eroticism. Come on, Sandie, keep up."

"Right, right. We're always coming back to the eroticism."

"Exactly." I shake my head. "God, he thought he was so good. He thought he could just skate on by, drive me nuts with his pectorals on display and his bulge ready to be unwrapped. Ohhhh no, I see right through him. When I said this is war, I meant it, Sandie. Time to strap on the war paint."

"You know, you sound a bit, um, unhinged at the moment, and I just want to make sure we're maintaining our goals."

"Oh, we're maintaining them all right. We're controlling our goals. We're taking the men by the dick, and we're making them all suffer."

"Okay, so when you say things like that, do you mean you're taking your dad by the dick as well? Because although I enjoy the play on words, I'm just afraid we're not thinking entirely straight here."

"I would never grab my dad by the dick."

"Good, okay, now I feel like we're—"

"But I would grab him by the man nipples."

"Ehh, okay, now we're back to me being concerned."

"No need to be concerned," I say, feeling slightly crazed. "Everything is on the up and up."

"What do you mean by that?"

The warrior inside me takes over as I say, "I mean, we're no longer going to sit back and be the good girl worker. Ohhhh no, if he wants to play with me, then I'll play with him. First one to cave loses."

"Ah, I see. So we're not going to tell him that you know he knows that you know? We're just going to continue this battle?"

"Battle? Ohhhh no, Sandie. This is war now. All of this is war. I was sidetracked for a second there, trying to please my dad, but not anymore. I'm doing this for me and me alone."

"I like that attitude, but what are you going to do?"

I squeeze the phone in my hand and say, "Erotic torture is back on."

"Oh dear God in heaven . . ."

Chapter Thirteen

LEVI

Levi: *She knows that I know that she knows.*

   Penny: *That strangely makes sense.*

   Ollie: *How do you know?*

   Levi: *Not much time. Out to dinner with her, she scuttled away and is talking on the phone. Probably to her friend. She keeps looking over at me. No doubt she knows.*

   Winnie: *Think she'll confront you?*

   Levi: *No, I think she's going to bring it.*

   Blakely: *What do you mean?*

   Penny: *Like fight your fire with her fire?*

   Levi: *Yup. Queens, prepare yourselves because I think this is the climax. We're about to walk into dangerous territories.*

   Ollie: *Why am I excited?*

   Winnie: *I'd be lying if I said I wasn't wishing I was a fly on the wall.*

   Penny: *Are you going to hold strong?*

   Blakely: *Or are you going to fold?*

Levi: *What do you guys think?*
Ollie: *Hold strong.*
Winnie: *Don't cave.*
Penny: *Do whatever you can not to fuck her, but almost fuck her.*
Blakely: *This is your moment. Prove to us that you can handle this!*
Levi: *I will. I can. I shall not break.*
Penny: *That's our boy!*
Blakely: *Make her sweat!*
Winnie: *Make her yearn.*
Ollie: *Spank her!*
Penny: *No spanking, Ollie. But . . . maybe a little accidental choking could work.*

Shaking my head, I put my phone in my pocket just as Wylie approaches, and from the gleam in her eye and the smirk on her lips, my assessment is confirmed. We're in this game together, both aware of what we're after and ready to play.

And there's a voice in the back of my head that's saying, *don't.*

That's reminding me of the repercussions.

That's telling me this is a bad, bad idea.

But fuck . . . just look at her.

Look at the way she's strutting toward me, full of confidence.

The grin that tugs at her plump lips.

The sway of those tempting hips.

How could I not play the game?

At least for a moment in time.

A moment when I can forget about what would happen if I took one simple taste.

Who am I kidding? Nothing about this woman is simple.

When she takes a seat at the table, I ask, "Everything okay?"

"Everything's great." She puts her phone face down and then adjusts her napkin on her lap. "I hope I wasn't gone too long. A craving of bagels didn't happen upon you, did it?"

I smile. "Not yet, but I'll be sure to let you know, maybe around two this morning."

"I can't wait. I love getting up in the middle of the night to fetch you breakfast carbs."

"You know"—I cross my arms over my chest—"I knew you liked it. It was a guess, but that's why I kept sending you because I thought it fulfilled something within you."

"Oh, it does. Nothing makes me happier than making you happy." And then, her foot rubs up against my leg under the table.

Yup.

She's playing, and I'm all fucking in.

Consider my will being snapped.

My strength weakened.

My need for her too strong.

The question is, who will break first? Because it sure as hell won't be me.

And just like that, this agony I've been living through just got a touch more fun.

"Besides making me happy, what brings you joy, Wylie? What are your hobbies? What do you like to do when you're not fetching bagels for me?"

She shrugs but continues to rub her foot over my leg under the table, and I just allow it. "Hobbies . . . I like trying new things."

"What kind of new things?" I ask.

Her foot runs up to my knee. "Experiences, going out to clubs, things like that."

"What kinds of clubs?" I wet my lips, letting my eyes flash to her mouth and back up.

"I think you know what kinds of clubs."

I smirk. Look at her turning on a dime. She was a bumbling mess before, and now she's ready to battle. Let's see how far I can push her because if anything, I'm a competitor, and I'll be damned if I don't win . . . whatever the hell this is.

"Yeah, have you ever fucked in one?"

She twists her lips to the side and shakes her head. "Just watched." Her eyes meet mine as she asks, "Have you?"

I rub my hands together and lean back in my chair. "What do you think, Wylie?"

Even though she's putting up a façade, her cheeks blush a pretty shade of pink. "I think you have."

I lift my glass of water to my lips. "You would be right."

"Do you prefer it that way? Keeping it at the club?"

I shake my head. "I have no preference as long as I have a good time and so does my partner."

She nods. "Well, if you ever need someone to go to one with you, I can go."

"Yeah. Maybe have a little company party?" I wiggle my brows. "Help your boss pick someone up?"

"I don't think you need help."

"Very true, but I'd love to see what your thoughts are on who you think I should be with."

She pauses for a moment and glances around the room. "You know, I think Jessica on the airplane was a very good option for you."

"Like I said, she's not my type."

"Then why did you take her number?" she asks, crossing her arms over her chest.

"It's called being polite," I answer. "I'm not about to be a dick to her and say no thanks."

"Instead, you're going to get her hopes up and make her wait by the phone?"

I shake my head. "No. I already texted her."

Wylie sits taller as her expression changes to surprise. "Wait, really?"

"Yup."

"So . . . uh . . . that means that you're going to meet up with her?"

"What makes you think that?" I ask.

"Well, you texted her. I'm assuming that means you plan to meet up with her."

I shake my head. "No, I texted her to tell her I was flattered, but I'm into someone else at the moment."

Her mouth slightly falls open, but then she masks her reaction and glances down at her silverware, quickly moving to look busy.

"That was, uh . . . that was nice of you to let her down like that."

"Yeah, thought it was the decent thing to do."

Her eyes meet mine again when she asks, "So if you're into someone else, then why do you want me to help you find someone at a club to fuck?"

"Because the person I'm into can't offer me what I want. What I need, therefore, I need to expel this energy somehow."

"Oh . . . makes sense."

"Don't you ever get so incredibly horny that you just need someone, anyone to fuck?"

She wets her lips softly. "I usually resort to my vibrator."

"A viable option, but sometimes, Wylie, that just isn't enough," I say just as our food arrives at our table.

Perfect timing.

———

LEVI: *Reporting in. I'm going full force. I jacked up the AC in the hotel room to force her into my bed.*

Ollie: *Clever.*

Penny: *What's the plan for sharing a bed?*

Winnie: *Levi, you realize her nipples are going to be incredibly hard. Can you handle it?*

Levi: *I want her nipples hard so they're more sensitive. And the plan . . . to tease the ever-living fuck out of her. I want this over by tonight. I want her begging me, so I can win and it all be done.*

Ollie: *Well, I just got horny.*

Penny: *You're always horny.*

Winnie: *I've never met anyone hornier than you, Ollie.*

Levi: *I'd agree with that statement. The horniest.*

Ollie: *I wear the label with pride.*

Penny: *Well, good luck. I approve.*

Winnie: *Approved.*

Ollie: *Go for it!*

Levi: *Where's Blakely?*

Blakely: *Trying to have phone sex with my man, so stop texting!*

Chuckling, I set my phone down on my nightstand and am plugging it in just as Wylie exits the bathroom. She's carrying her clothes from tonight and strutting around in a pair of tiny silk shorts and a tank top.

Her legs and ass fill out the shorts so when she walks, they ride up. Her shirt clings to her chest and stomach, leaving nothing to the imagination.

Fuck, she's so fine.

And I like her especially like this. No makeup, hair in a messy bun, casual. She looks cuddly and like I could wrap my entire body around her to keep her warm and protected.

"My goodness, it's chilly in here," she says as she sets her clothes down and looks around to find the thermostat. Her eyes zero in on it, then she glances over at me as I lie casually on the bed, the blankets barely covering my torso. "Did you want it to be an icebox in here?"

"Yeah, I was too hot in our last hotel room. I prefer it to be cold."

"Okay, well, it's freezing." She turns toward me and points at her chest. "Look at my nipples. They're hard as stone."

I wet my lips, very satisfied with looking at her nipples that I can nearly see through her shirt.

"Nipples look great to me," I say. "No complaints."

"Says my boss," she says.

"Hey, you're the one who told me to look at them. I'm just doing as I'm told."

She rolls her eyes and walks over to her cot where she slips under the covers. I turn out the light and sink into the mattress, just waiting for my moment to pop the question.

I listen as she moves on her cot, trying to get comfortable.

After the third jostle, I say, "Everything okay over there?"

"Fine, just trying to get warm."

I smile and place my hand behind my head as I stare up at

the ceiling. "You know, you can always join me in my bed if you're cold. I run hot."

I hear her still, and I can't contain my smile. She comes off tough, like she can hang in this sexual warfare, but I think it's all show. I don't think she can hang at all. I think she's trying to grasp anything to make it seem like she can hang, but in reality, I own this battle.

"You want me to sleep in your bed?" she finally asks.

"I don't want you to do anything. I'm just offering since you're so cold," I answer.

She's silent again, and I know she's thinking about it.

I hope she says yes because I want nothing more than to be able to sleep next to her, to hold her, to fucking drive her mad with need.

After a few seconds, she says, "If I go in your bed, I'll need to use your body warmth."

"Use me any way you want, Wylie," I say.

After another bout of silence, she leaves the cot and moves over to my side of the bed. Her silhouette comes into view, so I lift the bed sheets and let her in. She slips under the covers and then curls away from me and into one of my pillows.

Not even wanting to give her a second to reconsider, I wrap my arm around her waist and pull her into my bare chest, exposing her to my body heat.

"Warm?" I whisper into her ear.

I can feel her breathing hitch as she says, "Yes. That's, uh, that's better."

"Good," I say. "Can't have my assistant cold." I keep my arm around her as I press my chin up against her head, loving how she so easily fits right into the little spoon position, like she was made for me to hold her.

And hell, I know this was my choice, that I thought this was a good idea, but having her this close, feeling her in my arms, I fear that I might be the one who breaks.

But what does breaking even mean?

Because if I graze her boob, is that breaking? Or is that teasing? In my mind, breaking would be a kiss or going full throttle fucking. I think a graze here and a tease there never hurt anyone. That's all part of the game, part of the strategy, right?

My question is, what's going to be her move?

Sure, she's here in my bed, but she can't possibly just be here. She has to have a move. Any kind of move, something that's going to—

She wiggles her ass right against my crotch, getting comfortable.

And yup, there it is.

That's her fucking move and what a great one.

Because my dick immediately wants more.

My dick wants that to happen again. Multiple times.

"You good?" I slide my hand to her stomach.

"Yes," she says as her stomach contracts from my touch.

"Good, because I can't have you uncomfortable." I move my hand up her stomach to rest just below her breast. "Can't remember the last time I cuddled with someone," I say. "And I know I've never cuddled with an employee before."

"Would you consider this cuddling?" she asks. "I thought it would classify under trying to stay warm."

"Hmm, perhaps," I say. "But the ass wiggle against my dick, that wasn't keeping warm, was it?"

"It's called friction, Levi. We need some to stay warm."

"Hmm, okay, so then if I were to, I don't know, graze the underside of your breast like this"—I glide my hand under her heavy breast, causing her to inhale sharply—"that would be friction, right?"

"That, yes, that would be friction."

"Good to know. Well, I can offer you many types of friction, then. I can use just my thumb." I drag my thumb over the underside of her breast causing her to lean her head back against my shoulder. "I can use my whole hand." I drag the back of my hand under her breast. "Or I can use my palm," I say as I cup the underside of her breast, wanting so much more than these little teases. "You just let me know what you want."

I bring my hand back to her stomach, despite wanting to do so much more than that.

If I had it my way, I'd strip her out of her shirt, flip her to her back, and play with her tits until she came, then I'd tuck her into my chest and sleep like that for the rest of the night.

"Which was your favorite?" she asks.

"The thumb drag," I answer. "Not too much friction, but I enjoyed the way it made your body heat."

"How do you know I heated?" she asks as she presses her ass against my hardening dick. It's going to be a long fucking night.

"I could feel it," I answer as I run my thumb along the sensitive flesh of her breast again. She lets out a low breath as I graze her back and forth. "Your entire body stills, and I know in your mind, as your blood boils with need, you don't just want my thumb playing with your breast, but you want it passing over your nipple."

"You think highly of yourself," she says. "I don't think a nipple pass is creating that much friction."

"Friction, no, but will it skyrocket the heat level in your body?" I lean in close to her ear. "You'll be a fucking inferno." Then just to test her, I run my thumb just below her nipple, so close that I nearly groan.

"Fuck," she whispers as she tenses.

And I wait.

I wait for her to snap. For her to flip to her back, wrap her hand around the back of my neck, and pull me in for a kiss.

But when she doesn't move, when she doesn't do anything but rest against my chest, I realize that I'm going to have to do a hell of a lot more to get her to crack.

I'm impressed. I thought this would have done it.

Maybe . . .

Pulling on my bottom lip, I decide to try one more thing.

I slip my fingers under the hem of her shirt. I pause for a moment, wanting to make sure she's okay with this. When she doesn't say anything, I slip my entire hand under her shirt, letting my palm rest on her soft yet heated skin. There's no way in hell she's cold anymore.

"Now if you're still cold," I say quietly, "I can try doing some skin on skin." I drag her shirt up so it's just under her breasts, and I bring her bare back against my chest.

She's silent for a second before bringing her hand to her shirt. She sits up momentarily before dragging her shirt over her head and dropping it on the floor.

Holy.

Fuck.

She leans her back against my chest and says, "You're right, skin on skin really does make me warmer."

Now it's my time to pause.

To assess.

To tell myself to breathe and not freak out.

Not twist her to her back and take her tit into my mouth.

Have control, man.

Keep steady, don't fucking lose grip now.

But fuck, her skin is so soft.

So warm.

"Levi?"

"Hmm?" I ask as my palm presses against her stomach, bringing her in even closer.

"You're really hard." She rubs her ass against my erection.

"I know," I say.

"Do you need to take care of that?"

Yes, if you could sit on it and bounce up and down while I stare at your delicious body, that would be amazing, thanks.

"I'm good unless it makes you uncomfortable."

"No," she says softly. "I think it's hot." She twists just enough so she's looking back at me. "Incredibly hot."

And then she stays there, staring up at me.

I stare down at her.

My hand perched on her stomach, her bare breasts inches from my hand.

Her tongue peeks out and wets her lips.

I inwardly groan as I wet my lips as well.

And when neither one of us makes a move, neither one of us breaks for the kiss, feeling desperate for this to end, I let my thumb caress her bare breast.

Her eyes squeeze shut, so I do it again.

She twists just a touch more, and I curse that she's under the blankets covering her up.

When her eyes fall to my mouth, I push it a bit farther, then move my thumb just a little higher and stroke the underside of her hard nipples. *I need this to be over.*

"Fuck," she groans as I hold my breath, waiting for her to snap.

When she doesn't move, I do it again.

And again.

And fucking again, but she leans into it.

She pants.

Her chest fucking heaves, but she doesn't crack.

Instead, her teeth pull on her bottom lip as her hand moves between us and, to my surprise, presses against my cock.

Mother of fuck.

My eyes roll to the back of my head, a groan on the tip of my tongue.

With her palm flat on my length, I shift my pelvis into her hand where she squeezes me just enough to nearly make me choke on my own saliva.

And that's when I feel it, my will slipping.

My focus draining.

My mission failing.

Because I want more.

I want her to make me lose control.

I want to get lost in her.

I want to straddle her and play.

Play with her chest.

Her mouth.

Between her legs.

Fuck, I want this so bad.

I want it so bad, that my legs quiver, my cock swells, and I lose control.

I let out a deep breath, ready to take what I want just as I feel her slip out of the bed.

Nooooo . . .

With one arm, she covers her breasts as my cock pulses under the sheets. She stares down at me and says, "I'm warm now. Thank you, *Mr. Posey.*" And then she grabs her tank top from the ground and goes back to her cot.

My cock is throbbing with the need of release . . . while failure consumes me.

How did that not break her?

Because it sure as fuck broke me.

———

"YOU'RE eager to get back to your hotel room," Eli says as I jam my finger against the floor number.

"I'm not eager," I say even though I'm really fucking eager.

After a horrid loss tonight against a team we should have easily beat, everyone is pretty much on edge. Including myself.

I went to bed last night in so much fucking pain from no release that I woke up this morning hard as a goddamn stone. Thankfully, Wylie wasn't awake yet, so I nearly sprinted to the bathroom, turned on the shower, and stroked myself for a measly twenty fucking seconds before coming all over the shower tile.

Yeah, twenty seconds.

Fucking pathetic.

And my mind was so fucked from the night before that I felt like my head wasn't in the game today. Although, none of us played well so thank fuck it wasn't only me. And now that the game is over, I have one thing on my mind—breaking Wylie so we can end this fucking torture.

A smart person might say, hey, why don't you just break it yourself. End your own misery, but that would mean that she would win. *Losing is not an option.* Not when we've come this far.

No fucking way.

"You seem very eager," Eli says. "You sprinted off the bus."

"Sprinting is a bit of an exaggeration. And if I was sprinting, how the hell did we end up sharing an elevator?"

"Because I was sprinting too."

I roll my eyes. "You're really fucking annoying, you realize that?"

"You're calling me annoying? You're the most annoying person I know. The most annoying person the entire team knows."

"I beg to differ. You all obviously don't know how to look in the mirror."

"Denial is an ugly thing, Posey," Eli says in a scoff.

"Which is why you shouldn't be denying the fact that you're annoying." I pat him on the cheek. "That pretty boy face is going to turn into an ogre expression. Might even grow a single black hair on the tip of your nose."

Eli's expression falls flat. "My case in point."

"That's not annoying. That's just stating facts."

The elevator doors part open and I bolt out of the elevator and down the hall.

"Some might think you have a girl in your room," Eli calls out, but I just ignore him as I reach my room, open it with the key card, and then let myself in, only to find the room blistering hot.

"Jesus fuck," I say. "It's hot in here."

Wylie takes that moment to walk out of the bathroom in nothing but a pair of underwear and a white tank top with the hem tied up around her breasts.

What in the fuck is she doing?

"You're back," she says as she walks behind me. "Let me take your jacket for you."

"Why is it so hot in here?"

"I watched the game, and you know, I just thought you looked a little stiff. So I came up with an idea to help with that." She hangs my suit jacket in the closet, then guides me over to the bed. "I'm going to need you to strip out of your pants, though."

Oh, she has fucking plans. I can see it in her eyes. There's an evil gleam, and I realize that whatever is about to happen will be absolute hell.

"You seem a little shocked by the heat, so let me help you." She walks up to me and, before I comprehend what she's doing, she undoes my pants and leaves them open, then starts unbuttoning my dress shirt.

Her fingers play against my chest as I stare down at her deliciously curvy body. I take that moment to observe her as she works on my buttons. The way her body curves dramatically at her hips, giving her that hourglass figure is sexy as fuck. She's not model thin, something I love about her body. I want nothing more than to turn her around, bend her over, and grip those hips, that ass, and claim it as mine.

When she's done with the buttons, she pushes the shirt off and then brings me over to the bed where she sits me down. Hands on my knees, she kneels in front of me, causing my cock to jolt as she removes my shoes.

"Don't think I'm paying you for this kind of service," I say as she sets my shoes to the side. I lift so she can pull my pants off as well.

"This is something special." She winks, then lays me down on the bed, flat on my back.

"Does it have to be this hot?" I ask.

"Yes," she answers as she walks away.

"Where are you going?"

"Just rest there for a moment. Let the heat sink in."

"Wylie, it's already sunk in. I'm sweating."

"Good," she says as she reappears from the bathroom, but this time, she has the ice bucket in her arm.

She sets the ice bucket next to me.

"Like I said, you were quite stiff throughout the game, and I thought that maybe you needed some help relaxing your muscles and working through any tension you might be keeping in your shoulders."

And then, to my fucking surprise and joy, she straddles my lap and rests her center right on top of my now hardening cock.

She has to feel it. She smiles before picking up some ice and bringing it to my chest.

I suck in air as she moves the ice up my chest and around my pecs.

"Relax, Levi," she coos as I stare right down her shirt.

Hard to fucking relax when her hips are lightly rocking over my cock, I have the perfect view of her cleavage, and she's rubbing ice against my chest.

Nothing about this is relaxing.

And she fucking knows it.

She's had all goddamn day to plan this, and fuck has she outdone herself. This . . . this will make me break.

"God, your chest is incredible," she says as she brings the ice over my nipples. "You are so impressively large, Levi."

In what area?

Because right now, I know for a fact I'm getting impressively large in my boxer briefs.

She leans back, completely resting on my cock as she slides the ice down my abdomen, playing with the divots.

"Easily one of the hottest bodies I've ever seen." She lifts off my cock, leans forward, and places one hand on the mattress while the other runs ice over my left pec. She focuses entirely on that area, every once in a while moving the ice over my nipple and causing it to harden.

She sits back down and rubs her center over my length for a mere second before lifting back up and moving over to the other pec.

She continues this torture, slowly and methodically dry-humping me without actually dry-humping me.

It's one slow stroke after another.

One torturously slow stroke.

It's so fucking bad that I realize if I don't do something soon, if I let her take advantage of the situation, I'll snap, so I grab some ice from the bucket as well, and when she leans forward, I bring the ice to her chest.

She pauses in surprise. "You looked really hot, Wylie, so I thought I'd cool you down as well."

"Oh, no need. I can do that myself," she says as she sits back on my cock. Bringing the melting ice straight to her covered breasts, she rubs them a few times, dampening the fabric to where it's almost see-through.

Fuck . . .

Me . . .

Like a voyeur, I stare.

I watch as the gorgeous nipples harden from the cold of the ice. I watch intently as her head moves side to side and the way she gets lost in the feel of turning herself on.

I revel in the way she slowly rotates her hips over my cock, seeking her own pleasure.

And I nearly drool over the drop of her mouth when I lightly thrust my hips up into her.

Her eyes pop open as she realizes she's been seeking out her own pleasure. That's when I grip her hips and lightly guide them over my cock, up and down, up and down, showing her how hard she makes me but also tempting her. Giving her something that will tip her over the edge.

This has to do it. I know her clit is riding my length right now. I can feel how turned on she is. I can see it in her eyes. So I take more ice, slip my hand under her shirt, and as she moves forward to rub over my pecs again, I bring my palm to her breast, where I cup it with the ice.

She lets out a hiss and rotates her hips hard on my cock, causing me to buckle at the waist ever so slightly.

The ice falls from my palm to my stomach, leaving my hand on her bare breast. At this point, I don't fucking care. I squeeze her, feeling the weight of her in my palm, running my fingers over her hard nipple.

She curls in, her hands no longer gripping my stomach as her hips start moving faster over my cock.

Her eyes squeeze shut, and her fingers dig into my skin as my body lights up, my cock growing impossibly hard with every stroke, every rub.

"Fuck, baby," I say, unable to hold back, but it must snap her out of it because she pauses.

She stares down at me, and the hunger in her eyes morphs into realization.

"Jesus," she whispers before she scoots off me, leaving my cock nearly poking past my briefs. She hops off the bed, walks over to her suitcase, and doesn't even hide it as she takes her vibrator into the bathroom and shuts the door.

I stab my hand through my hair, pulling on the strands just as I hear her vibrator turn on.

And I don't have to listen intently as she starts moaning because it echoes against the tiles.

"Oh, fuck yes," she calls out. "Oh my God."

Not a chance I'm going to withstand this, so I push my briefs down, grab the base of my cock, and start pumping, using my precum as lube.

"God, Levi," she calls out. "Oh God, I'm going to come."

I bite on my bottom lip, my mind swirling, my body buzzing, the need for this woman so fucking strong. I squeeze tightly and pump hard, rocking my own goddamn world as Wylie gets off in the bathroom.

"Yes, yes, oh fuck, yes, oh God, I'm coming," she shouts. "I'm coming, fuck yes. Oh fuck!"

My brain goes dizzy, my legs go numb, and my balls tighten right before my orgasm shoots through my body, and I'm pumping my cock, coming all over my goddamn stomach.

I take a few seconds to catch my breath before I grab a tissue from the desk and wipe up my stomach . . . just as Wylie exits the bathroom.

She walks up to me, pats me on the chest, and says, "Relaxed now?"

Not even a fucking little.

―――

I GLANCE behind me and spot Wylie talking with Jeremiah, one of the rookies. He sat across from her on the plane, and on occasion, she's laughed at something he's said. And let me tell you, Jeremiah is not that fucking funny. I've heard him tell a story before—it's dragged out with barely a punchline. She's doing this on purpose, and I can tell you right fucking now, I don't like it.

I don't like anything at all. I'm in the worst fucking mood as we head back to Vancouver after a long-ass away trip. Thankfully, we won tonight's game, which means I can take a breather and collect myself, especially after last night. I'm still confused. Did both of us break? Technically, no. She dry-humped me for a few minutes, I grabbed her fucking spectacular breast, and then we both got off, separately.

And now, we haven't really said anything to each other, other than pleasantries. I don't think either of us knows where to go from here. But every time I hear her laugh, all I want is to take her somewhere and show her how into her I am.

"You look tense," Pacey says as he takes a seat in front of me but turns around to face me.

Silas joins him. "Very tense."

"Can we not do this?" I ask as I open my book of Washington state that I've somehow gotten into. Did you know that Washington has the largest ferry fleet in the United States? Found that fascinating. Also, it grows the most apples in the United States. I wonder if Eli knows that. It's a fun fact he could text Penny.

"Not do what?" Eli asks.

Speak of the devil.

"Posey doesn't want us bothering him apparently," Silas says. "Even though he bothers us all the time."

I study a picture of Mount Olympus. Just over seven thousand feet in elevation. Huh, seems like it would be taller than that.

"Posey isn't talking to us?" I hear OC say as he comes up from behind. "What did we do wrong?"

"I think we're annoying him," Pacey says.

"Even though he annoys us," Eli adds.

"Well, that doesn't seem like a reason not to talk to us," OC says. "We're friends. We should communicate."

"One would think, OC," Pacey says. "But it seems as though there has been a lack of communication lately with our good friend Posey. As Eli pointed out, he's very quick to flee the bus and get back to his hotel room."

"And he hasn't been hanging out with us as of late. The only time we see him is when we're getting ready for games," Silas points out.

"And there isn't an ounce of interest in our personal lives when usually there is," Eli continues.

OC leans in close and says, "And despite the write-up I did about Grace and me, I haven't heard a response."

That causes me to lift my head and pull away from my fascinating yet informative Washington book. "I didn't get a fucking write-up."

"Ha." OC points at me. "That's because I didn't turn it in yet, but I got you to look up."

I look him dead in the eyes and say, "That's going to be a mark against your name, good luck erasing it."

"Be serious for a second," Pacey says. "Something's going on and you're not telling us about it. For fuck's sake, you're reading a book, and that's very unlike you."

From the back, I hear Wylie laugh again, and it nearly makes me crumple this delectable book in my palm.

"I can read books," I defend. "Halsey does it all the time, and you don't say shit to him."

"Because he's been doing it for a long time, and he reads fiction. You're reading a book about Washington."

"What's wrong with that?" I ask. "What's wrong with wanting to gain knowledge about our neighbors, or just knowledge in general? Not everything is about living in a fantasy world like Halsey lives in. Books can be for both pleasure and knowledge. Don't make me feel bad for wanting to better myself."

"By learning about Washington?" Silas asks.

"It's a beautiful place," I practically yell. "Now get off my case and let me get back to learning about these goddamn apples they grow."

They all stare at me while I try to focus on the words in front of me, but they all jumble together.

"What if we don't try to involve ourselves in your life even though there's clearly something going on and instead, we just talk?" Pacey says. "Like we can talk about how Winnie wants to get married this Christmas Eve."

I glance up at him. "She does?"

He nods. "Yeah, I'm not sure about it, but she's dead set on the idea."

"Or how about how Penny wants to get married next summer?" Eli says. "When Holden is a little older and can be the ring bearer."

"Well . . . that's fucking adorable," I say.

"Or how about that I plan on proposing to Ollie soon?"

"Really?" I ask, feeling myself getting excited. Oh, the queens are making moves on their men, and I'm fucking here for it. "When do you plan on proposing?"

"Still trying to figure that out, but you would have been part of those discussions if you hadn't been ditching us. You don't even respond to group texts like you used to," Silas bemoans.

"I know." I drag my hand over my face. Guilt consumes me because unfortunately, they're right. I've been MIA when it comes to our friendships. I should really be better, but I've only been able to process so much. The queens take up a lot of my texting headspace, especially since they run rampant during some conversations, and it's really hard to pull them back. "I'm sorry," I say to the boys.

"We won't ask you why," Pacey says. "Because it seems like it's something you're not going to talk to us about, but we do want you to know that we miss you." *Crap. Talk about guilt.* But it's not only that, it's almost . . . sadness I feel. Understandably, there's been a slow shift in the dynamic of our relationship as each of my friends have fallen for their women, but it has meant that we spend less time with each other. It's been strange. Lonely at times. Dare I say, life had been simpler before the girls came along. Yet I'm also happy for my friends.

"And we made you this," Eli says, pulling a sandwich from behind him. "And when we say made, we mean we bought it for you." He sets it in front of me, and I don't even have to open it to know that it's a bologna sandwich.

I glance up at my friends and press my hand to my heart. "You did this for me?"

"We did," Pacey says. "Even Halsey, but he's reading in the back and told us not to disturb him because he just came to a plot twist. But he sends his love."

"Wow," I say, glancing down at the sandwich. "This means a lot. Thank you."

"Of course," Eli says. "And you know, you can always talk to us if you're going through something. You don't have to hide it."

"Dude, we said we wouldn't pressure him," Silas says.

"I know, but just reiterating that we're here for him."

I open the sandwich and take in the beautiful smell of bologna on white bread. God, they know me so well. The gesture almost, and I mean almost, makes me want to open up about what's happening, but at the moment, it feels way too complicated to even explain.

I'm not sure I even know what's going on, but what I do know is that it ends tomorrow.

This bullshit is over.

I lift the sandwich to my mouth and take a bite. I give it a few chews and look at Silas. "Tell me about the proposal. I want every detail because I know you're going to fuck it up, and

Daddy Posey is going to have to clean up your mess for you. So before that happens, let's make a plan."

"Don't refer to yourself as Daddy Posey," Silas deadpans.

"Don't make me, then," I say with a snarky bite of my sandwich, causing Pacey to laugh.

"And he's back . . ."

Chapter Fourteen

WYLIE

Levi: *Be dressed and ready by eight tonight. You're my wingman tonight.*

"That's what he wrote to you?" Sandie asks as she stares down at Levi's text message from this morning.

"Yes, what does that even mean?"

I'm perched on my bed, curlers in my hair, makeup done, and wearing nothing but a robe because I have no idea what to dress myself in as his wingman.

After Sandie got off work, she thankfully rushed over to my place, where I gave her the entire rundown of the past few days. We shared a large salad and some breadsticks from our favorite Italian restaurant, and I drank a hard seltzer or two to calm my nerves.

Sandie sets my phone down and says, "I think he'll try to break you tonight. After what happened the other night, I have no doubt that this is the crescendo. Tonight's the night that one of you is going to give in, and it looks like it will be in his favor."

We're both sitting on my bed, me against the headboard,

Sandie against the wall, our legs tangling in the middle. I bring my legs into a crisscross position and make sure to cover myself up so Sandie doesn't have to deal with a free show.

"So you think he'll flaunt another woman in front of me?"

"Yes." Sandie nods. "That's exactly what he's going to do. Think about what you did to him last time. You dry-humped him, then came loudly in the bathroom so he could hear you. He's reached his breaking point, and it doesn't seem like he wants to be the one who gives in."

"Trust me, if he was the one who gave in, I'd know at this point what it would feel like to have him inside me. This is a battle of wills, and he has the upper hand, Sandie. I don't think I can go through the night knowing that he might take someone else home."

"Then make it so he can't take someone else home. Make it so you're the one he's thinking about, not some random he finds at a bar."

"Yeah, I think I can do that." An idea pops into my head. "What if . . . what if I ask him to help me find someone?"

Sandie's eyes light up. "Yes, reverse it back on him. Maybe make some sort of deal where you both help each other out and see who breaks first."

"Yes, I can do that," I say, feeling more empowered. "I'm sure he'll hate if I flirt with someone else in front of him. Unless . . . what if he doesn't? What if he lets me go off with another guy, and he's with another girl?"

"He won't." Sandie shakes her head. "There is no way he's going to let you go off with any guy. Trust me on this. Someone will break tonight, and it's going to be him."

I smile to myself. "You're right, it's going to be him."

"That's the spirit." She pats my leg. "Now let's get you dressed." She hops off my bed and goes over to my clothes where she starts looking through my dresses. "I need you to look very indecent tonight. Like, nipple ready to pop out-type outfit."

"Do you think that's necessary?" I ask her.

She looks over her shoulder. "Uh, very necessary. Come on, let me try a few things on you."

I walk over to Sandie, who starts piling outfits onto my waiting hands.

This should be interesting.

⊏⊐

LEVI

I ADJUST my watch on my wrist and look at the time. She has one minute before I go barreling into her room to tell her that she's late.

I'm all business tonight. I have one thing on my mind, and that's breaking Wylie Wood. Like I said, this fucked-up game of wills ends tonight.

I chose to wear a pair of black jeans and a black button-up shirt, my typical club outfit. I styled my hair to look messy but also put together, left my scruff untouched, rolled my sleeves up, and made sure to put on the cologne I know she likes. I want to make it impossible for her to think of anyone but me. That's why I also left a few of my buttons undone so she has a peek of my chest throughout the night.

Now I just have to mentally prepare for what arsenal she's coming with. Lord knows she's going to dress to kill. I'm not fucking dumb. She's an incredibly sexy and sexual woman, and she'll dress provocatively—*sensually*—to make it impossible for me to look at any other woman. Lucky for me, I've already texted Samantha at the club. I told her what was going on, and she has no problem helping me out.

Samantha is a regular who I've played around with a bit. She's devastatingly gorgeous with long black hair, a killer body, and deep brown eyes. Being naked in front of people doesn't faze her, and she's been up on the main stage quite a few times, getting off for everyone to see. She's excited to play the part tonight.

So I have my bases covered.

Tonight, Wylie will break.

Just then, I hear heels clicking down the hallway, so I brace myself as Wylie appears in the kitchen. And yup . . . fuck . . . me. Jesus Christ, did she come to fucking play.

Her red hair is curled and voluminous, stretching past her shoulders and down her back. She went with a dark eyeliner, making her eyes pop, and a deep red lip that matches the vibrant color of her hair. And the outfit she chose, if you want to call it that, is a tight mini skirt that barely reaches her mid-thigh, and a single tube top that ties in the front and covers nothing but her breasts, and barely covers them if that. Pretty sure it's one of those bras she was talking about, but strapless.

Yup, she came to fucking play.

When she sees me, she pauses and wets her lips as she lets her eyes trail over me. "Ooo, boss man is looking to get fucked tonight, isn't he?"

By you, yes.

"I am," I say.

She walks up to me and pats me on the chest. "Don't worry, I'm going to be the best wingman you've ever had."

With that, she struts toward the front door, clutch in hand, ready to go.

Let the games begin.

WYLIE

"YOU'RE QUIET," I say after about ten minutes of silence in the car. "Are you mentally preparing to pick someone up?"

"I don't need to mentally prepare," he says, his grip on the steering wheel tight.

"Okay, well, can you tell me what you expect from me as your wingman?"

"Talk me up, make me look good, make sure the girl trying to get with me is worth my time."

I tug on my top, a habit I've acquired since the moment I put on this godforsaken bra that Sandie insisted I wear. It feels like it's going to fall off any second. "I can do that no problem. Is there anyone in particular you're looking for?"

He rubs the side of his jaw, the sound of his scruff bringing my attention to what it would feel like to have that scruff rubbing against my skin.

"Dark hair," he says. "Only requirement."

"Are you a boob man, ass man? Should I be looking for anything like that?"

"I like all bodies," he says and glances in my direction.

My cheeks heat, and I inwardly swear to keep it together. It's hard, though, when he looks like *that* and smells unbelievable. I swear his cologne was made to draw women toward him because even sitting in his car, I'm leaning toward him, wanting to get a better whiff.

He makes a right down a dark street, where he pulls up to a valet.

"Oh, I've never been here before," I say. "This is a bar?"

"No," he says as he glances at me. "A club."

He gets out of the car, and all the color drains from my face.

A club? As in . . . one of his clubs?

Fuck.

Before I can even think about texting Sandie for mental support, my car door opens, and Levi is on the other side, holding his hand out to me. I take it, and he helps me out of the car before letting go. He heads down the path toward the nearly pitch-black entrance, but I stop him before we enter. I tug on his hand, and when he turns to face me, I try not to show my nerves.

"Um, so is this one of those clubs you like to go to?"

"Yes," he answers, his jaw tense.

"And you plan on meeting a girl here and . . . taking her to a back room or something?"

"Yes," he answers again, making my stomach churn.

"Okay, and you want me to help you find that girl so that you can fuck in a back room?"

"Correct," he says.

I nod and look at the ground for a moment, clutching my purse as I try to find a way to deal with this. If this was a bar, that would be easier. I could pass some time and try to find the right person, but this is different. I've been to these clubs before—not this one in particular—but there is no fucking around. You find someone you like, you fuck, simple as that. No need to warm up, no need for small talk.

Which means the stakes are higher here. I have a lot less time.

"Okay, I can help with that, but you know, since we're here," I say, looking him in the eyes. "If I happen to see someone I might be compatible with, I hope you don't mind if I go off with them as well."

"If you're up for it, go for it," he says and heads toward the door.

Wait . . .

What?

If I'm up for it, go for it?

No tic of the jaw.

No anger in his expression.

No jealousy?

I would have at least thought that he'd show a hint of emotion over that, but I get nothing at all.

"Are you coming?" he asks from where he stands next to the entrance.

"Yes," I say, trying to shake the negative thoughts out of my head.

This is a game. He's playing the game.

Right?

That's what's happening.

That's what's happening. *But he's a man, Wylie. He's a virile, sex-loving, sexy man, who made you come after only dry-humping him.* He's told me that it's me he wants, but he's also told me that we can't cross that line. *But he touched me like he owned me the other night* . . . and then didn't take me.

"Dark hair," *he says.* "Only requirement."

Dark hair . . .

He opens the door for me, and I walk in before him only to stop at another door, the beat of the music on the other side making me nervous.

"Membership," the man at the door says, and Levi flashes him a card. The man nods and opens the door for us, leading us to a barely lit hallway. Levi guides me with his hand on my lower back until we're in front of a curtain. He pulls it back, and the view of the club is on full display.

Everything is black like Levi's room. The walls, the ceilings, the furniture, the only color is represented on the guests. Like other clubs I've been to, this one has a center stage with lounges and couches circling it. A bar is off to the left, and toward the back, there are large windows that give you a view of other private rooms for just couples. A few of them occupied.

On center stage is a woman currently undressing herself while a man sits in a chair, stroking his cock and staring at her.

Immediately, my nipples go hard, and a wave of heat passes through me. This is my element. *This is what I love.* Debauchery. I love everything about it. I love watching others. I love hearing others. I love touching others.

And from the way Levi glances around . . . he loves it too.

He leans in close to my ear. "Is this too much for you?"

"No," I say as my eyes fixate on the stage where the woman just fully undressed. "This is perfect."

"Good," he says as a few people pass us by, their eyes roaming us both.

Levi takes that moment to wrap his hand around the back of my neck, his fingers slightly curling around the front.

I shiver with arousal because I know what he's doing.

I know exactly what he's doing.

He's letting every man in this club know that I'm off limits. And just like that, the nerves are gone, the thrill of being here sets in, and I lean in toward him, ready to play.

He guides us through the club, toward the back where we have a view of the private windows and the center stage.

Currently, a woman is being fucked up against the window, her tits pressing into the glass as she moans loud enough for us to hear.

Incredibly hot.

A couple is next to us on a couch, the woman giving the man a lap dance, both clothed.

Off to the left is a woman on her knees, giving a man a blow job. That surprises me because I wouldn't think you could do anything like that out in the open on the main floor, but only in a private room.

Levi finds us a couch just as the woman on stage lets out a loud moan as she sits down on the man and starts moving up and down, her tits bouncing and her head falling back in ecstasy. I slowly take a seat, my eyes on them the entire time while the man takes her breast into his mouth and starts sucking.

"God, I'm already wet," I say without even thinking about it. "I love everything about this."

I glance over at Levi who's looking at me, his eyes seeming slightly dazed for a second before he focuses back on center stage.

"Are you hard?" I ask.

"Yeah," he answers.

"Is that weird to ask you?"

His brow raises as he says, "After everything we've been through? No."

"Well, let me find someone who can fulfill your needs."

His eyes shoot back to me, and I catch him glance at my mouth before he lets out a sigh and leans back on the couch.

Because it's so dark in here and he's wearing all black, I can't make out his bulge, which is a shame because I really want to know how much this turns him on.

Probably a lot.

"Oh fuck," the woman yells as she moves quickly over the man. "Oh, I'm coming," she shouts for everyone to hear, drawing attention to her.

Everyone seems to stop as our eyes focus toward the center and watch her and her alone.

My cheeks flame.

My temperature rises, and when she cries out in ecstasy, the man following closely behind, everything in my body throbs.

I want that.

I want to be that woman.

I want to be the one everyone watches.

"Would you ever do that?" I ask.

"Get up on stage?" he asks just as a server comes over to us.

"What can I get you, Mr. Posey? The usual?"

"That would be great," he says, then turns to me. "What would you like?"

"A hard lime seltzer, please."

She winks. "Be right back."

I turn toward Levi now while the couple clean up and switch out with another. His eyes flash to my chest briefly before up to my face. "Well," I ask. "Would you ever go up on stage?"

"No," he says.

"No?" I ask, my brow pinched. "Why not?"

"People know me, so I don't want to be on display like that. But one of the window rooms? Yes, because you can set the lighting where you can't see everything. Like room three." He points, and I look over where I can see the woman, but because the man is farther away, I can't quite make out who it is.

"That's really hot," I say. "I would totally do the stage or the window. Hell, I'd give someone a naked lap dance right here."

"Well, there's a single guy over there." He nods in the direction of a man casually touching himself while staring at the new couple on the stage.

"Are you allowed to come out here in the main room?"

"No, only on stage," he says. "Notice the blow job couple isn't here anymore?"

I glance over to the corner, and lo and behold, they've been removed.

"So what are you allowed to do?"

"Watch, feel, touch, undress your upper half, not lower. Lower half has to be covered. There are a lot of rooms in the back that are constantly being changed out and cleaned. They only allow so many patrons in the club at a time so they can keep up."

"So you've fucked in the back rooms?"

"Yes," he answers just as our drinks are brought to us. Levi is handed a tumbler, but it doesn't look like alcohol.

"What is that?" I ask.

"Club soda," he answers. "Game tomorrow, so I don't want to drink the night before. I try to avoid it as much as I can. Plus, I want to be present when I fuck."

"Understood," I say just as I spot a gorgeous woman in a pair of high-waisted pants and a bra walking toward us. Her long black hair swishes behind her as her hips sway side to side, her eyes set on one person and one person alone . . . Levi.

I take a large sip of my drink just before she arrives.

"Hey," she says in a seductive voice. She holds her hand out to Levi. "I'm Samantha."

He takes her hand and says, "Levi, nice to meet you."

She then turns to me and says, "I'm sorry, am I overstepping? I didn't even see you until I got up here. I guess I was just fixated on how handsome your boyfriend is."

"Oh, he's not my boyfriend," I say, waving my hand in dismissal. "He's my boss. Yup, at a sex club with my boss." I nod awkwardly. "Actually, I'm here to help him find someone to fuck."

"You're here . . . *helping* him?" Samantha asks and looks Levi up and down. "Doesn't seem like he needs help at all."

I shrug. "I'm just doing what he asks."

"Well then, let's see if I'm right for the job," she says as she sits beside me and holds out her hand. "I'm Samantha."

"Wylie," I say, taking her hand in mine and marveling at how soft it is. I look her in the eyes and say, "This might be bold, but you're gorgeous."

"Thank you," she says with a sweet smile. She crosses one leg over the other and places her hand on my thigh. "You're breathtaking." She touches my cheek and says, "Your eyes are so beautiful."

"Thank you," I reply as a hint of heat builds.

I'm very proud of my sexuality. I've been with men and women, and I find everything about the female body so sexy. It's why I love watching Patty Ford, and it's why I feel almost drawn toward Samantha at the moment. In college, I was very fluid—something my dad doesn't know—but I've had my fun.

"Tell me what your boss is looking for?"

"He said he likes all bodies but is looking for dark hair, which you have. So winning already." I glance behind me at Levi, who watches us intently. "But I know from experience he loves a great set of tits."

Samantha glances down at her chest, then back at me. "I think I can help in that department."

"I think so," I answer. "I think I'd also want him to have someone who could pleasure him seductively. Tease him. Edge him. He tends to edge himself a lot."

"Does he?" she asks, looking over at Levi. "You say that as if you have experience."

I shake my head. "No, but I know him well enough to understand he doesn't just come for release. He likes to come for a purpose."

"I like that," Samantha says as she drags her fingers up and down my thigh.

"Are you good at edging?" I ask her, the tingling sensation of her touch sending bolts of arousal straight between my legs.

"Very good," she whispers, leaning in. And then, to my surprise, she straddles my lap. Her legs fall on either side of mine, and her breasts are right at eye level as she brings her hands to my shoulders. "Let's pretend you're Levi. I'd start with conversation, touching him gently, making it absolutely clear how hot I think he is. After slowly unbuttoning his shirt, my hands would wander."

"He'd like that," I say as I place my hands on her thighs.

"And then I'd tell him that he could use me in any way he wants."

"He would," I say as I bite my lip.

"What do you think he'd do first?" she asks.

My cheeks heat as my mouth goes dry because . . . God, she's really hot.

And I don't know what prompts me, but before I can stop myself, I move my hands to the clasp of her bra and say, "He'd remove this. I know he'd want to see your tits."

"Then do it," she whispers.

Without thinking, I unclasp her bra and watch as it falls down her arms, revealing her breasts. Her beautiful breasts. They're not as big as mine, but they're firm and high with dark, pierced nipples.

God, I'm so jealous.

"You have amazing breasts," I say as I stare at them. "I love your nipple piercings."

"Do you think Levi would like them?" she asks, puffing her chest out.

I glance over at Levi, expecting him to be staring at Samantha, but I lock eyes with him instead. His attention is on me.

"Um, I think . . . he would," I say as I turn back to Samantha.

She rests her hands on my shoulders and starts moving her hips over mine. "Would he like this?"

I bite my bottom lip as I grow even wetter because, how could I not? The couple on stage is undressing each other, Samantha's on top of me—her beautiful breasts thrusting in front of me, her hips rotating over mine—and Levi's staring at us, watching every moment. It's checking all of my boxes and might be one of my best sexual experiences.

So I decide to take advantage of it.

"Can I touch you?" I ask her. "I want to make sure you're absolutely perfect for him."

"Please do," she says.

Excited, I move my hands up her sides to her breasts where I palm them and lightly drag my thumbs over her nipples, loving the feel of her piercings against the pad of my thumb.

I'm throbbing.

I'm so turned on. So hot. So ready for whatever comes next that I get lost in the feel of her breasts.

"Levi would love this," I say. "He'd play with your nipples all night."

"God, I hope so," Samantha breathes.

I squeeze her breasts again, pushing them together this time. "You're so hot," I tell her.

She looks down at me and says, "You are too."

Her teeth pull on her lip.

I lean close to her breast, ready to take one in my mouth, when she cups my chin.

"Have you ever kissed a girl, Wylie?"

"Yes," I say as I slide my hands down her back to the waistband of her pants.

She pushes me back on the couch and drags her fingers up my stomach to my breasts, where she draws a circle around my hardened nipple.

I nearly let out a loud, boisterous moan.

"Don't you think you should test to see how I kiss, to make sure I'm good enough for Levi?"

I nod my head. "Yeah, I think I should."

She leans forward, her tits pressing against mine as she grips my cheek.

I slide one hand over her ass and cup the back of her head with the other hand.

Every bit of me throbs as she lowers her mouth.

At the last second, I wet my lips, ready for her—and then feel her being pulled off my lap.

What?

My eyes flash open, and I catch Levi standing beside her, his hand in hers. He bends down, picks up her bra, and stuffs it in his back pocket.

Then he threads their fingers together and says, "Back room. Now."

Samantha smiles up at him . . . as realization hits me.

Wait, he's taking her?

She's . . . she's the one he's choosing?

And before I can say anything, they head back toward the private rooms.

No, that wasn't supposed to happen.

He's not supposed to go back there with her. He's supposed to . . . hell, what is he supposed to do?

Break.

That's what. I got so lost in sensation that I forgot what was going on. He was supposed to see me with her and want me, not her. And from the way he was watching me, I could have sworn he was going to ask me to be with him.

I look over at them and notice that his hand is now wrapped around *her* neck. *He's claiming her.*

Which means, he's no longer claiming me.

My stomach churns with anxiety.

Anxiety over Levi being with someone other than me.

With him being turned on by anyone other than me.

With him even touching another woman, *not* me.

My eyes well up with frustration.

With irritation.

With apprehension that if I don't do something, if I don't make a move, he'll fuck Samantha. Despite his attraction to me, he'll realize that he can and will find someone else . . . as if I'm invisible. *Replaceable.* God knows my mom found it just as easy to walk away from me as if I meant nothing.

I shouldn't be so emotionally invested in this, but I fucking like Levi

Posey. We click in so many ways, more than I have with any other guy. And if he does this, and I know I won't cope—I'll have to give up my job. *Is that what he wants? Me gone?* Was this not a game to him? Does he want me gone too?

Do not let her off the hook. Don't let her skate by. I want you to make her life a living hell, got it?

And mainly, don't forget that she's completely off limits.

No, I refuse to believe Levi truly doesn't want me.

Please choose me, Levi.

I hurry through the couches after them.

I trip over the leg of a patron watching someone in one of the windows, but I regain my balance and adjust my top as I make my way down the hall, where I find Levi leading Samantha into a back room. I chase them, and right before the door closes, I stop it with my hand.

"Wait," I say, feeling breathless.

Levi parts the door slightly and offers me a questioning brow. "What?" he asks.

I wet my lips and muster all the courage I can find. "Don't fuck her, Levi. Please . . . please don't fuck her."

He straightens up and asks, "Why?"

"Because." I twist my hands over my clutch as I try to find my words.

"Because. Why?" he asks, this time, taking a step forward and lifting my chin with his finger, forcing me to look at him.

"Because I don't want you fucking her."

"Why not?" He's not letting me get away with evasiveness. When I don't respond right away, he believes I won't answer and starts to shut the door again.

But I don't let him as I step inside the room where I spot Samantha sitting on the edge of the bed, hands propped behind her, enjoying the show between Levi and me.

"Wylie, unless you have a reason—"

"Because I want you," I say before I can stop myself. "I want you, Levi, for myself. So please, please don't do anything with her. It will . . ." I choke out the last few words. "It will gut me."

His hard-as-stone expression slowly softens before he turns to Samantha and says, "Give us space."

She nods, and as she walks past us, she plucks her bra from his back pocket and then twiddles her fingers at me before stepping out of the room.

Levi slams the door, locks it, then spins me against the wall. I stare up at him, my heart beating rapidly in my chest as he cups my cheek and lowers his forehead to mine.

"I wasn't going to fuck her," he says softly.

"Then why did you bring her in here?"

"Because I wanted you to crack. I wanted you to admit that you want this, that you want me."

My hand runs up his chest, and I say, "I've wanted you from the moment I saw you at the bar that one night. I've always wanted you, Levi."

His eyes squeeze shut as his hands smooth down my sides. "Fuck, I shouldn't." His eyes open, and there's clarity in them. "But I can't fucking stop myself," he says right before his mouth crashes down upon mine.

Thank God.

I could cry. This pent-up tension between us that's been building finally releases as his mouth moves over mine, taking everything we've wanted from each other for so long.

And it's just as electric as I remember.

He cups my ass and lifts me to pin me against the wall, giving him an easier angle. I wrap my legs around his waist and bring my hands to his face, where I marvel at his scruff and his carved jaw.

When his tongue runs across my lips, I part them open. He groans and presses into me more, his tongue dancing with mine, tangling, hungrily taking. I groan and shift my hand to the back of his head, playing with the short strands of his hair as he continues to own my mouth, showing me that I'm the one he wanted.

Not her.

Me.

He's not walking away from me but choosing me.

"Fuck," he grumbles as he wrenches his mouth from mine but then kisses along my jaw and then down my neck. His hands glide to my breasts, where he takes hold of the bra I'm wearing and tugs on it, tearing it right off my body. He tosses the fabric to the side, and then, with both hands, he cups my breasts, bringing one of my nipples to his mouth.

"Yes," I cry out as I hold his head down, wanting him to play with me. "God, yes, Levi."

His tongue swirls around my nipple, over and over again until he lightly nips on it, causing a hiss to escape my lips. Seemingly happy with my response, he repeats the same rhythm with his tongue, but instead of nibbling this time, he sucks . . . hard.

My fingers dig into his head, my legs quaking against him because it's been so long. So freaking long since I've been treated like this, where the attention has been on my pleasure, not my counterpart's.

"Your tits will be the death of me," he says before he moves to the other breast and repeats the process, but while he sucks on one, he twists the other with his fingers. Plucking and pinching.

Fuck, it feels so good.

So amazing.

He releases my breast and brings his mouth back up to my neck, where he rubs his rough scruff along my sensitive skin, marring me and making me his. When his mouth reaches mine again, he lets out a deep breath before saying, "I need to fuck you."

"Then fuck me," I whisper.

He lets out a deep growl before releasing me back to the floor. He reaches for me, but I drop to my knees before he can and bring my hands to the zipper and button of his jeans.

He braces his hand against the wall behind me as I undo his jeans and lower them. Next, I bring my hands to the elastic of his briefs and pull them down as well, revealing the sexiest penis I've ever seen.

Wide-eyed, I watch it stretch upward, revealing an intricate set of tattoos on the underside, a stack of triangles that move upward toward the head of his cock.

"Oh my God," I whisper before I look up at him.

He smirks.

"I need you in my mouth," I say as I sit up on my knees and angle his cock to my lips. I rub the tip along my lips, making him groan before I barely take the head inside. I play with the tip, just with my lips, teasing him and making him wet before I take in another inch, and then another . . . and another.

"Jesus fuck," he says as he leans farther into his propped-up arm.

I get him to spread his legs more, and as I suck him off, bobbing up and down over his length, I take his balls in my other hand and start fondling them, rolling them in my palm and lightly tugging, just enough to feel him grow in my mouth.

"That's it, Wylie," he mutters. "I like the pain."

Hearing that, I decide to scrape my teeth along his cock and see how he likes that.

His hand falls to my head, and he grips my hair, tugging on it as he groans.

"Uhhh, fuck, Wylie. Again."

Pleased, I dip my head forward, taking him to the back of my mouth, then I pull off, scraping my teeth along the underside while tugging on his balls at the same time.

"Yes," he says while pounding his hand against the wall. "Again, baby."

My skin prickles with heat, my pussy throbbing from his reaction as I bring him all the way back to my throat again. I swallow with him back there and apply more pressure as I drag him along my teeth and tug on his balls.

"Mother . . . fucker," he yells, then pulls away from me. He stares down at me, his eyes wild, his cock so large, so ready. "Stand up and turn around," he demands. "Now."

I do as I'm told and stand. Just as I turn around, he bends me at the waist. I prop my hands against the wall just as he flips my skirt up to find that I'm not wearing any underwear.

"Are you fucking kidding me with this?" he asks as he smooths his hand over my ass. "Fuck, Wylie, you're my dream girl."

Satisfaction pulses through me as his fingers slide over my crack and down between my legs, where he tests just how ready I am.

"Dripping, Wylie. You're fucking dripping." I glance over my shoulder as he brings his fingers up to his mouth and sucks on them. His eyes roll to the back of his head as he groans.

"Fucking perfect," he says before bringing the head of his cock to my entrance. "I'll eat you later, but I need this now." In one pulse, he thrusts inside me.

A long, satisfied groan falls past my lips as I adjust to his length and girth.

No one has ever made me feel this full before, and he must notice because he pauses. "Fuck, you're so goddamn tight. Are you okay?"

"Perfect," I say.

"Good," he replies right before he smacks me on the ass.

"Oh God," I yell just as he does it again.

"That's it, baby, squeeze my cock." He spanks me again, but this time on the other cheek, causing my inner walls to contract around him. "Squeeze it, Wylie." He does it again, and I squeeze him hard. "Such a good girl," he says before bringing his other hand up to my neck and lightly circling it. The soft pressure shows me that he's owning me, but it doesn't stop me from being able to breathe. It's perfect.

It's everything I want and need from him.

When he's ready, he pulls his hips back and slams into me.

"Your cunt, fuck, it's perfect. I want you coming all over me. Coat my cock, Wylie."

He leans forward and takes my breast into his hand, finely playing with my nipple, causing my arousal to spike in seconds as he continues to pulse inside me.

"Yes," I moan. "More."

He smooths his hand down my stomach to between my legs,

where he finds my clit and starts applying pressure, massaging it with two fingers.

I press my palm flat against the wall as a wave of pleasure rips through me, the beginning of my orgasm.

"Oh my God," I say as I shake under his touch.

"That's it, Wylie. Get loud, baby, let me hear you."

He continues to pulse into me, rocking me so hard that I start losing strength as my head knocks into the wall. His fingers are like magic, working over my clit, causing this tremendous sensation to beat through me, a sensation so great that I don't think I'm ready for it.

But he doesn't care.

He wants me to come.

He continues to rock into me, rub my clit . . . bite my shoulder.

"Oh God, Levi. Oh fuck," I say as my orgasm climbs and climbs and climbs until I hit the edge, and with one final pulse, I tip over, crying out his name in ecstasy as I convulse around him.

"Jesus fuck," he roars as he stills behind me, my pussy contracting, squeezing him. He groans and then pulls out of me, and his warm cum hits my ass. "Christ," he groans as I feel his hand smooth over my backside. "Fuck, Wylie." He breathes heavily and pulls away.

Holy fuck. That was . . . *I have no words.* All I know is that it was so worth the wait. Everything about that was incredible. His need for me. The way he smacked me. *"Fuck, Wylie, you're my dream girl."* His words. The feel of him stretching me, filling me. *Fucking. Me.* Nothing has ever felt that good. All I can do is shake my head, too breathless to speak. *Was it because of our insane attraction to each other? Or just the undeniable chemistry between us?*

From the corner of my eye, I see him grab a wet wipe from a drawer. He cleans himself up and then walks over to me and cleans me up as well. When he's done, he pulls my skirt down and tosses the wet wipe away. When I stand tall, I face him and watch him stuff himself back in his pants before zipping up.

I reach for my top and notice that it's completely broken. There's no way it's going back on me.

I hold it up to him, and he smiles. Cupping my chin, he presses a soft kiss to my lips before saying, "Sorry about that." He unbuttons his shirt and offers it to me. I slip my arms through it and then take the two ends and tie them together in a knot just below my breasts.

Levi's eyes watch in wonderment. When I'm done, I press my hand to his bare chest and stand on my toes, offering him a kiss on the chin.

"Let's get the hell out of here," he says before taking my hand and walking out of the private room, him shirtless and me feeling like I just walked on freaking water.

LEVI

I'M FUCKING BUZZING.

I've never felt more alive than at this moment, walking hand in hand with Wylie back to my apartment.

We were silent for the entire drive back, but I kept my hand on her thigh. When we arrived, I told her to wait in the car so I could open the door for her. Then I took her hand in mine and kept her close as we made our way up to my floor.

Now that we're back at my apartment, there is one thing on my mind . . . apologizing.

I let us in the apartment, lock up, and kick my shoes off. When she stands there, unsure, I take her hand and lead her to the couch, where I sit with her.

"I need to talk to you," I say, causing a pinch in her brow to form.

She wets her lips. "Listen, I know we crossed a line—"

"I'm sorry, Wylie."

She pauses, and her eyes start to well up. "Levi, please. Can we just take a second before we start claiming what happened was a mistake?"

Now it's my turn for my brow to crease. "What do you mean a mistake?" I ask. "I don't think any of that was a mistake."

"You don't?"

I shake my head as I lace our fingers together. "No, I'm apologizing because of what I've put you through." I shake my head again. "Fuck, Wylie, I never should have agreed to take you on as my assistant and let your dad use me. I . . . I feel fucking sick about it, and now that this is all fucking over, I'm realizing that the past couple of weeks have been a giant waste of our time." I let out a deep breath and look her in the eyes. "I never should have treated you the way that I did. I should have cherished you. I should have told you the truth right away. I should have worked with you instead of against you. It was foolish, and I was a scared motherfucker, and I'm sorry, Wylie. You deserve so much better."

This time, she shakes her head. "No, I should have told you I knew when I worked it out. *I* shouldn't have played this game. I was trying to prove something, prove my worth, that I'm better than the person my dad thinks I am . . . and I got lost. I'm sorry, Levi. This all happened because of me."

"Prove your worth?" I ask. "Wylie, you have nothing to prove."

"To you, maybe not. To my dad, I have everything to prove." She leans back against the couch and stares up at the ceiling. "And God, he probably predicted this would happen, that I'd fall into your bed and disappoint him all over again. He probably saw this happening a mile away."

Feeling like she's pulling away, I move closer. I'm not letting this go. Now that I've had her, I'm not allowing anything to get in the way of us being together, even if that means sacrificing a whole lot.

"I need to go," she says as she starts to get up, but I stop her.

"No," I say.

Her eyes meet mine. "No?"

I shake my head. "Fuck no, you're not leaving."

"Levi, I never should have—"

"Don't," I say. "Please fucking don't. Don't for one second regret any of this."

"But don't you see?" she says. "All of this has distracted me from what I'm truly supposed to be doing, focusing on my art and my career." She presses her hand to her forehead and lets out a deep sigh. Then she looks over at me. "I'm really sorry. This is on me, not you." She tries to stand again, but I keep her close.

"How about this," I say, not wanting to go around in circles and feeling a deep-rooted panic. *I can't lose her.* "We both take the blame and figure out how we can move forward from here."

"How could we move forward?" she asks. "We're both going to get into serious trouble for what happened. It might be best if we just . . . go our separate ways."

"No," I say.

"No?" she asks, looking like she's in complete disbelief.

"No," I repeat. "Not going to happen. Here's what we're going to do." I turn toward her and force her to keep her eyes on me. "We're going to date—"

"Levi." She shakes her head.

I hold my hand out. "Hear me out, okay?" She sighs but lets me proceed. "We're going to date. I'm going to woo the shit out of you so you won't ever consider dating another man again." That garners a smile. "You'll continue to work for me, but you won't be doing weird shit anymore. You'll focus heavily on social media and preparing me for away games. When you're not doing things for me, you'll do your art. You'll work on it and find what feels right. You won't live in the nanny hole anymore because you'll sleep in my bed." She raises a brow at me, so I add, "That's nonnegotiable, *not* sorry. And when the time comes, and you're ready, we'll tell your dad about us, but only when you feel like you have everything in place. Until then, we'll keep this between us and only us."

"Levi, you're risking a lot."

"Worth it," I say.

"You barely know me."

"I know enough about you to understand that I like you. That I want to get to know more about you. Wylie, I never stopped thinking about you after that night we first met. I feel such a genuine connection with you, and I'd regret not exploring this. If you want sex off the table, fine, we can take that off the table, but at least give this a chance, Wylie. Give us a chance." *I have never begged a woman for anything, so I seriously hope she doesn't ignore my plea.*

"You'd take sex off the table after what we just did?"

"I mean . . ." I scratch the back of my head. "It doesn't thrill me to know that I can't be inside you every night, but if that's what it takes, then yeah, sex is off the table."

She smiles demurely and looks down at our entwined fingers. "I wouldn't want sex off the table."

"Even better," I say, making her laugh. To my surprise, she moves on top of my lap and rests her hands on my chest. I run my palms over her thighs as I stare up at her.

"You think this could be something?"

"I know it can be something," I say. "Don't you feel it, Wylie? Doesn't it feel right to you?"

"Almost too right," she says.

"No such thing." I slide my hands under her skirt and bunch it around her waist.

She smirks. "You think we could pull this off?"

"Easy, babe. You work on your art during the day, dabble in some social media before my games, and when I get home, I'll make you scream my name until you no longer have a voice. Seems like a good deal to me, and hey, if you happen to make me a bologna sandwich here or there, that works too."

She chuckles and plays with the short strands of my chest hair.

"I love bologna sandwiches," she whispers.

"So do I," I whisper back. "That's how I know we're meant to be together."

"Seems too good to be true." I don't want her to doubt us.

"Having you sitting on me right now seems too good to be true," I say as I grab the knot she made in my shirt.

She pauses me. "Are you serious about this?"

"Never been more serious about anything," I say. "I want you, Wylie. All of you. I want to spoil you and show you that I'm the man you deserve. Let me do that. Give me a chance."

Her eyes lock with mine, and without saying anything, she undoes the knot of my shirt and flaps it open, revealing her perfect breasts. Groaning, I lay her down on the couch and move between her legs before pressing kisses along her neck, down to her collarbone, and across her chest. I pause for a moment, waiting for her to adjust her body to fit me better, and when she does, I kiss my way across her breasts, down her stomach, and right to her inner thighs, where I push up her skirt and marvel at her perfectly bare pussy.

"Fuck, you're so perfect," I say before I kiss her inner thighs and above her pussy. She squirms beneath me, looking for me to find her center, but I don't. Instead, I kiss down her leg to her knee and then back up, only to move to the other leg.

"Levi," she says on a groan. "Please don't tease me."

"Says the girl who dry-humped me a few nights ago."

She chuckles. "I can't believe you didn't budge."

"I can't believe I didn't come in my pants."

She laughs some more, and I continue to rain kisses over her legs until she lifts her pelvis, seeking my tongue. Feeling like she's had enough, I spread her with two fingers before bringing my tongue right to her glistening clit.

"Yes," she moans loudly as her hand falls to my head, keeping me in place. I love that. I love when a woman shows me what she wants and how she wants it. It's sexy.

I flatten my tongue against her clit and make long, languid strokes, sliding against her pussy so when I narrow my stroke, she cries out.

My other hand slides between her legs and inside her, angling to finger her G-spot. The moment I connect with it, she clenches around me on a gasp.

Perfect.

I lightly stroke it, causing her body to stiffen and her legs to fall open even wider.

"Oh fuck, Levi, what . . . where . . . oh my God."

I smile to myself and take that moment to make short strokes over her clit, flicking it and humming, mimicking the sensation she'd get from a vibrator, and it seems to be working as her chest heaves.

I pull away for a moment. "Play with your tits, Wylie. I want you coming in less than thirty seconds. Got it?"

She nods and plucks at her nipples. Immediately, her teeth pull on her bottom lip, so I pause to watch her, feeling my cock ache against the zipper of my jeans, wanting to play as well.

"Keep playing, Wylie," I say as she pinches her nipples now, making her wetter around my fingers. I decide to take that moment and match her pinching with short strokes against her G-spot. It proves to work as her eyes fly open, and she gasps. "That's it, baby. Fuck, it's so hot watching you. And watching you with Samantha, Jesus, fuck. I loved seeing you enjoy her." Her eyes fly shut as she continues to play with herself, her hips now rotating against my hand. "But that won't happen again because I don't share." I bring my mouth back down to her pussy, and I kiss her there, lingering and never giving her what she wants for release.

"Please," she pants. "Please, Levi."

"Please, you want to touch her again? Or please, you want me to touch you?"

"You," she says on a pained groan. "Oh fuck, please, please let me come."

Smiling, I spread her again, and this time, I suck her clit between my lips as I stroke her G-spot quickly.

It's all she needs.

She screams out my name, coming fast and hard, convulsing wildly beneath me. It's the sexiest thing I've ever experienced.

I lightly kiss her legs again, her pussy, and up her stomach as she comes back down to earth. When she opens her eyes and looks at me, I stand and undo my pants, pushing them all the way off, along with my briefs. I grip my hard cock and straddle her body on the couch. She must know exactly what I want because she presses her breasts together, and I slip my dick in her cleavage.

"Fuck, yes," I say as I pulse against her, my balls dragging along her stomach as I do so, creating a new sensation that feels fucking amazing.

Her eyes meet mine, and as I thrust against her breasts, while she gives me a good squeeze, I keep thinking how goddamn lucky I am. And why the hell did I play around for so long? This is what I should have been doing from day one. I'm a fucking idiot.

I brace my hand against the couch to give myself better leverage and start moving faster, my body already there, my arousal primed and ready to go as her soft breasts squeeze my cock hard.

"Jesus," I mutter as I move faster. "Fuck, feels amazing."

"Not as amazing as my mouth," she says before licking her lips, which makes me pause.

Her tits or her mouth.

Christ, I don't even know.

But she decides for me as she brings my cock to her mouth, where she sucks in the tip and swirls her tongue around it.

Oh fuck yes, her mouth . . . always her goddamn mouth.

She grips the root of my cock and squeezes hard, pumping as she sucks. The only thing better would be if . . .

Her hand presses the spot right behind my balls, causing my eyes to widen in pleasure as a pulse of arousal screams through me.

"Fuck, Wylie." I tighten my grip on the couch.

She smiles, her mouth full of my dick, then she takes me in farther, gagging slightly before pulling out.

"Not going to last," I say as I thrust my hips. She opens her mouth and lets me hit her in the back of the throat. I pull out as she sucks at the same time.

The space around us starts to go black as my balls tighten with my impending orgasm.

"Going to come," I say as I pull all the way out of her mouth. She presses her tits together, I pump my cock until it swells, and I come all over her gorgeous breasts. "Fuck . . . me," I breathe heavily as I slowly move my hand over my length, getting out every last drop.

After a few seconds, she says, "You've come on my ass and my tits. Now, you just need to come inside me, and you'll own every inch of my body."

My face heats as I stare down at her. "Give me a few minutes."

She chuckles and lifts up, my cum all over her beautiful body. With her hand on my chest, she leans in and presses the lightest of kisses to my lips. "I'm going to shower . . . alone."

"Alone?" I ask, feeling sad.

"Yes, alone. But I'll come back."

"Yeah?" I ask, feeling in a daze.

"Well, I'm supposed to sleep in your bed, right?"

"Damn right," I say.

"Let me gather myself and my things, and I'll be over in a little while."

"Do you need help cleaning?" I hopefully ask.

She smirks. "No."

When she takes off toward the kitchen, I call out to her before she's fully gone. "Wylie?"

"Yes?" she asks, pausing and turning toward me.

"You're mine."

She smirks again. "I know, Levi." And with that, she takes off down the hallway toward the nanny hole.

I collapse on the couch and grip my forehead.

Holy fucking shit.

Chapter Fifteen

WYLIE

"Thank God you answered," I say when Sandie's face pops up on my phone. She's already in bed, Dale next to her wearing his headphones and most likely listening to an audiobook.

"What's going on?"

"He took me to a sex club, I touched a woman's breasts, he was hard as stone, I broke, we fucked . . . twice, and now he's claimed me as his, and I'm about to go to his bedroom where I'll be sleeping for the foreseeable future."

Her mouth falls open as she stares back at me.

She blinks a few times. "Uh . . . how did this all happen in the matter of a few hours?"

"I have no idea but, oh my God, Sandie, the man can fuck. Like . . . really fuck. I've never experienced anything like it. And his hands are huge and his body is huge and his pecs are, ugh, God, they're so amazing, and his penis, Jesus, Sandie, his penis. It's tattooed and long and thick, and I swear he touched me in places I never knew existed."

"Wait, tattooed?"

"Yes, easily the hottest penis I've ever seen. And he was right, he has smooth balls. And I really like playing with them. I liked them so much that I truly believe I might suck them. I've never done that before, but his balls deserve to be sucked."

Sandie glances at Dale, who's thankfully oblivious to our conversation, and whispers, "You seriously want to suck his balls?"

"Desperately," I say. "Like I might just go into his room right now, strip him down, and dangle his balls like grapes over my mouth."

"Wow, okay, so really obsessed with his balls. Got it. Can I ask, though, how did you break?"

"He was going to take another girl to a private room in the sex club—and I know that sounds insane, but just go with it—and I asked him not to because I wanted him."

"You straight up told him?"

"Yes," I say. "I couldn't stomach the thought of it. Anyway, he made me come fast and hard, then when we got back to his apartment, he apologized for everything, and I apologized. He said he wanted to make this happen, and we'd figure out my dad later."

"Wow, okay so . . . how do you feel about that?"

I can't hide my smile. "I feel kind of amazing. I've never felt like this around a man before, and he's such a man, Sandie. Like this is why you should date older men because older men aren't idiots. They know what they're doing, and if the way I just came from his mouth doesn't prove that, I don't know what does."

"So you're all in then?"

"I guess so. He said I could still work for him, do the more serious things like his socials and calendar and packing, but the asinine shit is off the table. He wants me to focus on my art and what I want from my career, and when the time comes, we'll tell my dad. Until then, we're just going to be . . . us and, oh my God, as I say that to you right now, I remember him telling me that we'd keep this information between me and him. I hope he doesn't mind that I told you."

"Oh, I doubt that he'll mind."

"You can't tell anyone." I point my finger at her.

"Who the hell would I tell?" she asks.

"I don't know . . . Dale?"

She glances behind her to a now sleeping Dale with his headphones on, then back at me. "Trust me, Dale won't be finding out. Your secret is safe with me."

"I know. Thank you."

"Of course, anything for my girl. Are we okay with you being the one who broke? Are you excited about what's happening? Do I need to be gleefully clapping my hands and fawning over your new relationship?"

"Yes to everything," I answer. "This feels . . . it feels like it could be something, Sandie."

"If you feel that way, then nurture it. Don't let your worries or fears get to your head because I know you'll have them." *She knows me so well.* Because, deep down, I do fear that I'll go all in, and he'll grow bored of me. That I won't be good enough. That he'll get his fix and then leave.

But my fears are something I need to battle because I trust Levi.

"I've already started having them," I admit.

"Well, stop it," she says. "You deserve this. You deserve a man who'll care for you and support you. Lift you up. Soak him up and enjoy every second. Who knows, maybe he's the one."

I smirk and let out a sigh. "Is it weird that I've thought about that? We've barely been around each other, but something about him makes me feel like we belong together."

"I can see it. Mark my words, I think you're going to be Wylie Posey."

"Oh my God." I roll my eyes. "Please, one step at a time."

"And what would the first step be?" she asks.

"Go to bed with him tonight."

"Well, then, good luck and report back. Also, I'm happy for you, Wylie."

"Thanks." I blow her a kiss and hang up. I then stick my phone in my basket of things that I'm taking to Levi's room and head out of the nanny hole and down the hallway, through the kitchen and toward his bedroom where he meets me halfway down the hall.

I chose a simple pink tank top and matching pink shorts to wear to bed tonight, and he's already in his briefs. He smiles as he approaches and places a gentle kiss on my forehead.

"I like what I see," he says.

I give him a once-over. "I really like what I see."

He chuckles. "Going to double-check the locks. Make yourself comfortable, and I'll be right back."

While he heads toward the main living space, I move into his bedroom. I'm immediately transported back to the club with the black walls and furniture and carpet. But whereas the club felt almost cold, in some respects, Levi's room is comfortable.

I set my basket down and take my charger and cell phone to the unoccupied nightstand. I feel weird slipping into his bed without him, so I wait. Thankfully, he's quick and when he walks into the bedroom, spotting me just standing next to his bed and not climbing in it, he questions me.

"Everything okay?"

"Yes," I answer. "Just waiting for you." I pull on my bottom lip. "Last chance to change your mind about me being here."

"Change my mind?" he says as if it's the most insane thing he's ever heard. "There'll be no changing my mind. I'm dead set on this. If you chose not to sleep here, I'd follow you straight over to your twin bed."

I chuckle as he moves to his side and climbs in. He holds the sheets and bedding back for me, but I don't move right away.

"That would be quite the sight, you in my twin bed with me. Bet your feet would hang off the end as well."

"They would." He pats the mattress, but I don't move. He sits taller with a confused look on his face. "Everything okay?"

I twist my hands together. "Just nervous."

"Why are you nervous?" he asks.

"Because I like you," I say. "And that freaks me out. I haven't really liked anyone in a while. And you made me come hard, and that freaks me out as well because I really only know what an orgasm is from my own devices. It was rare a partner gave me one. And you're really, really hot, which freaks me out as well because I've never been with anyone as tall or attractive, or well-endowed as you." His smile stretches from ear to ear. "And I realize that you could have any girl you wanted and—"

"And I want you," he says as he moves across the bed and tugs on my hand, helping me join him in bed. "I want you, Wylie."

"Are you sure?" I ask on a wince.

He chuckles. "Fucking positive. Because if you haven't noticed, you're my fucking dream. Everything about you. I like your spunk and your attitude. I love your hair and your eyes, your fucking body. I love that you tell me what you want, when you want it. And I love how free you are, how open you are to new things. I've never truly been with someone before, someone I want in my bed, someone I want to wake up next to, and that should freak me out, but it doesn't because this feels right."

"It does," I say. "And that freaks me out."

He laughs, pulling me down on the bed with him. After turning out the light, he tugs me in close so I'm resting on his chest with his arm wrapped around me and his hand resting on my hip. My God, this feels nice. Given that Dad wasn't particularly tactile or demonstrative growing up, I often craved affection. And it looks like Levi Posey is a cuddler.

"Do you know what freaks me out?" he asks, the rumble of his chest right beneath my ear.

"What?" I ask as I rest my hand on his stomach.

"The fact that you like bologna. I've never met another person who likes bologna."

I chuckle softly. "I'm starting to think you have a real bologna problem."

"Babe, you should have realized that from day one."

"Apparently. Well, maybe our first date can be a picnic with bologna sandwiches."

"Don't tease me because that seems like the ultimate date."

I relax into his hold, loving how he can make me feel at ease, especially when all of this is sort of crazy and up in the air.

"Are you nervous about my dad?"

His thumb rubs over my skin as he says, "Yeah, of course. He told me several times to stay away from you, and look how well that worked out. I just need to figure out a way to make this right, to show him that it's okay, that we're okay. I mean, he can't really kill one of his best defensemen, can he?"

"I sure hope not. I know my dad will be disappointed in me."

"But why?" he asks. "I don't get it. And I don't mean that to sound heartless, but I don't understand why your dad treats you the way he does. Why doesn't he trust your judgment? Would it be so bad to date one of his players? Sure, there are a few bad eggs out there, but for the most part, we're good men, so wouldn't he want that for his daughter?"

I lightly run my fingers over his short chest hair. "I think it stems from my mom," I say. "I don't know much about what happened between them. I was far too young to know anything, but I do know she walked away. I haven't had any contact with her, and he never talks about her. I think he was hurt and has held on to that hurt for years. A part of me thinks because I'm a product of her, he feels apprehensive about me and what I'm going to do with my life. Maybe he doesn't trust me not to leave him. I really don't know. But it's been hard living under his regime. I've made the most of it and have found ways to connect with him, even if they're small, but those moments are few and far between."

"Do you ever think about just not listening to him, not trying to appease him?"

"Pretty sure being in your bed right now is me not listening to him."

Levi chuckles. "Yeah, I guess so. But do you ever want to stand up to him?"

"I've tried, but it just ends in a fight. It's like nothing gets through to him."

"Would you ever just . . . throw in the towel, give up on making anything of that relationship?" He slips his hand under the waistband of my shorts and soothingly strokes my hip. I love it.

I love this sense of possession.

"Maybe," I say. "I guess it would depend. If I truly couldn't get through to him, I probably would because I don't think it's fair for me to have a toxic and controlling relationship with my father rather than a loving one. I don't think it's at that point yet. I think there's hope, but it all depends."

"Is your career a deal breaker for you?" he asks.

"Yes," I answer without even having to think about it. "I don't want to do something that I hate for a living. How is that fair to me? And that's what he doesn't understand. Sure, I went to school for business, but that's because I was trying to make him happy. Last year, I started realizing that I can't please others for the benefit of their comfort and at the expense of my discomfort. It was a tough conversation I had with my dad, and I know he didn't take it well, hence the situation we're in, but I'm hoping that maybe if I make something of myself, if I can prove to him that I can do this, he might be okay with it."

"I know you will, Wylie. If anything, I know that you're determined. Learned that from the fucking torture you put me through these past few weeks."

I chuckle. "It was a fun kind of torture."

"For you, maybe. For me, I think my dick almost fell off."

Laughing, I kiss his chest and then sit up on my elbow to look down at him. "What made you say yes to helping him out?"

His hand smooths over my ass now as he says, "Didn't have much of a choice. Hate to admit it, but my dick has gotten me into some trouble in the past, and Coach Wood has helped me out of some potentially sticky situations. He's held that over my head."

"Ahh, I see. So it's not your typical nature to play around with assistants and make them do crazy things?"

"No," he says emphatically. "Christ, I didn't even want an assistant. I was fine with how I was handling things on my own. And it's not like I'm a big-ticket player like Taters, or Hornsby, or even OC now. I've skirted under the spotlight and done my own thing. But I didn't have a choice with your dad."

I draw a circle on his chest and say, "I can still see the look of shock on your face when I walked through the door of my dad's office. It took everything in me not to laugh."

"Yeah, it was a mixture of shock and relief since I'd been looking for you for God knows how long. I even had the hotel give me video of us that night at the bar to help me find you. Looks like my private investigator was a fucking moron, given the girl I was looking for was stealing my bologna this whole time."

I chuckle. "Yeah, he didn't look all too well."

"That night at the bar." He wets his lips. "I knew the moment I started talking to you that you'd make a lasting impression. I was planning on one night, but after five minutes with you, I was prepared to ask for your number."

"Are you just saying that?" I ask.

He shakes his head. "No, Wylie. I wouldn't just say something like that."

I smile down at him and run my finger over his nipple, which makes him bite down on his lip. "There was this one picture I found of you with your shirt off in the locker room. Your hair was wet, and you were looking off, a scowl in your brow. It was one of the sexiest pictures I'd ever seen. I can't tell you the number of times I got off to it."

His brow rises. "Really?"

I nod. "Yup. I had a big crush, Levi."

"Had . . . or have?"

I smirk. "Have."

"Good." He cups my ass and says, "And whose idea was it to torture me with not wearing a goddamn bra?"

"That was a combination of me and Sandie. She's my best friend. She's been along for this entire ride, and I, uh, I kind of told her about us. I hope that's okay."

"That's fine," he says as his finger drags along my crack, sparking an ember of heat inside me. So I drag my fingers down to his stomach where I play with the divots of his abs. "You need to be able to have that open relationship. So she helped you make me weep at night?"

"You wept?"

"Wylie," he says, looking dead serious. "You're the sexiest woman I've ever met. You check all the goddamn boxes, every single one of them. And you were walking around my apartment in a threadbare shirt with no bra. Yes, I fucking wept myself to sleep."

I laugh and pat his stomach. "You poor man. And yes, she aided in making you weep. It wasn't until after we found the email, though."

"What email?" he asks, looking confused.

"It was in the Vermont book," I say. "It was the first email I'm assuming my dad sent you because they were the first tasks you made me do."

"Oh shit," he says. "Fuck, that's right. You showed up when I was reading over the email I'd printed, and I just stuck it in the closest thing I could find. So from that email, you knew what was going on and decided to torture me?"

I nod. "Yup. Wanted to teach you a lesson and my father one as well. Then there was one night, after I walked in on you and Patty Ford . . ."

"A great but torturous night," he says while running his hand over my ass. "I got to see you come for the first time, and it was so fucking perfect, but I didn't get to be the one who did it."

"Yeah, that was quite the night." I smile softly, remembering it. "Well, after that, my dad called me, and we got in a fight. That made me change my perspective. I decided to stop messing around with you and instead focus on the job and my art. But then something in you switched."

He slowly nods. "Yeah, uh, I was actually chatting with some of the girls and asking for their advice. They suggested that you knew about the deal I had with your dad, so I turned the tables on you."

"They seem smart. Who are they?"

"Ollie, Penny, Blakely, and Winnie. So Silas's, Eli's, Halsey's, and Pacey's girls. I went to them because, frankly, my teammates are idiots when it comes to relationships. I figured they were the better option. I'll admit, we had some ups and downs, but they were helpful. I haven't told them about this yet. They'll freak out."

"Really?" I ask. "Tell them."

"Right now?" he asks.

"Yes, I want to see their reactions."

"Okay." He reaches for his phone, and I lie back down on his chest, moving my hand to the bottom of his stomach near the waistband of his briefs.

I watch him pull up a text thread, and he starts typing.

Levi: *ALERT. ALERT! Update.*

He presses send and then leaves it at that.

"That's how you're going to open a text message?" I ask.

"They like the dramatics," he says just as his phone starts buzzing. Together, we read the texts.

Blakely: *Oh God, what now?*

Penny: *I don't think I can handle any more alerts from you.*

Ollie: *Did you choke her, and it didn't go over well?*

I snort at that one.

Winnie: *Please tell me you didn't slip and accidentally penetrate her. Was she a willing participant?*

"Oh my God," I say on a laugh. "Are they always like this?"

"Always," he says as he texts back.

Levi: *I took her to a club, watched her feel up another woman, and then she told me not to fuck the woman she was feeling up, and then bam, my dick was inside her.*

"Jesus, Levi," I say.

"What? It's a good summary," he says.

"It's confusing."

"How so?"

His phone buzzes.

Penny: *Wait, what kind of club?*

Ollie: *That's what you're asking? What kind of club? I want to know where his dick went. Did you put it in the girl who was felt up, or the girl you've cried over at night?*

I let out a roar of a laugh as Levi's chest rumbles with mirth as well.

Winnie: *Please don't let it be the felt-up girl. This will be a huge setback.*

Blakely: *I will be so sick if it's the felt-up girl.*

"Told you it would be confusing," I say.

"It's all part of keeping them begging for more information," he says in a maniacal way as he texts them back.

Levi: ***Drum Roll** My dick was inside Wylie. I made her scream my name, then I came all over her ass.*

"Oh my God, Levi." I swat at his chest playfully. "I can't believe you said that."

"They'll love it. Just watch."

Ollie: *Um, can I get exact positioning? And were you in public?*

Blakely: *Hold on, you came on her ass?*

Winnie: *Was it a lot of cum?*

Penny: *Uh, hello, I think we're forgetting one major thing—he fucked Wylie.*

Ollie: *That's right, what does this mean?*

Blakely: *Was she happy about the fucking?*

Winnie: *Did you make her cross it off a to-do list? Fuck boss, check!*

Levi glances down at me. "Did you enjoy the fucking, babe?"

I slide my hand under his briefs and drag my fingers over his length. "Loved it."

He grumbles under his breath and grows hard in my hand.

Levi: *She loved the fucking, so much that she's right next to me, holding my dick.*

"Things you don't have to say to them," I say.

"They need all the details."

"If that's the case, tell them I like playing with your balls. Actually love it."

"See, I told them I had amazing balls, and they made fun of me."

His phone buzzes.

Penny: *What? You're texting us while she's holding your dick? What is wrong with you?*

Blakely: *Like legit, right now, she's gripping your cock?*

Winnie: *Why would you be texting us while she's doing that? Focus on what she's doing. Jesus, Levi.*

Ollie: *You know, I kind of like the idea of him texting us while she fondles him. Can you describe it to us?*

Penny: *Jesus, Ollie, go find Silas!*

"Ollie's the horny one," Levi says.

"I can see that. I think I might like her the most." I drag my nails over the underside of his length, and he groans before texting them back.

Levi: *She just started playing with my penis. I texted you first, then she stuck her hand down my briefs. She's really good at giving head, and her pussy is fucking incredible. I fucked her tits earlier, and she sucked me off. You should hear her come, it's the best sound ever. And she loves my balls. LOVES THEM. I have yet to come inside her, but hopefully, with her hand down my briefs now, that will lead to more. Fingers crossed.*

"You think I have an incredible pussy?" I ask as he spreads his legs, and I move my hand to his balls.

He sighs heavily. "The best, Wylie."

"Thank you," I say as his phone buzzes.

Penny: *I don't know how to respond to this.*

Ollie: *I do. Take a video!*

Winnie: *My God, Ollie!*

Blakely: *And I'm deleting this thread now. Bye.*

Chuckling, he sets his phone down as I tug his briefs off and pull down the sheets as well. I lift on my knees and remove my top and shorts, watching his gaze eagerly fall to my breasts. I take a moment to cup them and pinch my nipples, giving him a bit of a show before I move between his legs, spreading them and lowering myself so my mouth is right against his balls. I stick my tongue out and run it along the seam, which causes him to bend his legs and plant his feet on the mattress.

"Fuck, Wylie," he groans as I continue to play gently with his balls, not touching him anywhere else. I want to see if I can bring him to a climax without doing anything else, so I part my lips and bring them into my mouth, sucking on them one at a time, fascinated with how his cock bobs above, growing harder and harder as I continue to pull him against my tongue.

Wanting a little bit more, I lift and open his nightstand drawer. I move things around until I find a flat square. Curious, I pull it out and switch it on. It vibrates in my hand. *I know what this is for.*

Smiling, I bring it down between his legs, lift his sack, then rest it on the vibrator.

His hands immediately grip the sheets beneath him as his stomach rises and falls, his heavy breath leading the rhythm. I pull back and watch him, taking in the pulsing of his cock and the tension in his muscular body. His thick thighs bunching, the sinew in his forearms firing off. Everything about him is erotic. Everything about him is what I want in a man. Especially the fact that he lets me explore. That he's so open with his sexuality that he doesn't care what I do.

I go back to his nightstand and pull out a simple vibrator, just a wand, and I turn it on. I straddle his cock, letting the ridge press right against my wet clit.

"Baby, you're drenched," he says as he presses his hands to my thighs.

"I love turning you on. It turns me on," I say as I run the vibrating wand over his chest and across his nipples.

He sucks in a sharp breath and watches intently as I run it over my breasts as well, making them shake and shiver from the vibration.

"Christ," he says as he encourages me to move over his cock.

It wasn't my intention to get off on top of him, but with one bout of friction between us, I can't stop my hips from moving over him, not with how amazing it feels.

"You're so big, Levi," I say as my hips move faster, and I move the vibrator between my legs. "Oh God," I moan as the vibration pulses against my clit, making my entire insides clench.

"Wylie, are you close?"

I don't listen as I continue to move over him, my body tingling with anticipation. A burning desire builds up in the base of my stomach, and I lose all focus as I seek out this amazing feeling, this feeling that I've never felt other than with him.

"Wylie, baby . . ."

"Fuck," I grunt as I move even faster, abandoning the vibrator and just focusing on my clit rubbing against the ridge of his cock.

"Wylie, don't come," he says in a commanding voice that stops me.

I open my eyes to look down at him right before he flips me to my back, then climbs between my legs. He drapes one over his shoulder, positions himself at my entrance, and with one solid thrust, he's inside me.

"Oh fuck," I cry out from the angle.

And like a feral man, he goes wild. He pulses into me at a pace I've never experienced before.

In and out.

In and out.

With such force, such strength.

I feel him all the way to the hilt, bottoming out every freaking time. It sends me into a tailspin. My body sparks in every which way, my orgasm a frenzy as it builds and builds and builds.

"Fuck, I've never been this hard before," he says as he angles his body down, pounding into me now. "I can't handle how goddamn tight you are." He groans loudly and, to my surprise, flips us over so he's on his back again, and I'm on top. He brings his cock to my entrance and slams me down, causing me to yell out his name.

"Oh my God," I breathe. "Levi, you're . . . you're too big."

"No, baby, take me. Take all of me."

I let out a heavy breath, and that's when he sits up, handling me as if I weigh nothing. With his back against his headboard, our faces match up. He grabs my ass and assists me in moving up and down—and *fuck, that's so good.*

It's such an incredible sensation, being this full.

Gripping his cheeks, I bring his mouth to mine and move my hips up and down rapidly. He groans into my mouth, and I moan into his. He spreads my cheeks, and I grind against him. His tongue dances across mine, and I suck his tongue into my mouth.

Our connection becomes heated.

Our movements erratic.

And together, we build until white-hot pleasure bursts through me, seizing my body, making me convulse and contract over his cock with such force that he presses his mouth against my shoulder and bites down before he stills, and I feel him coming inside me.

And he comes hard . . . and long.

His moan carries on until nothing is left inside him.

After a few seconds, his head falls back against the bed, his neck and Adam's apple exposed as he takes deep breaths.

"Jesus fucking Christ," he says as he finally opens his eyes and meets mine.

He smiles adorably and grips the back of my head, bringing me in for a kiss. After a few seconds, he pulls away and says, "You own me, Wylie." He kisses the tip of my nose. "You fucking own me."

Chapter Sixteen

LEVI

"What do you want me to do for you today?" Wylie asks from where she's perched on the counter, wearing one of my shirts and looking disheveled from me running my hands through her hair all night, tugging on it, twisting it over my fist, even running it over my skin, loving the contrast of the red color on my skin.

Last night was . . . Christ, I feel like Jesus walking on water this morning. That's how amazing it was. Like nothing could penetrate this feeling, this amazing, glorious feeling. And it's all because of her.

People always say, there's nothing like love at first sight. Well, there sure as fuck is lust at first sight because I knew it. I knew she'd be perfect for me the moment I saw her. I could feel it deep within me, and last night was evidence of that.

She was playful.

Responsive.

And open to everything.

She took charge but also submitted to me.

And I realized last night that nothing will be better. No one will ever be better. She has ruined me in the best way possible.

"What do I want you to do for me?" I ask as I carry over a cup of coffee to her. "Uh, take naked pictures for me and put them in a book so I have something to take with me on away trips. That's going to be priority number one."

She chuckles and pulls me into her with her legs around my waist. She runs her fingers over my scruff and says, "Do you really think I'm going to do that?"

I slip my hands under her shirt and grip her hips. "If you were a good assistant, you would."

"Doesn't seem like the kind of task an assistant would do." Her fingers trail through my hair, and I find myself sighing into her touch. The control this woman has on me is incredible.

"It's the kind of task I require from you, so if you could get that done, that would be great."

She chuckles and leans in, pressing a sweet kiss to my lips. "I'll see what I can do."

I slide my hands up her back. "That's what I like to hear."

"In all seriousness, what can I do for you?"

"Make a post or two," I say, "and then work on your art. Seriously, babe, I don't need a lot of help, so focus on you."

"I can't take your money, Levi, if I'm not doing things for you."

"Then don't take it."

She pulls away slightly. "And how the hell am I supposed to afford anything if I'm not making money?"

I pause. "I'm going to guess me saying that I can pay for things isn't going to fly." She shakes her head. "Fine," I bemoan. "Uh, I guess just whatever you think needs to be done. I have nothing in particular, so if you think something needs to be done, then have at it."

"What about my dad's tasks?"

"Oh, he wants you to pick me up more books to rewrite. He's really into that idea. Looks like his creativity has run out."

"I can do that," she says. "Anything in particular?"

I tap my chin. "Maybe a book on Colorado?"

She chuckles. "Do you really read those?"

"I do now. I find them fascinating. Just don't copy and paste text so I'm rereading the same shit over and over again."

"You noticed that?" She winces.

"Yeah, I did and I missed out on some valuable information."

"Well, I don't plan on rewriting anything for you, so nothing to worry about," she says with a kiss to my nose. "I'll be sure to pick you up some more books about other states." She kisses me again, then pulls away. "Okay, you need to leave or else you're going to be late, and you don't want my dad questioning why you're late."

"I'll just tell him I was busy sticking my dick inside his daughter."

She smirks. "Not suggested."

"Shame." I let out a heavy sigh and kiss her nose before pulling away. "I better get out of here before I repeat what we did this morning."

"Probably should." She crosses one leg over the other, drawing my attention to her sexy thighs.

I push my hand through my hair and take a step back as I continue to stare at her. She notices, and to my dismay, she smirks, then uncrosses her legs and spreads them.

"Fuck," I mutter as her pussy comes into view. "Baby, don't do this to me."

She chuckles and then hops off the counter. She takes my hand in hers and guides me over to the door. With her hand on my chest, she stands on her toes and kisses my chin. "Go, I'll be here when you get back."

"Naked?"

"Naked," she confirms.

"Good." I kiss her one more time, and before I do something stupid, I take off, leaving her behind.

But I admit there's a large smile on my face because those words, *"I'll be here when you get back,"* gave me chills. I. Want. That. More than I thought I wanted.

⊂⊃

"GOOD MORNING, BOYS," I say as I walk into the locker room, feeling like that meme of Leonardo DiCaprio walking along the street, a gleeful pep in his step and a smirk on his face.

All my guys look up from where they sit and watch me sit on the bench of the locker room where I start removing my shoes.

They're silent for a moment and then Silas speaks up. "Someone sucked his dick."

"I agree," Eli says. "I haven't seen him this happy since the chef put an extra piece of bologna on his sandwich."

OC leans forward and examines me. "He has a permanent smile on his face. That's a *my dick was sucked* smile."

Pacey checks me out as well. "I concur."

Halsey remains quiet off to the side, but I do feel his gaze on me as I look up at all my boys. "You're being offensive."

"Dude, tell us it's not true," Pacey says.

"I don't have to tell you anything," I say. "Can't a guy just be nice to other guys without the assumption that his dick was sucked?"

"Yes," Silas says. "But when said guy has been a real bastard recently, evasive, basically MIA, then we have the right to question about the sucking of your dick."

"He's right. It's the law," Eli adds.

"The law of what?" I ask.

"Brotherhood," OC says. "It's the law of brotherhood."

"There's no such law," I defend.

"It's unspoken," Pacey says.

"Then how do we know it's enforceable?" I ask.

"Because . . ." Eli says. "Because we said so."

"Wow, great argument, remind me to use that when I'm in the pits of a controversy." I slip out of my sweats, leaving me in my compression pants.

"He's avoiding the topic," OC points out. "Makes me think that he really did get his dick sucked."

"Of course he did," Silas says. "Just look at his stupid grin.

The only time I've ever seen him grin like that is after a wild night with a woman and when he tried ground mustard with his bologna for the first time."

"He's right," Pacey says. "That grin is reserved for two occasions."

"The question we now pose is . . . who was it?" Silas asks.

"Great question," Eli says. "Could be a random . . . could be the assistant."

"It's not the assistant," I say, maybe a touch too quickly and a touch too defensively. "Don't even suggest that."

"Whoa," Pacey says as he looks around at the boys. "Just a joke, man."

"A joke that's not funny," I say.

"He seems pretty defensive," Silas says.

"Very defensive," OC adds as he leans in close to me and takes a sniff. "He doesn't smell like he's lying, though."

"What the fuck does that mean?" Pacey asks.

"Gross, dude," Silas says.

Eli points back and forth between OC and me. "The more you two hang out, the more you start to act like each other. I don't like it."

I glance over at OC and then back at the boys. "It's true, there's a certain scent people get when they lie."

"See?" OC thumbs toward me.

"Holmes, tell them they're idiots," Pacey says.

Halsey looks up from where he's taping his stick. "I'm not paying attention. Don't include me in this idiocy."

Grumbling, Silas says, "Just tell us who sucked your dick, Posey."

"What the fuck are you talking about?" Coach Wood shouts from the entrance of our locker room, scaring the shit out of all of us.

To my dismay, my teammates duck their heads, acting like they weren't just talking about Coach Wood's daughter sucking me off, leaving me looking like a deer in headlights.

"I, uh . . . you know—"

"My office, now," he says before turning away and walking to his office.

Fuck.

Me.

When he's out of earshot, Silas says, "That doesn't sound good."

"You think?" I shout. "Christ, here I was in a good mood—"

"Because of the dick sucking," OC says.

"Because I was just in a good mood, for fuck's sake," I yell. "And you guys ruined it."

I put my pants back on and then slip my feet into my slides before I head to Coach Wood's office.

I swear, if he heard anything about the assistant talk, I'm going to murder all my friends. *Sorry, Agitator fans, your starting lineup is now deceased.*

I walk past an assistant coach and give him a head nod before I knock on Coach Wood's office door.

"Get in here," he yells.

Great, he seems like he's in a good mood.

I let myself in and take a seat, not even waiting for him to tell me to do so.

Studying me, he leans back in his chair and says, "You fucking my daughter?"

Dear God in heaven.

Sweat creeps up the back of my neck as I try to remain calm and not give away anything. "No," I say. "Why would you think that?"

"What was Silas saying, then?"

I feel tempted to shift, to fidget, to do anything to help dispel my nerves, but I remain calm instead and try to relax the shake in my bones.

"He was being an idiot. All of them were. I arrive in a good mood, and they think that I had sex with someone."

"Did you?"

"No," I say, the lie flying out of my mouth before I can even think about it.

"So you're not doing anything with my daughter?"

"With all due respect, sir, I'm trying to avoid her as much as possible. I really don't think traveling with her and having her stay in my room was a good idea."

"Why?" he asks, his scowl growing.

"Because I was a goddamn nervous wreck the whole time, and I wasn't able to focus on my gameplay." Semi true. "I need my space and time to, you know . . . take care of myself, and having her there is not helping."

He slowly nods, still studying me. "You have been off your game lately."

"This whole arrangement has been stressful," I say. "Maybe we should, I don't know, call it quits."

"Not happening," he says. "Just apply pressure in other ways. Make her rewrite more books, make her repaint your place, decide you don't like the color and repaint it again."

I run my hand over my brow. "Isn't there something I can get her involved with here at the stadium? Like a charity or something? Maybe I can have her talk with Penny or Blakely, get her involved in a way that focuses more on the business side of things so she gets a taste of that, rather than making her do menial tasks." I clear my throat. "I think . . . I think she doesn't care about the work I'm giving her. She still finds time to do her art it seems. So maybe you're going about this the wrong way. Maybe you need to show her what a corporate job could be like. That it's not boring, that she could have fun with it."

He rocks back in his chair, pursing his lips together as he gives it some thought. After a few seconds, he says, "Might not be a bad idea."

Um . . . come again?

Did he just say my idea wasn't bad?

My God . . . did he have *his* dick sucked last night?

Trying to stay calm, I say, "I can talk to Blakely and Penny and see what they can come up with and report back to you."

He slowly nods. "Yes, do that. And make sure it's something that makes her use the skills she's acquired in school, but make it fun for her as well, something that applies to you and the work you're doing." Well, that's certainly a one-eighty. He wants his daughter to *have fun*.

"Yeah, we can work on that," I say.

"Good." He leans forward now and looks me in the eyes. "Good idea, Posey."

My right nipple just went erect.

"Thank you, Coach," I say as I casually cross one leg over the other. "You know, I was thinking about it the other night, and then bam, it came to me——"

"Get the fuck out," he says, pointing at his door.

"Sure. Yup, see you out on the ice."

PENNY: *I know you're getting ready for a game, but can we just pause for a moment and talk about last night? Were you drunk or was all that real?*

Ollie: *Penny! I was going to ask the same thing. I couldn't stop thinking about it.*

Winnie: *Did we really help you find your HEA?*

Blakely: *Were you really texting us when she was fondling you?*

Levi: *It was real, ladies. I told her about you guys, and she wanted to see your response to us getting together. You did not disappoint. Then yes, she started fondling me. She fondled me all night long.*

Ollie: *I don't think I could be happier.*

Winnie: *Eep. It's love!*

Blakely: *Are you happy?*

Levi: *I am, really happy. Definitely not love . . . yet, but I think she could easily be the one for me. She's amazing. Everything about her and yes, we are aware of the consequences. We're working it out and trying to figure out a way to make this all make sense so when we tell her dad, he doesn't kill us.*

Penny: *I think that's smart. Maybe don't tell him until you know that you're in love and what you guys have is the real deal.*

Blakely: *Solid advice. No need to disrupt the equilibrium if you don't have to.*

Winnie: *You can spend these weeks getting to know each other.*

Ollie: *And fucking each other.*

Levi: *Always so eloquent, Ollie.*

Ollie: *That's what I'm here for.*

Levi: *By the way, Penny and Blakely, do you think we can think of a role for Wylie to do that would incorporate what you guys do but will also introduce her to the corporate side of life and add a touch of charity in there as well?*

Penny: *I think we can think up something. Why?*

Levi: *To get Coach Wood off my back about making Wylie do strange tasks, I suggested she see the corporate side of life to see how she likes it. He thought it was a good idea.*

Blakely: *Oh, that was a good idea, Posey. I'm impressed.*

Ollie: *I'm impressed too.*

Levi: *I don't see why you're so surprised. I'm not an idiot.*

Penny: *Yes, you are.*

Blakely: *You most certainly are.*

Ollie: *Biggest idiot I know.*

Winnie: *Sorry to say, but you're an idiot.*

Levi: *Wow, says the happily-in-love women whom I helped form your relationships.*

Penny: *Not this again.*

Winnie: *I asked Pacey about that, and he said you were full of shit.*

Ollie: *Silas said the same.*

Penny: *Eli gave you credit for some of the texting, but that's it.*

Blakely: *Halsey still says he would have figured it all out on his own either way.*

Levi: *Erroneous! They are all liars, and I hope they burn in hell for it.*

Ollie: *Wow, a bit extreme, don't you think?*

Levi: *Extreme would have been wishing all of you to burn in hell. I just wished it upon them. I can wish it upon you too if you would like.*

Penny: *We'll pass.*

I JOG up to my apartment door and unlock it, my mind set on one thing . . . Wylie.

We won our game tonight, but it wasn't an easy win. OC scored a goal with an assist from Halsey in the last thirty seconds of the game to put us on top. It was fucking stressful, and I know Coach Wood wasn't happy with how it all went down.

At least we won. That's what should matter most.

And after the game, I got in a quick leg workout . . . and I mean quick before taking a shower and hurrying back to my car.

Now that I'm home, I'm fucking excited at the possibilities.

I open the door, and I'm surprised when I walk into a quiet and dark apartment. Fuck, is she not here? Panic seeps through me as I shut the door and lock it behind me.

"Wylie?" I call out as I take off my shoes.

"Bedroom," she says, causing my mouth to water.

I try to keep cool as I walk down the hallway to the bedroom. I part the door open and find her completely naked on my bed, her hands in soft cuffs that I had made specifically for my furniture. Long straps connect to the corner of the bedposts that can be adjusted, with soft cuffs that wrap around the wrists. Her feet are strapped in as well.

How the hell did she do this?

I slowly shut my bedroom door as I stare at her and how her legs are parted, waiting for me. Her submission a gift ready for me to explore.

Keeping my eyes on her, I shed my suit jacket and slowly unbutton my dress shirt, her eyes following my every movement. She watches intently as I work on every single button, taking my time because I'm addicted to her shameless perusal.

Wetting my lips, I ask, "How did you do this yourself, Wylie?"

"Took some time," she says, "but it was worth it. Worth it to see your reaction."

With my shirt parted open, I move in closer, testing the restraints. They're not quite tight enough, which I'll adjust, but nonetheless, it's exactly how I want to find her. Needing to feel her, I start at the top of her ankle and drag my finger across her smooth skin, running over her calf, to her knee, up her inner thigh and right between her legs where I press my finger along her slit.

Her slick . . . ready . . . cunt.

I wet my lips, my dick growing harder. "You're wet."

She nods. "I'm incredibly turned on."

"Good," I grunt out.

Keeping my eyes on her, I slowly undo my pants. I let them fall open and then push them down just far enough where I can pull my cock out. It peeks past my briefs, and I take in the greedy, hungry expression in her eyes as I run my hand over the tip.

"You want my cock?"

"Badly," she says.

"You want me in your mouth?"

"Everywhere," she says, wetting her lips.

Another good answer.

Wanting to be naked with her, I push my pants down along with my briefs and socks. My shirt is next and then I'm proudly naked where I let her take me in. With my gaze set on her, I tightly grip my length and stroke myself. The sound of my strokes fills the air as she shifts on the bed, clearly wanting to touch herself as well.

But I'm not going to let that happen. I'm the one touching her tonight.

As I run my hand down my length and back up again, I gaze at her hard nipples and how they're pebbled to the cool night air. "You're so fucking hot. I want to come all over you."

"Tell me where," she says breathlessly.

I stand on the bed and adjust the straps. When I feel that they're tightened to the point of no escape, I kneel and drag my cock over her lips.

"I want to come on this pretty mouth." I move over her cheeks. "On this gorgeous face." I move my cock over her tits. "Fuck, do I want to come on these again." I move farther down to her stomach. "I want to come here and watch it pool over your belly button." Then I bring my cock to her slit and run the tip along her slickness. She sucks in a sharp breath as I say, "I want to come here, and come inside you. I want you covered. I want you to know exactly who the fuck you belong to."

"You," she says as I test her entrance, just barely pushing inside her. "I belong to you."

"That's fucking right, Wylie."

I pull away and tug on her ankle straps one more time. "You comfortable?"

"Very," she says.

When I stare at her body, taking in her reddened cheeks, her dazed expression, and the heave of her chest as she anticipates my next move, I can't tear my eyes away from her tits, so I move back up her body and straddle her again.

This time, I run my fully erect cock over her hardened nubs. "Fuck, this feels good," I say as I enjoy how her nipples feel against my sensitive flesh. Like goddamn heaven.

But I need more, so I push her breasts together, slip my cock between them, and start fucking her tits again.

"These," I say on a grunt as I pump my hips. "These will be the death of me. These goddamn tits. Fuck, I love them." I pump harder, the soft flesh of her breasts enveloping my cock, bringing me so much goddamn pleasure that I could live here. I could spend hours here, my cock going in as I run my thumbs over her nipples, playing with them, toying with her, getting her hyped and ready for what's to come.

"I can't stop thinking about you," I say as I continue to pump, my balls tightening. Fuck, I need to stop, or I'm going to come way too soon. "Out on the ice, I think about you." I pause my strokes and let her breasts naturally fall. "I think about your fuckable mouth." I stare down at it as I move up her body and run the tip of my cock along her soft, plump mouth. "I dream about making you gag. Of you taking me to the back of your throat and swallowing." I tug on her chin with my thumb, parting her mouth open, and I slide my cock inside. I angle my body so I can better slip inside. "Take my cock. All the way, Wylie. Fucking take it."

She opens wider, and I slide inside, hitting the back of her throat where she gags, then I pull out.

"Yes, baby, like that. Eat this cock."

I pump in again, going a little farther. She gags harder, her eyes watering, and for a moment, I fear that I went too far until she sucks hard on my dick as I pull out. When I'm all the way out, she smiles and says, "More."

"Fuck," I grunt and then pulse into her mouth, twice in a row, loving the sound of her not being able to handle my girth.

I grip the headboard, and I thrust into her mouth again.

And again.

And again.

Each time, she gags and tugs on my cock on the way out to the point that my dick exits her mouth with a pop.

"Fuck, baby." I pulse into her again. "Even during the game, I kept thinking about this sinful mouth and your greedy cunt." She runs her teeth along the underside of my cock, and I see stars. I pull all the way out and breathe heavily, my cock throbbing, precum on the tip, my balls looking for a release.

But not yet.

Not fucking yet.

She needs to come with me.

So I go to my nightstand, where I pull out a vibrator and some lube, wanting to do some exploring.

"Has anyone played with your ass?" I ask. She shakes her head. "Will you let me?"

"Yes," she says breathlessly.

Satisfied with her response, I apply some lube to a thin vibrator and then reach under my bed where I pull out a triangular wedge pillow and place it under her hips, angling her upward. Then I adjust her leg straps again so they're pulling her tight and wide. When I'm pleased with her positioning, I bring the vibrator to her ass and slowly press it inside her.

"Oh God." She's resistant at first so I pause.

"Wylie, I need you to unclench."

"I'm sorry," she says as she takes a deep breath. "Just new."

I stop for a moment and look her in the eyes, wanting to earn her trust. "You know I won't hurt you, right?"

Her eyes connect with mine as she nods her head. "I know."

"Then trust me, okay?"

She nods and lets out another breath, unclenching. Once I believe she's ready, I inch the vibrator inside her, and when I feel like it's in a good spot, I ask her how she is.

Her breath is already labored as she says, "Good." Pleased with her response, I realize just how fucking fun this will be. The thought of her coming apart at my hands makes me want this so much more.

With her consent, I turn on the vibrator and watch her eyes widen as a new sensation pulses through her.

"Oh my God, Levi." Her expression is so fucking sexy. Confused. Elated. Turned on. "This is . . . oh God, I can't . . . this . . . oh fuck."

"Different, right, babe?"

"Very," she says as she squirms against her straps. "I . . . fuck, I like this."

Smiling to myself, I lower my mouth between her legs and bring my tongue right to her clit. I'm not playing around now, I'm ready to tease her. Edge her. Make her scream my name.

"Oh fuck," she cries as I suck her clit into my mouth. I want to bring her to her apex fast. I want her crying in desperation for me to make her come. I want her so fucking crazy mad for release that she lashes against the restraints and begs me.

I want her to remember this forever. *Wanting* this forever.

Keeping her spread with two fingers, I play around with her sensitive nub, swiping it with my tongue and making short, concise flicks, which I know will heighten her enjoyment quickly.

"God, Levi," she moans. "You're so good."

Pleased, I cup one breast and squeeze. Her hips lift, and her clit grows against my lips, letting me suck her in harder.

"Fuck me," she yells. "Yes, Levi. Oh fuck, again."

Loving her reaction, I continue to play with her clit while I circle her nipple with my finger, teasing her and testing how far I can push her.

Her breath becomes labored.

Her stomach begins to hollow out.

Her hips lift higher.

Her hands tug on the restraints.

And when she tenses beneath me, I pinch her nipple just as I flick my tongue over her clit. Her hips buck up and she lets out a cry of pleasure.

"I'm going to come," she yells.

Perfect.

I pull away and sit back on my calves, letting just the air of the room circulate around us as her eyes fly open. "Levi," she says desperately.

"What, baby?" I ask as I smooth my hand over her calf and then kiss it.

"I'm . . . I'm close."

"I don't want you coming yet." I straddle her stomach, press her tits together, and start fucking them again, loving the feel of driving through them. This will never get old. Ever. I'd say it's my third favorite way to get off with her. Number one being her pussy. Number two her mouth. Maybe one day she'll let me take her ass.

"Will you let me fuck your ass one day, Wylie?"

She gasps when I pulse hard against her tits, using her for my own pleasure. "Yes," she answers.

"Then I'd truly own you," I say as I pull away and move back down her body, checking on the vibrator. "Still feel good?"

"Amazing. I need more."

"I know," I say as I start massaging her clit, moving the pads of my fingers in circles.

"Yes," she says, her arms tugging on the restraints. "More, Levi."

Her hips rotate.

Her chest heaves.

And her fists clench as I bring her right to the edge again, her pussy so wet that my mouth waters to lick her up.

I pull away and remove myself from the bed as she cries out in frustration.

"Levi, why?"

"Because I can," I say as I move to the side of the bed and grab one of my favorite vibrators to use on a woman—a smart wand.

I bring it to my balls first and turn it on, letting it vibrate all the way up to my cock where precum comes out the tip again. I kneel on the bed and bring the tip to her mouth where she licks it off and tries to suck me into her mouth, but I don't let her. *Not yet.* I move back between her legs as I edge myself as well, removing the wand. One touch of her clit has her lifting her head and body in surprise as she cries out in pleasure.

"Oh my God, yes, Levi, yes."

Her skin breaks out in sweat as she moves her hips faster, and I can tell she's getting close. I let her ride out the wand, seeking her pleasure, keeping my eyes on her the entire time, and when I see her mouth fall open, ready to cry out, I turn off the vibrator and pull it away.

"No," she yells. "No, Levi. Please."

I turn off the other vibrator as well and remove it, leaving her buzzing but with no release. *I need to kiss her.* So I part her lips with my tongue and kiss her wildly. I love her mouth. I love how she kisses me because it feels so real, like with every stroke she means it. I could do this forever, so I get comfortable and play with her nipples.

I keep my mouth on hers, making out with her while I twist, pinch, and pluck at her nipples.

She groans against my mouth.

She tugs on her restraints.

And she lifts her chest, seeking more.

Her body is flush, sweaty. Her eyes are wild with hunger. And I'm fucking satisfied. This. With her. It's . . . *everything.* I've done this with other women, but *nothing* beats this connection with

Wylie. Nothing beats her reaction. Nothing beats her body. Her incredible cunt. It's beyond pleasure.

"What would you do if I left you like this, with no release?" I ask.

"Please don't, Levi. Please don't do that to me."

I stroke my cock, which is swollen, ready for release as well.

"I could make myself come." I tug tightly and lift so she can watch me. "I could come on your tits, on your neck, or on your face. Where do you want it?"

"Inside me," she says. "I want you inside me."

"What if I don't want to come inside you?"

Her eyes well up as she looks at me. "Please, Levi."

Well fuck, I can't deny that. *Her.*

I move to the end of the bed, undo her legs from the cuffs, and bend her legs so her knees are pressed against her chest. Then, thanks to the angle of the pillow, I enter her.

Immediately, she clenches around me, and my eyes roll to the back of my head from how slick, how warm she is.

"Baby, this cunt is mine, you hear me?" I push against her legs as I thrust into her. "No one else comes inside you, all mine."

"Yours," she pants out as I drive into her. Sliding along her inner walls, I feel her contract around me, squeeze me, make me see fucking stars. "Fuck, Levi, I'm . . . I'm ready."

I pull out of her, and she cries out in anger.

"Don't," she says, her eyes watering. "Please, Levi. Please fuck me. Please make me come."

Feeling wild, I undo her cuffs, flip her to her stomach, then push inside her again. This time, I lean forward and grip her neck, feeling her rapid pulse on my fingers as my hips fly wildly into her.

Over and over and over again.

Not stopping.

Not taking a breath.

But claiming everything about her.

Her delicate neck.

Her delicious body.

Her sweet cunt.

It's mine, all fucking mine.

"Yes, oh my God. Levi . . . ahh," she cries as her entire body convulses. She screams out in pleasure, her orgasm ripping through her at such a powerful rate as her pussy grips me like a vise.

"Motherfucker," I yell as I pulse one more time just as she clenches around me. I still as my cock swells and I spill into her, shooting my cum so hard that everything around me goes black, and my body floats as all feeling and sensation is directed toward my cock pulsing inside her. "Jesus Christ."

I take calming breaths as I twitch inside her, both of us catching our breath.

After a few seconds, I slowly remove myself and pick her up from the bed. She feels spent in my arms as I carry her into the bathroom where I set her on the counter and start a bath for us. While the water is running, I cup her cheek. She lazily smiles up at me as I kiss her lips.

"You okay?"

"Perfect," she says. "Really perfect."

"Good." I bring my hands to her hips and say, "We should have talked about this sooner, but are you on birth control?"

She chuckles and nods. "I wouldn't let you come like that if I wasn't. There's no doubt that would have made me pregnant."

I laugh and kiss her forehead. "Yeah, pretty sure that's the biggest orgasm I've ever had."

"Same," she says as she rests her head against my chest. "I'm . . . I'm exhausted."

"Then let me take care of you." I wrap my arms around her and rub her back. "You're all mine, Wylie, and I'll do everything to make sure you're protected and taken care of."

Everything.

LEVI: *There's going to be a delivery at the apartment soon. Wanted to let you know so you aren't alarmed when people knock on the door.*

Wylie: *Ooo, a delivery, what is it?*

Levi: *Something for you.*

Wylie: *Really?*

Levi: *Yup. I want you to be comfortable, and I want you to be inspired.*

Wylie: *Are you going to make me cry?*

Levi: *I hope not. The only crying I want from you is when you're calling out my name. By the way, how do you feel? Sore?*

Wylie: *Yeah, but it's a good kind of sore.*

Levi: *I'm sorry.*

Wylie: *Please don't apologize. I want to be sore from your cock. I want to walk around and still feel you inside me. I want to look in the mirror and see your beard burn. I want all of it.*

Levi: *Baby, don't get me hard in the locker room.*

Wylie: *When will you be home?*

Levi: *After a training session. Won't be long.*

Wylie: *Good because I want you again.*

Levi: *I want you every goddamn second.*

Chapter Seventeen

WYLIE

"May we come in?" one of the deliverymen asks.

"Of course," I say as I step aside. They roll in a large square box and a second smaller one.

"Over there in the corner," the other man says.

"Is that the corner he was talking about?" the other guy says.

"Yes, matches the picture."

What on earth did Levi get me?

I keep the door open as I watch the men open the box, peeling the sides down to reveal a camel-colored oversized leather chair. They set it in the corner, near the window, and then remove a side table that they place right next to it. Then they look around the room for a second until they spot the fiddle leaf fig tree and move it to the side table and place it on top.

My heart flutters.

They then pick everything up and hand me a card before leaving. When the door's shut, I open the letter and read it.

Wylie,

I wanted to offer you a space where you can curl up and let your art inspire. I know you're going to create beautiful things, and I can't wait to see it all.

Enjoy, baby.

Yours,

Levi

I clutch the letter to my chest and let out a deep sigh.

No one has ever done something so thoughtful for me. No prior boyfriend and certainly never my father . . . It makes me feel so cherished. As if what I need, what I feel, is extremely important. As I consider Levi's apology, his restraint—*and then his lack of restraint*—his complete focus on me? That's . . . incredible.

Oh God . . . I think I might be falling for him.

———

I'M SITTING cross-legged in my chair when Levi arrives home.

He walks through the door, and the largest smile spreads across his face when his eyes land on me.

"You didn't text me," he says.

"I wanted to show my appreciation in person," I say and pat the chair. "Come here."

He sets his things down, takes off his shoes, and walks over to me looking all kinds of good in a tight long-sleeved shirt and joggers.

He takes a seat next to me since the chair offers enough space for us both, and he puts his arm around me. I snuggle into his chest and lift to place a kiss on his cheek. "This was incredibly sweet, Levi. Thank you."

"You're welcome," he says, resting his hand on my hip. "I wanted you to have a comfortable place to draw, and I thought near the window and the fiddle leaf fig would be ideal."

I chuckle. "The fig tree was a nice addition. You should have seen them look for it and then carefully place it on the table."

"I'm glad you said carefully. I told them it was of the utmost importance that they were careful, and I tipped them well, so I'm glad they listened."

"They did." I draw small circles on his chest. "This was one of the nicest things anyone has ever done for me." I look up at him and try not to get emotional, but I can't help it. "I love that you believe in me, Levi."

He shifts to look at me as well. "Of course I do. If you're passionate about something, then I'm going to believe in you and support you. That's how it should work."

"You're right," I say softly. "That's how it should work."

Unfortunately, that's not how it works with my dad.

He must be able to tell what I'm thinking about because he lifts my chin and says, "He'll come around, Wylie."

"But what if he doesn't?" My eyes well up with tears, and I hate that I'm getting emotional over this.

"Hey," he says softly as he pulls me onto his lap so he can look at me better. I reach up to wipe at my tears, but he beats me to it. The pads of his strong thumbs run below my eyes, catching my tears. "Don't cry, Wylie."

"I'm sorry." I let out a low breath. "I just . . . I've never had someone believe in me like you do, other than Sandie, and you haven't even seen anything I've done. How can you so freely hand it over, and my dad can't?"

He runs his hands over my sides soothingly as he says, "I really don't know, Wylie. I wish I could give you a reason, but sometimes parents can be blinded by the future they planned out for their children, not realizing, that it's not up to them to plan it. It's up to them to nurture the plans you have for yourself."

My lip wobbles before more tears fall down my cheeks. "I wish he was different. I wish his love wasn't conditional. I wish he would accept me for who I am and what I want."

"I wish that too, Wylie," he says softly. "And maybe someday he will, but you have to keep being you. You have to keep being the person you want to be, and you have to keep working toward your goals, regardless of whether he approves. Allow him to catch up to you. Don't fall back to appease him."

I stare down at his handsome face and endearing eyes, and I think he's such a different man than I initially believed him to be. In my head, he was the playboy, the guy who fought on the ice and fucked at night, and I wanted a piece of that. It felt dangerous and exciting, but sitting here with him, being around him the last few weeks, I can see he's anything but that man.

He's kind.

He's hilarious.

He has a warm heart.

He's compassionate and supportive.

He's the complete and total opposite of my father, and I truly believe that's why I want to cling to him.

Why I need him in my life.

Why I want him so desperately because I want the comfort. I want the protection. I want the stability he offers so freely.

"Thank you," I say to him as I lean down and kiss him softly on the lips.

When I pull away, he says, "No need to thank me, babe. I'm here for you."

"I know you are, and I can't tell you how appreciative I am of that."

"You don't need to," he says. "We support each other. That's how it goes. At the end of the day, we're there for each other."

I play with the collar of his shirt. "You say that as if we're in a real relationship."

His brow quirks up. "Uh, we are."

I chuckle. "So . . . if presented with the opportunity, you'd introduce me to someone as Wylie, your girlfriend, not Wylie the wench who lives in the nanny hole?"

He lets out a laugh as he considers it. "Wylie, the wench who lives in the nanny hole, has a nice ring to it, honestly, but I'd have to go with Wylie, my girlfriend."

"Good answer." I smooth my hands up his chest and lean forward, making out with him for a few seconds, letting our mouths explore as his hands wander down my back to my ass.

That's when I pull up, and he groans in disappointment.

"Baby, keep kissing me," he complains.

"Can I show you something first?"

"Is it your tits?"

I chuckle. "No, it's a drawing I did."

"Then, hell yeah, show me." Smiling, I move off his lap, but he stops me. "You don't need to get off me to show me."

I roll my eyes. "Really? You know I'm a sure thing. You don't need to keep me on your lap."

"It's a comfort thing. I like you here," he says, those pleading eyes nearly cutting me in half.

Hard to say no to that. So instead of dismounting, I lean over to the other side of the chair where my iPad is and wake it up. Feeling slightly nervous, I stare down at the drawing I was working on, then hold it to my chest.

Looking Levi in the eyes, I say, "Please be honest with me. Don't say it's good just to spare my feelings."

"I'll tell you the truth."

"Promise?" I ask.

"Promise," he says.

I let out a pent-up breath and say, "So a little backstory, I've found great fun in drawing and not really focusing on graphic design for marketing purposes. That doesn't really excite me, but this does."

I turn the iPad around and watch Levi's expression as he takes in the erotic drawing I did of Patty Ford with a man between her legs, being pleasured.

His brows lift, and his mouth parts as he takes the iPad in hand and stares down at it.

"Holy fucking shit," he says as he takes it all in.

Excitement flows through me because *that* is an honest reaction. That's the kind of reaction I was hoping for.

I spent all day working on it, going back and forth between Patty Ford's website and envisioning what I thought she'd look like if she had someone else with her. I worked tirelessly on making sure her face was accurate and her proportions made sense, and I spent probably more time than I should have on her chest and refining her nipples.

"Wylie," he says as he shifts under me. "Fuck, this is really hot."

"Really?" I ask.

He looks up at me and nods. "And really good. Jesus." He drags his hand over his mouth and stares at it some more. "The shadowing is amazing, the way you contoured her body. Your lines are smooth. The expression on her face almost has movement to it. The whole drawing does. I can virtually see her panting if I stare at it long enough. Fuck. It's good." His eyes fall to mine. "And I'm not just saying that. This is really fucking amazing."

I can't help the smile that spreads across my face. "Thank you," I say. "I worked incredibly hard on it, and to be honest, it came to me while I was sitting in this chair."

"It's insane, like . . . fuck, babe, I'm hard."

I chuckle and wiggle on his lap, feeling exactly how hard he is.

He groans and sets the iPad down. He grips my hips and asks, "Are you going to send it to her?"

"Do you think I should?" I ask as he grabs the hem of my shirt and pulls it up and over my head, revealing my bare breasts. He sighs happily before reaching up to play with them.

"Yes, I think you should," he says.

I bring his shirt up and over his head as well and say, "What would she do with it?"

"Sell it," he says as I move down between his legs and pull down his joggers and briefs until he's fully naked on the new chair. His erection's stretched up to his navel, and instead of grabbing it, he rests his hands at his sides, letting me take charge, something that I love about him. He's very much a man in control, but he has no problem submitting every once in a while.

I smooth my hands up his thighs. "You think she'd sell that?"

"Fuck yes," he says as I spread his legs.

"Wait, was that a fuck yes to selling or a fuck yes to me spreading your legs?"

"Both." He chuckles.

I press kisses along his inner thigh and move up toward his aching cock. "Should I email her?"

"Yes." He swallows hard, then lifts my chin with his finger. "Let me finish this conversation before you finish me." He takes another breath and then says, "Email her with the idea that you could make more of these prints in different poses and fantasies, and she can sell them in bundles. Trust me, she'd make a fortune."

I sit back on my legs and say, "That's a good idea. Yeah, I think I will email her."

"Good." He cups my cheek. "I'm proud of you, Wylie."

I smile up at him, then bring my mouth to the head of his cock where I swirl my tongue around the tip.

He sinks deeper into the chair, and his muscles contract as I pleasure him with my mouth. The entire time, I can't help but think how lucky I am that my dad set this up. Little does he know, he set me up with the man of my dreams.

I REREAD my email for the tenth time, making sure my proposal makes sense.

After getting Levi off and him getting me off in return, we talked about what other images I could draw. I've been working tirelessly over those. I did one of her with her legs spread, completely naked, and her fingers playing with her clit while the other hand pinched her nipple. Levi really liked that one—it was his idea after all—and then he made me mimic the pose last night while we were FaceTiming. He had me angle the camera down and made me play with myself while he did the same. I'd much prefer for him to be here, but I'll be honest, my orgasm tore through me faster than I expected.

And when he's not home, he makes me sleep in his bed,

which I also love because it smells like him and reminds me of him.

The other drawing we decided on was of Patty wearing a white button-up business shirt and nothing else. She's pressed up against the wall, holding the bottom of the dress shirt up to show off her ass, while the top hangs off her shoulder, exposing one of her breasts. That's my favorite because there's mystery but also, it's tasteful. A tease.

And now that the images are done, I'm ready to send them.

Or am I?

I glance down at the time. Levi should still be in the hotel, so I call him.

He answers on the first ring.

The first thing I see is his abs with a towel wrapped around his waist. Then he comes more into view as he props his phone up and leans one hand against the bathroom counter, the other brushing his teeth.

"Hey, babe," he says before spitting his toothpaste in the sink. "You're up really early."

"I sleep better when you're here, and I have a lot on my mind."

"What's going on?" he asks before leaning down to look at me.

And there he is.

In his handsome glory, hair wet, eyes bright, ready to listen.

"I think I'm ready to send the email to Patty."

"I thought you sent it already," he says.

"I made some adjustments this morning. Just minor tweaks after you read it last night. I'm second-guessing everything."

"Don't. And what's the worst that can happen? She says no? Then we move on to the next idea, which I wanted to talk to you about." He picks up the phone and moves over to his bed. "Had dinner with the boys last night, and Halsey was telling us how his favorite author, W.J. Preston, put out a search for illustrators."

"Really?" I ask.

"Yeah, Halsey was excited about it because it seems like the author is looking to include illustrations in some of his books. Got me thinking. You should enter. I looked it up last night but didn't want to bother you because I knew you were working on this email. He gave prompts of what he's looking for, and I think it might be fun for you. There's also another author on the entry form as well. A romance writer. Rylee Ryan. Have you heard of her?"

I shake my head. "No."

"Well, she's looking to do the same thing, and they're teaming up. Anyway, I'll send you the link. I think the romance author is looking for more of a Patty Ford style, whereas W.J. Preston is looking for murder."

I chuckle. "I'll do both, I don't care. Oh my God, Levi, you are amazing." I press my hand to my heart. "Seriously, thank you."

"Anything for you, babe." He runs his hand through his hair. "I have to go. I have to meet the team in ten minutes. But send the email. I know she'll love the pictures and the ideas you have. You've got this, babe."

"Thank you, Levi."

He winks. "Talk tonight."

And then he hangs up.

I lean back in my chair and stare up at the ceiling.

You've got this.

I turn back to my computer just as a text comes through my phone.

Levi: *Here's the link. Proud of you, Wylie. <3*

I smile down at his text, and with my phone pressed to my heart, I send the email to Patty Ford. Now, only time will tell.

Meanwhile, I might as well check out this link and see what other types of work I can put out there.

―――

"THESE ARE INCREDIBLE," Sandie says as we sit on the couch

with bowls of ice cream on our laps. "Like . . . can you send these to me? I want to show Dale."

I wiggle my eyebrows at her. "Oh yeah?"

Sandie's cheeks blush. "Well, I was telling him about Patty Ford the other day and how you were drawing pictures for her. He had no idea who I was talking about, so I showed him, and well, one thing led to another."

I press my hand to my chest. "Sandie, did you and Dale get off to Patty Ford?"

"We did." She winces. "And oh my God, it was so much fun."

"See, she's fun for everyone."

"She really is." Sandie sets my iPad down. "So you haven't heard anything yet?"

"Not yet," I say, "but I figure it will take some time. I don't expect a response right away, especially since it was a cold call and not what she was asking for. She might just hate the idea altogether. But I have been working on those illustration entries for those authors. I think Levi was right. I might be a better fit for the romance author. He was helping me think up some different angles to draw last night."

Sandie lifts her spoon to her mouth. "He seems . . . amazing. Every time you talk about him, he's either doing something incredibly sweet for you, or helping you, encouraging you. I'm crushing, and he's not even my boyfriend."

I bring my knees into my chest and say, "Sandie, I've never been treated like this before. He's so different from any man I've ever had in my life. And we're not just talking about the sex, that's a definite plus, obviously, but the way he treats me, the things he says to me. He makes me feel special."

Sandie tilts her head and smiles. "That makes me happy, Wylie. You deserve someone like him."

"I do," I say.

"Are you worried at all what your dad might say?"

"I've honestly put it to the back of my mind because I don't want to think about it. I don't want to think about him. I haven't talked to him in a while, and it's not from a lack of trying on my end. I've sent him a few texts, and he hasn't responded. I know he's busy with the team, and they've been off and on with wins, so he's probably stressed and finding a way to level out the team, but . . . yeah, there hasn't been much communication." I shrug. "And I'm starting to see that I'm okay with that. Levi is showing me that I don't need to win the man's affection. He either loves me for who I am, or he can miss out on the great things I'm going to do." I had been ruminating on this a lot after Levi first asked me if it would really matter to my life if my dad didn't approve of my life choices. And it was a healthy wake-up call that if he can't believe in me, can't acknowledge that I want to be on a different trajectory, that I'm okay with that. His validation just doesn't have the same desired effect as say Levi's or Sandie's. I feel freer to be me.

Sandie reaches out and rests her hand on my knee. "Oh my God, look at you. He is seriously good for you."

"He is," I say, feeling my cheeks blush. "I think he's it for me, Sandie."

"Yeah?" she asks, her hope soaring. "Like . . . you could possibly love him?"

I nod. "Yes. I'm easily falling for him. I don't see how I can't. He's just . . . he's perfect."

"Wow." She shakes her head. "Never would have seen this coming, but I don't think I could be happier." She scoops up some ice cream and plops it in her mouth just as my phone buzzes. I glance down at it and see that it's Levi.

"Speak of the devil." I answer the phone. "Hey, you," I say.

"Babe, I need to see that pussy. Undress and grab a toy. I want you coming in seconds."

Sandie snorts and covers her nose.

I smile at Levi and say, "Uh, my friend Sandie is here with me."

I turn the phone toward Sandie who waves at him before I turn it back. The look on Levi's face is priceless.

"I might have to wait to undress unless Sandie wants a show."

"I prefer not to be here when you undress," Sandie says.

"Fuck, I'm sorry. Uh, sorry, Sandie. Nice to meet you."

"Nice to meet you too," Sandie says. "Thanks for being amazing to my girl."

I turn the phone so Levi can look at Sandie when he answers. "No need to thank me, although, I do have a bone to pick with you. That whole stunt you pulled with Wylie, having her walk around in your shirt that was too small. That nearly killed me."

Sandie casually shrugs. "Don't mess with my girl, and we won't mess with you."

"Lesson learned."

We all laugh, and I turn the phone back toward me. "I know I didn't ask, but is it okay that she came over?"

His brow pinches. "Wylie, you don't have to ask for permission. That's our apartment. Do what you want, just don't do anyone else."

"That's fair," Sandie says. *Our apartment. Shit. Ours . . .* Yes, I want that.

"Just wanted to check. Are you headed to bed soon?"

"Yeah, but I'll wait up. Take your time."

"Maybe you can play around with Patty Ford for a bit. Sandie and Dale did the other night."

"Oh my God." Sandie gasps and then pushes me with her foot. "Don't tell him those things."

"Why not? He'll think it's hot."

"It is hot," Levi says. "But I want the real thing tonight, so call me when you're done visiting and don't rush."

"Okay. I'll call you in a bit."

"See ya, babe, and bye, Sandie."

"Bye, Levi," Sandie says right before I hang up.

I set the phone down, but I can feel Sandie's eyes on me. "You are so freaking in love."

I cover my face with my hands. "I know!"

"FIRST THING'S FIRST," Penny says as she clasps her hands together and looks me in the eyes. "I need to know, has Posey eaten bologna off you as a sex thing?"

I nearly snort out the sip of coffee I just took. Instead, I swallow, then chuckle. "Uh, no."

"See, I told you he was classier than that," Blakely says as she takes a sip of her drink.

We all met at Café Peppermint, one of Levi's favorite places I found out, and we're discussing what I can do to help out the team, Levi's idea to get my dad to stop asking me to do crazy shit.

"You know, I'm kind of disappointed in him," Penny says. "I expected more."

"Did you want him to have bologna sex?" Blakely asks, almost horrified.

"I think I would have felt more at ease if he did."

I chuckle. "I think your perception of Levi is way different from the person he actually is. I understand the man you know because I've seen it too. Kind of goofy, but also tough and dangerous. He can be self-centered, thinking he is God's gift to the world, but I think that's how he is around his friends."

"Yes, that's exactly how I see him," Penny says. "The number of times I've rolled my eyes at that man."

"Same," Blakely says. "But I do believe there's a different side to him. Halsey said he sees it on occasion."

"I see it all the time," I say. "He's so not the guy he puts out there for the media and the fans. He's so different when it's just us. He's selfless, thinks of me all the time and my needs, not his."

Penny props her chin on her hand and leans on the table. "How so? Also, I know we are here to talk business, and we'll get to that, but I need to know more about this relationship. I'm fascinated."

"As long as you promise to tell me how you felt when Eli texted you that he just ate an apple."

Penny laughs. "Oh my God, he told you that?"

I nod. "He takes responsibility for all his friends being in love, and he went into great detail about it, but I'm sure what he didn't say to you guys is how each of you are the perfect counterpart."

"He said that?" Penny asks, looking surprised.

"He did. And he's really happy for all of you, especially his boys."

"See." Blakely swats at Penny. "He might be a little off, but he's a good guy."

"I never said he wasn't a good guy. I'm just perplexed by him. Is he good in bed?"

"Incredible," I say. "And adventurous."

"Huh." Penny looks over at Blakely. "Maybe it's in the Gatorade in the stadium or something."

Blakely chuckles. "That has to be it. Although, you're the only one with a baby."

"Trust me, everyone will be right behind me. I know it." Penny glances at me. "By the flush in her cheeks, I would say she's next."

"Ooo, not sure I'm ready for that yet, but I do want kids someday."

Penny shakes her head in disbelief. "She does seem perfect for him, don't you think?"

"I do," Blakely says. "And let me tell you, we are not kidding when we say that man is infatuated with you. Like absolutely crazy for you."

"He is," Penny says. "I'm sure he's showed you how crazy he is for you, but when he first needed our help, he was losing it. He wanted nothing more than to make a move on you, to make you his, to show you that he's not a playboy, that he can be a one-woman man. He also wanted to get to know you more, and not in the way where he was seeing how annoyed you would get over the asinine tasks he gave you. He hated everything he was making you do. It actually made him sick."

I smile softly. "Yeah, he told me, and he's apologized far too many times for it."

"Because he's a good guy," Blakely says. "Even though he says weird shit to us."

"Eh, we say weird shit to him," Penny says, then turns her attention back to me. "Okay, enough of that. I have an idea for you if you don't mind. I know you're struggling with your dad and him understanding what you want to do with your career. I hope it's okay that we know."

"It's totally okay," I say.

"Well, Blakely and I were thinking we have an upcoming charity event for American Thanksgiving. We call it a week of giving back. The fans bring in food donations, and we do themed nights. One of the nights is kind of stupid, but the fans love it— we turn the players into different dishes."

"Yes," I say. "I've seen this. I especially loved the one where my dad was turned into a cooked turkey."

"Exactly," Penny says. "I was thinking that maybe you could head up the graphics for those. The guy who did them last year left the organization, and we weren't going to do it, but then we thought, maybe we could ask you. We'll have you help out that night as well, so you get the feel of it. Posey is a big contributor to the week, so it all fits together. And you get to be involved in both business-focused activities, per your dad's request, and use that creative head of yours."

"Yes, I'd love to. But only if I can turn Eli into apple pie."

Penny and Blakely both snort.

"I wouldn't have it any other way," Penny says. "Although"— she taps her chin—"we did make a baby over a French silk pie, so maybe go with that."

"Consider it done."

Chapter Eighteen

LEVI

Penny: *She's on her way.*

    Levi: *Thanks. Did she like your idea?*

    Penny: *Loved it. She looks really happy, Posey, and I think a lot of that has to do with you.*

    Levi: *Wow, are you actually saying something nice to me?*

    Penny: *Stop it, you know I like you—even when you're being Posey.*

    Levi: *Well, thanks. I feel happy. She makes me happy.*

    Penny: *I'm glad. When are you going to tell the boys?*

    Levi: *Not yet. Once we figure out how to handle her dad, then I'll tell the boys. They're just too loud and obnoxious. I can't let them in on anything just yet.*

    Penny: *Better tell them soon. There's only so much we can keep from our men.*

    Levi: *I know. And I owe you queens big time.*

    Penny: *Glad you see it that way. Have fun tonight.*

    Levi: *Thanks, Penny.*

I set my phone down and look around the living room one

more time. I set up a few blankets in front of the lit fireplace that casts a nice glow through the room. And to add a touch more light, I set up candles throughout the living room—electric candles because I don't need to burn down my apartment. I chose to wear nothing but a pair of joggers because I know she likes it best when I'm shirtless. And I packed a delicious dinner into a picnic basket that I set on the blankets.

During our short stint away, I kept thinking about what I could do next for her. How I could woo her and show her that I deserve to be with her. I can't take her out in public right now, not until we tell Coach Wood, so I figured a date in the apartment would have to do. With of course, a surprise at the end. And by surprise, I don't mean my penis.

Shocking, I know.

But I planned this night to hopefully tell her how I've been feeling and see what she thinks about it all.

Am I a little nervous? Yes.

Terrified, actually. I've never dated much so this is all new to me. I'm shuffling through this with the education built off romance I've gathered from observing my parents and their long-lasting marriage and anything I've picked up from movies or TV shows. As well as the positive things my friends have done for their girls. I've seen the little gestures, the way they talk to them, hold them, pay close attention to everything in their lives. They've been good examples, even if they were slightly out of touch with solidifying the relationship—hence why they needed me. But looking around, I feel like I have a good handle on everything, at least I hope I do.

I pace the living room, waiting for her to come home, which I know won't take very long, given where she's coming from. She doesn't know that I'm home. She thinks I'm still at the arena. I told her I had to stay for a few team meetings, so this will be a total surprise.

After a few long, torturous moments of waiting, I finally hear the front door being unlocked and the door opens, revealing my girl in a pretty long-sleeved blue dress and heels.

When she spots me, she stutters for a second, shock on her face before her expression morphs into surprise and affection.

"Oh my God, you're home," she says as she sets her stuff down and comes up to me. Her hands go right to my pecs, just where I like them.

"Hey, baby," I say before kissing her and sliding my arm around her waist. "Fuck, you smell good."

She rubs my left pec as she says, "I'm so happy you're back. Are you here for the night?"

"I am," I say. "I'm all yours."

She glances around, taking in the candles and the instrumentals *Alexa* is playing in the background. When her eyes focus on the fireplace and the picnic basket, she says, "Aw, did you set up a date for us?"

"I did." I force her to look at me as I say, "I know I can't take you out in public out of fear that your dad would find out, but I wanted to do something nice for you, so we're having a picnic inside the apartment. Hopefully, that's not too lame."

She shakes her head. "Not at all, but could I possibly change real quick? I'm slightly overdressed."

"I think you look amazing," I say as I smooth my hands over her sides. "But if you want help getting changed, I can assist with that."

She smiles up at me and takes my hand. "You know I always want help." She guides me back to her old room where her clothes still are.

"We need to change this," I say as we walk into the small bedroom. "We need to move your clothes to my closet. I have plenty of room."

"You really want to do that?" she asks as she pulls one of my shirts out from where it's folded in a drawer. "You don't want to keep your space?"

My eyebrows knead together. "Space? I don't want space from you. Do you want space?"

Her eyes meet mine. "No," she says. "But I don't want to encroach."

"You're not when I'm saying I want you there."

"Hey," she says, coming up to me and pressing her hand to my heart. "Don't get upset. I just wanted to make sure you were ready for that."

"If I wasn't ready, I wouldn't have suggested it. I want you fully in my life, Wylie. I don't like this separation. I want you in our apartment, permanently there."

Her smile grows wide as she unzips her dress on the side and slips it off, leaving her in nothing but a high-waisted thong and bra.

"I think I can get on board with that."

I take her in as I place my hands on her hips. "Is this a new set?" I ask, running my fingers over the lace.

"It is," she says. "Want me to keep it on?"

"Yeah," I say, feeling all kinds of dizzy. "I do."

"Consider it done," she says as she slips my shirt over her head and lets it cover up her luscious body.

"Or maybe you lose the shirt," I say.

She chuckles. "I'm not about to eat a meal in just my lingerie. I would do a lot of things for you, but that is not one of them."

"Where's the romance?" I tease.

"Here," she says, slipping her hand down the front of my pants where she cups me.

I bend forward and let out a hiss as she works her fingers over my length right before removing her hand.

"Baby," I say in frustration. "You can't do that." I stand tall and gesture to my dick. "It's hard now."

"Just the way I like it." And like the tease she is, she takes my hand and leads me back toward the living room, me walking uncomfortably the entire time. "So tell me what you have set up for us."

I clear my throat and bring her over to the blanket, where I pull her down with me. I open the picnic basket and pull out two plates, each with a bologna sandwich.

She laughs out loud and shakes her head at me. "Oh my God, Levi."

"This is what our romance is built on."

"What are you talking about?" she asks.

"That night, when I found out you were the one stealing my bologna in the stadium, that was the night I knew you were meant for me."

"That's . . . oddly romantic."

I lean forward and kiss her lips before pulling back. Reaching into the basket, I pull out some champagne and glasses, as well as classic Lays.

"This is quite the meal," she says, looking down at it, then her eyes meet mine. "I don't think I could imagine anything else for our first date."

I pop the champagne and pour us each a glass. I hold out the flute to her, and I hold mine up. I clink her glass with mine and say, "You mean a lot to me, Wylie."

Her expression softens.

"And I wanted to have this night with you because you deserved a date, but also because I wanted to tell you that you make me really happy. Like happier than I ever thought I could be."

"You make me happy too, Levi."

I smile as my stomach churns. "I'm, uh, I'm glad."

Her brow pulls together. "Are you okay? You seem nervous."

"Yeah." I gulp, then set my champagne down. I set hers down as well and take her hand in mine. "I'm just trying to say something to you, and I've never done it before."

Her face brightens, and under the firelight, it's the sweetest, most beautiful thing I've ever seen. And for some reason, that settles the racing in my heart.

"I wanted to tell you that you make me really happy, Wylie, and these past few weeks, although complicated, have meant so much to me. And I know it's because I've found someone who understands me, who matches me in energy, and who cares but challenges me at the same time. I know it might be crazy, but from the night I first met you at the bar, I knew something was special between us. Something I didn't want to let go of." I wet my lips and look her in the eyes. "What I'm trying to tell you is that I'm in love with you, Wylie."

Her eyes well up as she moves in closer and sits on my lap. She cups my cheeks and gives me a soft yet full kiss. When she pulls away, she says, "I'm in love with you too, Levi."

Relief flashes through me as joy erupts inside my chest. I wrap my arms around her and pull her in even closer. "Really?"

"Really," she says. "How could I not when you're everything I've ever needed in my life? The goofiness, the protectiveness, the sexiness, the encouragement. You're so much more than I deserve, and I'm going to cling to you as long as you let me."

I press my forehead to hers and sigh. "Fuck, I'm so glad to hear that. I was nervous you'd think it was too soon."

"No," she says, dragging her thumb over my jaw. "To me, it almost feels like we've known each other for a while."

"Same," I say as I play with the strap of her thong under her shirt. "Feels like you were made for me." And then I drag her shirt up and over her head, leaving her in her lingerie set.

She smirks. "I thought I told you I didn't want to eat in this."

"You're not eating. I am, babe," I say before laying her down on the blanket. With a satisfied smile, she lets me peel off her thong before I spread her legs and make room for my large body.

Her hand lazily falls into my hair as I press lingering kisses along her inner thigh until I reach her arousal. I drape her legs over my shoulders, prop her up with my hands, and press kisses over her pussy, along her pubic bone, and when she squirms, I spread her with my tongue and lap at her clit.

"Fuck, yes," she groans as she shifts her hips, looking for more. "I love your tongue, Levi."

And I love you.

I love everything about you, Wylie.

And I will make sure there is nothing, and I mean nothing, that pulls us apart.

Making slow strokes with my tongue, I pull down one of her bra cups and glide my finger over her nipple until it's hard and pointed, then while I continue to go down on her, I roll the hard nub between my fingers.

She cries out.

She heaves.

She twists and turns under my hold.

And when I suck her clit between my lips, I pinch her nipple at the same time.

Her legs clench around me as she lets out a feral cry.

Loving her responsiveness, I do it again, sucking hard.

"Fuck, Levi," she calls out as her body stiffens, and her hand pulls on my hair. "Oh my God."

Her legs quiver.

Her mouth parts.

And when I think she's about to come, I pull away.

"No, Levi. Please."

I stand and push my pants off, then I move between her legs and lift her to pull off her bra. When we're both naked, I slowly take her mouth with mine, letting our lips mold together as I deliberately cup her breast and move from a frantic pace to a slow, thought-out one. She falls into my rhythm and brings her arms around my neck, holding me in place while she loops one of her legs around mine, making my erection press up against her soft center.

I lift from her mouth and kiss her cheek, then her jaw and down her neck. When I work back up to her lips, I stare down at her for a second before saying, "I love you, Wylie."

She smiles up at me. "I love you too, Levi."

This, *her*, this is all I fucking need.

Nothing else.

I slowly slide my cock inside her, taking my time and letting her adjust as we continue to make out. And with every inch that I move inside her, she squeezes me tight. Having her wrapped around me like this is the most incredible feeling. I will never get enough of it.

Never.

Slowly, I pulse into her, making short, concise strokes that create just enough friction to heighten our arousal. And as I pulse, I play with her tits because we both love it.

"I need . . . more," she says.

"Want it slow, baby," I say, bringing my lips to her jaw.

"I can't. Please, Levi."

Smiling, I sigh and forgo my plans of fucking her for at least a solid hour like this and flip her so I'm on my back, and she straddles me.

She falls flat on top of me, closing in on that last inch so I bottom out.

"Yes," she groans as she tilts her head back and plays with her hair.

And mother of fuck does she look hot.

So fucking hot.

I grip her hips as she places her hands on my stomach, pressing her tits together, and she starts rocking, grinding her clit against me.

"Oh fuck, yes," she says as her eyes squeeze shut and she picks up her pace.

I don't know what I was thinking.

This is so much better.

A thousand fucking times better.

I want her on top of me, fucking me all the goddamn time.

"That's it, baby," I say. "Use me, use my cock."

She sits up, places her hands on her breasts, and plays with herself while she continues to move over me. Nothing has been sexier than at this moment, with my girl, my love, riding my cock and loving every second of it.

"You're so big, Levi. I love your dick. I love it so much. No dick has ever made me feel this good."

"Then take what you want, baby. Take everything."

She places her hands behind her so they rest on my thighs, giving me a different angle of her, of our connection, and I watch it intently, my length going in and out of her as she rocks harder and faster.

Her tits bounce.

Her breath is erratic.

And her mouth parts as she quivers.

"Oh God, oh fuck," she says as she moves her hands to my chest again and steadies herself as she rides me hard and fast.

From the friction, the way she clenches around me, and the sheer sexiness of her, my legs and arms start to go numb. The room fades to black, and my balls tighten.

"Right there, baby," I cry out just as she screams my name and falls over the edge, her pussy contracting around me. It takes two more pulses over my cock before I'm coming with her. "Fuck me," I yell as I spill inside her, my orgasm lasting longer than I expected as she continues to contract around me.

After a few seconds, when we're both settled and our breaths are caught, she leans forward to lie flat against my chest. I wrap my arms around her and kiss her forehead as she holds on to me tightly.

She takes a few deep breaths and then says, "I . . . I've never said that to a man before."

"What part?" I ask. "We said a lot of things. Was it the dick part?"

She chuckles and shakes her head as she props up to look me in the eyes. "No, the I love you part."

"Oh." I smile at her. "Well, I've never said it to a woman either."

"I love that," she says.

I kiss the tip of her nose. "I love you."

She giggles and presses her head into the crook of my neck before squealing.

Chuckling, I say, "What the hell is that?"

When she looks back at me, she says, "A girly squeal because Levi Posey just said he loved me."

"Oh, if that's the case." I clear my throat, attempt a giggle, and then squeal as well.

She lets out a roar of a laugh. "What the hell?"

"That's my manly squeal because Wylie Wood just said she loved me."

She shakes her head in mirth. "God, you're ridiculous."

"But I'm all yours," I say while I roll her to her back and start kissing her all over.

⸻

LEVI: *Boys. I have something important to tell you, but I can't tell you yet, but when I tell you, it's going to be very special so get ready for special news. The most special.*

   Silas: ^^^ *Always with the dramatics.*

   Pacey: *Yeah, why can't you tell us?*

   Eli: *And why are you texting so late?*

   Halsey: *I'm silencing this thread right now.*

   Levi: *I'm texting because I can't get it off my mind. I'm so excited.*

   Pacey: *Then tell us.*

   Eli: *Please don't make this a thing.*

   Silas: *He's going to make it a thing. He always does.*

   Levi: *Taters is right, I'm going to make it a thing. Just prepare your-selves. It's huge, and I'm not talking about Halsey's giant dick.*

   Pacey: *It's too late for this.*

   Eli: *Remind me to punch you in the nuts tomorrow.*

   Silas: *You're probably my most annoying friend.*

   OC: *You know, just stepping in here to say, I live for the drama. Now I'm frothing, excited to find out what he has in store to tell us.*

   Pacey: *Jesus Christ.*

   Eli: *Shut the fuck up, OC.*

   Silas: *I was wrong. OC is the most annoying.*

   Levi: *And just like always . . . OC is my favorite.*

⸻

BAG IN HAND, I stuff my phone in it along with my wallet and stand from the bench where I just finished putting my shoes on.

Another win for the men tonight, but this time, it was special because Wylie was in the stands. She sat with Blakely and Penny, helping them with some random marketing shit to appease her father. The entire game, it felt like my penis led the way, and I know that might sound weird, but I was dead set on showing her how amazing I was on the ice. And sure, I know she's seen it before, but it was different this time. She was mine while watching me this time, and I wanted to make her proud. I wanted her to think in her head, there's my man.

And thankfully, I had one of my best games, and I didn't get in a fight, so all in all, a good fucking night. I have something special in my bag to clinch it.

"I'm out," I say to the boys. "Good game." I offer Pacey knuckles. "Amazing shutout, man."

"Couldn't have done it without you," he says as he leans back on the bench, looking stiffer than normal. Not sure how many years he has left in him. I know he's been considering retirement, and with his head injury, which I know still causes him some pain, I could see him retiring at the end of this year and starting a family with Winnie.

Makes me think what my future looks like.

To be the absolute dreamer where everything in life is perfect and not based in my current reality, it would look like this . . .

Wylie as my forever girl and Coach Wood by my side, shaking my hand for being the best son-in-law he could have asked for.

We'd joke over him blessing his underwear, and he'd poke fun at me for eating bologna, then we'd hug each other because that's what men do when they like each other.

Then he'd sit me down, look me in the eyes, and say how proud he is to call me son. I'd grip his shoulder and say something like, he's my second favorite father.

We would laugh.

And then of course . . . hug again.

It would be magical. He wouldn't want to kill me, he'd accept Wylie for all the greatness that she is, and he'd apologize for being an ignorant father and not recognizing how smart and talented Wylie is. We of course would forgive him and then spend Sunday nights during the summer playing Phase 10.

Sigh . . . keep dreaming, Posey.

I head out of the locker room where I find Wylie waiting for me while she talks to Blakely, Penny, and Winnie. Look at her fitting in so well.

And that's another thing, Coach Wood would tell me how he was such a fool for thinking she should finish school because that was his plan. He'd congratulate me on being a supportive boyfriend, then he'd one more time . . . hug me.

I'd sniff him.

He'd sniff me.

He'd say I smell amazing.

I'd joke around about buying him the same cologne for Christmas.

Our heads would fall back as he roared with laughter—

"Posey!" Coach Wood yells.

And yup, my balls just crawled up my ass.

I turn toward him as I feel the girls look over at me.

"Hey, Coach Wood," I say, trying to look like an ounce of man.

Coach Wood walks up to me, looks over my shoulder clearly where Wylie is standing, and says, "I need a progress report."

"Uh . . . here?" I ask.

"Yes," he says, keeping his voice low so I do the same.

"Uh, well, she seems to like working with the girls."

He glances over my shoulder, where Wylie says, "Hey, Dad."

Coach Wood just nods and whispers, "I need you to suggest she take classes again."

Yeah, okay, that's going to happen.

"Sure. Any particular rhetoric you'd like me to use?"

"No, you imbecile, just suggest it and encourage it."

"Right, I can do that."

"She seems to trust you," he says, almost skeptically. "Does she go to you with questions about life?"

Does asking if her bra makes her tits look big count? Because if so, that would be a yes.

"Uh, not really," I say.

He slowly nods but doesn't say anything, which feels off for him.

"So . . . is that all?" I ask.

"Yes," he says, straightening up.

"Great. Uh, good game, right, Coach?"

He doesn't answer. He just spins on his heel and walks away.

Okay, that was weird.

I wait for him to disappear farther down the hallway until I turn toward Wylie, who also stares off down the hallway. I slowly approach her and try to play it cool as I say, "Wylie, you ready to have that meeting?"

Her eyes find mine, and a smile appears on her face. "Yes. That would be great."

"Awesome, come with me." I nod at Penny and Blakely who roll their eyes at us.

"Talk to you later, Wylie," Penny calls out.

"I'll send you over the mocks tomorrow," Wylie says.

"Sounds good." They wave, and then Wylie and I are headed down the hallway and straight to the players' parking lot, which is thankfully closed off from the public. I open her car door for her and help her in before going to my side of the car. When we're inside, I turn toward her, grip the back of her head, and bring her mouth to mine.

We kiss for a solid thirty seconds before I pull away and smile lazily at her. "Hey, you."

She mirrors my expression. "Hey. Great game. You looked so hot out there."

"Yeah?"

She nods, her teeth pulling on her bottom lip. "Really hot."

"Well, hold on to that thought because I have a surprise for you."

"You do?"

I start pulling out of the parking spot while I say, "I do."

And then we head down the road.

I place my hand on her thigh, and she places her hand on top of mine. It's the kind of hold I would see my parents do all the time, and now I get to experience it.

"Is it bad that I was kind of hoping you got in a fight?" she says.

"What?" I laugh. "You wanted me to get in a fight?"

From the corner of my eye, I catch her wince. "I didn't want you to get hurt. I just wanted to see you dominate, is all."

"I can dominate you later tonight if that's what you need, baby."

Her hand squeezes around mine. "I guess that will do," she says playfully.

"Glad I could accommodate."

We sit in silence for a second before she asks, "What was my dad talking to you about?"

"You," I answer. "He wants me to encourage you to go back to school."

"Oh yeah? Are you going to?"

I stop at a red light and look over at her. "No, but I am going to say you need to do what you want to do with your life, despite what other people might want for you."

"Uh-huh, and what do you want for me?"

"If I had it my way?" I point at my chest and start driving again. "You'd be naked, primed, and ready for me every time I get home."

"So, your mistress?"

"I prefer the term sex wench."

Her head tilts back as she laughs. "Oh, sorry about that. You want me to be your sex wench?"

"With a pussy like yours, yeah, I really fucking do."

She chuckles, and I love seeing that smile on her face. "So where are we headed? I thought we weren't supposed to be seen in public."

I turn down a dark alleyway and say, "Don't worry, no one will see us." I park in front of a back door, and when she glances over at me, I can see the trepidation in her eyes. "Trust me?"

"Of course," she says.

"Then follow me." We both get out of the car and meet at the front of the hood. I take her hand and then walk up to the door where I knock on it.

A slot at the top opens up, and a man takes me in. "Mr. Posey," he says. "Good game tonight."

"Thank you," I say as he opens the door and gestures down a long, barely lit hallway.

Wylie clings close to me, and as we make our way down, she whispers, "Is this a sex dungeon?"

"No." I laugh as we reach a door where we're greeted by a balding man with a thick mustache.

"Mr. Posey." He shakes my hand. "I'm Harold and will be assisting you. We're so pleased to have you with us tonight."

"Call me Levi," I say and follow Harold into another room, this one much smaller and with a table and three chairs. In the center of the table is a large velvet box. Wylie looks all sorts of confused, so I turn toward Harold and ask, "Can you give us a minute?"

"Of course." Harold bows his head and then leaves the room, shutting the door behind him.

Turning toward Wylie, I take her hand in mine and look her in the eyes. "I wanted to do something for you, something to show you my dedication and commitment to you. And now that I know how you feel about me . . ." I turn her hand over and draw a circle on her palm. "I want to give you something that says that you're mine. If you're open to it, of course. I won't be offended if you're not ready for anything like that but—"

"I'd love it," she says with a smile, probably sensing my nerves because fuck, am I nervous.

I want this, I know I do, but that doesn't mean I'm not worried about what she might think about it. That she might think it's a horrible idea and want nothing to do with it.

"You . . . you do?" I ask, hope springing in my chest.

She cups my cheek and says, "Yes, I'm yours, Levi. If you want to give me something to represent that, then please, give it to me."

Fuck, I love this woman.

So damn much.

I lean my forehead against hers and press a soft kiss to her lips. "I'm so relieved to hear that." Then I tug her onto my lap where she fits comfortably. She plays with the hairs on the back of my neck as she beams down at me.

"Why are you relieved? You were there when I said I love you."

"I know," I say. "But remember, this is all new for me."

"This is new for me too," she says. "And we'll go through it together. But yes, whatever you have waiting for me, I want it. I want you."

"Good," I say as I reach for the velvet box. "Because I really want you to have these." I open the velvet box revealing quite a few gold and silver bracelets, all incredibly thin.

"Oh my gosh," she says as she looks through them. "Are these . . . bracelets?"

"Yes," I say.

"But they don't have clasps."

"Because they're permanent bracelets," I say. I look her in the eyes. "It's a way of me being able to tell people that you're mine." I pick one up. "You can take your pick. Some are generic, but there's one with my initials intertwined into the design and one with my number. If you don't like them, I can always get you something else. Maybe something less permanent—"

"I love these," she says as she studies the one with my initials closely. "It's beautiful. And the one with your number . . . and maybe this one." She picks up a generic one, but they look amazing together when she places them on her wrist. And because the number and initials are so subtle, her dad won't even know. "I love these so much. Am I allowed to get three?"

Relief washes through me as I say, "Get as many as you want, Wylie."

She pauses for a moment and gives them a long look. She even moves some around, grouping them together to see what works best. After a few minutes, she settles with the original three and cups my cheek.

"I love these so much. Thank you, Levi."

"Of course." I rub my hand up and down her back. "I'm glad you like them."

I lean in and offer her a kiss, which she takes, and I get lost in her mouth for a moment. I forget about the responsibilities around us, the trouble with her father, and the idea that all of this could be taken away with one wrong move.

Instead, I revel in the feel of her arms around me, in the passion in her kiss, in the gratefulness and love in her eyes.

When she pulls away, she tugs on my bottom lip with her thumb and says, "I'm so sucking your dick tonight."

I let out a roar of a laugh just as there's a knock on the door. "Come in," I call out.

Harold walks in and asks, "Are you ready?"

"We are," I say. "Wylie has picked three bracelets." Harold walks over to the right of the room where there's a small side table that he rolls close to us.

"Wonderful, and she understands they're permanent?"

"She does," I say, looking into Wylie's eyes.

"I wouldn't want them any other way," she says, giving me another kiss that I gladly take.

<hr />

"I LOVE THEM," Wylie says as we lie in bed, naked.

The moment we got home, she led me straight back to the bedroom where she tied my hands up—which I fucking loved—and pulled out my favorite vibrator. She made it pulse against my balls as she stood above me and stripped down to nothing in an erotic dance that had my dick bobbing for release.

She teased me by bringing her pussy to my mouth so I could lap at it, then she'd slide down my body, using her breasts to rub against my skin, and occasionally play with my cock. But she teased me, fucking terribly, with her mouth, her tongue, her hands. She brought me to my apex several times before stepping away and fingering herself, making herself come with one of my many toys. And then she'd start the process all over again, give me a small taste, rub her body over me, play with my cock, and pull away.

It was the best torture I've ever endured. I had precum all over my goddamn stomach, and when she finally let me come, she released my hands and let me come all over her tits and neck.

I was one happy motherfucker.

I run my finger over her bracelets and then kiss the top of her head. "I'm glad you like them. I like seeing them on you, knowing what they symbolize."

She turns toward me and sits up so her chest rests on mine, and I can look her in the eyes. "Have you always been a possessive man?"

I push some of her hair behind her ear. "I think a part of me has. Protective instincts have always been there. But possessive over a woman, never. Not until you."

She softly smirks. "Is it weird that I like that? That I enjoy the fact that you've never been with anyone else? But you find the need to be possessive over me?"

"No," I say. "I think you like to be cherished, and there's nothing wrong with that."

"I do like to be cherished. I like to feel special, and no one has made me feel that way besides you, Levi."

"Which is fucking ridiculous," I say. "All those idiots before me have no idea what they missed out on. Their loss, my gain."

She moves her fingers over my chest, something I've come to love with her. She has no problem touching me intimately, showing me affection, and she communicates what she wants to do to me. I couldn't have asked for anyone more perfect.

"I told Sandie about the bracelets."

"Yeah?" I ask. "What did she say?"

"That I can't ever let you go."

I run my hand over her back and let it rest on her bare ass. "You need to keep Sandie around. She's really smart."

"She is." She glances down at her finger playing with my chest hair as she says, "Are you going to tell your friends?"

"I want to," I say. "It's been killing me to keep this a secret. We've been playing together for a long time and tell each other everything. But this is different. I don't think I've ever kept anything like this from them, but . . . I'm worried. I don't want anything getting back to your dad."

"I don't either, but . . . I also want to figure this out because I don't want to hide."

"Me neither, babe. I hate not being able to take you out on dates or have you cheer for me at games. Fuck, I want nothing more than for you to wear my jersey and be my girl, yelling my name in the stands, but when I say that your dad is still very much on some sick, psychotic path to get you to go back to school, I'm not kidding. And I don't want to come clean to him until you're ready to face the backlash because there will be a lot."

"I know." She pauses for a moment and looks me in the eyes. "Are you worried that when he finds out that I'll leave you?"

My jaw tenses. I need to be honest with her. "I've thought about it. I've seen how these things work, how outside stresses can hurt a relationship. I've seen it with my guys, and yeah, I worry that you might not want to be with me because it's too hard."

"I think about that too," she says. "But with you leaving me. You thinking that I'm not worth the agony my dad will put you through when he finds out."

I shake my head. "Not going to happen."

"You say that now . . ."

"Wylie." I grip her chin, forcing her to look at me. "I was looking for you for a goddamn year with no name, no hope as to who you might be. I was working off a solid dick rubbing, sparring conversation, and life-altering kiss as my memory. I had a horrible private detective and some hotel camera footage, but I held out. Now that I've found you, there's no fucking way I'm letting you go, even if that means I'm put through hell. I'm not leaving. You can guarantee that."

That brings a smile to her face as she straddles my lap, stirring my cock awake. "Then maybe we figure out a way to talk to my dad."

"We're going at your pace, Wylie," I say as she rocks over my hardening dick.

"My pace? Promise?"

I slowly nod as I feel her arousal against my length. "You're in control, babe."

"Well, if that's the case . . ."

She slides down my body and swirls her tongue over my erection. Yup, she can be in charge all she wants.

⸺

"LEVI!" Wylie screams from the kitchen where she's toasting us bagels. "Levi, oh my God, Levi!"

Barely able to put on my briefs, I rush to the kitchen where Wylie stands in the middle of it, her hand covering her mouth and tears streaming down her face.

"Shit, what's going on?" I ask as I rush up to her, panic racing through my chest.

She doesn't say anything, she just cries, which is fucking terrifying, so I pick her up and place her on the counter so I can look her in the eyes.

"Baby, what's wrong? You're scaring me."

She takes a deep breath and then points behind me. "My phone."

I look over my shoulder at her phone that's on the counter and quickly grab it.

I turn the screen to her, and she plugs in her password, then turns it back around to me.

It takes me a second for my eyes to focus on the email.

Dear Wylie,

Thank you so much for sending over these incredible drawings of me.

To be honest, I was expecting another logo entry, but to my surprise, this was something incredibly different. I have to say, you are outstandingly talented. You captured my eroticism, the beauty in my job, and I've never felt sexier.

I spoke with my team, showed them the pictures, and we think your idea has a lot of merit. We'd love to talk to you about it in person. Think you can fly down to Los Angeles this week? I know it's short notice, but we'd like to run some things by you.

Let me know and we'll book you a flight. Look forward to hearing from you.

Yours truly,

Patty

I look up at her, my mouth agape.

"Holy fucking shit, Wylie."

"I know." Tears stream down her face. "Levi, this . . . this could be it."

"Wylie, this is it. Holy shit!" I lift her off the counter and spin her around the kitchen while her legs wrap around my waist. "This is amazing."

She cries into my shoulder, happy tears pouring out of her as I set her back on the counter. I wipe at her tears and when they're clear, she wraps her arms around my neck and pulls me into a kiss, mauling my mouth and not giving me a second to adjust. It's like a full-frontal attack as her fingers slip under the waistband of my briefs and push them down. With her mouth still making out with mine, she takes her shirt up and over her head, leaving us both naked.

She hops off the counter and turns around, looking over her shoulder. "Fuck me. Fuck me hard, Levi."

Well, Jesus.

"Baby—"

"Fuck me, Levi. I'm ready." She grips my cock and gives it a few pumps before she presses it up against her entrance. *She's already wet.* "Don't make me beg."

Christ.

I grip her hips and then slide into her slick pussy, groaning the whole time. She squeezes while I slip into her, making the pressure of my entrance fucking incredible.

I grip her hips and thrust into her.

"That's it. I want to feel your cock deep inside me."

A tingling sensation erupts on the back of my neck as I grip her harder and smack into her, bottoming out with every thrust.

"Yes, Levi. Fuck, yes." She angles her ass up, giving me better access, and I continue to pump into her, only letting go of her to spank her, which causes her pussy to contract around me. "Oh my God, again," she yells. "Please, again."

I listen. I spank her . . . over and over until her ass cheek is bright red, but she keeps begging for more, so I move over to the other side and spank her, marking her beautiful skin until she tightens around me. Before I know it, she's calling out my name and coming, convulsing around my cock.

"Fuck, baby, so good," I say as I pump harder while she's contracting, and after the fifth pump, my body stills, and I spill into her, my cum filling her until nothing is left inside me.

Feeling fucking faint, I lean over her body and pepper kisses over her back.

"Jesus, what was that?"

"That . . ." She lifts, and I release myself from her. She faces me and places her hands on my chest. "That was I-might-cry-from-excitement sex, so fuck me so I stop crying."

"Hell." I drag my hand over my face. "Well, I'll be more than happy to stop you from crying anytime you want." She chuckles, but I cup her face and grow serious. "I'm so fucking proud of you, Wylie. So goddamn proud. This is huge, and you worked hard at it. You tested what you wanted to do, and this is that foot in the door you were looking for. This is just the start."

"Thank you." She places her hands on top of mine. "I couldn't have done it without you."

"Yes, you could have," I say. "You did this all on your own. I was just here for the journey."

She stands on her toes and kisses me on the chin. "I love you so much."

"I love you too, Wylie."

Chapter Nineteen

WYLIE

Wylie: *I'm going to puke. Oh my God, I can feel it. I can feel the puke, Levi.*

Levi: *Take steady breaths, babe. It will be okay.*

Wylie: *But what if I have my hopes up, and she doesn't want anything to do with my drawings?*

Levi: *She wouldn't have contacted you and flown you to her office if she didn't want anything to do with your drawings. Be strong, baby. You've got this. Then come back home to me, and we'll celebrate in the best way possible.*

Wylie: *And what would this celebrating entail?*

Levi: *Your choice.*

Wylie: *Ooo, if that's the case, I want a vibrator in your ass.*

Levi: *Surprised you haven't done it yet. I'm all for it. Make me hard as stone, Wylie.*

Wylie: *God, I love how sexually open you are.*

Levi: *Whatever you want, I'm at your disposal.*

Wylie: *I can't wait.*

Levi: *Got to get out on the ice. Remember, you're mine. Don't let Patty hit on you.*

Wylie: *LOL. Can't make any promises. She's so hot.*

Levi: *I know, but remember who you belong to.*

Wylie: *Looking at my bracelets now. Only you.*

Levi: *Fucking right. Love you, Wylie. Good luck.*

Wylie: *Love you too.*

I stuff my phone in my purse and look up at the wall that's covered in framed photos of Patty Ford. Some clothed . . . some not. All of them are extremely hot.

God, to be that comfortable with your body, to have your office lobby decorated in naked pictures of yourself. It does give me an idea, though. I know Levi mentioned it, but I think it would be fun to take some boudoir pictures for him, print them in a small, bounded book so when he travels, he can slip it in his bag. It would be a lot of fun, and I know he'd love it.

I'll have to look into that when I get back home.

What is taking them so long? I feel like I've been sitting here for an hour. Is it an intimidation tactic? If so, it's working. I'm shivering in my skirt.

Not to mention, I'm sweating.

My nerves are getting the best of me, and I continue to sweep my hand over the fabric of my skirt so that when Patty Ford finally meets me, she won't be touching my clammy hand. No one likes a clam hand.

Not wanting to get myself worked up, I focus on the pictures in front of me, one in particular of her wearing nothing while she sits on the floor. Her hands are propped up behind her, her head is tilted back, and her breasts are pointed up at the ceiling.

It's so sensual. I could envision myself doing a pose like that for Levi.

"Miss Wood," the assistant, Deena, says, pulling me away from the picture. "Miss Ford is ready for you."

"Oh, great," I say as I stand.

I push down my skirt, grab my purse, and head toward the doors with Deena.

She leads me down a short hallway straight to a pink door she opens for me, revealing what I know as Patty's home.

Her bed is right in the middle of the room positioned in front of several cameras and lighting. There's a dining room table off to the side with an accompanying kitchen, and then to my shock, an open bathroom as well. It's all here, but unlike what you see on camera, it's just one giant studio. Holy shit, I had no idea.

And from the right, appearing in a lavender robe, comes Patty Ford.

"I'm so sorry about the wait," she says as she approaches me. I catch the subtle sway of her breasts, so she's clearly wearing nothing under the robe. And let me just say, she's even more gorgeous in person. She holds her hand out to me. "I'm Patty, you must be Wylie."

I take her hand in mine and say, "Yes, it's so nice to meet you."

Patty studies me for a second. "Have you ever considered going live on camera? You're gorgeous. People would pay great money to watch you take your clothes off."

My cheeks blush as I say, "Not sure my boyfriend would want to share me like that."

Patty smirks. "They never do." She gestures to a table off to the side that I hadn't noticed.

I follow her and take a seat at the table and notice the portfolio awaiting me. Deena asks, "Can I get you a drink?"

"Water would be great," I say as my mouth goes dry the moment Patty sits down and her robe wafts open. Good God, she really just doesn't care.

"Not a problem," Deena says and turns to Patty. She gestures to close her robe, and when Patty looks down, she smiles.

"Ooops, sorry about that. When you spend most of your day naked, you never really think about it."

"It's fine," I say. "Not to be weird or anything, but it's not like I haven't seen it before."

Patty laughs. "I guess you're right about that." She crosses one leg over the other and asks, "So you've watched my videos?"

"I have," I say. "Introduced my boyfriend to them. They're really good."

"Thank you. I appreciate that and love that you're a woman who watches them. My clientele is mostly men, so I love knowing a female is enjoying them as well."

"Well, my best friend enjoys them with her boyfriend too."

"I love that." She glances at the time on Deena's phone and sighs as Deena places water in front of us. "I hate to rush, but I'm between private sessions right now. I'm sorry the last one ran late, but I offer my patrons the opportunity to buy bonus time, and well, the man I was with last was stacking up bonus time. So I apologize."

"Not a problem at all."

"Well, let's get down to business. I loved the pictures. You are incredibly talented, and I thought your proposal, offering these prints to patrons who buy into a subscription every month, was genius. Deena and I were talking, and we both agree that this would be a very lucrative opportunity. But she came up with the idea where patrons, for an extra price, can send in a picture of themselves to have you draw an erotic scene of me with that person. Is that something you could do?"

"Oh my goodness, that's such an innovative idea." I wonder if they'd be willing to send pictures of them on their hands and knees. "And yes, I'd possibly need to have a fairly specific photo of the person to get their body accurate. Positioning. Proportions, that sort of thing."

"Totally agree, and we could provide specifics to patrons once they sign and pay perhaps?"

"Definitely," Deena adds.

"We're thinking that there'd only be a certain amount of those available every month. So there would be tiered packages. The top tier would be offered all the prints for that month, plus the personalized one. This would be an extravagant price, and we'd only have five available."

"Ooo, you could have them outbid each other," I say, and Patty's eyes light up.

"That's brilliant."

"They'd bid high," Deena says.

"Yes, they would." Keeping her eyes on me, Patty says, "We can work out the details, but I'd love to get you on board . . . exclusively. Meaning, I wouldn't want you doing this for anyone else, especially since some people have already copied the model I've developed."

"Wait, you want to hire me?"

"Yes," Patty says. "And offer you forty percent of any purchases of your prints on my website, including all tiers."

"F-forty?" I ask, utterly shocked.

"Yes, Deena and I, which, I'm sorry I didn't introduce you, but Deena is my wife. We both believe that women should support women, and with your talent, we want to make sure you're compensated properly, especially since this was your idea."

Uh, my mind is racing.

First of all . . . wife?

I had no idea.

Second of all . . . forty percent?

Holy shit.

If Patty even sold two prints for five thousand each per month, that's four thousand dollars. That's three grand after tax. And I know she'd sell more than that. Possibly double. *I can live on that.* And if my name is associated with Patty's in the art world . . . *this is incredible.* "Thank you, Patty. I'm speechless. That's such a generous offer. I feel so affirmed . . . in my art . . . as a potential businesswoman. It's amazing."

"We want to thank you, Wylie. We're thrilled." She looks at her wife, who looks at her watch. "Deena can walk you through all of the details because I have to jump on this call, but I hope you accept. I'd love to work with you on this idea." She reaches out and clasps my hand for a second before she turns to Deena, kisses her, then heads over to the bed where she sets up her camera and removes her robe.

Dear God.

I look away as Deena says, "Why don't we leave her to it so we can discuss details?"

"Sounds great," I say as Deena leads me out of the room.

How is this actually happening? This is not only insane but also so unbelievably lucrative.

And the one thing that comes to mind is Levi.

This is happening because he believed in me.

He's the reason, and I can't wait to thank him.

LEVI

LEVI: *At the arena, got an extra leg workout in. Can't wait to hear from you. Love you.*

I set my phone down and lean against the bench, nervous as fuck to hear from Wylie. We kept missing each other yesterday so I haven't talked to her. I tried texting her a few times, but she's been quiet, which makes me feel ill. Her distance leads me to believe that things didn't go the way she wanted them to.

And if that's the case, I need to be ready. Thankfully, we're on a long home stretch, so I'll have time to be with her, and I'll even fly her out to our next away trip if need be.

"What are you doing?" Halsey asks as he comes into the locker room, straight from the showers. When I sent a text to the boys saying I was going in for another leg workout, Halsey offered to join me.

"Just thinking," I say.

"Thinking about what?" He sits down and runs another towel through his hair, drying off the short strands.

"Nothing I think I can share right now."

He sets the towel on the bench next to him and slides a pair of briefs under his towel. Not sure why he's being shy. The man has a fucking monster of a cock. He should be flapping that thing around every chance he gets.

"You're in a relationship, aren't you?"

"Why do you think that?" I ask.

"Because," he says, his voice even, no joking or teasing anywhere in sight. "You've been happy. Genuinely happy. You've looked smooth on the ice. And you haven't been around a lot, which I completely understand. The only reason I'm here is because Blakely is having a girls' night with her roommate from college." He stands and straightens out his briefs. "Seriously, dude, just tell me. I swear I won't say anything."

I need to talk to someone about this. And if I'm honest, I know I can trust Halsey with this. Sighing, I stare up at the ceiling and say, "In all seriousness, I'm in love, dude. And she's in love with me. We've been seeing each other for a while now and well . . ."

"It's Coach Wood's daughter, isn't it?" he asks, keeping his voice low.

I look over at him and nod.

He takes a seat on the bench and whispers, "Christ."

"Tell me about it. I'm in way over my goddamn head, and even though on paper, I made a huge mistake, I don't feel bad, not one goddamn second because she's . . . fuck, Halsey, she's everything I want. She's—"

"Are you the only two left?" Coach Wood says, popping his head in the locker room and making my entire body seize. Christ, how long has he been here? Did he hear anything?

"We are," Halsey says, acting normal, thank God. I feel like I would squeak out a response if I was left to it.

Coach Wood looks at us, then knocks on and pats the door-jamb. "Good work getting extra reps in. See you tomorrow." Then he takes off.

After a few seconds, I turn to Halsey and whisper, "He terri-fies me."

"He terrifies everyone," Halsey says and puts on his sweat-pants, then his sweatshirt. "What are you going to do about it?"

"No fucking clue," I say. "But I sure as shit don't want to talk about it here."

"Understandable." He slides his shoes on and picks up his phone, wallet, and keys. "Let's have breakfast tomorrow or meet up somewhere else so we can talk about it."

"Yeah, I'd like that. Thanks, man."

"Hey, you helped me with Blakely. I might as well return the favor."

I press my hand to my heart and say, "Jesus, fuck, I think that's the first time you've ever admitted that."

"And it will be the last." He offers me a fist bump and takes off, leaving me alone in the locker room.

At least one of my friends can admit to my hard work. I knew I always liked Halsey the most.

I glance at my phone and check to see if Wylie's responded. When there are still no messages, I groan and strip down to my briefs before heading into the shower room with the idea that this will be the quickest shower of my lifetime. Maybe I can stop by the store on the way home and pick up a cake or a cookie or a cookie cake. Either way, I'll get something that could double as a celebration and a way to fight off the depression.

I switch on the showerhead and suffer through the water warming up so I can be fast. As I work shampoo through my hair, I consider how it could be possible that they'd fly her there but then not offer her a job. That seems insane to me. Unless they did and the terms weren't right. If that were the case, I might have to write Patty Ford an email and tell her to change her tune.

I rinse out my hair and start soaping my body.

Then again, she wouldn't want me to do that. I know for a fact if I stepped in and tried to help her, Wylie would be pissed, and rightfully so. She should do this on her own. It doesn't stop me from having protective instincts, though.

I rinse my body and turn off the water then grab a towel from the shelf across from the shower stalls and dry off. Then I wrap my towel around my waist and turn toward the locker room just to come face to face with another human.

I scream bloody murder.

A pitch so high only dogs can hear as I shrivel backward, hand to heart.

"Levi, oh my God, I didn't mean to scare you."

My eyes adjust, and I see that it's Wylie in a towel.

"Jesus fuck, babe." I take a few heavy breaths, then pull her into a hug. "Fuck, you startled me."

"I'm sorry." She chuckles. "I said your name."

"Did you?" I say. "Christ, I must have been in my own head." I lift her chin and place a kiss on her lips . . . her wobbly lips.

Confused, I pull away, and that's when I see the tears in her eyes.

Oh fuck.

I take her hand and lead her into the empty locker room and sit down on the bench. That's where I see her clothes next to mine. Wait, she's in a towel . . . naked. What the hell is going on?

"Wylie, what's—"

She undoes my towel, then stands in front of me and drops hers, leaving her completely bare. I immediately go hard because how could I not? She's the sexiest woman I've ever met.

She straddles my lap and grips my shoulders, her pussy rubbing against my cock. "I got the job, Levi. She wants me to work for her."

"Wait." I grip her waist. "Holy fuck, are you serious?"

Her eyes well up again, and she nods. "Yes. She loved the idea, and I was able to come up with a few more ideas as well. I start tomorrow."

"Holy shit, Wylie. Fuck, I'm so happy for you." I wrap my arms around her and give her a hug. When I pull away, she grips my cheeks and starts kissing me . . . passionately.

Her tongue is immediately in my mouth, and her hips start rocking over me.

"Whoa, slow down, hold on," I say, pulling away. "Babe, we shouldn't do this here."

"No one's in the arena," she says. "The parking lot was empty when Sandie dropped me off. It was just your car."

"Are you sure?" I ask.

She nods. "Let me fulfill this fantasy for you, Levi. I know you want it. And I want to celebrate."

Well . . . when she puts it like that . . .

I grip her face and bring her mouth to mine again before lowering my palms down her body to her breasts, where I massage them in my palm, squeezing and playing with them as she rocks over my erection.

"I'm so proud of you," I say between kisses.

"It's because of you," she says as she kisses down my neck. "I love you so much."

"I love you too," I say as she lifts and grips my cock. She angles it at her entrance, then sits down on me.

"Mother . . . fucker," I breathe. "Christ, I've missed you."

I help her hips rock over me while our mouths meld again.

And it's the best feeling ever.

This right here, being inside my girl, knowing that her future is bright from her hard work. Nothing could ruin this.

Absolutely nothing.

She moans into my ear, and I roar up inside her, just about ready to lay her on the floor.

Yup, this is perfect. All of this is so fucking—

"What the fuck are you doing?" Coach Wood's voice booms from the door of the locker room.

Everything in my body seizes as a tidal wave of dread nearly drowns me. I clench my arms around Wylie as I look over her shoulder at her steaming father.

Hands are clenched at his sides.

Eyebrows are slanted.

His neck veins look ready to pop right off his body.

And the only thing that comes to mind?

I'm absolutely fucked.

WYLIE

"WHAT THE FUCK WERE YOU THINKING?" my dad roars as he paces the small space of his office. "You weren't, and that's the problem. You weren't thinking. You never think. You just do whatever is good for *you* at the moment." He looks me in the eyes. "That's my player, Wylie. My goddamn player, and you were fucking him in my locker room."

I shrink into my chair. He does have a valid point about the locker room. Everything else, not so much.

"That was reckless. Careless. Stupid. And all the more reason you are clearly not mature enough to handle your own decisions."

"Dad—"

"No, don't even start with me. I let you have your little vacation from reality, but it's over. You're going back to school, and that's final. I'll set up an internship in the meantime with one of my friends, and you are by no means allowed to see him anymore." He points toward the door, where I know Levi is waiting outside. "And you're moving back in . . ." He turns on me. "Wait, where have you been living? With him?"

I wince, and that's all the indication he needs.

"Jesus Christ, how long has this been going on? This whole fucking time? Have you just been having some sort of sex vacation away from school?"

"No, Dad," I say. "It isn't like that."

"It isn't?" he yells. "Then explain to me what it is because right now, it seems like you've been ignoring your responsibilities to fuck one of my players."

"I haven't been ignoring them," I say, angry at his assumptions. "I've been working my ass off—"

"Doing what? Fucking my player?"

"No," I yell as I stand from my chair. "I wasn't just fucking him, Dad. I love him."

His brows shoot up before he starts shaking his head. "There is no way you love him. You're too young to understand what love is."

"Too young? Dad, I'm twenty-two. I'm old enough to make my own decisions, date whoever I want, and live with whoever I want."

He shakes his head and laughs, which in return dials up my anger. "You have no idea what real life is, kid. You've been blessed to have a successful father who has provided for you your entire life. You are clueless as to what the real world really is."

"Really? How would you know?" I ask. "You rarely talk to me anymore. You're so busy with your own job that you've failed to realize that I've been trying to have a relationship with you, but you refuse to acknowledge it. I've called, texted, and attempted to show you that *despite* the dictator role you've taken up rather than a fatherly one, I still love you, and I still want to have a bond with you. But you can't see that. You're so blinded by your own hurt that you've switched off your ability to show affection to your own daughter. God, you won't even accept it *from* your daughter." I move toward the door. "And you know what? I'm done trying. I'm done with all of this. Send me the bill for my tuition. I'll pay it off with my own money that I'm earning from an art job I just secured. Every month, send me a bill, and I'll pay it immediately. Other than that, don't bother communicating with me. Your chance at having a relationship with me is done."

And with that, I walk out of his office where I find Levi leaning against the opposite wall. I walk up to him and place my hand on his chest. Whispering, I say, "I love you. Nothing is changing that. It's you and me, okay?"

He nods, but I can feel his nerves rattle him.

"Say it, say you love me," I plead.

"I love you, baby." He cups my cheek.

"And nothing is splitting us up . . ."

He wets his lips. "Nothing is splitting us up. I promise."

And then he lowers his mouth to mine and presses a very soft

So This is War

kiss. As he pulls away, I hear a throat clear. When I look to the side, I see Andie, the GM, looking at us.

Oh no, that can't be good.

"Posey," she says. "I think we should have a conversation with Will."

Levi nods, offers me one more kiss, and moves toward the office. He glances over his shoulder and says, "Have Sandie pick you up. I'll see you at home."

"I want to wait."

He shakes his head. "Please, Wylie, meet me at home."

From the sincerity and pleading in his expression, I know he's serious, so I nod and move away from the office. I then text Sandie and ask her to come pick me up.

I wait outside, my anger and my nerves coming to a crashing point, making me feel all kinds of nauseous. *What's going to happen to Levi?* Is he going to get in trouble? Will he be traded?

The thought of him being traded really makes me want to throw up. But could they trade him over this? Andie didn't look too pleased, but then again, she was called into the office late at night, probably not wanting to deal with this. Either way, I don't think it will be good for him, and he's going to take the fall. I know he will. That's the kind of man he is.

If he wasn't one of my dad's players, I'd be in there with him, standing up to my father with him, but I know this situation runs deeper than that. This very well could be a conflict of interest. I have no idea.

Ugh, what was I thinking?

My dad was right about one thing. I wasn't thinking. I was just so happy, so excited. I wanted to celebrate. I wanted to be with Levi and show him how much I appreciate his support. And I was positive there was no one else here. Looks like my dad parked somewhere else.

Thankfully, Sandie doesn't take too long to pick me up since she was already out and about from dropping me off.

I meet her outside the players' parking lot since she doesn't

401

have access like I do, and when she pulls up, I hop into her car, turn to her, and burst into tears.

"Come here," she says as she pulls me into a hug. "What's going on? Did he break up with you? Because if he did, I will make sure he feels the brunt of my wrath."

"No." I shake my head as I pull away. I didn't tell her anything, just asked her to pick me up as soon as possible. "My dad caught us," I say. "It was stupid, and I shouldn't have done it, but when I saw him, I just needed him so—"

"Oh God." Sandie winces. "He saw you guys doing it?"

I nod, tears falling down my face. "In the locker room. He lost it completely and said some really awful things to me."

"Who? Levi?"

"No, my dad. Levi has been . . . God, he's been amazing. I know he's taking the fall for all of this right now, and I can't stomach it. He told me to meet him at home."

"Do you think this is going to hurt you guys?"

"I really hope not," I say. "He told me he loved me before I took off." But then worry races up my spine. "Do you think he's going to break up with me?"

"I don't know," Sandie says. "What kind of trouble is he in?"

"I have no idea. He just said he'd meet me back at home, but God, what if he's kicked off the team and resents me? After everything he's done for me, I couldn't forgive myself."

"How about this," Sandie says, placing her hand on my hand. "Let's not put unrealistic thoughts and ideas in our heads. Let's just go back to your place and wait for him to return. No use making yourself sick over the *what ifs.*"

My lip wobbles as I nod. "Yeah, you're right."

"It will be okay," Sandie says reassuringly. "Everything will be okay."

Chapter Twenty

LEVI

"He violated the code of conduct," Coach Wood yells, still not letting up.

"Unfortunately, Will, we don't have a code of conduct regarding sharing relations with family members of staff or players," Andie says, clearly wanting to be anywhere but in the middle of this.

"Then what the fuck am I supposed to do?" Coach Wood asks. "There has to be something. He was fucking my daughter in the team locker room."

"Yes, and we'll issue a warning for using team property in such a manner, but unfortunately, that's all we can do."

Coach Wood picks a mug off his table and slams it into the wall before sitting in his office chair. He stares at me in a menacing way. "I hate you," he says. "I fucking hate you. I never should have trusted you in the first place. I should have known you were going to be a horny motherfucker and take advantage of my daughter."

"Hold on a second," I say. "I did not take advantage of her. Everything between us has been strictly consensual."

"Really? Consensual? My daughter said that she loves you. There's no way she came to that conclusion on her own. You've manipulated her."

"I didn't," I say. "We just . . . we fell for each other. Is that too hard to believe?"

"Yes," Coach Wood shouts as he stands again. "It is. You are *not* worthy of her. You're a dumbass jock with a right hook. You've only been kept on this team because you've held your ground on the ice, taking the punches so other players, especially Hornsby, our *leading* defenseman, don't have to. You're overrated, and trust me when I say, I'll do everything in my goddamn power to make sure you're off this team." With that, he charges out of his office and slams the door behind him.

Fuck.

I smooth my hand over my forehead and glance at Andie, who leans against the wall with her arms crossed.

After a few seconds of silence, she says, "Did you really have to go after his daughter?"

"There was an attraction there before I even knew she was the coach's daughter. It was inevitable, Andie."

She nods and pushes off the wall. "The team will fine you for having sex in the locker room."

"I understand," I say.

When she starts to walk away, I say, "Am I going to be kicked off the team?"

She looks over at me and shakes her head. "No, Levi, despite what Coach said in anger, you're a valuable asset to this team. But I do suggest you find a way to calm down your coach because he's going to make your life a living hell."

And with that, she's out of the office as well.

I lean back in my chair and pull my phone out of my pocket. I need help, and there's only one place to look for it.

Levi: *I need help. It's bad . . . really bad. Meet me at Café Peppermint in half an hour.*

—

"OH LOOK, HE GOT US DRINKS," Silas says as he takes a seat in the private room I secured.

"Is it decaf?" Eli asks. "I won't sleep if it's caffeine."

"It's peppermint hot cocoa," I say as Pacey, Halsey, and OC all sit down as well.

Halsey offers me a sympathetic look while taking one of the cups of hot cocoa.

"Is this going to be something dramatic?" Silas asks. "Because I don't enjoy being pulled away from my girl."

"Yeah, this better not be a bologna emergency," Pacey says.

"Guys, I think it's serious," Halsey says, looking concerned.

They all look at Halsey.

"Do you know something?" Eli asks.

"Did he tell you something he didn't tell us?" Silas asks.

"This hot cocoa is fantastic," OC says after taking a sip.

"He told me just tonight, something he's been holding in. I'm assuming what you called us here for has to do with that?" Halsey asks.

"Yes," I say and let out a deep breath. "I, uh . . . I'm in love with Coach Wood's daughter. And I mean that, actually in love, no bullshit, no joking."

Their mouths fall open as they stare back at me.

"I thought maybe you were just fucking her," Eli says. "But in love?"

"Yeah, I mean, it was obvious something was going on," Silas says. "He's had that stupid smile on his face for the past few weeks."

"And he's missed some dinners we've invited him to," Pacey says.

"Is that why you haven't been able to help me with Grace?" OC asks.

"I've been preoccupied." I drag my hand through my hair. "To keep it short, Coach asked me to hire his daughter to teach her a lesson about what her life would look like if she left college.

He virtually blackmailed me into it, and I followed along because, well, I didn't feel like I had an option. She needed a place to stay, so I offered her the nanny bedroom in my apartment. One thing led to another, and despite trying to keep my feelings to myself—since she's the girl I've been pining over for the last year—"

"Wait, the girl you told me about, that's Coach Wood's daughter?" OC asks.

"Yes," I say. "That's her. And well, we fell for each other. And we'd been trying to figure out a way to tell Coach Wood but hadn't. And then today, fuck." I pinch my brow. "Wylie came home from a business trip where she was hired for this amazing opportunity, and in her excitement, came to the arena to find me. She found me in the shower, and well, we, uh, we started fucking in the locker room."

"Jesus Christ," Halsey murmurs.

"Fuck," Silas says. "Did Coach Wood find you?"

I slowly nod, and all the guys mumble under their breath.

"Yeah, and it's not good. He yelled at Wylie, said some pretty awful shit, then threatened to kick me off the team, bench me, trade me, everything under the fucking sun."

"Can he do that?" OC asks.

I shake my head. "No, Andie was there thankfully, and she reassured me that I'd just be fined and issued a warning for having sex on the team's property. But Coach Wood is fucking pissed, and he told me to my face that he hates me, and that . . . that I'm overrated, and the team doesn't need me."

"That's not fucking true," Pacey says. "Without you, so many more goals would get through the defense."

"There's no way in fuck you're overrated," Eli says. "He didn't mean that."

"I know," I say. "Doesn't mean it doesn't sting, but I can get over that. I'm not sure Wylie will get over some of the things he said to her." I shake my head. "I need to make this right, and I don't know how." I look up at the boys. "I need your help."

Silence falls over the table for a moment, and surprisingly,

Silas is the first one to speak up. "I know this is not a solution, but I do want to say I'm happy for you, man."

"Same," Eli says. "That's what I was thinking. It's about time you found someone."

"I was going to say the same thing," Pacey cuts in. "You've seemed really happy, and now that we know why, I don't want this situation to freak you out. Don't give up on Wylie or try to break up because you think it's the right thing to do."

"I couldn't," I say. "I wouldn't do that to her. I just hope . . . fuck, I hope she doesn't think the same thing, like to help me, she would break up."

"If that happens, we'll help you out," Eli says. "Honestly, I'm shocked you didn't include us when you started dating her."

"Yeah, about that," I say, knowing they won't be happy about this. "I've actually been texting your significant others, and they're the ones who helped me with Wylie."

"What?" Pacey says.

"Wait," Silas says, looking pissed. "Ollie knew about your relationship before I did?"

"Even Blakely?" Halsey asks, looking hurt.

"To be fair," I say before Eli can say anything. "I told them not to say anything to you guys because I didn't think your advice would be helpful."

Eli crosses his arms over his chest. "What about the Frozen Fellas? Did that mean nothing to you?"

"It did. It's why I called upon you now," I say. "Because I knew that this was a different level. I don't think the girls can help me with this. This requires insider information." I blow out a heavy breath and say, "I think I need you to help me woo our coach."

"Jesus Christ," Silas says as he leans back in his chair.

"Not what I had in mind," Pacey says.

"I'm still hurt that we weren't good enough to help with Wylie," Eli says.

"Honestly, I'm still shivering over the knowledge that Coach Wood caught you having sex with his daughter. Yikes," OC adds.

"Guys," Halsey says. "I don't think we can joke around about this. I know Posey thinks that Andie has his back, but Coach Wood has pull, and as much as this bologna-loving asshole drives us nuts at times, we don't want to lose him, so we do need to come up with a plan. And I don't think wooing him is the way to go. I think it needs to be serious. We need to put our foot down." He looks between us. "We're his starting lineup. He fucks with one of us, he fucks with all of us."

I slowly turn to Halsey and touch his hand. "Dude, my nipples just got hard."

"Yeah . . . this is the guy you want to stick your neck out for," Silas says while thumbing toward me. "Mr. Hard Nipples. Jesus." He shakes his head and leans forward. "Okay, what are we going to do?"

———

IT'S REALLY FUCKING late by the time I get back to the apartment. So when I walk in and see that it's dark, I'm not surprised, but I am surprised when Wylie's not waiting for me in the bedroom.

Panic sets in, and I call out her name. When I don't get a response, I set my phone down on the nightstand and head into the living room. I turn on the light, checking her chair, the couch . . . the kitchen.

Nothing.

Fuck.

I head to the nanny hole, open the door . . . and find Wylie lying on the bed, curled into her pillow.

"Wylie," I say as I take a seat on the edge of her bed. "What are you doing over here?"

She looks at me with puffy eyes. "I thought . . . you weren't coming home and—"

I pull her onto my lap and scoot back against the wall, gently stroking her hair as I hold her in place. "I'm sorry it took me so long. I had to chat with the boys. Figure things out."

"What do you mean?" she asks. "Are you off the team?"

I shake my head. "No. I have an iron-clad contract. Your dad has sway, but not that much sway."

"So . . . what happened?"

"The GM issued a warning, and I'll be fined, but that's it. Your dad wants me gone, but like I said, that can't happen."

"What's the fine? I'll pay you back. This is all my fault." Her eyes meet mine. "I'm sorry, Levi, and if you need to . . . take a break or whatever, I understand. I put you in a bad position—"

"Stop," I say, gripping her chin. "This is my fault too. I let it happen. It takes two to make that kind of mistake, so don't blame yourself, and like I said earlier, I love you. I'm not going anywhere."

"But if you want to—"

"Do you want me to break this off?" My brow creases.

She nibbles on her bottom lip. "I've had some time to think, some time to wonder what's going to happen to you, and I just feel, even though I don't want this to happen, I feel like it might be better if we just . . . go our separate ways."

"That's not fucking happening," I say. "No fucking way. That solves nothing other than making us miserable and prolonging the inevitable."

"What's the inevitable?" she asks.

"You and I being together. I told you, I found you, and now you're stuck with me." I bring her wrist to my lips and kiss the permanent bracelets. "I meant everything I said when I gave these to you. It's you and me, babe. You're not going anywhere." To prove it, I scoot off the bed, keeping her in my arms. Surprised, she wraps her arms around my neck, as I carry her down the hallway, through the kitchen, and down another hallway to our bedroom where I lay her softly on the bed.

With one thing on my mind, I start undressing her, but she pauses me. "Levi, you don't have to prove anything."

"I'm not proving anything," I say and then pull my shirt over my head. Her eyes move to my chest before going back up to my eyes. "I'm showing you how proud I am of you, Wylie." I push down my pants and my briefs along with my socks. Then I move back to her and undress her. I have her naked in seconds, and I'm climbing onto the bed.

"But . . . what about my dad?"

"Let me worry about that," I say as I crawl between her legs.

"Wait . . . Levi," she says, worry in her gaze. "Please, I don't want you to have to do this alone."

"I'm not," I say. "I have a plan. Now let me celebrate the fact that you're fucking amazing, and you got the opportunity of a lifetime."

"But—"

"No buts, babe. What happened at the arena is done. It's just you and me now, and that's what I want you to focus on."

I spread her legs and press my mouth against her pussy. She's stiff for a moment, but when I start lapping at her, she relaxes in my arms.

That's all I need right now . . . for her to relax. The rest will come.

━━

WYLIE

DAD: *Are you with him? Is that why you didn't come home?*

I stare at his text as I sit on the couch in the dark, not wanting to wake Levi. Last night, I let the events of everything fall to the back of my mind, but after he fell asleep, spooning me, I found it incredibly hard to stop thinking about the day's events. They came roaring back, keeping me up, so finally, I gave up on trying to sleep and came out here, only to see the text from my dad.

Does he really think that I'm going to return to his house? I told him I wasn't. I told him to send me the bill for my tuition.

With what I'll be making working for Patty Ford, I know that I can pay off those bills. It will take time, but I know I can.

Deciding to call instead of text, I dial his phone number and sink deeper into the couch as I wait for him to answer.

It's past six, so he should be awake.

After three rings, he picks up. "Where are you?" he asks sternly into the phone.

Sighing, I say, "I'm at Levi's place, Dad."

"Wylie, I swear to God—"

"What are you going to do?" I ask, remaining calm. "It's not like you can ground me. Or cut me off. You already did that."

"I'll hurt him," Dad says in a threatening voice. That would have shaken me to my core last night, but after talking with Levi, I know there really isn't anything he can do.

"Dad, can I ask you something?"

"Is it if you can move back into my house? That shouldn't be a question, that's a demand on my part."

Trying not to grow frustrated, I ask, "Why did Mom leave you?"

There's silence.

Prolonged silence that would normally crack me, but I stay firm in wanting to dig deeper with my father.

Finally, he says, "We're not talking about your mother. We're talking about you."

"But why?" I ask. "Why did she leave you? You've told me nothing about her."

"Wylie, I don't have time for this."

"You don't have time for your daughter?" I ask, my voice shaking. "I love you, Dad. I have loved you unconditionally ever since I can remember. I've looked up to you, I've followed you, I've listened, and I've honored you. But when it comes to our relationship, it can't be one-sided. I can't be the one always trying, always trying to connect. It goes both ways."

"What are you talking about?" he says, growing angry. "Why do you think I'm so angry? It's because I care."

"But why does it matter if I date Levi?" I ask. "He's a good guy. A sweet and caring guy. He's supportive and—"

"He's not good enough for you."

"To what standards?" I ask.

"To my standards," he replies.

"And what standards are those? Do you not want me to find someone who makes me happy? Who will spend hours every night talking to me about my dreams? Who will support me rather than tear me down? Who will hold me and comfort me when my dad is being a dick, and who will celebrate me when I find a job? Would you rather him treat me like Gareth? The boy who cheated on me in high school that you ask about every once in a while. Would you rather me be with Brett, who I dated in college and who thought that partying was more important than me? Or would you rather I be with a man who is more like you, someone cold and unaffectionate? Someone I have to work to earn their love, because it isn't handed over automatically."

"That is not how I treat you."

"Isn't it, though?" I ask. "When was the last time you said you loved me? When was the last time you asked me out to dinner to just chat and see what I'm up to? When was the last time you gave me a gift that you put thought into, rather than a check at Christmas with a note that says to spend it wisely? You think that your overbearing parenting style is loving me, but it's suffocating me. You're not letting me be who I am, and . . . and you're going to lose me, Dad." Tears fill my eyes as my voice breaks. "You are going to lose me just like you lost Mom."

And that right there makes him silent.

So I continue. "I don't want that to happen. I want to build a relationship with you. I want to make you proud. I want you to look at me and not think how you can mold me to be the daughter you want, but rather celebrate me for my individuality. You're making it hard to love you, Dad. You're making it hard for me to want to keep trying. I think . . . I think the pain you *cause me* is worse than actually losing you."

I hear him clear his throat before saying, "Well, if that's how you feel—"

"I don't want to lose you, Dad," I plead. "But you make it hard to stay."

"Then maybe you should just . . . leave. Go your separate way."

"Because I don't want to," I say. "I love—"

But the phone goes dead. *The hell? Did he hang up on me?* My thoughts are confirmed when I look at the screen.

He hung up on me. Even when given the choice, he's letting me go. No, he's pushing me away.

"Then maybe, you should just . . . leave. Go your separate way."

I drop my phone to the side and bury my head in my hands, letting my tears fall.

I don't want to lose him.

I really don't.

But I don't think he's giving me any other choice.

"Hey," Levi says as he sits next to me, surprising me. He places his strong arm around my shoulders and holds me tightly. "Wylie, what's going on?"

I turn toward him and press my head to his shoulder. "Just talked to my dad." My voice shudders. "He . . . he thinks it's best if he and I just part ways." I wipe at my eyes as I take a few deep breaths. "I don't get it, Levi. I'm trying. I don't understand why he won't try with me."

"I don't know either," he says, "but I'm going to make it right."

"This isn't your fight," I say to him.

"The fuck it's not," he replies. "You're mine. Therefore your baggage and your battles are mine to shoulder."

"It's a lost cause."

"It's not," he says with such confidence that I'm definitely shocked. "I'm going to make this right. The boys and I have a plan. Just let us work our magic."

I pull away to look up at him. "Getting the boys involved, I don't know if that is a good idea."

"Trust me . . . it is." He winks, scoops me up, and carries me back to the bedroom.

Chapter Twenty-One

COACH WOOD

"You have to play Posey," my assistant coach, Sterling, says.

I move my hand over my jaw. "Put him on second string."

Sterling shifts in his seat. "Will, I understand you're upset—"

"Upset? He was fucking my daughter," I say through clenched teeth. "In the locker room where anyone could have seen."

"Yes, a mistake for sure, but you'll only punish the team, our record, and chance at the Cup if you take him out. Like it or not, we need him."

I feel like punching a wall because I know he's right. Unfortunately for me, Posey is one of the best defensemen in the league, despite what I said to him last night. We need him. Pacey needs him because he's slowing down. It's showing. This very well might be his last season. Hell, it should be his last season. If I take out Posey, Pacey will have a hell of a time keeping up.

"This is bullshit," I say through clenched teeth just as there's a knock on the door. "Come in," I shout.

The door opens and in walks Halsey Holmes. Easily one of our best drafts in Agitators history. The man is a machine on the ice—precise, sharp, and quick. He can see plays three steps ahead, and he capitalizes on that natural instinct. We're fucking lucky to have him.

"Coach," he says with a curt nod.

"What do you need?" I ask him.

He tosses a card on my desk, then stuffs his hands in his pockets. "That's for you."

I glance down at the card and back at him. "What the hell is this?"

"Read it. You'll figure it out."

I pick up the envelope but don't open it. "If this is about Posey, I want nothing to do with it."

"If you don't read it, then your starting line wants nothing to do with you," Halsey says, standing his ground. "Fuck with one, fuck with all." With that, he leaves my office.

I look over at Sterling, who has the smallest, and I mean smallest, fucking smirk on his face.

"Get the fuck out," I yell at him.

He stands and gathers his things before leaving. When the door is shut, I open the stupid envelope and read it.

Two things you need to know about Levi Posey:

When I was at my lowest, in a very dark place after losing my brother, Posey often slept on my couch just so I wasn't alone. When I was reading in a corner, feeling so desperately alone, missing my brother, he'd sit next to me and stare into nothing. When I thought I couldn't make it through Holden's funeral, he held me up. Your daughter would be lucky to have a man like him.

This is the first time I've ever seen him in love. This is the first time he's ever told me he was in love. And I'll hang up my skates before I let you take that away from him.

Holmes

I stare at the letter, reading the first paragraph a few times over. I remember when Halsey lost his brother. It was devastating to the entire hockey community, but mostly to Halsey. I remember the way he focused on nothing but hockey. At the time, I considered it a wise way to channel his energy. But now . . . now that he's out of that fog, I don't think I've ever seen him play better.

Although, he can't credit that to Posey so . . . nice fucking try.

I toss the letter in the garbage and go back to my starting lineup.

Can I bench Posey?

———

"GOOD GAME, COACH," Sterling says as he heads out of the rink and down the tunnel to the locker room. "Are you going to say anything?"

"No," I answer as I ignore the fans looking for a high five.

"Interesting, because this is the most cohesive I've ever seen them play. Five to one is one hell of a game, especially for a team that should have, on paper, given us a battle."

I pause and turn toward Sterling. "Are you trying to imply something?"

He shrugs. He never backs down to my grouchiness. "Just interesting is all." He moves faster down the hallway and into the locker room. I head straight to my office where another envelope waits for me.

"Jesus Christ," I mutter as I take a seat and open it up.

I will deny this until the day I fucking die, but the reason I'm a happy motherfucker with the girl of my dreams has a lot to do with Posey. He might pretend he's indifferent when helping, and he might offer terrible advice at times, but that advice always seems to turn into something worth listening to. If you think Posey is the worst thing for your daughter, you couldn't be more wrong. He'll treat her well. He'll support her how she needs. And most importantly, he'll give her the love she deserves. I've seen it. I've seen the way he talks about her. How he's so fucking proud of her.

Trust me when I say, if you fuck with him, if you fuck with them, you're fucking with all of us. She's part of the family now, and we won't go down without a fight.

Silas

I crumple up the letter and toss it into the trash can.

Fucking annoyed.

Really fucking annoyed.

A note from Holmes, sure. But a note from one of the biggest assholes on the team? Is Posey paying them to do this?

Either way, makes no difference.

Over my dead body will I be okay with Posey dating my daughter.

"COACH WOOD," someone calls when I'm a few feet away from my car.

I turn to find Eli and OC standing behind me.

"Jesus fuck," I say as I grip my head. "If this has to do with Posey, I don't want to fucking hear it."

"That's fair," OC says. He's been a huge addition to the team since we lost Rivers, but seeing that he's on the Posey train makes me rethink that decision. "But you're going to listen."

The fuck?

Where does he get off talking to me like that?

Eli Hornsby, the prettiest motherfucker on the team, steps up and says, "Posey is one of the main reasons I put my skates back on after losing Holden Holmes." He wets his lips and continues, "I never said this, but I was ready to quit after I found out about his death. I was there that night, and I didn't stop him from drinking too much or from driving under the influence. I blamed myself, endlessly. It was fucking torture. And every time I stepped out on the ice, I kept thinking about how he should be out here too. I was done, but Posey . . . he stood by me. He knew I didn't want to talk, so instead, he made me laugh. He joked about the good times we had with Holden. He joked about anything and everything. He even made me fucking bologna sandwiches. He pulled every trick out of his back pocket to make things easier . . . a little less painful. I know he's done the same for your daughter."

My brow turns into a scowl at the mention of Wylie.

"I haven't known him as long as the other guys," OC says, "but I will say this. I've never seen a more loyal friend. He cares about each one of the players on the team, he offers them help, even if it means helping a friend pick up breakfast because they're running late. You might see him as the playboy you've had to help out of some disagreeable situations, but that's not what defines him. What defines him is the loyalty he carries in his heart, the loyalty he's already shown your daughter. He loves her, simple as that. And he'll give up everything just to make her happy."

I twist my lips to the side. I'm getting really fucking sick of this bullshit.

"Are you done?" I ask.

"We are," Eli says. "Good game tonight, Coach. Shame our leadership couldn't enjoy it."

They turn around and walk away.

When the hell did I start losing the respect of my players?

I pause, the question sounding off in my head. What the fuck did Posey say to them?

What did he tell them about my relationship with my daughter?

They probably perceive me as an angry tyrant. But they don't know the whole story.

No one knows the whole fucking story.

I'm not in the wrong. I know I'm not . . .

⸻

"HEY COACH, CAN I JOIN YOU?" Pacey Lawes says as he stands next to my chair on the plane.

I look up at him, knowing exactly what this will be about.

"Don't want to hear it," I say.

"It's about my retirement," he says.

When I look up at him again, he lifts my bag from the seat next to me and sets it in the aisle as he sits.

I knew this was coming, but why would he address this on our way to Nashville on an airplane?

He rests his head against the headrest and says, "I'm barely holding on, Coach Wood. The pain is starting to take over, and every day, I wake up more and more stiff. I still have headaches on occasion that are absolutely debilitating. There are days when I feel like I can't put on my gear one more goddamn time." He looks over at me. "I can't do this for another year. This is . . . this is it for me."

I swallow, knowing this will be a huge loss to the team. Lawes has been our backbone, our foundation, some might say the start of something great. With him in front of the goal, we've had more championship wins than in franchise history.

"I can respect your decision," I say. "But if you're in this much pain, why haven't you said anything?"

"Because I've been able to power through," he answers. "But not because of sheer will." He looks me in the eyes. "Because of Posey." Motherfucker. I look away, but Pacey keeps talking. "He's the one who stays in the ice baths longer with me so I'm not alone. He's the one bringing me all kinds of vitamins and powders to help me with recovery. He's the one who checks on me at night when we're on away trips to make sure I don't have a headache or to make sure I have everything I need to wake up fresh the next day. I know you think of me as the backbone of the team, but the fact of the matter is, Posey is the one who keeps us together. And it's about fucking time you realize that." He rubs his hands together and says, "And your daughter . . . she's so talented. She's intelligent. She has a good head on her shoulders, and the fact that she fell for a good man shows that. He's a solid man. A man you can trust."

"Trust?" I shoot back, losing my patience. "A man I can trust? If I can trust him, then why did he go behind my back and date my daughter?"

"I can't answer that for him," Pacey says. "But what I can say is that Posey has a reason for everything he does. You might not agree with it, but there is a reason. Maybe you should ask him.

Maybe you should give him a second to explain what happened. That's what good leaders do, after all. Right, Coach? They listen."

He stands from his seat but doesn't leave. Instead, he leans in again and says, "You're the best coach I've ever played for. You're a smart man, and you have the kind of drive that gets his players moving. Don't fuck that up over this. We respect you, but the way you're treating Posey and your daughter? That's causing a lot of players to lose their respect for you."

He pats the back of the chair and then takes off.

I look away, focusing on the clouds out the window, his words registering harder than any of the other ones said to me.

"But what I can say is that Posey has a reason for everything he does. Maybe you should give him a second to explain what happened. That's what good leaders do, after all. Right, Coach? They listen."

Fuck. I'm not blind. I've seen everything these boys have mentioned about Posey. On and off the ice. But I refuse to ignore his blatant disrespect, his lies about what he was doing behind my back with my daughter. *Why should I?*

But . . . to be called out for not being a good leader.

That hits hard.

Harder than I want it to.

THERE'S a knock on my door just as I set my bag down. Sterling and I had a two-hour meeting about tomorrow's game and how we want to match up with the Renegades. They're known to be quick on the ice so we determined ways to keep our legs fresh.

After two hours, I'm exhausted, and the last thing I want to do is hear about fucking Levi Posey again.

There's another knock, and it seems like they won't go away, so I head over to the door, open it, and—lo and behold—Posey is standing on the other side.

I run my hand over my brow. "I can't do this tonight."

"Hear me out, Coach."

"Why?" I ask. "Don't you think your teammates have done enough?"

"I don't think so," Halsey Holmes says, stepping behind him. Following closely are the rest of the guys.

God Almighty.

This is starting to feel like an after school special.

"I think our friend here was looking for a nightcap . . . of water," Pacey says. "And he wanted to spend it with you, his leader. Don't you think it would be a good idea to listen to him?"

These fuckheads.

Christ.

I walk over to the dresser and grab my key card and stick it in my pocket before moving out of my room. I walk ahead of them straight to the elevator, where I punch the down button. I feel them all gather behind me, and I'm wondering if this will be a team thing.

I sure as hell hope not. When the elevator dings, *we* get on it and ride down to the main lobby where *we* get off and head straight to the restaurant bar. *We nod at the hostess who allows us to choose our table. We go for one in the far back, away from everyone. Fucking hell. They should be leaving me the fuck alone.* I take a seat in the booth while Posey sits across from me. I half expect the other guys to take up the rest of the booth and the top of the table, but instead, they sit a few tables over, watching.

Lurking.

"Quite the extravagant way to boost your image," I say to Posey.

"Wasn't trying to boost the image, was trying to portray the truth."

"Okay, so they said you were a good guy, that you put people first. That was the general consensus. Tell me, why should I give a fuck about that?"

He places his hand on the table and looks me in the eye. "Coach Wood, I'm not here to win your approval. What the boys said was their choice, their decision, and frankly, I have no idea what was said to you. But when I told them I needed help, they came to my side. But like I said, I'm not here to get you to like me. You either do or you don't. I'm here to show you this."

He pulls out his phone and pushes it toward the middle of the table.

I glance down at it and feel my heart sink as I stare at a drawing of one of my favorite pictures. It's of me and Wylie and we're out on a frozen lake. She's about five in the picture, and I'm holding her hands as she shakily skates across the ice.

I pick up the phone and observe the drawing and how realistic it is, how it feels like the picture, but also isn't quite the same.

"Why do you have this?" I ask.

"I took it . . . from your daughter. I emailed it to myself. She's been working on it the last few days as a therapeutic way to stay connected to you, and I wanted to show you. This is what your daughter is capable of. This is the talent she possesses."

I stare at the photo, studying the lines she used and the shading to create dimension. It truly is remarkable. *Wylie did this? Impossible.* This is the work of an established artist, not a young girl.

"You might not believe in her chosen career path, but don't downplay her talent. A talent that she used to secure a very high-paying job, one that will offer her the opportunity to support herself and pay you back for the schooling you paid for. This . . ."—he points at the phone—"this is her passion. This is what she's good at. And you needed to see it. You need to see the heart she has, because it comes through in every drawing. She's really fucking good, and I'll be damned if you don't acknowledge how goddamn lucky you are to have such a beautiful and talented daughter." He clears his throat. "I couldn't give two shits if you like me, but don't throw away a relationship with your daughter over this. She loves you. She wants to be a part of your life. Let her, Will."

"I don't need you telling me how to raise my daughter."

Posey stands from the table and places his knuckles on the edge. Leaning in, he replies, "You don't. But you do need someone to tell you when you're being an ass, and you're being an ass. That's something I won't stand by. I love your daughter, I've loved her longer than you probably know. I've searched high and low for a woman like her, and I've waited a long fucking time. I won't watch you tear her apart. I won't fucking stand for it." He knocks his knuckles on the table. "Don't lose the best thing that's ever happened to you over pride. You're better than that."

Posey moves away from the table and the others join him, walking behind him as a group. Pacey places his hand on his back while Halsey says something to him. Posey nods, and they disappear toward the elevators.

I drag my hands over my face and let out a deep breath.

Fuck.

Chapter Twenty-Two

WYLIE

"Babe," Levi calls out when he enters the apartment.

"Right here." I'm in my chair where I've been working on a drawing for Patty all day. I was struggling with the angle, but after staring at her vagina for two hours straight, I figured it out.

"Oh." Levi laughs and kicks off his shoes before walking up to me with a gift bag in hand.

They got home from their away game late last night and had to report to the stadium today for some light training. Levi texted me from the ice bath, explaining to me the anatomy of his man parts and how they shrunk into nothing while he iced his body.

Something I didn't need to read, but it was entertaining to say the least.

The one thing that Levi never fails to do is make me laugh or roll my eyes, and he's done a lot of that in the past few days. He hasn't let me sulk or question. Instead, he's made me feel loved and protected—cherished—like he does every day.

He leans and cups my cheek before kissing me on the lips. "You smell fucking amazing."

I smile. "Thank you. Sandie brought me a new perfume because she thought I needed some cheering up."

"Well, tell her thank you." He sniffs along my neck. "Jesus Christ, that is . . . that's making me hard."

I chuckle and set my iPad down. "I think I can take care of that for you," I say as I move my hand between us, but he stops me.

"Hold that thought." He holds up the gift bag. "I got you something."

"You did?" I take the bag from him and ask, "Is it that vibrator we were looking at the other day?"

"No, but I did order it, and it's been shipped. Counting down the days for that to arrive." He taps the bag. "This will be better, though."

"Better than the Magician? That's what it was called, right?"

He nods his head. "Yup, better than the Magician."

"How could anything be better than the Magician?" I open the bag and look inside to find a jersey. "Levi," I say on a gasp as I pull it out. A full-on Agitators—women's cut—jersey and on the back . . . it says Posey. I squeeze the shirt to my chest in a hug and say, "Oh my God, I love it. Thank you."

"There's one more thing." He nods at the bag, so I look inside.

At the bottom is a ticket. I pull it out, and it's for tomorrow's game. "What's this?" I ask.

He takes my hand. "Will you cheer me on at tomorrow's game officially as my girlfriend?"

"Are you serious?" I ask.

He nods. "Yes. Dead serious. I want you there, representing me. I want to look up in the stands and see your face. No more hiding, no more secrets. Tomorrow, I want it to be about us."

I tilt my head to the side as I stare at the most handsome, caring, and loving man I've ever met. "Yes, Levi, of course I will."

A large smile spreads across his face as he loops his hand behind my head and brings me in for a kiss. When he pulls away, he says, "Winnie and Ollie will be sitting next to you. Everyone knows who they are, so if people see you between them with my jersey on your back, it's like announcing to the world that you're mine." He lifts my wrist and kisses my bracelets.

"Possessive much?" I tease.

"When it comes to you . . . yes."

Then he lifts me and carries me to the dining room table, where he spreads me out.

"Now, excuse me while I feast." He pulls down my pants and thong. "I'm fucking starving."

———

"HAVE you ever been to a game before?" Winnie asks.

"Did you really just ask her that?" Ollie says while we carry our pretzels and drinks down to our seats. "She's the coach's daughter. Of course she's been to a game."

"I meant as Posey's girl. Maybe she hasn't, you don't know," Winnie counters as she shuffles down our row and finds our three seats. "She could have been banned from all games like she was banned from all penises on the ice."

"And look how that turned out," Ollie says with a wink.

I chuckle. "Yes, I've been to several games, but I've never sat three rows back, and I've never cheered on a boyfriend."

"Ooo," Winnie says while bumping her shoulder with mine. "This is so exciting. I feel like I go feral at games."

"She does," Ollie says as she takes a bite of her pretzel. "It can be scary at times."

I look out toward the ice, where the boys stretch and warm up. It takes me a second, but I spot Levi over with Eli. They're both stretching their hip flexers and chatting it up. I glance around the arena, taking in the energy and, for the first time, fully appreciate the love for these men. Grown men cheer, children wave their hands, and women toast their beers. There are signs asking for pucks, telling the players how much they love them, and even a few proposals. There's one for Levi that makes me chuckle.

It truly is a sight to see, and I can understand why someone like my dad would revel in such impassioned energy all the time. It's addicting.

Speaking of Dad. He's behind the bench in his standard black-on-black-on-black attire, hands behind his back, looking out over the rink. Sterling, his assistant, talks to a few players on the bench while the staff prepares for the game around them.

But my eyes remain fixated on my dad, as I take in the stoic yet intimidating set of his shoulders. The way he casually observes but is calculating every little advantage in his head. He's conniving and smart, one of the many reasons the Agitators are the team to beat this year.

"You okay?" Winnie asks.

"What? Oh yeah. Just thinking."

"About your dad?" Ollie asks, mouth full of pretzel.

"Yeah," I answer.

"Have you spoken to him since everything went down?"

I shake my head. "No, and that's okay. I've come to terms with it. It sucks, but like Levi has said, it's his loss if he doesn't want to be a part of my life."

"He's right," Ollie replies. "And I don't say that very often."

"It's taken me a second, but I'm coming to terms with that train of thought."

"Good," Winnie says. "If anything, you've gained a whole bunch of brothers and sisters."

I smile. "I can get on board with that."

"I CAN BARELY TALK," Winnie says, her voice hoarse.

I rub my ear. "Yeah, and I think I can barely hear."

"Glad you were the one in the middle," Ollie says as we walk toward the players' locker room. "Usually I'm the one with a ringing in my ear after a game. Told you she was loud."

"Like, way louder than I ever could have imagined." I glance at Winnie. "You're so small. How do you do it?"

"Blessed with powerful lungs, I guess," she answers.

"It was a good game, though. I will admit that," Ollie says. "Do you think Posey got in that fight because you were watching? He was barely checked into the boards, and it looked like he lost his cool."

"I don't know," I say. "But it was really hot." I bite the corner of my lip, recalling the fight. Levi was hardly touched, but he got the other player a few times in the ribs and once on the face. Levi went to the penalty box with a sweaty head of hair and a ripped jersey, while the other player went in with a bloody nose and a dazed expression.

"Posey could have given him a few more wallops. I think he held back. He was showing off but not being barbaric about it."

"I'm sure it will aid in tonight's festivities," Ollie says.

"Most definitely." Winnie winks just as the locker room door opens, and Silas pops out, looking fresh from the shower. When he spots Ollie, he walks right up to her and wraps her up in his arms before placing a big kiss on her lips.

"Need you, babe," he says, barely loud enough for us to hear. And then he whispers something in her ear that makes her cheeks flush.

She twiddles her fingers at us. "Got to go. Talk to you later, ladies."

"Bye," Winnie and I say together with a laugh.

When they're gone, Winnie leans over and whispers, "Bet they do it in the car in a parking lot somewhere."

"Seriously?" I ask.

Winnie nods. "Yup, they've been into this voyeur, almost getting caught situation lately. I don't know. I prefer the privacy of my own home where Pacey can bend me over the counter."

I laugh just as the door opens again, and this time, it's Levi.

He's wearing the same green suit he showed up in, but unlike the image I saw of him on social media, walking into the arena, this time, he has a smile on his face as he spots me.

He scoops me up into his arms, spins me around once, and plants a huge kiss on my lips. When he pulls away, he groans quietly. "Fuck, I love seeing you here, waiting for me in my jersey. It feels like everything is right in the world."

I cup his cheek. "Everything is right in the world." Then I stand on my toes and kiss him one more time before pulling away. "Ready to go home?" I ask.

"Ready."

I turn toward Winnie. "Thanks for tonight. My ears will never be the same."

"Anytime." She winks, and then, hand in hand, Levi and I start heading toward the parking lot, but stop when we see my dad staring back at us.

I knew this would happen at some point, but I wish it didn't happen tonight. Not when we're both on such a high from the game.

Dad crosses his arms over his chest. "Wylie, may I have a word?"

That doesn't sound great.

"Uh . . . sure," I say as I look up at Levi. He nods and then leans down and gives me one more kiss before he encourages me to go with my father.

I head toward his office, but my dad moves toward the rink instead.

"Where are you going?" I ask him.

"Follow me," he says. So I do as I'm told and follow him through the players' tunnel and onto the bench, where he takes a seat.

He leans his forearms on his thighs as he stares out at the ice. Uneasy and unsure of what he's going to do, I keep some distance from him and prepare my heart for whatever he has to say.

After a few seconds of silence, he says, "Did he get you that jersey?"

I look down at it. "He did."

Dad slowly nods his head. "Seems like he really cares about you."

"He does," I answer. "We, uh, we actually have known each other longer than what you might think."

Dad glances over at me. "How so?"

"We met a year prior at a hotel bar. It was when I caught a ride with you to visit Sandie in college. Levi and I got to talking, and well, I didn't let him know who I was out of fear that he'd stop talking to me. It was honestly one of the best nights. I felt an immediate connection with him, which surprised me because I too had a preconceived idea of who he was. But when I saw you come into the bar, I bolted before I could tell him my name. I only recently found out that he'd felt the same attraction, as he spent the better part of a year looking for me. Using a private investigator and everything. He was so shocked when he then found out I was your daughter in your office a few weeks ago."

Dad runs his hand over his bald head. "What a moron."

I don't know why, but that makes me laugh. "He can be at times," I say, "but he's a loveable moron."

"Did he tell you what he and his teammates have been doing these past few days?"

"No," I say, brow pinched. "What did they do?"

Dad sits up, and I watch his strong, usually tense jaw relax. This *genuine* conversation is the first we've had in a long time. "His teammates went on some sort of Posey campaign where they chatted him up with letters to me and personal conversations, telling me what a great guy he is. How he's the backbone of the team. How he would do anything for anyone."

"They're right," I say.

"Well, I didn't believe them," Dad says, making my heart sink. "Not until Posey came to me himself."

"He did?" I ask.

Dad nods. "When we were in Nashville. He showed me a picture you were working on, one of you and me." My cheeks flame with embarrassment.

"I'm not done with that one yet. I was actually kind of practicing. It's not my best—"

"It nearly made me cry," Dad says, stunning me. He then looks out at the ice again and quietly says, "Your mother was an artist, Wylie. She was incredible. It was one of the things that I fell in love with. She could see the beauty in everything . . . well, everything but me." He lets out a deep sigh, and I inch closer toward him as I comprehend how vulnerable he's being. When I'm close enough, I place my hand on his back. "I was a fool back then. She wanted to paint around the world, and I wanted to build my career, make something of myself. She tried to live a simple life with me, being the coach's wife, but it wasn't enough. She told me I wasn't enough, and it cut me. She wanted to leave, and I told her she could, but if she left, she wasn't to ever come back. And her relationship with you was terminated. She cut me so I wanted to cut her. Little did I know, she would take the deal."

"Dad, I'm sorry."

He shakes his head. "It was my own fault. My own selfish fault." He looks at me now. "When you told me you wanted to drop everything and pursue art, I had this sick, boiling feeling erupt inside me that it would happen all over again. That my world would crumble around me, and I'd lose another thing I loved so much." He scratches his beard as his eyes meet mine. "Little did I realize I was losing you just like I lost your mom, and I'm ashamed to say that it wasn't until Posey showed me his undying loyalty toward you that I realized my head wasn't on straight. He was right. I was losing the best thing to ever happen to me out of fear that . . . well, I'd lose you like I lost your mother."

"Dad," I say as I take his hand in mine. "I would never intentionally leave you like that. We might have had our ups and downs, but you're my father, and I will always love you. I just . . .

I wish that you would treat me more like your daughter and less like your prisoner."

"I know. I'm sorry. There's no excuse for my behavior. But I do need you to know that I was trying to hang on to you and ensure that you'd always be there by my side."

"I get that, and I'm sorry if I scared you in any way. Please know, though, I want to have a relationship with you, Dad. A healthy relationship. I want to hang out. I want to have dinner where it's just you and me, and we chat about what's going on in our lives. I want a connection. And I hope you could maybe open your heart to that."

"I can," he says. "I want to." He wraps his arm around me and pulls me into a hug. "And I'm sorry for everything I put you through. You deserve better."

"I deserve a father who wants the best for me. I know that's you, even though you lost sight of that for a moment."

"I did, but I think I figured it out." He squeezes me. *Thank God.* I am so thankful he's softened his heart and actually wants what I want. Wants to love me and keep me in his life. "Now, about that boy. You're telling me that you love somebody who might possibly love bologna more than you?"

I let out a laugh and curl in closer to my dad. "I do. And I'm willing to play second fiddle to lunch meat if it means I can be with him."

"Well," Dad says. "If that's not true love, I don't know what is."

⊏⊐

DAD GIVES me one more hug, then heads toward his office while I go to the players' parking lot, where I know Levi waits for me in his car. He texted me to let me know.

When I spot his car, I rush over to the passenger side and hop in when he sees me.

"What did he——"

He doesn't even get a second to finish his sentence as I lean over the center console and kiss him wildly. I kiss him for loving me. For making everything right for my dad. For believing in me. And for not letting one man's bitterness change the trajectory of who he is.

My dad's awful words, not to mention the way he handled the situation, could have deterred anyone into writing him off, but instead, Levi chose the high road because he knew how important my dad was to me. Instead of cutting him out of my life, he went out of his way to patch things up, and that's why I will forever and always love this man.

When I pull away, I cup his cheeks. "You are the best thing to ever happen to me. You are my rock, my strength, my everything, and I'm so beyond grateful you have chosen me."

He studies me for a moment, confusion laced through his expression.

"How could I have chosen anyone else?" he says. "You were clearly made for me."

I smile and stroke my thumb over his cheek. "My dad told me what you did for me, for us." I shake my head in disbelief. "I can't believe you did that, Levi."

"I love you, Wylie. I'd do anything for you." He laces our fingers together. "Please tell me that you were able to come to some sort of understanding."

I nod. "More so. He apologized. Explained to me that my mom left him to be an artist, and well, he didn't handle it properly, but he was scared I was going to do the same."

"Makes sense," Levi says.

"But either way, I told him about the job. He was a little uneasy about what I would be drawing, but he did tell me I did beautiful work. He congratulated me, then gave us his blessing. Called you a good guy."

"Did he now?" Levi says, puffing his chest.

"Oh yes, seems like he might be a fan. Then again, not sure he'd ever show it."

"I'll take a secret fan as long as you remain my number one."

"Always," I say as I lean in again. "Forever and always, Levi."

"Never forget it," he says as he kisses me again, and this time, the kiss bounces all the way down to the tips of my toes.

After ditching him at a bar, never in a million years did I imagine I'd end up here—being loved and cherished by Levi Posey. I was looking for one night of fun, and he's offering me an endless eternity of love.

Epilogue

LEVI

"Levi, are you really going to be on your phone right now?"

"I'm sorry," I say as I set my phone down, worry etching through my chest. I blow out a heavy breath. "OC sent an article. A damning one."

"Is it about the expansion team?" Wylie asks.

I nod as I grab a box from under the Christmas tree. "Yeah, he's freaking out. Rumors are swirling about what might happen and since we heard there's a possibility Rivers might come back, he's nervous he's going to be traded at the end of the season."

"Well, nothing is set in stone."

I wince. "The article was written by a reputable source. Looks like the team could be collecting some serious bad blood."

"What do you mean?" she asks, thankfully being amazing as I hand her my favorite Christmas present I got her. Last thing I want to do is talk about the team on our first Christmas, but OC is freaking out.

When we heard of the expansion team, the San Francisco

Rogue, a few years ago, we never thought much of it, but with a heavy set of investors, willing and ready to throw down cash for the toughest position players, there was some worry that started to develop. But OC recently has ramped up that worry.

"The owners are a collective who want to win. And they will do it any means necessary, meaning, they're looking for the best of the best. The ones who are willing to do anything to win and I mean anything. Cheap shots, hell on ice type shit."

"But that's not OC, so why is he worried?"

"Because Rivers might come back and if he does, that makes OC a free agent and given his talent, the Rogue would be dumb not to scoop him up."

"Oh . . ." she stares down at her present. "That would be sad, I really like OC."

"We all do." I drag my hand over my face. "Shit, babe, I'm sorry. I shouldn't have looked at that text in the middle of our Christmas."

She smooths her hand over my bare chest and says, "It's okay. It's one of the reasons why I love you, because you care so much about your friends, even if it's on a freaky close level."

I chuckle and pull her onto my lap. "Okay, blocking that out, now open your gift."

I kiss her neck and while she giggles, she unwraps the present I got her. She parts the jewelry box open and gasps.

"Levi, oh my God. I love it so much," Wylie says as she stares down at the gold necklace I got her.

Bing Crosby croons in the background about a white Christmas that, unfortunately, we don't have. Now, a rainy and cloudy Christmas, Vancouver went all in this year.

We're spending the morning here, just her and me, in front of our Christmas tree that we decorated together, opening presents and eating the cookies we made last night while we ate bologna sandwiches with potato chips between the slices. It was Wylie's personal touch, which I had never done before, but after the subtle combination of the soft and crunchy, I know I'll never go back.

Later this afternoon, we're heading over to her dad's, where we plan on exchanging gifts and having dinner. We'll also be mingling with Giselle, who'll be stopping by as well.

Yeah, Giselle, the flight attendant.

Apparently, Coach Wood was flirting with her. Took him a bit, but he finally got up the nerve to ask her out, and according to Wylie, sparks flew after the first date. And I have to admit, the scary vein in Coach Wood's head that usually has its own heartbeat . . . has significantly calmed down since Giselle entered into the mix. OC even told me that he saw her going into Coach Wood's hotel room one night. When I told Wylie, she gave her dad a round of applause and said he needed to get some ass.

God, I love her so much.

"I love having your initials on me," she says as she holds it out to me and turns around. "Put it on for me?"

I slip it around her neck and clasp the necklace together. She then turns toward me and asks, "How does it look?"

"Perfect," I say.

Wylie has been hard at work, drawing every day and coming up with new and exciting sketches for Patty, who gobbles them up . . . as are her patrons. I can't even remember the number they've sold, but Patty and Deena were blown away. And now they're coming up with different packages and incentives that could be sold with the drawings. They thought the more exclusive they can be with certain packages, the higher the bidding.

Frankly, I'm all for this business model. Seeing women kill it as entrepreneurs is always great to see. She also got a call back from Rylee Ryan about her drawings for her book, but given the workload Wylie has taken on for Patty, she had to turn down the opportunity. Rylee told her to keep her in mind if her workload ever lightens up.

From the way things have been going, we don't think it's going to lighten up anytime soon.

"My turn," Wylie says as she reaches under the tree and hands me a gift. "I worked very hard on this one."

She takes a seat on my lap again, and I kiss her shoulder

before I open the present. It's a flat box. I pull off the top, push back some tissue paper, and reveal a black-bound book.

"Did you finally write up the Vermont book in Arial?"

She chuckles and shakes her head. Although, she did buy me a book on Maine that I'm frothing at the mouth to dive into. Can't wait to see all that lobster. Plus, when I was flipping through it, there was a section about this little town called Port Snow and how they have tons of Lovemark movies being made there. Tell me more about that!

I lift the book out of the box and flip open the cover, only to have my breath escape my lungs. *It's Wylie* . . . in nothing but an Agitators jersey, cut up the middle and showing off a dangerous amount of cleavage.

"What . . . the . . . fuck," I say as my dick starts to go hard. "Baby, what is this?"

"Keep flipping through."

I go to the next page, and it's a picture of Wylie, lying on the ground, her fingers barely covering her nipples as she looks up at the camera.

"Holy shit, babe."

I flip through, page after page, getting harder and harder as we go on until the last two pages, where she's leaning against a bed, a vibrator in hand with a look of pure ecstasy across her face as she masturbates.

"Please, baby, please tell me a woman took these."

She laughs as I look at the last picture. It's of her, with her hands propped behind her, her chest up, and her tits pointed toward the ceiling.

Fuck . . . she's so hot.

"Deena and Patty took them for me while I was down there a few weeks ago."

"Jesus," I murmur as I flip through them again. "Babe, this is . . . this is the best gift you could have given me."

"Better than the bologna in the fridge?"

"Way better," I say.

"Well, then, let me give you the accompanying present that

goes with this." She gets off my lap, turns around, and pushes me onto my back. She tugs on my Christmas pajama pants and releases my hard cock from its confines. She wets her lips and leans down, running her tongue along my tattoo.

I groan as she circles her tongue around the tip.

"I want you looking at the pictures while I suck your cock, so when you go on away trips and take this book with you, you have a memory of this moment."

"Fuck, I love you," I say as I rub my thumb over her cheek.

"I love you too," she says right before she sucks me all the way to the back of her throat.

Christ.

And here I thought I'd be at war with this girl forever, a mad battle of erotic torture. Instead, I won the battle. I won the best prize of all time.

I get to call Wylie Wood mine and share the rest of my life with this precious gift.

Nothing beats that.

Made in the USA
Middletown, DE
14 October 2024

62567475R00249